"POWERFUL . . . EXHILARATING . . .

Here is a writer of intelligence and tenderness, a rare combination in a cynical, doubting world."

"When a book is this successful, it's artistic struggle. The narrative seems thrilling ease. Jack is such an absorb fact, that it's easy to overlook the real-life multifacetedness of the novel's other characters, both major and minor. Its pitch-perfect dialogue, skillfully contrived plot, and authentically wintry atmosphere are all exceptional, but a great deal of its strength comes from the moral complexity of its characters."

—*The Washington Post Book World*

"Lyric . . . Memorable . . . Frederick Busch is such a fine writer. In his new novel *Girls*, he marries love and sorrow, memory and guilt in a story that will break your heart."

—*Orlando Sentinel*

"Busch is a master and those who don't know his name should."

—*The Baltimore Sun*

"Powerful . . . Though the crime story is intriguing, it is Jack's growing insight about his marriage, his town, and himself that transforms this page-turner about lost children into a tender and eloquent examination of the even greater mystery that is the human heart."

—*Glamour*

"*Girls* is about as close to perfect as a novel gets. Its prose is clean and strong but never advertises its own quiet brilliance, its characters are sharply defined and irresistible, and its plot is suspenseful enough to keep you up until dawn. . . . Jack is a superb creation: troubled, desperate, angry, capable of violence, even more capable of kindness. Fanny is equally compelling, a quintessentially tough/tender American woman. . . . *Girls* is an achievement, powerful and true."

—*Men's Journal*

Please turn the page for more acclaim. . . .

"A TOUR-DE-FORCE . . .

This is the finest literary thriller since William Trevor's *Felicia's Journey*. . . . It is a dark tale, but it's told with an economical mastery and intensity that only a few current novelists can command."

—*Publishers Weekly* (starred review)

"The novel's social realism gives it the page-turning pace of a mystery. But Busch's masterly pairing of dark wit and tender mercy is what makes *Girls* a great work."

—*US Magazine*

"Combining the quick pace of a detective story with the bold poetics of a literary work, Frederick Busch's taut new novel, *Girls*, is a dark, compulsively readable drama."

—*Elle*

"Some writers get by on artifice. Other writers depend on something deeper and more difficult; when they core the apple of human behavior, they throw away the apple and keep the core. Frederick Busch is one such writer. Busch has proven himself an able and sometimes spectacular chronicler of the serious business of life. Short on gimmick and long on emotional truth . . . this novel finds him working at the top of his form. . . . A chilling story about the impossibility of preserving the innocence of childhood and the discomfort of embracing the guilt of adulthood."

—*Time Out*

"A complex and disturbing vision of the world as a place filled with danger powers this fascinating novel, another blistering drama of family relations from one of our most productive and passionately serious writers. . . . It all works superbly as a conventional thriller, though the story's most effective as a harrowing expression of the fragility of our defenses against loss and death, and a moving characterization of its memorable protagonist, a decent man who struggles against powerful odds to remain one. An impressive demonstration of Busch's continuing mastery of realistic narrative."

—*Kirkus Reviews* (starred review)

"Engrossing . . . Busch has a wonderful ear for dialogue and a remarkable talent for creating nuanced characters whose behavior rings painfully true."

girls

Fiction

A Memory of War (2003)
Don't Tell Anyone (2000)
The Night Inspector (1999)
Girls (1997)
The Children in the Woods (1994)
Long Way from Home (1993)
Closing Arguments (1991)
Harry and Catherine (1990)
War Babies (1989)
Absent Friends (1989)
Sometimes I Live in the Country (1986)
Too Late American Boyhood Blues (1984)
Invisible Mending (1984)
Take This Man (1981)
Rounds (1979)
Hardwater Country (1979)
The Mutual Friend (1978)
Domestic Particulars (1976)
Manual Labor (1974)
Breathing Trouble (1973)
I Wanted a Year Without Fall (1971)

Nonfiction

Letters to a Fiction Writer (2000)
A Dangerous Profession (1999)
When People Publish (1986)
Hawkes (1973)

girls

A novel

Frederick Busch

Fawcett Books
The Random House Ballantine Publishing Group • New York

A Fawcett Book
Published by The Random House Ballantine Publishing Group

Copyright © 1997 by Frederick Busch

Reader's Guide copyright © 1998 by The Ballantine Publishing Group,
a division of Random House, Inc.

All rights reserved under International and Pan-American Copyright Conventions. Published in the United States by The Random House Ballantine Publishing Group, a division of Random House, Inc., New York, and simultaneously in Canada by Random House of Canada Limited, Toronto.

Grateful acknowledgment is made to Alfred A. Knopf, Inc. for permission to adapt "Ralph the Duck" (chapter 2, "Ralph") from *Absent Friends*. Copyright © 1989 by Frederick Busch. Adapted by permission of Alfred A. Knopf, Inc.

Fawcett is a registered trademark and the Fawcett colophon is a trademark of Random House, Inc.

www.ballantinebooks.com/BRC/
www.randomhouse.com

Library of Congress Catalog Card Number: 97-97063

ISBN: 0-449-91263-9

This edition published by arrangement with Harmony Books,
a division of Crown Publishers, Inc.

Cover photo by Gary Isaacs

Manufactured in the United States of America

First Ballantine Books Edition: March 1998

10 9 8

JUDY

—

I intend to portray none of the too many families who search for their children. While writing this book, I wished that I were working on their behalf. But this is, of course, a novel, and it can speak at last only about these characters, all of whom I have invented.

—

flash

W E STARTED CLEARING the field with shovels and buckets and of course our cupped, gloved hands. The idea was to not break any frozen parts of her away. Then, when we had a broad hole in the top of the snow that covered the field and we were a foot or two of snow above where she might have been set down to wait for spring, we started using poles. Some of us used rake handles and the long hafts of shovels. One used a five-foot iron pry bar. He was a big man, and the bar weighed twenty-five pounds, anyway, but he used it gently, I remember, like a doctor with his hands in someone's wound. We came together to try to find her and we did what we needed to, and then we seemed to separate as quickly as we could.

At Mrs. Tanner's funeral, they sang "Shall We Gather at the River," and I sang, too. It was like that in the field. Everyone gathered, and it was something to see. Then we all came apart. Fanny went where she needed to, and Rosalie Piri did, and Archie Halpern. I did, too. Most of them, I think, remained within a few miles of the field.

The dog and I live where it doesn't snow. I can't look at snow and stay calm. Sometimes it gets so warm, I wear navy blue uniform shorts with a reinforced long pocket down the left hip for the radio.

I patrol on foot and sometimes on a white motor scooter, and it's hard for me to believe, a cop on a scooter in shorts. But someone who enforces the law, laws, somebody's laws, falls down like that. Whether it's because he drinks or takes money or swallows amphetamines or has to be powerful, or he's one of those people who is always scared, or because he's me, that's how he goes—state or federal agency or a big-city police force, down to working large towns or the dead little cities underneath the Great Lakes, say, then down to smaller towns, then maybe a campus, maybe a mall, or a hotel that used to be fine.

I've moved a few times, changing my job but trying to stay on a kind of level vocationally. I would like not to sink very much more. And she traces me, and she calls. The first time, I was surprised. I was south and west, looking at a map while lying on a bed in the Arroyo Motel, where they gave good residential rates and didn't care what species your roommate was. The dog was in the bathroom, lying against the coolness of the tub and panting, and I was reading the map of New York State. At one time, I marked the areas with a felt-tip pen where girls had disappeared. Most of them were under the snow and ice up there, I figured, and I didn't know why I had to look at months-old guesses about burial sites. I distrusted this kind of recreation.

It was my third week on the new job, and I continued not to know where to go or what to do for what might be thought of as pleasure. I was supposed to have fun or relax, the duty sergeant made clear, because I had been reported for menacing a citizen and obviously I needed some time to get right.

"Gritting your teeth isn't menacing," I told him.

"In *your* face," he said, "it is." Then he told me, "Jack, go and get unfucked."

So I was off duty and getting unfucked with a daydream I often had about her. Facedown on my chest was a map marked with places where someone took people's daughters and killed them.

I am talking here about being lost or found. You can be a small child and get lost, and maybe I will find you. God knows, I'll try. Or you can be a large and ordinary man and get lost in everything usual about your life. Maybe you will try to find yourself, and so might someone else. It ends up being about the ordinary days you are hidden inside of, whether or not you want to hide.

I didn't flinch when the phone rang, and I didn't run to pick it up. On the fifth ring, I said, "All right." On the seventh or eighth, I answered it. The dog, I noticed, had moved from between the toilet and the tub to lie with his nose at the threshold of the bathroom door.

She said, "I knew I'd get you. There you are."

All I could think to say was, "Aren't you something."

"Given my family connection to the finding-people profession, no. I wouldn't expect any less of me. Neither should you."

"No. I think I won't."

She said, "I prepared a list of remarks to fall back on in case I couldn't think of anything to say that would keep you on the line."

I could hear the hum and hiss of the open connection, but I couldn't hear anything of her. Then she came back and I felt her on the line. A piece of paper rattled, and then she recited, the way you do when you read something out loud, "Are you eating well? Are you sleeping well? Are you, in general, looking after yourself?"

I said, "Are you all right?"

"No. Are you?"

"Sure."

"Really?"

"No. I guess, really, no."

"Good," she said. "In a way. You come back here, Jack. Will you come back?" She gave me a little time to answer, and then she said, "Never mind. You wouldn't. Maybe I can get there. Wherever in the world it really is. Jack, it's so far away."

"I believe that's why I came here."

"Yes. Except you had to leave me behind when you did that."

"You couldn't have come with me. The dog could barely stand it. *I* could barely stand it. I haven't been really friendly, these days."

"But you're some kind of a *fugitive*, Jack. From *me*. Consider that.

You and your dog, in the middle of the night, you drive away in the world's oldest station wagon to—"

"Daylight. I left in daylight. But I know what you mean. And the Torino did finally die. Get this: outside of Buffalo, New York. I never even got it out of the state."

"I can't imagine you driving anything else," she said.

"I drive a Subaru DL, 1980. I had to pay extra for a rearview mirror you can tilt against the headlights behind you. You have to replace the struts every few miles, but the engine's good and the body only shifts on the frame when you turn a corner or pull out to pass."

She said, with a kind of a wobble, "Is there room for the dog?"

"He gets the backseat."

"You and him."

"Me and him," I said. By then, I think, I was messed up, too, and my voice must have showed it, because the dog banged his tail on the floor. It was a trick he used to do with my wife. Now he was promiscuous, and he would slam his tail against the floor if anyone gave the slightest signal of distress. Apparently, I was signaling, and he was signaling back.

Thinking about the way we came apart, all of us, Fanny and Rosalie and Archie and me and the Tanners and their daughter and every man and woman who worked in the field between the houses and the river, was like watching something explode, but slowed down.

I saw it on the job, early in my rotation, when my work consisted of rousting disorderly American teenaged boys in uniform in Phu Lam when they overacted their role as savior. I was giving directions to a somewhat shit-faced marine just back from Operation Utah in I Corps. He was so chiseled down and locked tight, I would not have challenged him to a bet on a ball game. I was pointing, I remember, when a car bomb took down a hotel across the street. I kept seeing it afterward. Traumatic flashback, a doctor taught me to call it.

But that day, directly after the explosion, I didn't know its name, and I sat on the curb and I kept watching the hotel go out and up. The marine, who got very sober very fast, squatted behind me where I sat. I was wondering out loud for him whether what we might be thinking of as oil or gasoline that pooled beneath my legs in the street could actually be the blood of whores and janitors and cleaning ladies. He patted my shoulder over and over, and he kept saying, "Uh-huh," and "That's right," and "You got it." After a while, I didn't see blood, but I did keep seeing the slow coming apart of the back end of the little gray Fiat, and then the stick-by-stick dismantling of the two-story hotel, slat by gallery banister, window mullion by floorboard, everything coming toward us from the inside out.

"Uh-huh," the marine said, patting me, "you saying hello to Flash."

She said, "Jack."

"The chances weren't terrific, you know," I told her.

"For what?"

"Well, what you're calling about."

"You and me. That's what I'm calling about."

The dog was pounding away with his tail. He sounded like the drummer on an antique recording of a slow, surrendering song.

"But you were hoping they'd get better," she said. "Weren't you?"

I said, "Not at first."

ralph

YOU CAN'T SAY ONCE upon a time to tell the story of how we got to where we are. You have to say winter. Once, in winter, you say, because winter was our only season, and it felt like we would live in winter all our lives.

I was awake in the darkness and the sound of wind against the house when the dog began to retch at 5:25. I hustled ninety pounds of heaving chocolate Lab to the door and rolled him onto the snow that looked silver in the fading moonlight.

"Good boy," I said, because he'd done his only trick.

Outside he vomited, and I went back up, passing the sofa Fanny lay on. I tiptoed with enough weight on my toes to let her know how considerate I was. She blinked her eyes. I know I heard her blink her eyes. Whenever I told her I could hear her blink her eyes, she said I was lying. But I could hear the damp slap of lash after I made her cry.

I got into bed to get warm again. I saw the red digital numbers, 5:29, and I knew I wouldn't fall asleep. I didn't. I read a book about men who kill one another for pay or for their honor. I forget which, and so did they. It was 5:45, the alarm would buzz at 6:00, and I would make a pot of coffee and start the woodstove. I would call

Fanny and pour her coffee into her mug. I would apologize because I always did. Then she would forgive me. We would stagger through the day, exhausted but pretty sure we were more or less all right. We would probably sleep that night. We would probably wake in the same bed to the alarm at 6:00, or to the dog, if he'd returned to the frozen deer carcass he'd been eating in the forest on our land. He loved what made him sick. The alarm went off, I got into jeans and woolen socks and a sweatshirt, and I went downstairs to let the dog in. He'd be hungry, of course.

I was the oldest college student in America, I sometimes said. But of course I wasn't. There were always ancient women with parchment skin who graduated at seventy-nine from places like Barnard and the University of Alabama. I was only forty-four, and I hardly qualified as a student. I patrolled the college at night in a Jeep with a leaky exhaust system, and I went from room to room in the classroom buildings, kicking out students who were studying or humping in chairs—they do it *anywhere*—and answering emergency calls, with my little blue light winking on top of the roof. I didn't carry a gun or a billy, but I had a heavy black flashlight that took three batteries, and I'd used it twice on some of my overprivileged northeastern-playboy part-time classmates. On Tuesdays and Thursdays, I would waken at 6:00 with my wife, and I'd do my homework, and then patrol at school and go to class at 11:30, to sit there for an hour and a half while thirty-five stomachs growled and this guy gave instruction about books. Because I was on the staff, the college let me take a course for nothing every term. I was getting educated, in a kind of slow-motion way. It was going to take me something like fifteen or sixteen years to graduate. I predicted to Fanny I would no doubt get an F in gym in my last semester and have to repeat. There were times when I respected myself for going to school. Fanny often did, and that had served as fair incentive.

I am not unintelligent. "You are not an unintelligent writer," my professor wrote on my paper about Nathaniel Hawthorne. We had to read short stories, I and the other students, and then we had to write little essays about them. I told how I saw Kafka and Hawthorne in a

similar light, and I was not unintelligent, he said. He ran into me at
dusk one time, when I answered a call about a dead battery and
found out it was him. I jumped his Buick from the Jeep's battery, and
he was looking me over, I could tell, while I clamped onto the termi-
nals and cranked it up. He was tall and handsome, like someone in a
clothing catalog. He never wore a suit. He wore khakis and sweaters,
loafers or sneakers, and he was always talking to the female students
with the brightest hair and best builds. But he couldn't get a Buick
going on an ice-cold night, and he didn't know enough to look for
cells going bad. I told him he was going to need a new battery, and
he looked me over the way men sometimes do with other men who
fix their cars for them.

"Vietnam?"

I said, "No way."

"You have that look sometimes. Were you one of the Phoenix
Project fellas?"

I was wearing a watch cap made of navy wool and an old fatigue
jacket. Slick characters like my professor enjoy it if you're a killer or
at least a onetime middleweight fighter. I smiled as if I knew something. "Take it easy," I said, and I went back to the Jeep to swing
around the cemetery at the top of the campus. They'd been known to
screw in down-filled sleeping bags on horizontal stones up there, and
the dean of students didn't want anybody dying of frostbite while
joined at the hip to a matriculating fellow resident of our northeast-
ern camp for the overindulged.

He blinked his high beams at me as I went. "You are not an
unintelligent driver," I said.

———

Fanny had left me a bowl of something made with sausages and
sauerkraut and potatoes, and the dog hadn't eaten too much more
than his fair share. He watched me eat his leftovers and then make
myself a king-size drink composed of sour mash and ice. In our back
room, which is on the northern end of the house, and cold for sitting

in that close to dawn, I sat and I watched the texture of the sky change. It was going to snow, and I wanted to see the storm come up the valley. I woke up that way, sitting in the rocker with its loose right arm, holding a watery drink, and thinking right away of the girl I'd convinced to go back inside. She'd been standing outside her dormitory, looking up at a window that was dark in the midst of all those lighted panes. They never turned a light off; they would let the faucets run half the night. She was crying onto her bathrobe. She was sockless in rubber-bottomed boots, the brown ones so many of them wore unlaced, and for all I know, she might have been naked under the robe. She was beautiful, I thought, and she was somebody's red-headed daughter, standing in a quadrangle how many miles from home and weeping.

"He doesn't love anyone," the kid told me. "He doesn't love his wife—I mean, his ex-wife. And he doesn't love the ex-wife before that, or the one before that. And you know what? He doesn't love me. I don't know anyone who *does!*"

"It isn't your fault if he isn't smart enough to love you," I said, steering her toward the Jeep.

She stopped. She turned. "You know him?"

I couldn't help it. I hugged her hard, and she let me, and then she stepped back, and of course I let her go. "Don't you *touch* me! Is this sexual harassment? Do you know the rules? Isn't this sexual harassment?"

"I'm sorry," I said at the door to the truck. "But I think I have to be able to give you a grade before it counts as harassment."

She got in. I told her we were driving to the dean of students' house. She smelled like marijuana and something very sweet, maybe one of those coffee-with-cream liqueurs you don't buy unless you hate to drink.

As the heat of the truck struck her, she started going kind of clay gray-green, and I reached across her to open the window.

"You touched my breast!" she said.

I said, "Does it count if it wasn't on purpose?"

She leaned out the window and gave her rendition of my dog.

But in my rocker, waking up at whatever time in the morning in my silent house, I thought of her as someone's child. Which made me think of ours, of course. I went for more ice, and I started on a wet breakfast. At the door of the dean of students' house, she'd turned her chalky face to me and asked, "What grade would you give me, then?"

———

It was a week like this: two teachers locked out of their offices late at night, a Toyota with a flat and no spare, an attempted rape on a senior girl walking home from the library, a major fight outside a town bar (broken wrist, probable concussion), and variations on breaking and entering. I was scolded by my vice president of nonacademic services for thumping softly on a student who got drunk and disorderly and tried to take me down. I told him to keep his job, but he called me back because I was right to swat the kid a little, he said, but also wrong, but what the hell, and he'd promised to admonish me, and now he had, and would I please stay on. I thought of the fringe benefits—graduation in only sixteen years—so I went back to work.

My professor assigned a story called "A Rose for Emily," and I wrote him a paper about the mechanics of corpse fucking, and how, since Emily clearly couldn't screw her dead boyfriend, she was keeping his rotten body in bed because she truly loved him. I called the paper "True Love." He gave me a B and wrote, "See me, pls." In his office after class, his feet up on his desk, he trimmed a cigar with a giant folding knife he kept in his drawer.

"You got to clean the hole out," he said, "or they don't draw."

"I don't smoke," I said.

"Bad habit. Real *habit*, though. I started smoking 'em in Germany, in the service. My CO smoked 'em. We collaborated on a brothel inspection one time, and we ended up smoking these with a couple of women." He waggled his eyebrows at me, now that his manhood was established.

"Were the women smoking them, too?"

He snorted laughter through his nose while the greasy smoke came curling off his thin, dry lips. "They were pretty smoky, I'll tell ya!" He was wearing cowboy boots that day, and he propped them on his desk and sat forward. "It's a little hard to explain. But—hell. You just don't say *fuck* when you write an essay for a college prof. Okay?" He sounded like a scoutmaster with a kid he'd caught jerking off in the outhouse. "All right? You don't wanna do that."

"Did it shock you?"

"Fuck no, it didn't shock me. I just told you. It violates certain proprieties."

"But if I'm writing it to you, like a letter—"

"You're writing it for posterity. For some mythical reader some-place, not just me. You're making a *statement*."

"Right. My statement said how hard it must be for a woman to fuck with a corpse."

"And a point worth making. I said so. Here."

"But you said I shouldn't say it."

"No. Listen. Just because you're talking about fucking, you don't have to say *fuck*. Does that make it any clearer?"

"No."

"I wish you'd lied to me just now," he said.

I nodded. I did, too.

"Where'd you do your service?" he asked.

"Baltimore. Baltimore, Maryland."

"What's in Baltimore?"

"Railroads. I liaised on freight runs of army matériel. I killed a couple of bums on the rod with my bare hands, though."

He snorted again, but I could see how disappointed he was. He'd been banking on my having been a murderer. Interesting guy in one of my classes, he must have told some terrific woman at an overpriced meal: I just *know* the guy was a rubout specialist in the Nam. I figured I should come to work wearing my fatigue jacket and a red bandanna tied around my head. Say "man" to him a couple of times, hang a fist in the air for grief and solidarity, and look worn out, exhausted from experiences he was fairly certain he envied my having. His dungarees were ironed, I noticed.

———

On Saturday, we went back to the campus because Fanny wanted to see a movie called *Seven Samurai*. I fell asleep, and I'm afraid I snored. She let me sleep until the auditorium was almost empty. I asked her, "Who was screaming in my dream?"

"Kurosawa," she said.

"Who?"

"Ask your professor friend."

I looked around, but he wasn't there. "Not an unweird man," I said.

We went home and cleaned up after the dog and put him out. I drank a little sour mash and we went upstairs and didn't make love. It got to be Sunday morning, maybe four or five, and the dog was howling at another dog someplace, or at the moon, or maybe just his shadow thrown by the moon onto snow. I did not strangle him when I opened the back door, and he limped happily past me and stumbled up the stairs. I followed him into our bedroom and I made myself not groan a happy groan for being satisfied Fanny hadn't shifted out of it yet.

———

He stopped me in the hall after class on a Thursday and asked me, "How's it goin'?"—just one of the kickers drinking sour beer and eating pickled eggs and watching the tube in a country bar. How's it goin'? I nodded. I wanted a grade from the man, and I did want to learn about expressing myself. I nodded and made what I thought was a smile. He'd let his mustache grow out and his hair was longer. He was starting to wear dark shirts with lighter ties. I thought he looked like someone in *The Godfather*. He was wearing his high-heeled cowboy boots. His corduroy pants looked baggy. I guess he wanted them to look that way. He motioned me to the wall of the hallway, and he looked confidential and said, "How about the Baltimore stuff?"

I said, "Yeah?"

"Was that really true?" He was almost blinking, he wanted so much for me to be a damaged Vietnam vet just looking for a bell tower to climb into and start firing from. The college didn't have a bell tower, though I'd once spent an ugly hour chasing a drunken ATO down from the roof of the observatory. "You were just clocking through boxcars in Baltimore?"

I said, "Nah."

"I thought so!" He gave a kind of sigh.

"I killed people," I said.

"You know, I could have sworn you did," he said.

I nodded, and he nodded back. I'd made him so happy.

———

The assignment was to write something to influence somebody. He called it "Rhetoric and Persuasion." We read an essay by George Orwell and *A Modest Proposal* by Jonathan Swift. I liked the Orwell better, but I wasn't comfortable with it. He talked about natives and I felt him saying it two ways.

I wrote "Ralph the Duck."

Once upon a time, there was a duck named Ralph who didn't have any feathers on his wings. So when the cold wind blew, Ralph said, Brr, and he shivered and shook.

What's the matter? Ralph's mommy asked.

I'm *cold*, Ralph said.

Oh, the mommy said. Here. I'll keep you warm.

So she spread her big, feathery wings, and hugged Ralph tight, and when the cold wind blew, Ralph was warm and snuggly, and he fell fast asleep.

The next Thursday, he was wearing canvas pants and hiking boots. He mentioned kind of casually to some of the girls in the class how whenever there was a storm, he wore his Lake District walking outfit. He had a big hairy sweater on. I kept waiting for him to make a noise like a mountain goat. But the girls seemed to like it. His boots made a creaky squeak on the linoleum of the hall when he caught up with me after class.

"As I told you," he said, "it isn't unappealing. It's just—not a college theme."

"Right," I said. "Okay. You want me to do it over?"

"No," he said. "Not at all. The D will remain your grade. But I'll read something else if you want to write it."

"This'll be fine," I said.

"Did you understand the assignment?"

"Write something to influence someone—'Rhetoric and Persuasion.' "

We were at his office door and the redheaded kid who got sick in my truck was waiting for him. She looked at me as if one of us was in the wrong place, which struck me as accurate enough. He was interested in getting into his office with the redhead, but he remembered to turn around and flash me a grin he seemed to think he was known for.

Instead of going on shift a few hours after class, the way I'm supposed to, I told the dispatcher I was sick, and I went home. Fanny was frightened when I came in, because I don't get sick and I don't miss work. She looked at my face and got sad. I went upstairs to change. When I was a kid, I always changed my clothes as soon as I came home from school. I put on jeans and a flannel shirt and thick wool socks, and I made myself a dark drink of sour mash. Fanny poured herself some wine and came into the cold northern room a few minutes later. I was sitting in the rocker, looking over the valley. The wind was lining up a lot of rows of cloud, so the sky looked like a baked trout when you lift the skin off. "It'll snow," I said to her.

She sat on the old sofa and waited. After a while, she said, "I wonder why they always call it a mackerel sky?"

"Good eating, mackerel," I said.

Fanny said, "Shit! You're never that laconic unless you feel crazy. What's wrong? Who'd you punch out at the playground?"

"We had to write a composition," I said.

"Did he like it?"

"He gave me a D."

"Well, you're familiar enough with D's. I never saw you get low about a grade."

"I wrote about Ralph the Duck."

She said, "You did?" She said, "Honey." She came over and stood beside the rocker and leaned into me and hugged my head and neck. "Honey," she said. "Honey."

———

It was a terrible storm, the worst of the long, terrible winter so far. That afternoon, they closed the college, which they almost never do. But the roads were jammed with snow over ice, and now it was freezing rain on top of that, and the only people working at the school that night were the dispatcher and Anthony Berberich in the other truck and me. Everyone else had gone home except the students, and most of them were inside. The ones who weren't were drunk, and I kept on sending them in and telling them to act like grown-ups. A number of them said they were, and I really couldn't argue. I had the bright beams on, the defroster set high, the little blue light winking, and a thermos of sour mash and hot coffee that I sipped from every time I had to get out of the truck or every time I realized how cold all that wetness was.

About eight o'clock, when the rain was turning back to snow and the cold was worse and the road was impossible, just when I was done helping a county sander on the edge of the campus pull a panel truck out of a snowbank, I got the emergency call from the dispatcher. We had a student missing. The roommates thought the girl was headed for the quarry. This meant I had to get the Jeep up on a narrow road above the campus, above the old cemetery, into all kinds of woods and rough track that I figured would be choked with ice and snow. Any kid up there would really have to want to be there, and I couldn't go in on foot, because you'd only want to be there on account of drugs, booze, or craziness, and either way I'd be needing blankets and heat, and then a fast ride down to the hospital. So I dropped into four-wheel drive to get me up the hill above the campus, bucking snow and sliding on ice, putting all the heater's warmth up on the windshield because I couldn't see much more than swarming snow. My feet were still cold from the tow job, and it didn't seem to matter that I had on heavy socks and insulated boots I'd coated with waterproofing. I shivered, and I thought of Ralph the Duck.

I had to grind the rest of the way, from the cemetery, in four-wheel low, and in spite of the cold, I was smoking my gearbox by the time I was close enough to the quarry to see I'd have to make my way on foot to where she was. It was a kind of hollowed-out shape, maybe four or five stories high, where she stood, wobbling. She was as chalky as she'd been the last time, and her red hair didn't catch the light anymore. It just lay on her like something that had died on top of her head. She was in a white nightgown that looked like her sloughing skin. She had her arms crossed like she wanted to be warm. She swayed, kind of, in front of the big, dark, scooped-out rock face, where the trees and brush had been cleared for trucks and earthmovers. She looked tiny against all the darkness. From where I stood, I could see the snow driving down in front of the lights I'd left on, but I couldn't see it near her. All it looked like around her was dark. She was shaking with the cold, and she was crying.

I had a blanket with me, and I shoved it down the front of my coat to keep it dry for her, and because I was so cold. I waved. I stood in the lights and waved. I don't know what she saw—a big shadow, maybe. I surely didn't reassure her, because when she saw me, she backed up, until she was near the face of the quarry. She couldn't go any farther.

I called, "Hello! I brought a blanket. Are you cold? I thought you might want a blanket."

Her roommates had told the dispatcher about pills, so I didn't bring her the coffee laced with mash. I figured I didn't have all that much time, anyway, to get her down and pumped out. The booze with whatever pills she'd taken would make her die that much faster.

I hated that word. *Die.* It made me furious with her. I heard myself seething when I breathed. I pulled my scarf and collar up above my mouth. I didn't want her to see how angry I was because she wanted to die.

I called, "Remember me?"

I was closer now. I could see the purple mottling of her skin. I didn't know if it was cold or dying. It probably didn't matter much to distinguish between them right now, I thought. That made me smile. I felt the smile, and I pulled the scarf down so she could look at it. She didn't seem awfully reassured.

"You're the sexual harassment guy," she said. She said it very slowly. Her lips were clumsy. It was like looking at a ventriloquist's dummy.

"I gave you an A," I said.

"When?"

"It's a joke," I said. "You don't want me making jokes. You want me to give you a nice warm blanket, though. And then you want me to take you home."

She leaned against the rock face when I approached. I pulled the blanket out, then zipped my jacket back up. The snow was stopping, I realized, and that wasn't really a very good sign. An arctic cold was descending in its place. I held the blanket out to her, but she only looked at it.

"You'll just have to turn me in," I said. "I'm gonna hug you again."

She screamed, "No more! I don't want any more hugs!"

But she kept her arms on her chest, and I wrapped the blanket around her and stuffed a piece into each of her tight, small fists. I didn't know what to do for her feet. Finally, I got down on my haunches in front of her. She crouched down, too, protecting herself.

"No," I said. "No. You're fine."

I took off the woolen mittens I'd been wearing. Mittens keep you warmer than gloves because they trap your hand's heat around the fingers and palm at once. Fanny knitted them for me. I put a mitten as far onto each of her feet as I could. She let me. She was going to collapse, I thought.

"Now, let's go home," I said. "Let's get you better."

With her funny, stiff lips, she said, "I've been very self-indulgent and weird and I'm sorry. But I'd really like to die." She sounded so reasonable, I found myself nodding agreement.

But I said, "You can't just die."

"Aren't I dying already? I took all of them, and then"—she giggled like a child, which of course is what she was—"I borrowed different ones from other people's rooms. See, this isn't some like teenage cry for *help*. Understand? I'm seriously interested in death and I have to stay out here a little longer and fall asleep. All right?"

"You can't do that," I said. "You ever hear of Vietnam?"

"I saw the movie," she said. "With the opera in it? *Apocalypse*? Whatever."

"I was there!" I said. "I killed people! I helped to kill them! And when they die, you see their bones later on. You dream about their bones in splinters and with blood on the ends, and this kind of mucous stuff coming out of their eyes. You probably heard of guys having dreams like that, didn't you? Whacked-out Vietnam vets? That's me, see? So I'm telling you, I know about dead people and their stomachs falling out. And people keep dreaming about the dead people that they knew, see? You can't make people dream about you like that! It isn't fair!"

"You dream about me?" She was ready to go. She was ready to fall down, and I was going to lift her up and get her to the truck.

"I will," I said, "if you die."

"I want you to," she said. Her lips were hardly moving now. Her eyes were closed. "I want you all to."

I dropped my shoulder and put it into her waist and picked her up and carried her down to the Jeep. She was talking, but not a lot, and her voice leaked down my back. I jammed her into the truck and wrapped the blanket around her better and then put another one down around her feet. I strapped her in with the seat belt. She was shaking; her eyes were closed and her mouth was open. She was breathing. I checked that twice, once when I strapped her in, and then again when I strapped myself in and backed up hard into a sapling and took it down. I got us into first gear, held the clutch in, leaned over to listen for breathing, heard it—shallow panting, like a kid asleep on your lap for a nap—and then I put the gear in and howled down the hillside on what I thought might be the road.

We passed the cemetery. I told her that was a good sign. She didn't respond. I found myself panting, too. It was like we were breathing for each other. It made me dizzy, but I couldn't stop. We passed the highest dorm, and I got back up into four-wheel high. The cab smelled like burnt oil and hot metal. We were past the chapel now, and the observatory, the president's house, then the bookstore. I had the blue light winking, the V-6 was roaring, and I drove on the edge of out of control, sensing the skids just before I slid into them, then getting back out of them the way I needed to. I took a little fender off once, and a bit of the corner of a classroom building, but I worked us back on course, and all I needed to do now was negotiate the sharp left turn around the administration building, past the library, then floor it for the straight run to the town's main street and then the hospital.

I was panting into the mike, and the dispatcher kept saying, "Say again?"

I made myself slow my talking. I said we'd need a stomach pump, and to get the names of the pills from her friends in the dorm, and I'd be there in less than five minutes.

"Roger," the dispatcher said. "Roger all that. Over." My throat tightened and tears came into my eyes. I felt a kind of stupid gratitude.

I said to the girl, whose head was slumped and whose face looked too blue all through its whiteness, "You know, I had a baby once. My wife, Fanny. She and I had a little girl one time."

I reached over and touched her cheek. It was cold. The truck swerved, and I got my hands on the wheel. I'd made the turn past the ad building using just my left. "I can do it in the dark," I sang to no tune I'd ever heard. "I can do it with one hand." I said to her, "We had a girl child, very small. I used to tell her stories she didn't understand. She liked them anyway. Now, I do *not* want you dying."

I came to the campus gates going fifty on the ice and snow,

smoking the engine, grinding the clutch, and I bounced off a wrought-iron fence to give me the curve going left that I needed. On a pool table, it would have been a bank shot worth applause. The town cop picked me up and got out ahead of me. He used his growler, then his siren, and I leaned on the horn. We banged up to the emergency room entrance and I was out and at the other door before the cop on duty, Elmo St. John, could loosen his seat belt. I loosened hers, and I carried her into the lobby of the ER. They had a gurney, and doctors, and they took her away from me. I tried to talk to them, but they made me sit down and do my shaking on a dirty sofa decorated with drawings of little spinning wheels. Somebody brought me hot coffee—I think it was Elmo—but I couldn't hold it.

"They won't," he kept saying to me. "They won't."

"What?"

"You just been sitting there for a minute and a half, shaking, telling me, 'Don't let her die. Don't let her die.' "

"Oh."

"You all *right?*"

"How about the kid?"

"They'll tell us soon."

"She better be all right."

"That's right."

"She—somebody's really gonna have to explain it to me if she isn't."

"That's right."

"She better not die this time," I said.

———

Fanny came downstairs to look for me. I was at the northern windows, looking past the mullions, down the valley to the faint red line along the mounds and little peaks of the ridge beyond the valley. The sun was going to come up, and I was looking for it.

Fanny stood behind me. I could hear her. I could smell her hair and the sleep on her. The crimson line widened, and I squinted at it.

I heard the dog come in behind her, catching up. He panted and I knew why his panting sounded familiar. She put her hands on my shoulders and arms. I made muscles to impress her with, and then I let them go, and let my head drop down until my chin was on my chest.

"I didn't think you'd be able to sleep after that," Fanny said.

"I brought enough adrenaline home to run a football team."

"But you can't be a hero, huh? You can't be discovered. You're hiding in here because somebody's going to call, or come over, and want to talk to you—her parents for shooting sure, sooner or later. Or is that supposed to be part of the service at the playground? Saving their suicidal daughters. Freeze to death finding them in the woods and driving too fast for *any* weather, much less what we had last night. Getting their babies home. The bastards." She was crying. I could hear the soft sound of her lashes. She sniffed and I could feel her arm move as she pawed for the tissues on the coffee table.

"I have them over here," I said. "On the windowsill."

"Yes." She blew her nose, and the dog thumped his tail. He seemed to think it one of Fanny's finer tricks, and he had wagged for her for years whenever she'd wept or sniffed or blown her nose. "Well, you're going to have to talk to them."

"I will," I said. "I will." The sun was in our sky now, climbing. "I think that guy with the smile, my prof? She showed up a lot at his office the last few weeks. He called her 'my advisee,' you know? The way those guys sound about what they're getting done by being just a little bit better than mortals? Well, she was his advisee, I bet. He was shoving home the old advice."

"She'll be okay," Fanny said. "Her parents will take her home and love her up and get her some help." She began to cry again. Then she stopped. She blew her nose, and the dog's tail thumped. She said, "So tell me what you'll tell a waiting world. How'd you talk her out?"

"Well, I didn't, really. I got up close and picked her up and carried her."

"You didn't say *anything*?"

"Sure I did. Kid's standing in the snow outside of a lot of pills, you're gonna say something."

"So what'd you *say?*"

"I told her some lies about the war. I ogred and howled. I don't know, Fanny. I told her stories," I said. "I did 'Rhetoric and Persuasion.' "

A couple of weeks later, Fanny volunteered for the 11:00 P.M. to 7:00 A.M. shift. We saw each other when she was coming home and I was heading out. I timed my leaving for work so we'd say hello. "Good morning," we'd say. We'd sing it, to prove we weren't angry or embarrassed or scared. The dog got a little confused about who was supposed to feed him his breakfast. We'd talk about that in the blue-cold mornings at the cars outside the house, and then I'd drive to work and she'd go in. Of course, we'd be home together in the house at night, but she'd be trying to sleep when I came in or I'd be sleeping when she was getting ready to leave. You can make a routine out of it, and that's what we did.

Here's what I thought. I thought, Once upon a time.

And I was not a dishonorable student, I guess. At the end of the term, he gave me a C+ for the course.

bloom

WAS UP EARLY. I'd been up a good deal of the night. I let the dog out, then fed him and thought about feeding myself. Instead, I watched the early news from Syracuse. It was the same news I'd seen at two in the morning. A plane had landed in a river. A deputy had confessed to crimes. Arson was suspected in a fire. The President was not a crook. I didn't want to taste my own coffee. I put a little extra weatherproofing on my boots, took a thermos that might be clean, and went out to the car to warm it up. As I knew she would, Fanny settled her car into the icy ruts in the drive. She turned the engine off and did what she usually did: sat with her head back, not moving, like she'd fallen asleep. I opened her door and said, "Hey."

"Hey," she said, her eyes still closed.

"Lousy night?"

"Good one. Nobody died. Nothing got amputated. We had a blue baby, but he's all right. The doctor's scared to death because he gave him oxygen, but what could he do? Last time he did that, the kid went blind and he got sued for ten million bucks or something. Of course, they settled. It's what you do. Kid doesn't breathe, you flood him with it and you pray, and then you settle."

"So you're sitting here praying? Or settling?"

"I'm sitting here is all, Jack."

The sun was rising on the other side of the house, but the skies were overcast and it still felt like nighttime. I said, "The dog's fed. I don't remember whether I turned the heat up or not."

"I'll figure it out," she said. "If I'm cold, I'll turn it up."

Her face was pale, and her eyelids looked dark, like her eyes were sore. "I better go," I said.

She nodded.

I said, "I'll see you later."

She nodded. She said, "Bye, Jack." With her eyes still closed, she raised a hand in its mitten and waved.

I said, "Bye."

The car I drove to work was possibly the last surviving Gran Torino station wagon manufactured by Ford in 1974. It was chocolate brown and rusted nearly through at a number of key points. At each of those points, where metal that simulated wood for an old-fashioned station wagon appearance was hanging off, I had laid on silvery duct tape. There was nearly nothing duct tape wouldn't hold together. Among the exceptions would be people, I suppose. The car was heavy enough to get me over our unpaved and usually unplowed road. I could see ice glinting on the road through the floorboards on the passenger's side of the front. While I slithered and slid, I leaned over and pushed the cocoa fiber doormat back into place over the hole. My breath hung around me in a cold cloud, so I felt like I was driving in the outside weather while I was staring through my private weather inside the car. I kept the high beams on for the outside stuff, and hoped for the best with what was in.

I stopped at the Blue Bird to fill up with coffee for the day. Two broad streets met at the top of town, and the Blue Bird looked out on them both. Local contractors and snowplow drivers and nurses coming on and off shift and the old people, who didn't sleep a lot, came into the Bird and drank the oily coffee and ate yeasty cakes and slippery eggs. There was a no smoking section in the back, and because it consisted of only two booths, most of the college people went to another joint, where they had less fun but better air. I sat at the counter and asked skinny Verna with her high voice and wattled throat for a cup of coffee and a full thermos, and I looked for Archie Halpern. He was the gentlest of them. He was the best of them.

When I saw him in a window seat, I took my coffee and went over.

He moved around the pepper and salt, the napkin holder, the menu, and a dirty spoon.

"I started out trying to make room for you," he said, "but you're really *not* going to sit on the table, are you?"

I shook my head and sat down.

He had a very short crew cut and a sloppy shave, so his round head looked fuller than usual. He ran his thick hand over his head and his smile looked embarrassed. "I swore I'd cut my hair off if the hockey team made it to the tournament."

"Who'd you promise?"

"Can't tell you."

"A counselor deal," I said.

"A kid's doing his best to fuck his life up, and I've been doing some work with him."

"You're good at it."

He shrugged. He said, "I'm not sure I'm that good. I wouldn't call *you* too well-adjusted, you taciturn son of a bitch. Is that face for me or the coffee?"

"Both."

"How's Fanny?"

I nodded.

He said, "Yeah?"

"Yeah what?"

"Yeah, what in fuck are we talking about is what," he said.

He began to sweat. At first, I used to think it was a trick. I learned after a while that when he began to concentrate, his metabolism speeded up. Often enough, by the end of an hour or so, his clothes would be wet. I said, "You don't need to go to work on me, Archie."

"Fine."

"I didn't come over here to freeload a little psychological health."

"Jack," he said, "I couldn't do it for you with a wheelbarrow and shovel, you're so fucked up."

I nodded.

"I was joking," he said.

"No, you weren't." I shrugged to show him how I didn't care.

"Jack," he said pleasantly and low, "you're so full of shit. You look like you got run over before you got out of bed."

I leaned down to my coffee and then sat up. I looked at his little eyes in his big face. He kept it deadpan when he worked. I said, "I guess I was looking for you. But it wasn't to make you work. I was just looking for a no-stress breakfast."

He laughed, a high, choppy sound I liked. "Like no cholesterol," he said.

I tried to laugh with him.

He said, "Are you talking to Fanny any more than you're talking to me?"

I shook my head. Then I said, "This morning. I tried again."

"You sad motherfucker," he said. "You tried talking English and she didn't jump up and down, right? Remember what I said about you have to *live* communicating? Remember? All the time, not just when you get frightened?"

I said, "How'd you know about the frightened?"

There was sweat on his upper lip. He wiped at it.

"Archie," I said.

He clasped his hands. I did the same, but my cup was in the way and I spilled it onto the table and jumped up.

He said, "It's fine, Jack. It's all right."

Verna, bringing my filled thermos, came with a big yellow sponge. "Don't you listen to him," she said. "It's not all right. And you didn't eat nothing, neither."

Archie said, "She wants a bigger tip." She swatted at him with the sponge.

People went back to eating and talking and smoking, and Verna left. I stood beside the table, laying money on it and zipping my coat.

Archie asked, "You want to come by the office, Jack? Or the house?"

"I'll see," I said. "You know. Thank you."

He looked sad. I couldn't imagine what I looked like. He gave me half a wave, and I waved back like he was a hundred yards of snow and ice away from me. When I was outside the Blue Bird and looking back up at the window tables, I saw the poster, taped to the back of the storefront so people walking by could read it. That was the first one I remember.

———

I saw another one in the window of a pickup truck parked at the curb, and there was one in the window of the Radio Shack. When I got to the security building, there was a poster tacked to the door. The signs were eight and a half by eleven, in black and white. In large letters at the top was MISSING. Underneath was the face of a little girl —fourteen, according to the sign—with a sweet smile and white teeth and wide eyes. She weighed ninety-six pounds. She was five feet tall. She had gone from Sunday school to her house in one of the little towns south of the college, and she had never arrived. She looked happy and fragile. It was easy to think of a large man with his hands around her upper arms, compelling her into a car or truck or doorway. It became such a huge county, when you looked at the picture, in the hugeness of New York State, in such a big continent. You could cry, looking at her face.

It had bloomed overnight, and I saw it everyplace. Anthony Berberich had a poster taped to the window of his Jeep, and every building I had occasion to enter that morning had posters taped and tacked onto doors and bulletin boards and corridor walls. Her family was doing what they could, and I wished I knew them so I could tell them so. My throat ached at the thought of seeing their faces, or hearing them talk. I'd have given a lot to know, without having to ask them, what they did to erase from their minds the idea of the fear she must have felt. Of course, I didn't have to ask. They didn't erase it because they couldn't. I wondered if Fanny had seen the posters at the hospital, and I nearly phoned. But she might have been able to sleep, I thought, and probably that was why I didn't call.

I wanted not to see the picture of the missing child, but wherever I went, she was looking back. Her name was Janice Tanner. I knew a Tanner Hill in the vicinity, and I wondered if it was named after her family. On the way home once after work, I had driven up the road over Tanner Hill. It had looked pleasant and far from everyplace else, and I hadn't seen a child in skirt and sweater and sneakers who was in jeopardy. I saw my English professor, but I pretended not to. I waved to a kid who was a friend of mine, Everett Stark, who'd come to school after four years in the navy. I once asked him how he was doing, and he said, "Man, ain't nothin around here but white folks and cows."

I had to park up behind a little tan Chevrolet import that kept rolling down the worst part of the classroom building hill. I stopped the Jeep in the middle of the road, with the bumper just touching the car, and I hit the roof light to keep student traffic off us. They raced up the hill to get to their illegal parking places and they believed that death and maiming were limited by law to people over twenty-two. Once I looked at the little car's tires, I understood. They were almost bald. I walked around to the driver's side and she looked at me the way I sometimes look at sheriff's deputies filling their quota of speeding tickets.

"Morning," I said.

"I'm late for class," she said. Her voice was harsh, but in an interesting way. She had a big mouth and a beaky nose and hair sprouting all over the place from under her dark woolen cap.

"I can get out of your way and let you roll back down," I said, "or I can try and push you up, or I can chock your wheels and drive you to class if it's a real emergency, or we can hang around a little and you can be abusive."

"I'm not being abusive," she said.

"I know. I figured you were thinking about it."

Her smile was very broad.

"You might get angry when I point out that your tires are shot. If I was a cop, I'd cite you for that."

"But you're not."

I shook my head. "I'm a campus cop. Like an usher in the movies."

"When did you ever go to a movie with an usher? You must be old."

"You wouldn't believe how old," I said. "I'll try and push you up. Let go your brake when you feel me behind you and give it just a little bit of power. I'll do the rest."

She blushed and looked away, then smiled the smile. "I assume that was not a double entendre."

"Doobel what?"

"Never mind," she said. "Forgive me. Yes. I'll—what you said before." She rolled her window up and, like a child, waved a small hand in a leather mitten.

Everyone was waving good-bye to me, I thought as I released my parking brake and put it in first and made contact with her car. She slid back down into me, but I held in four-wheel drive and we made it up to the social sciences parking lot. I put it back into two-wheel drive and pulled out before she could wave again.

I radioed in what I'd done so they could add it to the day's log. The dispatcher told me that a professor was asking for me.

"Is that an emergency? Over."

"Negative, Jack. Professor Strodemaster says when you can. Over."

"So anytime I get what they like to call a spare minute? Over."

"That's a roger, Jack. Soon as you empty out somebody's ashtray for them and, you know, spread the peanut butter on their sandwich, you can drop in. He'll be there all day, he said to tell you. Over."

I wondered if the vice president for administrative affairs had monitored our frequency. I figured class warfare was nothing new to him, but I thought I should tell the dispatcher we might tighten our procedures just a little. It never hurt to pretend you were a professional.

———

I saw one of the cars I thought came over the hill from Masonville, which was north and west from town, in the direction of Syracuse. The school there was an agricultural and technical two-year-degree college that I had heard was often the difference in the lives of local kids. They learned computer skills, or took degrees in cosmetology or nutrition or modern farming methods. Recently, it had begun to receive large numbers of kids from the New York City area. Their high school guidance counselors thought or hoped or made believe that the hundreds of miles from New York were a buffer. They weren't, and the trade in weapons and pharmaceuticals was large.

It was an old, scuffed black Trans Am fitted out with an air scoop and a spoiler, and it probably sounded, running flat out, like the Concord jet clearing its throat. It was parked outside the student union, nose to the low brick wall, and I pulled up behind it tight, so I knew it would stay there. I asked the dispatcher to run a check with the state police, and to ask Big Pete, who was barely five foot six, to back me up, no lights or sirens. The car had a Masonville sticker on the rear window, a Grateful Dead head on the right rear, and a big silver crucifix hanging from the rearview mirror. I saw three crumpled brown paper bags on the floor of the passenger's side. I knew I could safely bet a week's wages that the kid who owned or drove the car had carried such a sack inside the union with him. I mean, these were upper-middle-class students, and they were accustomed to service. You sell them grass, you have to deliver. And the kids at Masonville, who were the children of parents supporting themselves through service jobs, if they lived with their parents and their parents worked, didn't mind making a call.

"You got a problem with my car?" the kid said. He'd come limping up after pausing only once—long enough to see I had his car and I'd seen him approach and he was mine.

"If I use my best party manners, would you open it up and show me what's in the bags in front on the floor?"

He was short, broad, pale, a fine-boned Irish kid with curly dark hair and an angry mouth. His limp was the city stud's tough-guy walk, and it grew even more exaggerated as he came closer. He said, "Would you like to maybe go fuck yourself? Or you got a warrant lets you look in my car? Or would you maybe want to show a little respect for a private citizen's constitutional rights?"

By then, Big Pete was there and sizing us up. He came over after a minute, and I said, "Pete, this visitor to the campus has been making a delivery. I asked to see the goodies he brought, but he said I should go fuck myself."

"*Maybe* fuck yourself," the kid corrected, smiling. "A suggestion made with manners, same as you. It was just an idea. Maybe you got a better idea. I'll listen." He was under twenty, I thought. He seemed to consider himself an independent businessman, and he seemed to think of Pete and me as make-believe cops. He was right. The wind was shaking the vehicles and moving us around.

"Get into my car," I said, "so we don't freeze. We can talk in there."

"Now, I got a choice? Or this is a show of force? Or what?"

"Pete, you want to call in we're having a conference and then wait in your vehicle awhile?"

"Watch him," Pete told me, with his gift for talking uselessly.

When we were in my Jeep, the kid said, "We gonna deal?"

"I don't know what you think a deal is. If we're trading, I've got your car, and I know you'd like it back eventually. What've you got for me?"

"You can't keep the car. It's private property. I bought it, I paid for it, and I pay the insurance on it. I'm on my lawful way, good-bye. You keep smiling when I talk. I'm funny? All *I* got to do is call a cop. You can't. You're breaking the law. I studied up on this shit in college, man."

"I'll give you my radio and help you make the call. Then I'll tell the cop what's in the front of your car."

"You don't know."

"We'll let the cops find out. What do you like, local guys, sheriff's deputies, or state troopers?"

"No, see, they got to obey the law, too. It's to protect a citizen like me from guys like you, they throw their weight around. I got a professor could tell you this shit like he told it to me." He had a sweet smile. He must have destroyed the girls with his lost outlaw number. "Any kind of cop," he said, "they *got* to have a warrant."

"What's your name, Mr. Bill of Rights? It's coming in on the radio any minute."

"You ran me?"

"I saw it in a movie one time, so, yeah, I made the same noises they did. And guess what?" I was hoping the dispatcher would call back with the registration.

"You fucking *ran* me? You can do that?"

Dispatch came in with it. William Franklin of Staten Island, New York. He had enough points on his license so that one more ticket would ground him.

I said, "Dispatch, this is Jack. Over."

"Dispatch."

"Ask Elmo St. John to stand by. Nothing yet, just stand by. I think I may need him to write a town citation for disturbing the peace. Or dangerous driving on a county road. Or reckless you name it. Something you could detain someone for. Over."

"Elmo to stand by. Roger."

"He's the village cop," I told William Franklin. "He's a prick like me in a silly uniform. Except he can write something besides parking tickets," I said. "We'll get your license canceled for a year or so. It'd hurt your education in constitutional law. Wouldn't it?"

"What'll it cost?" he said. He sounded older than me.

"Who you deal to here."

"Names?"

"Unless you prefer to go by the customer number on the label of their L. L. Bean catalog."

He breathed out a long, sour breath.

I picked up the microphone and clicked it.

"Dispatch. Somebody in trouble? Over."

"This is Jack. Is Elmo ready? Over."

"Dispatch. Elmo's curious. He says to tell you he never wrote a dangerous-driving. He's curious, and he's on his way."

I said to the kid, "You ready?"

He nodded. "You made up your mind," he said. "You own my ass and that's that."

"That's that." I canceled the local police, I sent Big Pete back on his rounds, and I wrote down the names the kid from Masonville gave me. I knew he was lying and so did he, but short of some kind of savagery, some battery and mayhem, I was getting nothing from him but a little hesitation, the tiniest beginning of fear. He might shy away after this, though I wouldn't have sworn it.

William Franklin was in the right-hand seat in front, half-turned to me, and he was telling me lies.

I said, "That's everyone?"

"That's everyone, boss."

"You need to see this from my point of view," I said. "I'm supposed to protect these kids. Their mommies and daddies want me to, you know, watch over them a little."

He smiled what was really an attractive smile. He had a nicely textured complexion and clear dark eyes.

I turned to face him directly. I squared up on the seat and laid into his left cheek and temple with my right forearm. It was a short chop, which is how you want to do it. Long, loopy blows diminish the power that a short one will focus. His head snapped back and struck the passenger-side window and his eyes rolled up. They didn't stay shut. They fluttered, so I knew he wasn't quite out.

"Please don't come back to campus," I said.

He said, "I—"

"Please," I said. "Don't call me anything. Don't threaten me with lawsuits or the real police. Just go away. Leave these boys and girls to spend their money on booze and prophylactics and carfare to wherever they go to get their tans. Just leave, please." Then I said, "You feel all right to drive?"

I reached across him and opened the door and shoved him. He spilled but landed on his feet, holding on to the door frame.

I said, "Don't *dare* to slam the door."

He left it. I reached across and shut it, then backed up. He unlocked his car and sat in it awhile. I backed up farther, and he came back, then drove downhill. At first, he went quickly, but I stuck my hand out my window and made the downward-pressing signal to go slow, and after a while he saw it and cut his speed. I followed him until he was at the light across from the Blue Bird. When he drove out of town, he lifted his hand out the window and hoisted his third finger into the air above the roof. I went back to the campus, telling the dispatcher where I'd been. My arm felt a little strained under my coat, but I knew it was my imagination. The body was just remembering the blow it had delivered. It had been an excellent shot. And the rest of me, that minute, sad to say, felt exceptionally good.

———

The teacher who sent for me, Randolph Strodemaster, was a big, noisy man who couldn't decide whether to be a small-town local booster or a big-shot physics professor. He lived in a hamlet a few miles from school. It straddled a river and once supported a leatherworking industry. He knew its history and told it, he was a member of its volunteer fire department, he served bready meatballs and sticky spaghetti at their fund-raising dinners, and he was said to incorporate small-town lore into his lectures on quasars and quarks. He was supposed to be important for his work, at least in his department. He liked me, I figured, because I was as big as he was, and because I was local and because I didn't know anything about his profession and because I was a campus cop. He was the kind of man who made it his business to know the deputies and EMTs and the men who hauled gravel from the bed to the construction site. He did his own masonry, and he had rented a backhoe and run it himself when he had to lay in a leach field for his waste-disposal system. He was famous in his town, I was told, for making a mess of his sewage.

"Randy," I said at his door. He was in the new science building, which, as far as I could see, consisted of empty classrooms and small offices with expensive-looking furniture. It smelled of electricity.

"Jack, boy," he said. "Thank you."

"What'd I do?"

"You came up."

"You *sent* for me."

"Tell me you came because we're friends."

I said, "Randy, damned right."

"Good man." He stood, took a sport coat from an upholstered chair, moved the chair a quarter of an inch, and motioned me to sit in it. He was wearing a long-sleeved T-shirt that showed the bunchy muscles in his arms and shoulders. I should have known that he lifted. He probably worked out with the football team. His gold-rimmed glasses had slipped down his nose and as he sat he pushed them back up.

"I'm not just an asshole who teaches hard science, Jack."

I waited.

"I'm a pretty good guy."

Why not? I nodded.

"I live in a pretty good town."

"I heard it was nice there."

"Heaven on earth," he chanted. "You know who else lives there?"

I shook my head.

"The Tanners," he said.

"Who? Oh, the family. Of the—"

"The little girl, Janice. The one who's missing," he said. His big, hard face looked like a slab of light oak with a line of dark grain where the mouth should be. He looked like those movie heroes who swing through windows on a rope, gun firing, muscles jumping, the hard lines of the mouth showing how upset they are with evildoers. He had big hands with long fingers and thick, broad nails. They moved on each other, like he had a rash or like each hand gave the other one comfort. I didn't know him well and I didn't want to. I never trusted men who tried too hard to make me like them. I never knew why they would. And he looked as sad as anyone I'd seen since sunrise.

I said, "The state guys might find her. They're good."

"They're good," he said.

"You think she's in trouble? You think she didn't just run away?"

"They waited a week, Jack. They had the cops in two days, state the same night, they waited until a week was out, and then they did the posters up and started running ads—you know, they did what you can do. Meanwhile, the fuzz are doing what they can do. And it's not enough. And they know their child. She's one of those 'go to church, join the cheerleaders, do your homework and help Mom with the chores' kids. She wouldn't run away. I know her. I really think they're right. A lot of us do. The fuzz keep hoping she took off, so then they won't have to run a search and try to find her and admit they can't."

It was when he said "fuzz" that I remembered. He'd been very active in the seventies, I'd heard, protesting against the war. I'd been told how he prided himself on getting arrested a couple of times for demonstrating against Richard Nixon. His glasses caught the light, his muscles moved heavily under the tight cotton shirt, and he smiled, like we shared a feeling.

"I guess that's it," I said. "Everybody's doing whatever you can do when a kid disappears. She looks like a sweet kid in the posters."

"She's terrific. She's like my own daughter, Jack. I'm wondering about one thing more. The pigs are grunting—no offense, all right? —and I think maybe they'll get the FBI involved. After a while. But that's mostly big-pigs stuff. And meanwhile, there's this splendid family and their gorgeous little missing daughter, and the parents don't understand law enforcement. They're very simple people. Quite brilliant in certain ways. They're religious, and I don't understand religion, but I understand people. Teaching's about people. Right? So's your line of work, here on campus. We know about people, don't we? You can imagine the agony they're in."

I wanted to say that I did, but I heard myself say, "I can?"

"Don't bullshit a bullshitter, Jack. I know what you did when you went after that kid who walked up into the woods, all coked out or whatever, and she nearly died and you got her down. Archie said what you were was *tender*. You mind being called that? You think it damages your reputation? You're a man called tender by a man who ought to know."

"My good friend Archie."

"This shit matters, Jack. It's a little *girl*. They're so frightened. They're so thrown by this."

"The state guys are good," I said. "They're excellent."

"Can you explain that to the Tanners?"

"Why do you need me to do that? Because I'm so tender?"

"Because of your history."

I was standing then. "What's that supposed to mean."

"I know about the child. Your child."

"What's *that* supposed to mean? And who told you about our life?"

"Archie Halpern."

"He wants me involved in this?"

"I talked to him before I talked to you."

"So he could leak my life to you."

"All he did was tell me a little about your service record and that you lost someone—a child. Because we need to help the Tanners find *theirs*. Now, given your history, and seeing your face now, I can understand your not wanting to get involved. You're a human being, too, and it makes sense. You want to stay out, you stay out. You feel this way, *I* think you should. You sit it out because you need to, that's what you do and you get my vote. All right? Hey. I'm your friend either way."

"I thought you needed me, because I'm so terribly tender and an ex-MP, to tell them how the state cops will work very hard to try to find her."

"Then that," he said. "The point is, you can do that or not. You call it. What I don't want is you hurting yourself over this. This is me and you, Jack." He didn't look like a smiling small-town Rotarian in training. He didn't look like one of the goofier professors. He looked like a very serious man with a terrible headache and red-shot eyes and oily skin.

I said, "No."

"You can say that and nobody respects you any the less."

"And I really don't give a goddamn about what you can do about my job. I get fired, I get fired. So get this completely straight. Don't you talk about me and my wife and our—our— Don't talk about us like we're some kind of *story* to tell when you and your friends drink sherry. Understand me?"

"I hate sherry," he said.

"Not cute. Don't. And don't ever talk to me about it. All right? Go do your life and leave me in mine, and we're finished. No more after now, *starting* now. We're done."

He sat back and looked at his desk. He raised his hand. I knew what he was going to do. My day had been nothing but. He waved good-bye.

———

It was beginning to snow when I got back in the Jeep and told the dispatcher I was patrolling. I went to the top of the campus and worked my route down, then drove to the dormitories and sports buildings that were adjacent to the campus. I wrote out tickets to two Saabs and a Toyota 4Runner, then ticketed some shabby old American cars to show that I would treat the professors the same as their students. I drove a kid with a busted leg from his classroom building to his dorm. He complained about the pressure of the crutches under his arms. Then I came back to the social sciences building to pick up a coed and her wheelchair and take her to her apartment. She made jokes about her legs that didn't work, and she didn't complain about the chair.

The snow grew denser, and I worried about how bad it would be for Fanny on our road. They often didn't plow it in heavy snows because very few people lived on it. She was a competent woman, an emergency room head nurse who could handle any sort of disaster I'd heard of. She was tall and square-shouldered and had level, bushy eyebrows that were the same dark brown as her hair. She wore her hair up at work, and when she came home, she let it drop, saying, "Ahhh." I used to watch her do it, and I'd feel my muscles let go, knowing we were home, both of us together, and now it was all right. She was a terrible driver, though, especially in snow, because she was so used to being in control. When you drive on ice and snow, you have to know there are certain kinds—the loose-packed, wet, slick-surfaced snow—that can kill you. You have to know how the dense stuff will let you control a lot of the motion of your car. But, whatever kind it is, you have to be able to let go just a little, stop steering at certain kinds of slide, stop overcontrolling because it looks treacherous, and simply permit the weight of the car, plus its momentum, plus a tiny adjustment of the wheel, plus *accelerator,* not brake, to take you through the turn. But Fanny was used to controlling situations. It was her job. I'd pulled her out of snowdrifts, embankments, roadside ditches filled with slush. She'd telephoned from strangers' farmhouses and from public phones in the center of town. I worried as much about the strangers in the farmhouses as I did about the skids.

I wondered what degree of sleeplessness she'd have to reach before it affected her work and a doctor would report her. But who'd they report her to? You don't find good nurses from good programs very easily in upstate New York. They couldn't afford to lose her, so they might leave her alone and she might commit some terrible mistake. And driving home, with so little sleep, after the constant push of the ER, what might she drive into, given an unlighted country road and her hands squeezed too tight on the wheel? I saw her leaning forward, steering with tired, jerky motions. I saw the car, on a slithery hill, going into a long, fast loop.

We were going to have to talk. Archie was right. But he'd sold me to Strodemaster. Well, not completely, not really. He told the guy I'd had some experience in the loss of children. It wasn't a secret, really. We just didn't talk about it. Strodemaster wanted the girl found, and that was all right. Archie thought I could help because he trusted me. All right. And what he had told me, again and again, casually, as casually as a round-faced, sweating man who looked like a hog in love could be casual, was that Fanny and I needed to talk all the time, not just when it exploded in us.

About our child.

So we would have to talk. So that Fanny wouldn't turn her knuckles white against the steering wheel and come off the road and pitch through her windshield. I couldn't help seeing what the glass of a windshield looks like after someone has gone into it in a collision. There's always so much blood, and it ends up in the starred but not shattered off-white sections. It's like a jigsaw puzzle joined with blood.

I parked outside the humanities building and started in the basement, trying doors, making a note of who was working in an isolated corner of the building as late afternoon got dark and the snow intensified. It was too early, really, to be checking the building, but I needed to be out of the car and out of the thoughts about Fanny that hung inside it like someone's cigarette smoke. The posters about Janice Tanner were on the walls and many office doors. Her smile had a downward tug to it, like she might be someone who would easily cry. But it was a bright smile, and her dark eyes seemed to be smiling, too. She was very small and fragile-looking. After a while, after seeing the smiles, and the eyes, and the word MISSING, I couldn't look at her. When I saw one of the posters, and its promise of a reward for information, I had to look away.

I went back to the Jeep and answered a call about a disturbance at one of the fraternities. The row of them, very large houses, very well kempt, lined the street across from the bottom of the campus and its hill. The disturbance was a fight. By the time I arrived, it was a fight that was over. One boy was on his hands and knees, bleeding from the nose and mouth into the snow. The boy who had apparently put him down stood with his arms at his sides, his shirt torn open, and he wailed. He was like a dog, with his head pointed up, and with shrill yipping noises coming from his face.

I got the boy who was down to sit on my running board, and I stopped the bleeding from his nose. I used his shirt to stanch it, then wrapped him in a blanket. I took his name and told him to stay put. I talked to the one who was making all the noise. I took his name and told him to stay where he was. According to the president of the house, a big handsome kid who looked like he could have taken either of them, and who seemed more upset than either of them, they had fought over a girl. "A woman," they called her. I made them shake hands. They embraced and wept together. I heard one of them say, "Fuckin' bitch," so I knew American manhood was defended again. I took the bloodied one to the college infirmary. His assailant insisted on coming. I wrapped him in a second blanket. I had thought of taking them to the hospital. I thought I might see Fanny in case she was in before her shift for some reason. But the infirmary was closer, and it was open, and I followed the rules. I wrote a report while I waited, and then I took them back.

The snow was very, very bad now, and I thought seriously about calling Fanny or stopping at the hospital. She hated it when I said she drove badly, because she insisted on doing everything well. So I finished the rest of my paperwork at the security building and I started home. The worst of our weather was in February and March. It dawned at twenty below, often enough, and often enough it didn't reach zero. On February afternoons, I drove home in purple-blue darkness, the headlights making the ice sparkle. This afternoon, it was black, and the snow was thick, and I couldn't see with the lights on their high beam. I kept the headlights low, made sure the cocoa doormat was squarely over the hole through which exhaust as well as cold air leaked in, and I did a steady twenty miles per hour off the campus and north, instead of south toward home. There was a small, shabby lumberyard I knew, endangered by the hardware chains that also sold wood, and I gave them my business in the name of general revenge. I had to estimate the dimensions and quantities of drywall and studs, nails and drywall screws and joint compound. I should have known it by heart, since Fanny and I had talked off and on for months about almost making the decision to do the room.

Lumber with a red flag stapled to the end of a stud protruded through the open back window. Freezing air and carbon monoxide were sucked in, mixing with what was coming through the floor. I kept the full blast of warm air blowing onto the windshield, I kept the wipers clacking, and I drove slowly, hoping for the best. I got home. Every mile closer to it, I thought I ought to go back for Fanny. She didn't want me to. I knew that. I thought I should. She knew *that*.

How good that we knew what we knew.

Our road was getting axle-high in snow, and I thought the town crews would decide to stay in until the snow stopped. Why plow twice?

I answered: Because of Fanny coming home.

I let the dog out, and we stayed outside awhile, tossing snowballs and talking about the day. He butted me in the thigh a few times and dashed around the yard in the snow, then went up on the side porch because it was time to get fed. I poured out his kibble, and after he inhaled it, I let him out again to roam. Then I propped the door open and unloaded the wagon, carrying the materials directly upstairs so I wouldn't change my mind. It took me quite a few trips. Then I closed the car up, got the mail from the roadside box, brought the dog in, and turned on the porch lights in case Fanny came home early. I turned up the heat so she would be warm.

The studs and firring strips for cleats and pine one-by-tens for shelves were on the hallway floor outside the room, and the plaster-board and compound and drywall tape and sacks of nails and screws were leaning against the hallway door. Inside, there was the closet, the little writing table, the small bed, the shelf unit. We had given the toys and books away. The plan had evolved to this: We would build bookshelves along the long outer wall, we would build a unit of storage shelves along the opposite wall next to the closet, and the room would become a kind of office. Fanny could keep professional records here, and we would do the bills together, she sitting at a desk and I in a rocker. The idea was to make us stop feeling what wasn't in the room. In our bedroom, or carrying woolens in plastic bags filled with mothballs to store in the big closet at the end of the hall, we felt it. It was like a bruise. If you hurt your arm, you could run your hand along it and then you'd suddenly wince. It was a part of our house that made us wince.

I put down some blue plastic tarpaulins to protect the floor. I brought in extension cords and my circular saw. I made sure the battery in the drill was charged. I looked at the wallpaper that Fanny had put up. She was good with wallpaper. I had forgotten paint. I would have to use the heat gun and a putty knife and take the wallpa-per down, because you can't pay bills and balance your checkbook in any hardheaded way with Bambi smiling at you from the wall.

So I sat on a ladder and, with the heat gun roaring, taking care not to cook the walls or the studs behind them, I took Bambi down, a square at a time. When I let the heat gun focus too long and the wallpaper began to smoke, the smell made me hungry and I remembered I hadn't eaten dinner or lunch. I thought about Archie Halpern at the Blue Bird and remembered I hadn't had breakfast, either. I thought I'd start to drool and drip on the heat gun and electrocute myself. The dog waited in the hall, and he escorted me to the refrigerator. There was a plastic-wrapped bowl of noodles with some kind of green peas and cheese and bacon in them. There was another bowl, this one filled with Fanny's winter vegetable soup. I looked at the cheese in its wrap. I looked at eggs and at pickles in a jar. I took a glass of orange juice and went back upstairs to eliminate Bambi.

I woke up when the heat gun fell out of my hand.

"Okay," I said. Outside, in the hallway, the dog thumped his tail. I said, "You're right. It's a sign. You fall asleep, you know it's a signal to get a little sleep." The dog banged back. I unplugged the heat gun, ran my hand along the wall to make sure it was cool. I had taken most of the long wall down; it was a good night's work. I went downstairs and sat in the back room with the lights off. I heard the snow hitting the windows, the wind gusting, the tikkety-tak of a dog's nails on the wooden floor.

I told him, "Come lie down." He hit the floor beside the sofa. I lay down on it and said, "I'll get you out to pee later on. You let me know if I forget." His tail thumped twice. I closed my eyes and felt the day.

Days.

Longer than that.

I let my breath go out and out and out. I said, my mouth so tired that I barely moved it, "Thank you, God, for all this shit you've given us, you son of a bitch." I waited. I waited a minute more as my arms and legs got heavy while my brain filled like a sail with what I was thinking. "You son of a bitch," I said. I got up, went to the side door, and let the dog out. I made myself some toast and, when I couldn't decide what to spread on it, I ate it dry. When the dog came in, I went back up and worked on stripping the walls.

jelly

HEARD A ROARING sound in the road and I woke up on the floor of the room. The dog was beside me, waiting. At the window, I saw the wrecker drive off, yellow lights whirling. He had left Fanny's car outside our little drive. The road was unplowed and so was the drive. When the town plows did come, they'd have to detour her car, but they would, and there we were, both of us home and nobody killed. I heard her walk slowly through the house. I went into the bathroom, and by the time I came out, the dog had found her and had been released to go outside.

I made coffee while she changed from her uniform. I called in sick.

She came back downstairs while I was doing that, and she said, "What?"

I told the dispatcher, "Tomorrow. Guaranteed."

Fanny waited. She was wearing jeans and a thick black turtleneck and wool-lined moccasins over woolen socks. She kept rubbing her hands together like she was cold. Her eyebrows were up over her pale face, and her lips looked bitten. Her green eyes were wide. She was waiting to hear bad news.

"I just got too tired," I said. "It isn't anything. I got tired."

"Depression makes you tired," she said.

"Then everybody I know is tired."

She smiled a little and nodded.

"Coffee's up pretty soon," I said. She sat at the table and folded her hands. "Was it rough?"

"No," she said. "A lot of car wrecks, nothing too terrible. Did you hear the tow truck?"

"You didn't get hurt."

"No," she said, "no. I'm fine. I came down Potter Road and I wasn't thinking, I was half back in ER and halfway home, I guess. I did what I always do. I hit the brakes at the last minute, and I sailed through the T junction and into where the plows dropped off these huge loads of snow they were moving. I couldn't back out."

"So you went to the farmhouse up there where the vampires live—"

"They were very nice to me."

"And instead of calling me, you called a stranger from a stranger's house."

"The stranger," she said, "was a tow truck stranger. You do not offer a tow truck, among your attractions."

"I have towed you out of every other snowbank in the county."

"I thought you'd be in the shower."

"Or shaving," I suggested.

She said, "Balancing the checkbook."

I said, "We're joking about this, right? We're being relaxed and friendly and we're joking about this?"

"He got me home, Jack. And he was polite and helpful. He kept calling me ma'am."

"Did you correct him?"

She put her head down on her hands and rolled her head to signify no.

I poured coffee for us, then let the dog in and rewarded him with a biscuit for identifying his own door. He lapped a lot of water from his dish, groaned, and lay down under the table. I knew he was on Fanny's feet. She lifted her head and looked at her coffee, then leaned back in the chair.

"And you're only tired?" she said. "Not sick?"

"Not sick. I started in doing the room."

She put her cup down.

I said, "We'd pretty much decided."

"Pretty much," she said. "I thought we might talk about it again."

"All right," I said.

"Well, there isn't much point. Not if you've begun. What'd you do?"

"There *is* a point. We can talk. I can stop. It doesn't have to happen."

"What made you begin?"

I shook my head. I shrugged.

"And what did you do?"

"I took a lot of wallpaper down."

"The Bambi?"

"That's the wallpaper."

"Why does it have to come *down?*" Her eyes were full.

"So I can build the bookshelves we talked about." I sounded to myself like a reasonable man, but I'm not sure that's who she heard.

"But Bambi doesn't have to come down for us to make bookshelves. We could've seen the paper through the shelves. That wouldn't have hurt anybody, Jack. She used to look at the wallpaper. She used to make noises at Bambi, Jack. She would have learned to *talk* to him. How can you take it down?"

I did not tell her that I'd done only two walls and that there were plenty of fawns with big eyes. I took a sip of coffee and I sat an instant. Then I said, "I'm sorry. I think I didn't understand. I have to get a shower and change my clothes." I went upstairs.

When I came down, the dog was lying behind the living room sofa, slapping his tail against the floor, which meant Fanny was on it and blowing her nose. I put my boots on and I went out to shovel snow. It took me an hour of sweating in the very cold, very still day to clear the area between my car and the road. I dug around the axles to make sure they were clear. Then I started up the old bomber and went in to tell Fanny she was snowbound. The tow truck had left her car in the road, and the plows had gone around it, sealing it behind

a thick wall of snow. She wasn't in the living room. I heard her
upstairs, and I heard the dog's nails. I tracked the sounds and knew
she was in the room, looking at what I'd erased.

I heard something shatter and I figured it might be a coffee cup.
I hoped it wasn't a window. I heard objects against a wall. I heard—I
barely could hear it—the sound of Fanny breathing hard while she
lifted things. The studs clattered and there was a thick, solid noise
that could have been a sheet of plasterboard getting holed. I knew
what she looked like. Her eyes would be huge. Her face would be wet
with her tears. It would be very pale. She would lift and push like a
man. She was trained to be physical. She knew about wreckage. Right
now, she wanted some. When she went like this, her lips curled in
on each other and she looked through whatever she was moving into
the air and onto walls and floors. She was there, but she also wasn't,
and her empty eyes were frightening.

I knew she had waited until she thought I was gone. She was
never not fair. She had waited so that I wouldn't think of what she
did as warfare. It wasn't. I knew that. It was mourning. It was grief. It
was some kind of general rage. I thought there had to be a difference
between those feelings. I thought I could ask Archie Halpern what
the difference might mean. Or Fanny, I thought. Archie would tell
me how she'd be someone to ask. I sipped a little hot coffee and I
called Strodemaster. He shouted into the phone. I took one of our
telephone pads and a pen. It seemed to make sense to take notes.
You take notes, I'd learned on my jobs, and you can focus on something besides your feelings. That would be a sound idea today.

———

The tiny village Janice Tanner's parents lived in was like a long crossroads separated from an ice-choked river by a cornfield that ran about
a third of a mile. Under all that heavy whiteness was corn stubble. In
the spring, I thought, deer would wander down from the hills and
across the river and into the field. It would be good to see them doing
that if spring ever came. I didn't believe it would.

Most of the population here was in the houses that lay parallel to the river on either side of the road. I'd seen dozens of hamlets like this one. The children, some very young and some almost teenaged, shifted in clusters from lawn to yard to lawn to yard, from game to game. Kids grew up here, before they moved to driving and drinking and sex, by fishing together and torturing frogs and picking the worms from tomatoes in gardens, and when you drove through and saw them in noisy clusters, it occurred to you that human life was possible.

I drove to Strodemaster's house and went in the back door. He was in a heavy blue woolen bathrobe and unlaced boots. "*Here* he is!" he called. He acted embarrassed. He didn't want to meet my eyes. I tried to think of a way to get him off the hook, but I couldn't. I'm not very good at that. He shouted, "Damn it, Jack, I'm glad as hell. Good man!"

He brought me coffee I didn't want, and breakfast cake in a supermarket wrapper. When I looked at his kitchen and the toothpaste stains down the front of his bathrobe, I remembered that his wife had left him. She had taken their kids, a daughter and a son. I remembered that gossip had him driving her out. He periodically moved in local women, but they left promptly enough, and he was a handsome-looking, lonely-looking, shabby middle-aged man. Let that be a lesson to you, I thought, tracking the green-white drip marks on his bathrobe.

There was a stale, sweet smell in the kitchen, or leaking into it from elsewhere in the house. He might have profited from taking the garbage out, I thought. I got used to it soon enough. The birch-veneer kitchen suite had been bought at Sears, I figured, with a coupon booklet for paying it off. The floor was linoleum, a kind of vines and sticks pattern that made me feel I was going to fall through the flimsy sticks. The wallpaper complemented the floor, though there seemed to be very large bugs on whatever the tiny white flowers were. I didn't want to know about wallpaper. He was talking about the police, finding it necessary to call them "the fuzz," and I realized that at about the time I was doing my work in the war, he was probably calling me some kind of killer.

On the far wall, next to the telephone, was a large black chalk-board surrounded by cork. There were curled notes and cartoons tacked in the cork. A piece of chalk attached to the board by red string hung straight down. On the board, someone had written "Oreg-ano" and, under it, a different hand had written "de Bergerac."

Strodemaster called, "*Here* they are!" and Janice Tanner's parents came in. They were shy-looking people, tall and a little stooped. They looked like brother and sister. I could see the daughter's pointed chin in their faces, and her large eyes, though neither of them had eyes that drew you as hers did. The husband had very long arms and legs, a short torso, and a long neck. The wife was better proportioned, and at first I thought she was tanned. I realized, after a while, that she was brown-yellow from cancer or the treatments.

They sat at the table and we all had to have cups of coffee and doughnuts and pastry. Mr. Tanner nodded at the plate before him and said, "Piece of cake, you could say."

Mrs. Tanner ignored him. Strodemaster said, "You're a gutsy man, Reverend."

Mrs. Tanner seemed to be shivering. She looked up and caught my stare. She gave me a little smile.

Like a kid, and despising myself right away, I blew on my hands to show her it was really the temperature, not the dying.

Strodemaster saw, and he moved out of his chair to the living room. I heard his footsteps and then the furnace coming on. He returned, chafing his hands. He sat, and the silence began.

Finally, I said, "I'm not an investigator."

The father looked at my pad and my pen. "I'm a campus cop," I said, "a security person. I have some training, but I got it twenty years ago. I don't carry a weapon. I don't have a license to investigate. I have a pistol permit, but I can't imagine what good it would do us. I did a little investigating in the service—this was years ago. Not too much, not that successfully. What I mostly did was bully drunk sol-diers and drug addicts and men who were sad about their marriages. That kind of thing. What I do now is run after college kids who drink too much, mostly. So you shouldn't expect me to know a lot, or to be able to find out a lot. You need to understand how little I can offer you."

They stared at me. The father blinked, the mother seemed hardly to move her eyes from me, and Strodemaster ate a jelly doughnut and drank with a lot of noise. His doughnut leaked on his fingers and as he licked them he made a kind of low hum. He seemed very happy in a strange way. It annoyed me. I thought he ought to be sad. But he was enjoying this. I guessed because he wanted it so much. He seemed to have appetites for everything. His bathrobe picked up blots of coffee mixed with milk and crumbs of cake.

"Are you religious?" the father asked.

"Well," I said. "No."

"I'm a pastor. That's my church you passed, driving in. Sunday school is taught in the basement by my wife here. Our daughter came out of God's house and she disappeared. You wouldn't see that part of it as meaningful, I take it. Or would you?"

"I don't know yet. But I wouldn't take it up with God, if that's what you're asking."

"She's alive," the mother said.

I nodded.

"No, she is. I feel her. I felt her after we conceived her, and I feel her stirring now. She's alive. She's well. She's frightened, but she's coping. She always could."

"She looks lovely. In the picture. You've done a wonderful job of getting the posters out."

"Everybody's helping," the mother said. "How could you not help a child that good?"

I nodded. "And what, exactly, did you think I might be able to help with?"

"Oh," the father said, "sort of interpreting for us, in a way. I don't know what the authorities mean when they tell us things. They're very busy; they're a little unwilling to talk too much about their work, I think."

"Habit," I said. "They don't mean to be cruel."

Strodemaster raised his eyebrows. He wanted them to mean to

be cruel, because he'd lived a life on the assumption that anyone not sleeping with him might be working against him. He must have been a child of ferocious appetites and pretty basic satisfactions, I thought.

I said, "Look. I can get names from you, investigators on the case, and I can visit them and ask what they know. I can tell you what they tell me, *if* they tell me. I was wondering. I drew this up in the car." I turned the pad over and showed them my little note. It asked whomever it might concern to tell me as their agent whatever the Tanners were allowed to know about the search for their child. I asked them to sign and date their signature and they did.

The mother said, "Do we pay you a retainer?"

"No, Mrs. Tanner. I'm not a lawyer or a detective. I'm just a friendly volunteer. I want you to have your daughter back." My throat tightened up when I said it, and I shut up.

Mrs. Tanner said, "There is a cosmological dimension, you know."

I said, pretty stupidly, "Like a—something about God?"

She nodded, smiling very tiredly. "A manifestation of His intelligence. A plan. Perhaps a test. It might be a desperate woman who needs a child," she said. "I feel something like that. Somebody who doesn't want to hurt anyone. Somebody with a very deep need."

I had to say it. "No, it's a man. It nearly always is."

Mr. Tanner said, "You know that."

I wanted not to answer that, so I said to her, "A plan, you said. God has a plan? Is that what you mean?"

She said, "I pray for it. If not Janice back, and safe with us, and whole, then God's design."

Her husband nodded, but his eyes were closed, and I know he was weeping or working not to.

She took my left hand in both of hers. Her skin felt clammy. Her fingers felt light, powerless. She didn't seize me; she only held. She said, "You're very decent to help. It makes you sad, doesn't it?"

"It's a sad business," I said.

"I think you're dealing with more than that," she said. Her voice had a tendency to lift, a lightness that I associated with her limbs. She was being cooked from the inside out by the radiation or the chemicals, and now she had to carry this. Three cheers for God's design, I thought.

They gave me names and telephone numbers and, like an investigator, I wrote them down. When I looked up, I saw that all of them were watching me. The expectation in their eyes reminded me of the wallpaper I should not have taken down.

———

The Tanner family printed more posters. The amount of the reward was now five thousand dollars, and I wondered where a preacher with a very sick wife finds that kind of money. The new posters were on yellow paper, and some were a foot and a half or two feet high, so there was another crop, a new flowering of her face. It was the same photograph, and the enlargement made it coarser, like she'd aged while I watched. Her mouth looked more vulnerable in the new version, and I found that I couldn't meet her eyes.

Girls run away, and not only to the Port Authority bus terminal on Forty-second Street in New York, and not only from the country. Boys and girls run away. I knew no statistics, and I hadn't talked to a cop about it, but I assumed they ran away a lot and were stolen very little. You read about it, of course, but it's usually an infant taken from a stroller or a carriage. Once in a while, a drunken father or boyfriend punches an infant to death, or burns it, or the mother kills and buries it. If the child is older, I thought, and a girl, and she hasn't run away, she's dead. I remembered a few cases of kidnapping and the rest were murder, or rape and then murder. I worked not to think about Janice Tanner in some maniac's car or trailer or furnished apartment. I tried not to think of her blood on bathroom tiles or her body in a crawl space, moving a little every time he slammed the door going out or coming home, like she still was alive and very badly hurt and frightened. I worked not to imagine her alive. I tried not to observe her fright.

I went to work every day. Sometimes at home, after a while, I slept. One day, I took the dog for a long walk over the hill behind the house, pushing myself through it until the snow, which was the height of my knees a dozen yards from the door, was up to my waist. The dog leapt, tearing himself loose, then sank in, then worked himself free, jumping again. His tongue hung out, stiff and pink, like he'd been running for an hour. I was heaving and blowing, gasping with high sounds.

"We're a couple of old guys," I told him.

He breathed in choppy pantings and his winking, friendly, alien eyes stayed on me. He was a dog bred for errands, and he waited for me to find one. The spittle turned to ice around his long, blunt muzzle, and he seemed content to pause before the next episode of our mission. I wanted to be like that. I wanted to know that orders were coming and that I'd soon perform them, and then the job would be done, and I would dive slowly into the curving path made by my flanks while I circled and circled, as if I was clearing away a nest, and lie down and sleep.

My feet were numb and my hands were cold. The winds drove past the collar of my parka and up my sleeves. My nose and cheeks hurt and even my eyeballs felt cold. It was time to turn around. The milkiness of the broad hill before us and around us was getting darker, which meant more weather coming on. It was time to fill his aluminum water dish and lock the dog in the kitchen and go to work. I tried to turn around, and my feet were slow to move. I had difficulty lifting them and wasn't surprised when I fell. He was over and at my face, licking me, delighted with our new game. I lay where I was and closed my eyes. He shoved his muzzle into my face and I felt his paw on my chest.

"Good game, huh?"

I heard myself breathe out noisily, then take in icy air with less pleasure. I listened to that for a while, and the little snorts of the dog.

I said, "Okay."

He left off, because he knew the tone. It meant *not* okay. He was waiting nearby, and I ought to be standing by now, in motion. Of course, a man doesn't walk away from his house through a field of deep snow one morning in February just before work and lie down until the winds cover him with blown snow and then die.

"I didn't say anything about dying," I said. My mouth wasn't working right, or I didn't want it to be. That was it. I sounded like someone trying hard to be drunk. I didn't like that sound, and I rolled onto my side and, when the dog returned, because he suspected action, I leaned a little of my weight on his shoulders and I got to my knees and then stood.

"Good trick," I told us. "Good." I took my glove off and found the biscuits in the pocket of my coat, and I gave him one.

"Aren't we clever," I said.

Fanny's car was in the drive, which had been plowed twice since she'd been stuck. The winter was the worst I could remember for snow, and for getting up to fight through the cold and ice and balky motors and the difficulty of simply walking between two points, a feeling in the air of not enough oxygen. Drivers on campus were cranky and less and less thoughtful. The snowplows seemed to come less frequently, though we needed them more. Fanny still drove, I was certain, with her knuckles white and her mind not focused on the surface of the road. I was glad to see her car, to know she'd made it home. But I was also a little sneaky in my approach to the side porch, because I had a need to come and go unnoticed.

She was in the kitchen, though, waiting, still in her uniform, with a heavy white sweater tied by its sleeves around her shoulders.

"You look terrible," she said. "What happened?"

"I took him for a walk," I said. "I haven't been very good, the last few days, about exercise and stuff."

"And stuff," she said.

I said, "Stuff." I saw that she'd made coffee, and I went for a cup. "How was work?"

"Quiet."

"Good."

"Dr. Kalubia's wife came to the ambulatory clinic and announced that her husband was a frequenter of whores and a carrier of diseases. He gave her venereal warts, apparently."

"That doesn't sound terribly quiet."

"Warts are *very* quiet. You wake up quietly one morning and you have them. No noise."

"But *she* wasn't quiet."

Fanny shook her head and smiled her tired smile. "But she got done pretty quickly," she said.

"What'd Kalubia say?"

"He asked if I would like, some night, to meet him at the Red Roof Inn and have a drink."

"Warts and all."

"It takes a lot of energy and will to be a doctor, I guess."

The dog lay on his round bed, panting, looking pleased to have extended himself that much. His stiff tongue stuck out dopily, and he watched us like he understood what we said.

I said, "I'll be late if I don't leave now."

She nodded. She looked so sad.

"Winter camp for the overindulged," I said.

"You like them."

"Some of them."

"You're good with kids."

Which had unwittingly led us, of course, to where we didn't want to be. Dear Archie: What do you do when everyplace you try to go ends up the place you didn't want to get to?

I said, "I had the funniest thing happen outside."

She clasped her hands and moved them below the surface of the table. I knew she was holding them in her lap. I had seen her do it at the doctor's office, waiting for news.

"No," I said, "I just fell down and it was so deep, I could barely get up. Old friend to man over there ambled up and I leaned on him. That was all. It was like one of those 'what weather we're having' remarks is all. About how much snow we've got in the back field, on the hill."

"What were you doing on the hill? There's nothing *there* this time of year except snow."

I stood to carry my cup to the sink. "Exercise," I said. "And I wanted to confirm the rumor about there being so much snow out there."

She hung her head like she was very nearsighted and trying to study the tabletop. She said, "Jack, you're a little insane."

I went over to her. "It's better than being a lot insane," I said.

I was talking to the back of her head. I leaned down and kissed it. I put my hand on it and felt the shape of her skull, the springiness of her hair, the heat of all her life going on. I was surprised. I had expected to find it cool underneath my fingers. I kept my hand there, and what I wanted was for information to flow between us. I wasn't thinking so much about facts, because there weren't many. Her, me, the house that nobody lived in with us except for a noble, unbrilliant dog—those were the facts. The rest was more like feelings, except it wasn't anything simple like love or hate. It was in between feelings and facts and we needed to know them, I thought.

She said, "You're squeezing the back of my neck, Jack."

She kept her head down. I rubbed at the soft flesh under the base of her skull. I said in the voice of the half-drunk marine who had squatted behind me in Phu Lam, "Well, we're just seeing Flash."

———

I caught what I wasn't meant to. I didn't know all 2,200 of them, of course, but I was familiar with a lot of faces and ways of walking. I knew the habits of some of them—the kids who walked alone at night with a heavy rhythm, the ones who sat on the steps of the bookstore and chain-smoked, the students approaching the library with their heads down because they were defeated before they began. Usually, they paid no attention to us. But this one noticed me. She didn't want me to see her. Any kind of cop will feel it. I had seen her at the other end of the first-floor lounge of the freshman dorms as she woke up. They call them first-years now. The *man* in *freshman* isn't fair. It isn't female.

But she was female and young and as deep in trouble as anyone I knew. I saw her there. Later, I saw her smoking outside the dining hall. She was dressed like the rest of them, but she wasn't. Jeans jacket and a sweatshirt, jeans torn at the knees, bright woolen gloves. But the students here were mostly clean and so were their clothes. Hers weren't and her hair looked lousy. I only saw their hair dirty if they did hard drugs or were writing poetry that semester or wanted to die. They wore their long-billed hats backward when their hair was dirty. This one didn't look like any of them. Her face was supposed to be tough, I think, but mostly it looked sad and cold and worried.

I saw her again in the morning, when I was investigating an open door at the receiving dock down at the foot of the campus. I took some notes and I left. That was when I saw somebody leaning against a wall near the tennis courts that were at right angles to the dock. It was the same kid. She tried to look like she was waiting for someone. Anyone playing tennis was under about four feet of snow. I smiled and walked slowly when I approached her.

"Hi," I said. "How are you on this cold morning?"

She tapped against her cigarette like a first-time smoker, knocking off ash that hadn't yet accumulated. She was vibrating with chill, standing on her backpack to keep her sneakers out of the snow.

"Hi," she said, but with no welcome.

"I can give you a lift to the main campus," I said.

"I'm waiting for someone," she said.

Her chin was a little thick and rounded. Her nose was too small. Her shoulders looked bony under the thin jacket that her sweatshirt hardly padded up. She wasn't pretty, she was about fifteen, and she was someone's daughter who had run away.

"You've been waiting for a week or so," I said.

She threw the cigarette at me and her shoulders slumped. She said, "Shit. Bastard. Don't do this? Please?" Then she said, "Shit," because she knew, whatever *this* was, I was going to do it.

I said, "You need to get warm. You need to get fed. You need to go home."

"You know about my home?"

I shook my head.

"Maybe you wouldn't make me go back if you knew about it."

"I can't let you stay here," I said. "Listen. Somebody loves you."

She put her hands over her face. I knew the face, with its thick chin and displeased eyes. I had seen it on a milk carton. They put photos of the lost and runaway kids on milk cartons, and people never look at them as if they are pictures of people they might see. She was ordinary. But I remembered her. She looked like somebody's daughter.

From under her hands came "Why do you have to *do* this?"

"Because someone loves you," I said.

I carried her knapsack to the Jeep. I helped her in and I fastened the seat belt. I drove her over to Elmo St. John's little office in what's known as the municipal building. As the heat rose, her smell of dirt and oil and dried perspiration came over to me. She had taken out another cigarette and was lighting it.

I said, "I can buy you a meal before we—"

"Turn me over to Social Services," she said.

"How many times have you done this?"

"Eleven? Twenty-one? I don't know. It isn't a *this*. I have to get out of there. I'm getting better at it. I'll make it work. It was the weather, for a change, that fucked me."

"You want food?"

"No."

"You want to tell me your name?"

"Check the milk carton."

"How long have you been out?"

She sighed. She said, "Not long enough."

"Look," I said, "I don't want you hating me. I'm just—this is what I'm supposed to do."

"You go round up all us milk carton kids."

"It's really the right thing," I said.

She blew out smoke when she said, "Sure." She continued to shiver.

I said, "It is. You need a doctor or anything? You feel okay, more or less, physically? Look in the thermos on the floor in front of you," I said. "There's hot coffee. Maybe it'll get you warm."

She opened it, and when she smelled the coffee, she closed her eyes and leaned her head back.

"Just like home in the morning," I said.

I was looking at the street and I couldn't see her face when she said, "No. My house smells like K-Y jelly in the morning. And the night. You can slide downstairs on it. My daddy lays it on thick."

I said, "What?"

I heard her pour out coffee.

I said, *"What?"*

I heard her put the top on the thermos, and then I heard her laugh into the coffee. It was to punish me, and she had been fighting all of us long enough to know it did.

Elmo St. John was as nice a man as Archie Halpern, but a lot less gentle. And he never sweated, not that I had seen. He was so lean, he was always tucking in his shirt, and that involved pulling up the cheap plastic belt that supported his plastic holster and his handcuffs. He never carried extra cartridges in the belt loops because their weight pulled down on his trousers. His shoes were also plastic, bright and glossy, like the shoes you get when you hire a tuxedo from a cheap franchise rental outfit. His feet were very wide and very long. His hands were big, and his wrists protruded from his cuffs. He was in a town cruiser in the parking lot behind the municipal building. We had turned the runaway over to a woman from Social Services. The kid hadn't talked to me again. Every time I thought of her laughter, I wished I could ask Fanny what she thought.

We were about to head off, but I didn't want to leave yet. I was thinking about the runaway. I was thinking about Janice Tanner. My Jeep was parked so my left window was next to his. Our engines idled as we sat and sipped coffee from paper containers and talked. There was a lot of smoke around, what with the idling exhaust of each car and the smoke from the coffee and from our mouths and Elmo's cigarette.

"She was just sweet," he said of Janice Tanner. "Just the nicest child. My nephew knew her. Had his ninth-grade crush on her, I believe. Although they never tell you these things. *You* know," he said, as if Fanny and I had raised a child to be fourteen.

I nodded. Then I said, "You said *was* just now. You think—"

He said, "Don't you say I said it."

"No."

"Well, I said it. Was. Was. Was. She's torn up crotch to neckbone someplace. Or strangled. Or maybe beat until her bones are sandy."

"Jesus, Elmo."

"It's what happens. I know a fellow in the FBI. I told you I lived a couple of years in Fort Drum, right? Talk about winter. Yeah. He had me come in for a lecture they gave for 'local constabulary,' they called it. That's me and you, Jack. Local constabulary. There's a pattern they got, nearly as predictable as a cookie cutter. Like one of those gingerbread men. It's a male between, I forget, thirty-five and fifty-five, and he was, let's see, abused by his mother or father or both of them, and, one way or another, it was the mother's fault. Well, he *blames* her for it, anyway. Poor mothers. They catch all the shit, you know? And he kills girls. He's what they call—"

"A sociopath."

"Right. He don't have a conscience, the way I understand it."

"He goes on these benders. Binges. Except instead of drinking, he murders whoever he needs to. Boys, girls, pussycats, frogs, whatever it is. And he does it a way he needs to do it to scratch his itch, except it doesn't stay scratched."

"See? You know this shit, too. You military guys. You probably got the same lecture from the FBI."

"Just not in Fort Drum," I said.

"I always wished I could get over there when it was happening," Elmo said. "Too old. Too married. Too many kids. Too pretty damned much useless, as a matter of fact. I always wanted to get there, though. When the hippies were lifting their legs on soldiers rotating back. It happened here. It made me mad as hell."

"It made them mad a little, too," I said. "Elmo. You're pretty sure she's dead, right?"

"I am, Jack. How about you?"

"She might have run away. They do. Jesus, Elmo, one of them just did."

"Not Janice. Guaranteed."

"Damn."

"She was lifted, Jack. 'Hi, sweet child, can you read this here name on the map and tell me how to find it?' " He made a slicing noise between his teeth. "That's all it takes." He dropped his cigarette butt into his coffee cup and I heard it hiss. "But you believe otherwise, I take it."

"She might be alive. Maybe it isn't a psycho job. Maybe he isn't a killer. Or she. Maybe it's a woman who needs a child, the mother thinks. Or a man who needs one?"

Elmo said, "I sure do hear you, and I said I'm on my way. Now: ten fucking *four*." He hung up his handset. "A catastrophe of major dimensions. Kid in an old camper bus from the college slid sideways through Celia's Floral Arrangements on her way to make a delivery. We've got hothouse roses all over Route Eight. You and I show up Code Three, that'll make a deputy, my other patrol car, and us. Jack, do you think the four of us can handle this one?"

"Who's hurt?"

"Celia's feelings, the right leg of the student, and the flowers, of course. See you there."

I realized that he had one of the original small posters taped to the inside of the patrol car's side window.

He said, "Jack?"

———

The bomb scare was in the social sciences building, so I was outside with history professors and anthropologists and political scientists. They were very good about staying where I and the other security people and Elmo and his two deputies had put them. I noticed that about college people. They got pretty surly about parking regulations and running electric gizmos off too little wiring in their offices, but otherwise, when it came to standing in line, they tended to be obedient. I recognized the woman with the big mouth and nice nose. She was shivering and smiling at the same time, her arms crossed in front of her, mittens on her hands. Her lipstick was bright red and so was her stocking cap.

She said, "Hi. I thought of you when I was sliding backward down the hill again this morning. Do you know my name?"

"No, ma'am," I said. "You ought to call me if you have trouble on the road surface."

"All right," she said, looking at me steadily. "I'd need to know your name." A couple of students were watching us, and so was the poet from the humanities building. He was standing behind her, with a bare finger touching the cloth of her coat. I wondered if she knew that. He saw me watching, and he brought the hand to near his lips and blew on the finger, as if her coat had heated it up.

"Just ask for Jack," I said.

"My name's Rosalie Piri," she said. Her cheeks were bright from the cold. I thought it made sense, holding your hand out to her to get warm. I disliked that he had done it, though.

I said, "Professor Piri."

"Rosalie," she said.

Two state police cars pulled in, and a red-and-white car and truck from the sheriff's department. A dog jumped down from the van, a giant black Labrador with a rolling, broad chest and thick forepaws. He seemed glad. They all went into the building. The new president of the college came up from his office, walking in clumsy steps in his thin rubber galoshes. Then his vice president for administrative services came over. A television truck with a minicam antenna rolled in. It was going to be a prank, of course, a false alarm. Nobody blew up college buildings anymore. There wasn't enough at stake, now that the war was done, and the days of rage. If you were black, you might want to do it, I thought. Except they don't bring that kind of black kid into these schools. They used to, but they'd stopped. Things were tidier now.

Though not, of course, in Janice Tanner's life, and not in her parents'. Except for that, though, except for the screaming and screaming her parents wanted to do and she had maybe done or was doing, it was a calm time, and no one was political. The Vice President of the United States would be here in a month, and the campus cops would help to spy on the faculty and report curious characters and foreigners. Some feelings would be hurt; some people on certain lists might be asked to get off campus by the Secret Service for the sake of the Vice President's safety. But no one would be violent.

Except in Janice Tanner's life.

Classes were canceled and the students were sent on their way. The professors waited for the bomb-sniffing dog to clear their offices so they could retrieve their work. Two of us stayed behind, and the rest of us left. The sky dropped before darkness fell, and then more snow came. I thought I saw, under the hood of a thick down-filled parka, the red hair of the girl who had tried to kill herself. But I remembered that her parents, at Archie's suggestion, had kept her out on a leave of absence. I thought about Archie talking to people about my military record and our life and our child.

But he did it on account of the Tanners' daughter, I thought. Sometimes you have to do it for the ones still alive. I ought to tell him I'd forgiven him. He'd know how angry I'd have been.

I drove off the campus in a borrowed security Jeep. The little clapped-out tan car of Professor Piri was ahead of me. She skidded, then obviously released the brakes and rolled until she gathered too much momentum for comfort, then braked and of course went into a skid. She seemed to go sideways as much as ahead. I followed her until she made it to the stop sign at the bottom of the hill where it joined Route 8, which was also the town's main street. I felt a little bit like a shepherd, and when she turned onto the street, I stayed behind. Her car stopped some yards down, so I drove alongside her and leaned across to roll down my passenger-side window.

"You all right, Professor?"

"Rosalie. I thought you were escorting me home, Jack. It was very reassuring and then, when you stayed back there, not so reassuring." Her car was a litter of books and papers and fast-food sacks. Her defroster made a very loud roar. Looking down from the Jeep into the squat car, I saw that her coat and skirt were pulled back for easier driving. I looked at her legs, then back to her face.

I said, "Sorry. I didn't mean to press you. I was worried about those tires. You really need to replace them."

"And I am going to. I was going to ask with what?"

"With what?"

"Replace the tires with what?" She grinned widely, enjoying her joke.

"Other tires, I think. Newer ones."

"Ah," she said seriously, "other tires. Well, then, I will. Thank you, Jack."

"Yes, ma'am."

Her face was solemn, and then the grin came back. " 'Yes, ma'am,' " she said. "Thank you for guarding me. Good night."

She drove on slowly and unsteadily. I turned myself around and drove out of town toward the long, greasy hill that would end in Masonville. I didn't know what I would look for and, a half an hour later, as I came in slowly, in four-wheel drive, down the long approach to the small business district a few streets beyond the squat cement buildings of the campus, I found myself turning my head a little quickly, looking for strange behavior, like someone on patrol. They had their own security force, of course, a lot larger than ours, and I ought to report to them. But this wasn't college business. This was, as Randy Strodemaster would say, community business. There was gown and there was town, and this was town, he would say. I thought of his handsome face and his filthy bathrobe. I looked for anything and I found nothing. Snow blew across the streetlamps, and sparse traffic lit the dirty slush in the road. The windows of bars and a diner were fogged. People were in there, generating heat, and, according to Elmo St. John, Janice Tanner was under the ice of a lake some- where, or stuffed in a barrel, wrapped in a sack.

He was right, I thought. He was probably right. I saw the over- sized air scoop that ruined the profile of the Trans Am, and I pulled into the curb and parked and shut my lights off. I left the engine on to run the heater. He was probably right, but maybe she lived in spite of the FBI profile and the experience we all shared, which insisted that what these men are in love with is death. The suffering is inci- dental, much as they enjoy provoking it. The fear, much as they might relish it, was also incidental—no, it was secondary. What they loved was death, because what they feared was their deadness. And if you

can give death, you're alive, you're in power over who you've fastened
to the tabletop or floor, you're a little bit of a god.

I thought of Mrs. Tanner. Whoever took Janice had a different
notion of gods.

Power, I thought. I had to remember that and ask Elmo and
maybe Fanny, though I didn't think she could talk about this a lot. It
was power, and then the child was dead and the power was gone and
you had, after some time, to start again. That was for the cops, I
thought. All I wanted was Janice Tanner back, I told myself, and I
knew it wasn't true.

William Franklin's car, parked around the corner of a long clapboard bar, wasn't empty like I'd thought. A head moved up in the
front seat, on the passenger's side, and then what I'd thought was a
headrest began to move on the driver's side. They had been engaging
in recreation, and their posture suggested what it was. I felt a little
jump in my own body. The doors opened and a short girl walked
around the car to the driver's side. Franklin got out and they embraced, leaning against the door he'd closed.

I had no authority to follow him or roust him, and I thought he'd
come after me if I beat on him in front of his girlfriend. Then the
local cops would come, and the state police, and I'd be in the shit,
with nothing learned. I'd known this in advance, hadn't I? So why, on
a night so terrible for driving, had I driven here?

"You don't know that," I said, "you're stupider than I thought."

And because of the eyes in the wallpaper, Jack. I leaned forward
to turn on my lights and shift into first, and my body ached like I'd
been beaten by the kid I was about to start roughing up. Go home, I
told myself, thinking about the wallpaper. You go home and go upstairs and you look back at them.

———

The dog and I were outside next morning, and as I watched him roll
on his back, grinding at a piece of rabbit several decades old that he'd
brought back as a trophy, Fanny wobbled over the crisp ice to park

her car. He was up and waiting, paws on the door, his big brush of a tail wagging. I thought of the Labrador sniffing for the bomb they hadn't found. There was this optimism in dogs. They got up and charged into the day with a confidence I wanted to have. Looking at the rabbit haunch, I was grateful my nostrils were sealed by the cold.

Fanny's, apparently, weren't. She held her nose.

"I think it goes back to Lyndon Johnson's administration."

With her hand away from her face, she said, "All those presidents smell the same to me."

We stood in the deep cold and nodded in agreement.

"I have to go soon," I said. "I've been getting in later and later, and I believe I'm going to be reprimanded. I needed to talk to you. Have you got a minute?"

"Have I got a minute," she said. "You and I spend a dozen hours a day chasing after strangers to mop their blood up and rescue their vehicles and generally smooth the way—"

"Smoothing the way. That's good."

"That's what we do. We're utilities. Like electricity."

"Smoothing the way. I can't think of anything rough I've turned smooth."

"Like goddamned sandpaper," she said.

"The tears will freeze on your eyes," I said.

"Except I'm not crying," she said. "Come inside. Have I got a minute. God, Jack." She was inside the door, reaching back to hold it open for me. The dog went in, and I followed. She stood in the mudroom with her coat halfway off her shoulders. "Have I got a minute. And we're passing each other, going back and forth like little ferries. Where was it, before you reported to Fort Leonard Wood, and we got a week—where did we go, where the ferries kept going there and back, there and back?"

"Seattle."

"Vashon-Seattle, Seattle-Vashon. They were going to Canada, right?"

"We stayed in a hotel you said didn't have mice or rats because the boa constrictors ate them."

She let her coat slide down her arms and back. It pooled on the floor around her feet. I picked it up.

"Jack. Yes. I've got a minute." She stood in front of me with her arms hanging, her shoulders sloped. It was a perfect picture of exhaustion. I think she could have slept standing before me. I knew it wasn't only fatigue from work. We were grinding each other away with a kind of friction that didn't involve our touching each other.

I said, "You know the little kid who disappeared? The one they're offering a reward on?"

"I see her face all day. Everyplace. It's a terrible little face. It's so open."

"One of the professors hooked her parents up with me. He was talking to Archie Halpern and I guess Archie said something about me and the MPs and some of the work I did, so this professor decided· he needed my help. The Tanners asked me to do something. I don't know what to do."

"Just talking to them is something. You're doing it, I assume."

"I don't know. That's what I wanted to talk to you about."

"You know how they feel."

"No, it isn't the same."

"It isn't the *same*. But you know how they feel."

I nodded, and I could swear she knew I was going to drop on her, because I heard her feet move, as if she had set them. I leaned over onto her. I let my head fall onto her shoulder where it runs up into the neck. It must have hurt. She winced. But I felt, all of a sudden, the way she had looked a moment before. I thought my bones couldn't hold me anymore. We got locked up like that, my empty left hand and my right still holding her coat in a fist, both of them behind her now, one of her arms around the small of my back, the other on my arm, and each of us at the same time trying to let our weight go and hold each other up.

The dog heard her sniff, and he thumped his tail. It hit the washing machine behind her and made a resonating noise. He did it again.

I said, "Oh boy."

He probably thought I said, "Good boy," because he slammed his tail against the washer.

Fanny said, "Poor, poor people."

"Poor people," I said.

Fanny said, "I was referring to us."

She stepped out from under me, and I moved away. We avoided each other's eyes.

"Listen," I said. "A thing happened yesterday. Did you hear about the runaway girl?"

"They brought her over for a physical. They were sending her home. Yonkers, New York. She'd been gone for months, and then she lost some diddly job she shouldn't have been given in the first place and she ended up here."

"Sleeping at school."

"You found her?"

"Yeah. She didn't think I was doing her a service."

"How'd you know about her?"

"I saw her on one of those supermarket milk cartons."

"We don't drink milk," Fanny said. She went to the refrigerator and she opened the door. "See?" she said. "No milk. You never go into the supermarket. So why would you notice a milk container in the market, Jack?"

"I went in there one time, I guess. I guess I noticed them. How can I go in there and *not* notice them?"

"This does not help, Jack."

"It helped her parents. But listen—there was something she said I wanted to ask you about."

"They did a physical on her. Whatever he did had healed. She'd been gone awhile."

"You think he did it? Her *father*?"

"You are not a guard at a nursery school, Jack. You *know* about these things."

"But I had to send her back, right?"

Fanny sat at the kitchen table. Her chin was in her palm, her elbow was on the table, and she looked more tired than anyone I'd seen since the war.

I said, "Right?"

She might have moved her head. I couldn't tell.

"Am I nuts, Fanny?"

"Sometimes—I don't know. Maybe *I'm* crazy. Maybe we're both crazy and our marriage went crazy and the only sane thing in our lives is a dog. That's what I sometimes think."

I remembered, once, telling her how fortunate we were not to keep a gun in the house, because one of us would use it for sure on the other someday. She'd reminded me we *did* have a gun in the house and I had to admit I thought I'd kept it hidden from her.

I wondered why I was thinking of the gun. I moved myself back to her and drew her by the waist. She lifted her arms to my shoulders, and I thought of how old couples, when the right music comes on the kitchen radio, can fit together so easily and start to dance. I kept my eyes closed and I matched us, chest and belly and groin and thigh. I pulled her to me the strongest I could.

"Fanny," I said "Tell me what to do. Tell me what to *know.*"

We rocked at one another, and it was like getting a memory back, except in the flesh.

She pulled me. I thought we were going to fall onto the floor. I felt the heat of her mouth when she whispered, "Tell me why our baby died."

I tried to answer. I don't remember the words I wanted. The dog began to bang his tail along the floor because I was doing Fanny's trick. I couldn't hear if she had also begun to cry, because I made so much noise against her shoulder and her neck.

FRIDAY NIGHT, after I fed the dog and walked along our road with him for a half an hour or so, I made myself a burger out of turkey meat. It was a new ingredient for me. Fanny thought we ought to eat healthier foods, so I was trying to get used to patties of ground bird and to yogurt that, even with fruit, tasted to me like something gone rotten. The dog and I shared three-quarters of a pound of partially fried meat. He showed more enthusiasm than I did. Then I washed the dishes and went upstairs to make a decision about the room.

Fanny had done the rest of the wallpaper. She hadn't cleaned up, so charred strips and chunks, some still attached to the old gypsum board, lay in a track about ten inches from the two walls that she'd worked on with the putty knife and heat gun. The gun, which looked like a bulky, more dangerous hair dryer, lay on the floor, still plugged in. The putty knife was a foot away from it. She had worked steadily, I would have bet, probably crying through part if not all of the job. Then she'd have tossed her tools down and thrown a curse at me or something larger and walked out of the room to shower.

She could have told me, I thought, remembering the eyes that had lived on the wall. It occurred to me that this had been no kind of wallpaper for a child to grow up staring at. I tried to imagine how it would feel, in the weak glow of a night-light, to lie in a crib with the eyes on you over and over along the wall, ceiling to floor, looking at you through the slats and over the headboard again and again. I'd been required to qualify for a license to drive and I'd had to apply for a permit to keep my handgun, but no one had asked me a question about my abilities to be a father to a small girl. On the floor, in ragged, worried strips, was more evidence that I oughtn't ever to have started.

She should have been sleeping, of course. She should have come home from work and walked through the house, maybe puttered awhile, and then she should have showered and slept, waking up in time to leave while I was sleeping. Instead, she had come into this room and finished what I'd begun. It was a kind of talk, I thought. It was the way we'd been talking for some years now. When she took down the paper, she was giving something to me, I knew. I wasn't sure what it was. I thought it must have cost her a lot.

While she slept in our bedroom at the end of the hall, I sawed by hand instead of using the power saw, and instead of driving eight-penny nails by hand, I used inch-and-a-half Sheetrock screws that I sank with my battery-driven drill. She was in her deepest sleep now, and if her brain was going to let her sleep, my noise wouldn't waken her. I framed up an alcove that came at right angles out of the wall between the closet door and the window corner. I eyeballed the studs but used a right-angle measure to be sure I had the footers level. Then I measured gypsum board, cutting it with a razor knife, and I screwed it, using the drill, into the studs that I had fastened at ceiling and floor as well as to headers and footers.

I had five gallons of joint compound there, and I taped so the seams were tight. I went on the toes of my stocking feet to the bathroom and made a thick soup of the compound by adding more water than you would for taping joins. I stirred the soup with my hand and the sponge, then did a heavy wash of the wallboard. Once I got the mixture and the pressure right, the stuff worked and the new right angle of wall looked like an old-fashioned plasterer had done it.

I would install a heavy-duty outlet with a built-in reset, and we'd go to barn sales and antique dealers and find a perfect writing table for her. This would be her office. She'd have privacy here. I thought maybe we could find one of those old brass lamps with a green glass shade and I could rewire it for her. I thought of buying her a cracked felt eyeshade as a joke.

The rest of the room would be for guests. Maybe someone would stay with us sometime. We'd have a convertible sofa bed and a chair and a reading lamp and pictures on the painted walls. Maybe I would sit and read while Fanny sat at her desk on a weekend morning when we both worked the same shift. It would be an ordinary room. Maybe we could put in a television set and I'd watch the football games. She might watch one with me. We'd just be a married couple who sat in a room.

Fanny was behind me. I heard her voice, still slow with sleep, say, "What's this?"

"Where your office goes," I said, turning around. She'd slept in her uniform. She hadn't showered. Her hair looked greasy and her skin was dull. There were bits of wallpaper stuck to her uniform pants and shirt. Her white shoes were laced, and I wondered if she'd slept in them.

"Not any office *I'm* working in," she said. "Thank you, but this is really—well, Jack, how could you even *think* I'd work in here? And what's that coffin for? That's my office? So I can be dead in here, too?"

I couldn't fasten to enough of what she said. I couldn't answer. There wasn't any answer. I felt like I had a sore throat, and I couldn't swallow because it hurt too much. So when I talked, it sounded to me like I had a sandwich in my mouth and the words came around it. "A slight miscalculation," I said. "I can take it down."

She said, "Please."

"I can take it down *now*," I said.

"Fine."

It was easy. I stuck the blade of my pry bar into the corner seam near the ceiling and I struck it, hard, with the palm of my left hand. The bar slid in through the thick, even paste of compound. I angled it toward a screw, and I pulled toward me with both hands. A lot of wallboard and a lot of compound and a snake of wet, heavy tape came away. I inserted the pry in the seam near the floor and pulled out and up. A lot of the board tore. I could have located the Sheetrock screws and put the drill in reverse and taken them out. But I didn't want to take care. I wanted to break things. I pulled away more of the board, slopping the compound on my hands and onto the floor, spattering it up onto my face. When I had the outside stud at the corner partially exposed, I approached it and raised my leg. I could hear myself breathing hard. I didn't look at Fanny. I kicked the stud and tore it away from the ceiling. It fell, still fastened to the floor. Some of the ceiling tore away. I kicked the other stud, and it went over, wallboard and all. I knocked each stud down. I laid the pry bar under the footers, two by four by thirty-six inches, and tore them up and out. The screws came up, tearing away subfloor, thin plywood on which I had planned to lay carpet.

I stood in the mess, my knees bent and my back strained, panting. "There," I said. "A little dramatic. A little messy. A little destructive. But, Fanny, fucking *there:* The alcove is down. You have any further wishes for the room?"

As I looked at her, as she rocked back and forth and looked at me, I thought I should have started by thanking her for stripping the rest of the wallpaper.

What I said was, "You want me to find the same pattern of paper and put it back on the walls?"

I put my head down as soon as I'd said it. I couldn't any longer find satisfaction in a fight with her. We were both too beat up for this. I started to say it but found when I looked up that she had left the room. I followed her. That was how our fights had always gone, Fanny walking off and me following. We had done it in cities on the West Coast and in the Middle West and even in Manhattan, where I'd finished up my stateside rotation and mustered out. She'd stood at a cement wall in Battery Park, looking down into the dirty water. She'd been wearing an ugly bronze raincoat I'd always hated because it made her skin look gray. She'd move, and I'd move with her. We went that way along the embankment. Finally, at the navy monument, she said, "If you'd tell me how to get home, I could stalk away and you could follow me there and get this damned thing over with." I'd shown her the right subway entrance, but by then she wanted me with her, and we went home together. Now we *were* home together, and no one knew where else to go.

I went down the hall to the bathroom and listened at the door. I heard the shower. I banged on the door.

She said, "What?"

"I'm sorry."

I banged again after I'd waited half a minute.

"What?"

"I said I was sorry."

"I heard you."

"Fanny, are *you* sorry?"

She said, "What do you think?"

"Don't cry," I said.

"So what should I do?"

"Come out."

"In a while."

"Fanny, I'm lonely for you."

"What?"

"I miss you. It's like I'm in Tokyo or someplace and talking on the phone. I keep missing you."

Then she said, "I miss you, too."

I was sitting on the floor outside the bathroom, my back against the linen closet door, and I'd been sleeping. She had put a blanket over me. The dog was on the floor beside me, with his back wedged hard against my leg. We were littermates. When I moved again, I woke him, and he looked over his shoulder with a kind of stupid glare, and then he thumped his tail.

"We missed again," I said.

He rolled to his feet and shook himself head to foot as if to throw off water, and he planted himself. He was ready. Good dog.

The college was digging out after days of storm. Pickup trucks with plows in front and salt distributors in the bed worked the narrow lanes and paths while big trucks with highway plows cleared the larger roads. Grounds crew on ladders and a cherry picker crane worked to lever ice off the roofs before it melted enough to come down in avalanches. We'd had students buried under slides like that. The sky was bright and the sun, though it hadn't any weight on your skin, was good to see, especially if you believed in winter ending, which I did not. From high up on the campus roads, you could look into neighboring counties. I was patrolling near the graveyard where they used to sell lots to the faculty. It was my suggestion, since my English professor's girlfriend had hiked up here to try killing herself, that we include the cemetery and the quarry in our rounds. I wasn't really patrolling. I sat in the idling car and looked over the campus, over the bright hills, and I stared without focusing.

I was counting my credit hours. Since I wasn't taking a course this semester, I was a little behind schedule. According to my calculations, the sun would get very, very old and explode, incinerating all the planets in the solar system, a year and a half before my degree was in hand. This was not a viable self-improvement program, and I was going to have to step up the pace. On the other hand, I couldn't imagine taking another course as long as I lived. I kept seeing myself as I used a yellow crayon to draw a picture of Ralph for Introduction to Art. I heard myself making up songs about Ralph for Music 101. I was too disgusted to think for long about my having written a paper and handing it in and letting myself be graded for what I had to say about a story I had told a baby girl about a duck.

I was grateful when they called me on the radio and asked me to come in. My vice president for administrative services made me head of security. I was given a raise of a thousand dollars. I asked if I got any more courses free, and he regretfully reported that I got what everyone else got: one per term. I asked if I could work plainclothes and he said we could try that. I had come in early because I didn't think Fanny ought to have to deal with me. I knew what was bad for her. I was sad because I knew, and probably that was what my vice president felt. He was a pleasant man with a taste for bold tweeds and what he had assured me were English neckties. He wore tinted glasses in dark plastic frames and looked like he ought to be a teacher.

"Does this please you, Jack? You seem a little subdued."

"No, sir," I said. "I'm pleased. I'm grateful. I'm a little worried about the responsibility, but no, there's nothing wrong. Thank you very much. And we can use the money."

He looked at the papers before him. "How's Mrs.—how's Fanny?" he asked.

"Hanging in there," I said.

"All right, though," he said.

"Yes, sir. Fine."

"Well, that's fine," he said. "Congratulations, and, you know, fine. Stay in touch."

The dispatcher kissed me on the cheek, and the other three on patrol shook my hand. They were former policemen from villages in upstate New York, and they were envious of the money but had no desire to make out shift schedules and answer to angry students about their slack attitude toward date rape.

The call came from the library, early, around half past eight, and I drove over.

I'd never liked going there. It was built into the side of a hill, and you climbed a lot of stone steps with short risers and somehow you were always out of breath, going in the heavy glass doors past the electronic apparatus that wailed if you didn't check a book out properly. It was full of angles and corners. You didn't get a good look at a long vista you could inspect and become familiar with until you hit the reference room. Standing near the circulation desk in the entrance hall, breathing a little too hard, I always felt I had come into someone else's house. I tried to make my breathing normal. I saw walls and angles and shelves of new books on display, and I heard the clattery, hollow, plastic sound of computer keys. The catalog was on computer, and almost every long table I saw had computers on it. I didn't like to use them unless I was forced to. No matter how I made my way through the computers or in the stacks among the students, I knew I didn't belong there.

Through a glass wall with a door in it, near long tables with computers, I saw Rosalie Piri, who had bald tires, and a tall man and a taller woman. Professor Piri looked little between them. She saw me and lifted her chin and smiled. The others looked over, waved me in and then on. I followed them to an office on the far side of the reference room, where I was introduced to the circulation librarian, Donald Gombricz, and Irene Horstmuller, the head librarian. We sat around a conference table in Horstmuller's office. There were pads, pencils, and a small book in a navy blue binding closer to where I'd been placed.

The head librarian said, "Professor Piri borrowed a book. It contains some possibly distressing information. We're calling the authorities, but Professor Piri suggested that strict procedure would involve your input first."

I looked at Piri. She looked at me and colored. She shrugged. "My father's a cop," she said. "He's a New York cop. I learned the preferences of the Police Benevolent Association before I learned to read. You *always* talk to the local man."

"I'm the local man," I said.

She said, "I know. That's why you're here."

"Thanks," I said. "Maybe. Somebody vandalized—what, *defaced* the book?"

"No," Horstmuller said. Her face was full and stern and tan, her long hair wound in a knot. She wore a necklace with red stones in a silver setting, and she was conscious of it, adjusting it while she spoke. "We don't get hysterical about damaged books. We get angry and sad, but we don't call for security over that."

"Sorry," I said.

"There's a threat," Gombricz said.

Piri said, maybe noticing Horstmuller's necklace, touching her own bare neck with the yoke of her small left hand, "You know about the Veep?"

I shook my head. I thought they were talking about a book or an author or a computer program.

"The Vice President," she said.

"He's coming to talk. In the chapel. We've been working with the Secret Service."

"You will be plenty more, I guess," Piri said, smiling. Her mouth was remarkably broad and kind of curly. "This book has some writing in the back."

She made a flexible, bending gesture with her wrist. In the hum of the fluorescent lights on the ceiling, squinting against the glare of the bright February sky coming in the office's two large windows, I examined the book. It was called *Indispensable Superfluity: A History of the Vice Presidency in the United States*. A piece of gummed memorandum paper led me to open to the back cover, and on what Piri referred to as an endpaper, I read:

> *The veep will weep*
> *And then he'll sleep*
> *He'll never wake up*
> *Till called by St. Pete.*

I said, "Would that be considered a legitimate rhyme?"

Piri laughed. Gombricz frowned. Horstmuller said, pretending that I wasn't a thorough pain in the ass, but talking like I was mildly retarded, "I believe the 'Pete/sleep' would be called slant rhyme. But of course we're concerned about the threat."

I said, "You consider this a *threat?*"

She said, "Yes, I consider it a threat. He's predicting the death of a Vice President in a book borrowed from the library of a college that the Vice President is going to visit. I telephoned the Secret Service. I faxed them a photocopy, and I can tell you that *they* consider it a threat. They arrive this afternoon."

"I can't believe they're at work this early," I said.

"My call was relayed to the office in New York City. They had someone at a night desk."

"Good operation," I said.

Piri, the cop's daughter, nodded.

"So," I said to her, "you found this?"

"I had the book out, and I noticed the little poem. I called Irene here"—the head librarian looked at me with very large light blue eyes—"and she set things in motion."

"So now we're in motion," I said. "Where are we going?"

Professor Piri said, "I guess you'll want to be here when the Secret Service arrives."

"I can get Elmo St. John—he's the local cop. He and I can have the person waiting for them. Look up who had this book out before the professor and we can go get him. It's someone either on the faculty or administration or in town, right?"

Gombricz, who had very little hair on top of his slender head but who wore a very carefully trimmed fringe of beard that followed the lines of his manly jaw, folded his hands and said in a deep and resonant voice, "Not doable."

I thought I ought to forgive the "doable" once. I'd have bet he sang in a community choir. He probably took the starring roles when the little civic theater association did musicals. I looked at him so he would understand the need to explain. He waited, though, to make me ask.

I dutifully said, "Why?"

"Federal statutes passed, after extensive lobbying by the ALA, and subscribed to by the CLA, dictate that a library cannot disclose, without violating the constitutional right to privacy, who has taken out what book. Period."

Horstmuller nodded. I waited until Piri nodded, and then I believed it.

"Jesus," I said. "So we know who this person is."

Horstmuller nodded. "We can know," she said.

"And we can't tell the Secret Service?"

"And we won't," Gombricz sang.

"And the Vice President's life, you figure, is in danger. What if it was the President?"

"The same scenario," Horstmuller said.

"Does the Secret Service buy this?"

Horstmuller said, "It doesn't matter if they don't."

"It's probably a crank. A prank. Whatever that is. It probably isn't true."

Piri smiled and shrugged. Horstmuller gave no opinion. Gombricz chanted, "We've no way of knowing."

"It isn't your field," I said. "Okay. It isn't mine, either. I'll come over when the *federales* get here, if you like. I can pistol-whip them when they start abusing you, which I imagine they will."

"I didn't know campus security carried guns," Gombricz said.

"Maybe I'll let you touch my pistol," I told him. Piri, grinning, ducked her head. Horstmuller pretended not to have heard. "Call me when they kick in the door," I said. I left then because I knew I wouldn't have a better exit line in a week of being clever.

As I drove the campus, I tried to imagine the long white chapel and its hard benches occupied by students, some there because they were interested, the majority of them driven in by their history and political science teachers. Rosalie Piri would be there, I thought. She was a woman who showed respect when she felt it. And I thought of the Vice President's attractive face and less appealing voice, and the nervous Secret Service men in front of the podium as he leaned into the lectern and kept leaning, slumping over it and falling forward on top of it, the report disappearing into the plain high ceiling of the old Baptist church.

It would be a pity, I thought, performing the literary criticism in which I'd been trained on this very campus, to lose a good Vice President to a poem as bad as the one in the back of that book.

———

I drove through the parking lot behind the humanities building and I ticketed some cars. One of them wouldn't turn over, and after I wrote the student a ticket, he asked me for a jump start. It was one of the services they required us to give, so I helped him roll it away from the building he'd nosed against, and then I connected the cables. I signaled him to crank it, he did, his engine started, and, as I removed the cables and carried them back to the Jeep, he honked his horn. I looked over and saw him tearing the ticket into halves, then quarters, and throwing them over his shoulder into the back of his car. It was when I looked at the back of his car that I came away from the Jeep, the cables still in my hands. I pointed at him as if drawing a bead, and I said, "You wait."

He was puzzled, and perhaps frightened. They always are when you act like they aren't quite as far beyond your reach as they think their money takes them. I went over, but not to his window. I wanted the window behind it.

I said, "Stay."

I leaned on the roof and read the poster. It was light blue, maybe a kind of lavender. It said REWARD OFFERED, and under it was a photograph, but not of Janice Tanner. This was a smaller girl. She was nine years old, the poster said. Under her photograph were the words *In Jeopardy*. It didn't tell how a child that small could be allowed to get there. It described her, height and weight and clothing she'd last been in, and it said *Please Help Us*.

"Where'd you get the poster?" I asked the kid. He was the usual: tall, sandy-haired, healthy, Caucasian, dressed from one of the better catalogs.

"A lady taped it on."

"Today?"

"Yesterday. Hey, I didn't mean that, about the ticket."

"No? Why not? It's your right to behave like an overprivileged candy-ass. Stop shaking. I'm supposed to pretend to show you respect. You can go."

I left him and stowed the jumper cables. I knew what I'd be finding on the campus today. Another face would have grown overnight on the walls and doors. On the corkboard wall of the student union, where kids advertised their need for lifts to important social centers of the Northeast, there would be this new face, these new eyes I wouldn't be able to meet.

I thought, as I got back in and put the Jeep in gear, of how Professor Piri had looked at me when she'd said her father was a New York cop. She had looked like someone surrendering.

And how do you mean *surrender*?

The little girl was from Onondaga County, miles away. There was nothing to do here except look for someone shifty with a little girl. And I wouldn't see them together, I thought, because the child was probably dead. As Janice Tanner probably was.

I thought of the yellow-gray of her mother's skin, and I thought of her belief that our lives' events are orderly, somehow part of a pattern. I also thought I had promised to make an effort.

But how did you mean *surrender*?

And why not, starting now, name the efforts you can make?

I made my list. Elmo St. John had left word that the investigator for the state police was a sergeant named Bird. I didn't know him, but I could call, and we could play phone tag for a few days and then maybe talk a little. I knew what he'd tell me. It would add up to being very watchful. There was no physical evidence, but the posters were everywhere, and they would help keep some pressure on. I had called the Tanners and suggested they call the Syracuse, Utica, and Binghamton papers and TV. Mr. Tanner had sounded strangely glad when I asked if he minded doing some recorded messages for the local radio stations to play. I knew there wasn't a lot that Bird could do, and I was afraid I had done my best in a few phone calls. Still, I hated the druggies in Masonville, and I wouldn't mind driving there again and this time leaning on some people, especially if Bird gave me his blessing. I doubted he would, but I could ask. Though the last thing the drugheads would want was a girl as young as Janice Tanner. Sex was secondary to most of them. Money came first and last and mostly in between. Drugs filled the hollows. Kids traded energetic, expert sex for drugs when they had to, and when the trade was—I thought of the circulation librarian and his fine tenor voice—doable.

So that was a nothing I could perform.

And I could tell them their girl was under a repair bay in a truck stop someplace. Or in a frozen-over lake, I could say. Or eaten by wolves if out of doors, by rats if in.

She was a local girl. I thought of bracing local thugs, except we didn't have any. We had violaters of labor laws and health codes, we

had income-tax evaders, and we probably had some wife beaters and
child abusers, but I didn't know out-and-out bad guys whose names
I could toss around.

I thought, Call Sergeant Bird.

I thought, You call your wife.

From a secretary's phone in Admissions, I called Elmo's dispatcher and asked her to relay my request. The boys and girls and
their parents were looking at videotapes of the campus they sat in. I
went down to the basement to show the flag at the cash-payment
window and the soda machines and the bursar's office and then I
drove down to the physical education complex. They had step machines and free weights and lifting machines that cost more than our
fleet of four-wheel-drive vehicles. They had an Olympic-size swim-
ming pool and Olympic-quality kids to dive into it and swim it end to
end. I was good enough to sink like a weighted sack of cats and
thrash and drown.

I did a turn through the off-campus apartments and looked into
the lighting in the laundry rooms. We'd had an incident there. Someone had talked too aggressively to a girl. She described herself as a
woman in the interview room, and I called her that in my report. But
she was a girl. She had freckles across the top of her nose, and she
was skinny, but with nice shoulders. She wore one of those floppy-
topped sweaters that purposely fell by accident off half of the shoulders and chest of the girl or woman who wore one. I did not mention
costume in the interview or report. It was considered bad form. She'd
been frightened by a big boy, and she had a right not to be, and I was
making sure Buildings and Grounds had increased the lighting and
put in a phone.

Next was the cluster of science buildings. They looked like factor-
ies. Outside of the physics building, I saw Strodemaster's high, battered old Land Rover. It looked like it had just come off the desert,
pursued by Bedouin shooting movie rifles. I think maybe Strodemaster wished it had. He was parked in the no parking zone in front of
the loading dock. I took out one of the cards my administrative vice
president had given me as part of the promotion package. It cost
them about eleven cents to print the cards up, and you were supposed

to feel important—instant cheap morale. On the card, I wrote "Naughty." I'd give him the ticket next time. He was the kind of man who made you want to provoke him, maybe even hurt him, and partly because he acted like everybody was born with glands, lungs, heart, liver, and the need to make Randy Strodemaster happy.

I drove along to the humanities building, and Dispatch let me know that the New York State Police would meet me at a diner called Junior's a couple of miles north of town. The cop who'd meet me would be there near one, and he could stay for half an hour. I made sure to be on time. The state policeman had gotten there early. Sergeant Bird was tall, slender, tough, and very politely careful about me. His blue-black skin made the purple of his necktie against the gray of his uniform shirt seem brighter. He drank coffee and chewed on a grilled cheese with tomato sandwich. I became so hungry, I thought I was going to drool. I ordered the same. Junior's was a big square room with small tables and comfortable wide wooden chairs. The waitress kept pouring extra coffee into cups, and Junior, in the kitchen, listened to tape cassettes of opera while he cooked. His whole name was Ruggiero Nazitto, and he liked to talk about coming to America *not* to make pizza.

"Good food here," Bird said.

"He puts garlic on everything."

"Smart move. So, what's your interest in my missing kids?"

"The family of Janice Tanner would like more information. They don't know how to get it. You aren't volunteering much, apparently. So they asked me to do something. What they asked for is anything, actually."

"Well, you're doing anything," Sergeant Bird said. "What qualifies you to ride the same horse as me?"

"I didn't say I was. I had a little experience in the service."

"Which, judging from what I see, was not the day before yesterday."

"A while ago," I said. "I was an MP. I got into some stuff and I ended up attached to Intelligence. It was mostly surveillance and, right before I was done, some interrogation."

"Army?"

I nodded.

"They're a joke," he said.

"No," I said, "Navy Intelligence is a joke. Army's almost competent. And I was all right. Really. I did some stuff. I found a truckload of missing weapons. I stuffed an outfit of pharmaceuticals merchandisers. You can check me out."

"The request is already in and working."

"So you wanted to look me over."

"Small college security cop has the police chief, who is one of a staff of four in a tiny upstate town, request full cooperation, which means disclosure of physical evidence as well as a siphon on my time? You bet your paper white ass I look you over."

I was wrestling with strings of hot melted cheese and boiling tomato. I said, "Mmmm."

He nodded like I'd told him something, and he wiped his hands on his paper napkin, which he'd folded into sixteenths. His fingers were long, the nails pale, and he moved his hands with tremendous certainty. They looked like he could go from wiping his fingers to performing surgery.

"I'll read your jacket when it comes in," he said.

"Okay."

"I'll think about it. Because I can use . . . well, I can actually use anything. I can tell you that much. Anything. One answered question I might not get to ask."

"You're buffaloed," I said.

"We have a little."

"I doubt it," I said. "You don't have time, I figure, to take a leak more than once a day. So you get a request from Elmo St. John, who is not J. Edgar Hoover—"

"Thank Christ," he said.

"And you drive over here, you take a lunch break when you look like you eat one meal a day, and that's late at night, alone, because your wife doesn't talk to you, she's so pissed off about your work schedule. And you're here because you got zero on the Tanner thing, and then the little kid a county over. . . ."

"There's another one," he said.

I put the other half of my sandwich down.

"You'll see the posters soon. I think it's unrelated. It might be. It's outside of Buffalo, near the Canadian border. I hope it's Buffalo's. It feels like a fucking plague, doesn't it?"

"Their faces," I said.

He said, "I hate it. I have two daughters. And the pissed-off wife, you're right. I think of my daughters. It seems to be white kids who get snatched, except in Atlanta or the Apple. But you never know. Here's one of those times you sink down onto your knees and pray for bigotry."

"Amen," I said. "We really have to stop him."

"Them."

"You're pretty sure they're unrelated? There's more than one guy doing this? Isn't that worse?"

"I know what you mean. It's like a condition. It's like . . . weather. If it's just a crazy person, we've got a possible shot."

I said, "Will you catch the call if there's a threat against the Vice President? He's coming to campus in a month or two, and we might have an incident."

"Anything I need to know?"

"I'll brief you on it. When you get back to me on this."

"Slyly done," he said. "I'll read your file. I'd bet I'll be back in touch with my quid for your little pro quo."

"That Latin's Greek to me," I said. "Can I pay for this?"

"I'd rather you owe me, just in case I get pissed off at you down the road, Jack."

"What's your first name again?" I asked.

"Sergeant," he told me.

———

I went to Strodemaster's house after work, but he didn't answer. I opened the back door and called for him, but I still didn't get an answer. The kitchen was as smelly as last time, which meant he still hadn't taken his trash out. You get that way, living in the country, because the more trash you take out, usually to the barn or garage, the sooner you have to stick your pails or bags in the truck and get them to the county waste-management site—dump, as we once used to say.

On the chalkboard, in the *Oregano* hand, but under *de Bergerac*, someone had written *Bring more stuff!*

I called, "Randy!" There wasn't an answer, and I left.

I almost went to his barn to look for him, but I wanted to get my visit over and go home. I loved his barn. It was set about twenty yards behind the house. It had a thick dry-point foundation wall, and the wood that went a story above it looked to be in wonderful shape. Inside, a fine-gauge tongue and groove divided it into bins and stalls. There were corners to go around, two sets of stairs to the upstairs loft, and several areas of floor that were cobbled. I'd often thought that with enough land around it, I'd consider buying the barn and converting it to a house. Fanny and I could do the job, I thought, and I still had it in mind—buying the property, selling off the house, keeping the rest of the land and the barn. I didn't know if we could move back into a town, though. Small towns sap your strength because you lose your privacy. We needed ours. We hadn't strength to spare.

I drove a few houses over to the Tanners'. She answered the door, saying that her husband was at his church, having a painting bee with a few retired people who had volunteered to do the walls of the Sunday school.

"The paint in churches, we've found, gets worn away quicker than in other buildings. I think it's the friction of the souls. They grind themselves against the ceiling and walls. Come in here, if you would, Jack, so I can lie down."

We went into their small living room with its bold Victorian wallpaper of blowsy, fat flowers in vertical stripes. Water simmered in a speckled blue basin set on top of an airtight stove, and music was playing from a radio on the windowsill. Mrs. Tanner lay on a long blue sofa, her head on a boldly patterned pillow of yellow, maroon, and blue. "I was listening to Ralph Vaughan Williams. I was trying to find out why the English say Ralph as Rafe."

"I didn't know they did," I said.

"They do seem to."

"Well," I said.

"What, dear?"

"Nothing, ma'am."

"You look so uneasy. Do you"—she sat up and put her palms on the sofa—"do you know something?"

"I'm sorry," I said, shaking my head. "No."

She lay back down very quickly, as if she didn't have the strength to sit up.

"I met today with one of the state investigators. He's very determined. He wants to find your daughter."

"Janice," she said.

"Janice."

"Someone said there was another missing child. I had the most dreadfully selfish thought."

"You were afraid it would—"

"Dilute the search for Janice. Yes. I'm ashamed. How did you know?"

"I just thought like a parent, I suppose."

"Yet you're not one, you said."

"I am not a parent," I said.

"That's too bad. You ought to be."

"I guess I wasn't meant to be one, Mrs. Tanner."

"You see? You knew perfectly well all along what I meant about patterns and plans."

"How do you feel, Mrs. Tanner? How's your health?"

"You mean the cancer?"

"Yes, ma'am."

"Did your wife tell you we met last night? I felt poorly—it was the treatment, not the disease—and poor Mr. Tanner decided he had to rush me through the night and snow and ice into the emergency room. And there was your wife. She is the loveliest, kindest, most competent woman. Some people are simply born to give care, aren't they? Oh, *she* should be a mother!"

"Yes," I said.

"But I'm all right. I'm not bedridden yet. It hasn't blown me up or torn me down yet. I've decided that Janice will be returned to us between now and her birthday. It's in March, the twenty-second. I'll be alive."

"Of course," I said.

"Of course. And Janice will be home."

I didn't know what to do. I sat on the ottoman with my legs out in front of me and I squeezed my palms into my kneecaps and agreed.

She said, "Really, Jack. I assure you."

"I thought I was supposed to be assuring you."

She didn't answer, and I stood. "Mrs. Tanner?"

"It's fine," she said after what felt like a long wait. "Don't worry. And I feel certain you'll get your turn."

———

The weekend was long and quiet and icy and long. Temperatures fell by Friday night to twenty-five below zero, and they didn't rise more than twelve degrees during Saturday. We had long ago sealed the fireplace up with an insert, a small iron stove from Vermont, and Fanny and I carried in load after load of wood. We had the thermostat set high for the oil burner, and, in the back room, which was heated by electric baseboard units, we turned the thermostat all the way up. Fanny wore an old woolen shirt of mine under a thick wool sweater, flannel pajama pants under her jeans, and heavy ragg socks inside of her wool-lined moccasins. I wore the down-filled vest I used for outdoor chores in autumn. Nothing much helped. One of us was always looking through the kitchen window at the thermometer and reporting on how bad it was, or turning from the radio or television set to repeat a number always ending in below zero. The windows frosted up in fan shapes. On Saturday afternoon, when the temperature rose closest to zero, I started our cars and kept them running a good while. Then, shutting them down, I set old blankets and tarpau-

lins over the engines to insulate the batteries and wiring. I ran a
droplight on an extension cord from the mudroom, where we plugged
in the washer and dryer, out to my old Ford, and I arranged the bulb
to lie above the battery, under blankets, to provide a little heat.

The rest was moving slowly, going to windows to look at the
threat, and sitting in the house near the stove and talking about the
cold. We did not discuss the room upstairs, or our daughter, or
the errand that Strodemaster invited me into, though we talked in
general about the missing girls.

Fanny said, late on Saturday afternoon, when we drank chicken
broth in mugs near the fire, "What if she ran away and she's outside
in this?"

"It would have to be hell in the Tanners' house to want to be
outside in this, wouldn't it? I don't know about him, but she seems a
gentle woman. Strong person, you know, but gentle. I don't know
what in hell the preacher's up to. Probably raping her every night."

"They don't quite rape them," Fanny said. "They seduce them.
Daddy *needs* you. Why are you so *beautiful*, I can't stay away from
you—so it's the girl's fault. It isn't as violent as rape. But it's also
more violent."

"You get them in the ER?"

She shook her head. "Not usually. They don't come in hurt, as a
rule. Sometimes they go wild, and they kill him, and *he* comes in all
cut or bleeding or burned. Once, this was when I was in nursing
school, they brought a guy in—his sister-in-law had done him. She
waited until after he worked the daughter over and he was sleeping.
She tied his hands and feet to the bed. He was on his back. And she
hammered nails into him. She said he twisted a lot, and his wife kept
trying to rescue him, and the nails banged off his ribs, but she did a
lot of damage. She was trying to sink these big spikes, they looked
like, into his heart. The wife kept saying she would press charges, she
would press charges."

"Against her sister, right?"

"Oh, of course." Then Fanny said, "When you talk to Archie—
are you his patient?"

Fanny was in the morris chair I had pulled over. She had her legs up under her, and I'd put a comforter over her lap. For a while, she had looked relaxed. But now her brow, which had looked pale but relaxed, almost smooth, was a furrow of twisted parallel lines pushed up by her wonderful eyebrows, which had risen as I rocked. The dog felt the tension increase. He sat up, then laid his head on his paws and watched us.

"Not a patient. No. Sometimes, going in, when I stop at the Blue Bird to fill up on coffee, if I'm early, we have a cup together and we talk."

"About us."

"About the salary cap in the NBA. About campus politics that percolate down to the infrastructure people like me. About the weather. Sometimes—"

"It was the sometimes that I think I was asking about."

"Sometimes we talk about emotions."

"Because you're such a garrulous fellow and you just can't stop pondering out loud about the way folks emote?"

"Exactly," I said. The lines on her forehead were slightly less bunched.

"Tell me."

I closed my eyes so I could say it. "Sometimes I worry about if I'm smart enough, educated enough. I don't know. Strong enough? *Something* enough. To be useful to you."

I rubbed my face like I was tired. It kept my hand in front of me, and it kept my eyes shut.

"Useful," she said.

I made the sound you make when you agree with someone.

She said, "Jack."

We still didn't talk about the wreckage upstairs in the room. Sunday night, we got Fanny's car running, and her wheels squeaked off on the frozen road. In the morning, the dog wandered away while I worked on starting the Ford. The oil sounded like sludge and the starter sounded like a very weak cough, but it turned over, and I let the engine run while I stumped around on numb feet, trying to get the dog in. He burst up from the woods below the house with snow powdering off him like water in the wake of a fast-moving ship. His head was high and his jaw was clamped. He was full of victory and pride, and he carried a loop of frozen blue-maroon intestines two feet long. He had clearly been to the mother lode of all sickness-provoking snacks for dogs, and he'd returned in glory. I let him run around the yard a few times, circling me to make sure it was understood that an event of major importance had taken place. Then, when he fell to his belly a few feet away to begin his meal, I made him drop it. I carried the guts in, put them inside a plastic bag, and hauled them out to the trash pails in the garage. I didn't want us smelling them while they defrosted.

The dog escorted me and his fading triumph, and I thought of kitchens and rotten garbage, and I wondered again what Strodemaster kept beneath his sink. Probably it was a matter of how long he kept it more than what he kept. He was the kind of man whose wife had a long job description, I figured, and it included trash removal, pest control, and bathrobe cleaning. Now that his wife was gone, he couldn't ask his girlfriends to shovel and sweep. Fanny had nothing but scorn for women like his wife who let themselves get run like appliances.

I thought of how I'd lied to Fanny and then told the truth. I couldn't stay angry at Archie, because he knew too much about us. And because he'd worked so hard, with such delicacy, to help me out. I left early, apologizing to the dog, as I always did, for locking him in the kitchen for the day. I realized that I wanted to get to the Blue Bird and have an early cup.

His side of the window table was dusty with powdered sugar and crumbs and little crumpled sugar packages. He was wearing a huge, thick turtleneck sweater that had a collar that came almost up to his ears.

"Jesus," I said, "you look like one of those U-boat captains in a movie."

"I was told at home this morning that I look like Erich von Stroheim," he said. "Have a pastry. They frosted them with maple this morning."

I handed my thermos to Verna and I burned my mouth on coffee. I said, "Your pal Randy Strodemaster asked me to help out with something."

"Something," Archie said.

"This missing girl, Janice Tanner, you son of a bitch."

"I take it that you don't agree with me that talking with her parents would be beneficial."

"Periodic discussions about dead girls. *Are Ex,*" I said, making the sign for a prescription in some of his pastry crumbs and spilled sugar. "Hang around the parents of a dead girl and exchange little recognition signs about misery."

"So, then, you *don't* appreciate the idea."

"You son of a bitch."

"But you said yes?"

"Yeah."

"Why?"

I said, "Why?"

"Don't stall," he said. "Why'd you agree? I made the suggestion to Strodemaster. But I didn't tell you to do it. I can't make you take on chores. That part was your idea. Why?"

"I felt like I had to, I guess. I don't know. I—to tell you the truth, I was—something about it made me want to. I couldn't stay away. I hated it. I hate it. The idea—it was like stopping someone's death, if I could. I'm a goddamned nuthead, aren't I?"

"You sound pretty savvy to me," he said. "If you're not careful, you'll sound healthy."

I said in almost a whisper, "Fanny asked me if I was your patient."

"What'd you tell her?"

"I lied."

"Of course you did. But what did you say?"

"I said I didn't talk to you about her."

He stared at me hard, his beautiful piggy face dead serious, his little eyes focused. "You don't," he said at last. "You talk about you. A lot of you's about Fanny. That's all right. Because one of these days, you're going to tell her, 'We both need to talk to Archie,' and because you ask her to, she will, and then you'll have told her the truth."

"And this is ethical?"

He ate a huge mouthful of something shaped like a cowpie filled with almond slivers and glistening raisins.

"Don't you fucking worry about ethics," he said. "You worry about your wife and yourself and *fuck* your quibbles." Crumbs flew as he spoke. He paused, he sipped a big bubbly mouthful of coffee and swallowed it. He waved his thick, short forefinger between us and he said, "Somebody comes in bleeding, Fanny does what?"

"She calls the doctor."

"Don't fuck with me, Jack."

"Stops the bleeding," I said.

"That's what we want to do. *Then* we can worry about correct behavior. Are you working?"

"You mean with Fanny?"

"Are you fucking at *work* on the little missing girl?"

I nodded.

"Tell me how you feel."

"It isn't—"

"Tell me."

"I need to go, Arch. I'm late."

"You piss artist."

"I know."

"You find me this week, the next couple of days, and you and I talk. Yes?"

He was sweating, and I had ruined one more breakfast for him. I was no better than any recidivist. You arrest them, try them, send them up, parole them, and they're back inside in a week, habitual offenders. Granted, Fanny and I had grappled a little with—let's say with us. But we hadn't addressed the event, and we wouldn't. That was what, for the sake of some kind of honesty, some kind of friendship, I would have to tell Archie Halpern one day. I wanted his help, but I could never—and I never would—do what he would advise.

————

When I came in, the dispatcher told me that Big Pete was in an interview room with a woman who had a complaint. I could hear her voice ranging low to high, then Pete's even bass. His voice would enrage her. She'd think he was being calm on purpose, so she'd assume he thought she was being hysterical, and she'd be furious with him, and neither one would know why.

I asked the dispatcher to request, on the intercom phone, that he come out and see me. When he did, rolling his eyes and loosening his necktie, I suggested that he take my campus loop while I talked to the student. Since he had to do what I suggested, he did.

We had built two small interview rooms, each with chairs and a small table that was large enough for the student being interviewed not to feel like one of us was looming over. I left my coat hanging outside and when I went in, before I took the clipboard with the incident report from the shelf, I said, "Hi. I'm Jack. Who're you?"

She was Niva. She was in her third year. She had a crew cut almost as flat as Archie Halpern's, and she wore a little golden ring through her nose. It was hard not to talk directly to the ring. Her scoop-necked sweater was a hazy kind of purple and her pants had once been black. There were various colors of paint on them. She wore high thick-soled leather boots. Her hands and feet were big, and the rest of her was very skinny. She was almost copper-colored, and her eyes had a coppery touch to them, too.

The complaint was about a senior boy who no doubt called himself a man. His name was Roger Gambrelle. He shared studio space with Niva in a section of the arts building they let the kids use for what I guess was art.

"He plays this heavy rap," Niva said.

"Too loud?"

"He's trying to fuck me, Jack."

"You mean—"

Niva didn't smile. I'd hoped she would. Her face had deep frown lines and it seemed to live in a kind of scowl.

"That's exactly what I mean," she said.

"Right," I said. "I'm trying to figure it out for this report. My associate has written 'To promote sexual intercourse.' "

She smiled, but it went away too fast for me to enjoy it. She said, "That's the fucking, Jack."

"So, Niva, are you complaining about the moves he's putting on you, or—this seems to be about the music."

"He's a stupid racist asshole. He thinks all people of color dig rap, and what you do, you want to get in one of us's pants, you send the music up. Like perfume, understand? Like you're laying flowers on a woman you want. *This* hyena is doing this mealy shit music can't *no* one get into on account of it sours your *mind,* listening to it hour after hour. It's antifemale, it's violent, it brings us down, and I'm trying to move some paint on a surface to *mean* something. You understand."

"Yeah," I said. "I do. It's easy. I'm going to make sure Mr. Gambrelle turns the music down." She shook her head. "Doesn't play the music at all is going to be very tough. I can try for it, but I can get it turned down. Low. Next part's a little hairy. If you want me to, if you ask, I can kind of hint—I can't do more than that—about how you would appreciate his laying off. But students don't like anyone meddling in their lives, and some guy from security—"

"You feel inadequate for the job?"

"I'm pretty sure it *isn't* my job," I said. "Can you ask one of the student deans to talk to Mr. Gambrelle? Have you got a friend who can do it for you?"

"You're friendly," she said.

"Let me think about it. I'll do the music. I'll *maybe* drop the hint about the other. Is that all right?"

She stood up. She was taller than I was. "That's all right," she said. The smile came and went, and then she left.

"Watusi princess," the dispatcher said.

"No," I said. "Don't talk like that. We can't talk like that in here."

"Excuse *me,*" she said.

"Slow down," I told her. "Don't get mad. Just don't talk like that. A favor to me, all right? Never mind it's the rules, that we're supposed to be courteous servants et cetera. Just as a favor to me, okay?"

I believe her face turned into dough with coal bits for eyes and sticks for the mouth. Something wonderful and strange happened to it because the door opened in, and Sergeant Bird of the New York

State Police walked into the office. She stared at his lustrous dark skin. He winked at her, and she turned away, like a dog when you look into his eyes.

He shook my hand and gave me a very thin envelope. "Two photocopied sheets," he said. "A summary. There's nothing else to give you."

"Can the parents know?"

He sighed, buttoning his open coat and putting his gloves on. "If they have to."

"It's their kid, Sergeant. Stop. Don't give me the lecture. I apologize. I know you know it's their kid. I retract it. Tell me what you want me to do or not do or what."

"Tell them what you think could possibly comfort them. I guess you'd want to do that. There isn't much. There really isn't."

"You holding anything back for later? I guess it wouldn't be in here."

"No, it wouldn't."

"I thought you trusted me."

"Well, I guess I do," he said. "That doesn't mean I have to *count* on you."

"No. I wouldn't, either. You on your way someplace, or can I give you some coffee?"

"Another crime scene." He saw my face. "Not another girl," he said. "This is a kid drove into his girlfriend's house. I mean *in*."

"It'll be pretty."

"And I look forward to it," he said. "We'll talk."

After he left, the dispatcher said, "You planned that, right?"

"Timing is everything," I said. I opened the envelope, but both our lines rang, and I reached for my coat.

"Library," she said. "My God. They said something about the Secret Service. Do we have *spies*?"

I got my coat and I made a hushing sign, finger to lips, then suggested with motions that it wasn't safe to talk. Often enough, it isn't.

———

At a college that size, the dean of faculty is also the provost, the head goose in the flock. The president was away in New York City, probably to beg money, so the dean was grim with his responsibility. He was tan all year, and handsome the way local Realtors are, a little pudgy but full of stories about how many K's he almost ran. He was full of congratulations and powerful handshakes, and I didn't trust him. The library people were there, and Professor Piri, and a jock who worked in Alumni Relations and had a law degree but no bar exam. He was there, apparently, in place of the college lawyer, who was flying back with the president. Everyone sat tall in his or her chair, except Piri, who couldn't be tall, and who I kept thinking of as cute. You can lose a couple of inches of flesh for saying that word these days to a woman, especially if she looks like a girl.

We sat in a long, narrow room with windows that faced the hillside behind the library. I felt like I'd been here before or someplace similar. Winds took snow off the hill and the windows shook. I felt the light shrink as clouds dropped into place. We sat in a dimness that suggested being underwater. The Secret Service men came in, and fluorescent light flared at the door, and then darkness rolled over us.

I don't remember their names. I was introduced and my job was named, and I stood so they could nod, and then I sat. The others didn't stand. The men from Secret Service acknowledged them, and we all leaned forward in our chairs. The dean was master of ceremonies. Everyone was praised, our concern for the safety of the Vice President was described.

It was the light. That was why the room felt familiar. I had been in light so much like this before that my nerves and brain and spine were thinking for me. My skin, which had been underneath this light before, was remembering it.

Head librarian Horstmuller: "The dilemma is, we can't examine any records that might say who—student, teacher, guest on the campus, friend of the school—borrowed the book."

The Secret Service agent with slightly long hair: "If only we could, you see, since it is, after all, the life of the second in command, then we could walk the dog, as we say, backward through the list and

clear them one by one until we've interviewed them all and know—
we *will* know—who made this threat and lock them away."

"We could get a subpoena for the records": more conventional-
looking agent.

"It wouldn't hold up": Professor Piri.

Fanny, at thirty-nine, a feisty scrub nurse, pregnant for, it felt
like, a year and a half, swollen and damp all over and hating her
body but loving its one pregnancy, said by a doctor to be impossible,
swearing at her friends in Obstetrics, "Wait just a goddamned minute!
Nobody told me virgin birth *hurt!*" They laughed at that until one of
them cried, but I knew she was crying with gladness because Fanny
and I, who had tried so long to beat the odds of uterus tilt and
husbandly sperm count, were going to have our child.

"Give me the *fucking* anesthetic," she bellowed. They didn't.
They wouldn't. It wasn't time, they said, but the doctor was on his
way in and she could talk to him.

"I don't have time to *learn* a foreign language," she said.

They laughed some more, and I tried to smile while I gripped her
sweaty, strong hand and pretended there was a use for me.

"There's a judge right now, in Syracuse, waiting for the phone
call. We can get the subpoena": short-haired agent.

"I won't honor it": head librarian.

"Fanny," I told her, "you're a genius. You're a hero. Look at you.
You're a hero."

"Jack," she said, "I thought these sluts were my friends. They're
trying to kill me."

"We want Jack's body," one of them said.

"You give me the gas, I'll let you have him for a week every
month," she said. Her hair was pasted to her forehead. I wiped her
face with a washcloth.

"Once we serve you, there isn't a choice. I'll have a technician
into your records and you in a federal prison cell if you like. So don't
you threaten the United States government": longer-haired agent.

"Yeah, well, I *am* the United States government": Piri.

The clouds were sealing in the dim green light. The windows had gone dark. Darkness had lain against the windows of our house months later, when we'd come home with our child and I had told her again, after the hours of labor, "You're such a hero, Fanny. Look at you. Look at what you did."

We were home with our sick, unhappy child. Our baby had to return to the hospital, and then stay in a larger one, because she was jaundiced. But then we brought her home again. She was small, she was undersized, but she was going to thrive, Fanny said. Her eyes were never merry. That was what I expected, merry eyes like Fanny's when she laughed or when we made love and she rode on top of me and looked down, waiting for me to open my eyes and come out. Our baby's eyes were either sad or steady, like she looked me over and sized me up. She studied us. She was judging the odds, I thought later on.

She seemed allergic to her mother's milk. "It happens," Fanny said. So we fed her formula together. We sat in the night and at dawn with the warm white bottle, and we fed her. She lay in Fanny's lap and drank. Or she lay along my arm, her head in my palm, her feet leaning up against my bicep and shoulder, and she pulled at the nipple, sometimes looking into my face. She was thinking it over, and sometimes, when she did that, I wanted to cry.

At first, I tried props—the stuffed bear, the rubber duck. And then I made up the story about the yellow duck named Ralph. She seemed to like it, and I told it again and again. She looked at my lips as I recited it, and I looked at hers.

And then when she was five or six months old, she wouldn't sleep. She started to not sleep, and we used the tricks our friends taught us and we followed the advice of nurses and doctors, and she didn't sleep. We were hung over from wakefulness, from the sawing on our nerves of her thin, high, constant raging. She wanted something and she couldn't tell us what. "She *wouldn't* tell us," Fanny once said to me. We played cassettes of singing with no accompaniment, of music with no voices, of men singing, of women singing, of guitars alone, of solo piano, of storytellers narrating *Winnie-the-Pooh,* of Mr. Rogers talking about darkness, of an English woman giving advice to children worried about being alone. I told and I told and I told about Ralph and the missing feathers and the cold winds blowing and the mother's downy wings.

We asked each other what we were doing wrong. We worried together that she suffered, that she felt forsaken, that she needed help we didn't provide. Fanny had refused to go to work, so I stayed home that day as well, and we took turns walking around the house with our baby held against our shoulders and chests. We sang low to her and once in a while she slept. She didn't eat very well, and her face felt hot by evening. Her dark eyes watched us. Her skin and hair smelled oily instead of perfumed.

"We take her to the doctor now."

"I can't go back again, Jack. It's like I'm this shit mother who can't take care of her kid."

"No," I told her, "you're a great mother. You do everything, Fanny. You're fabulous. It's just, she's sick. Let's take her to the doctor."

"If she's like this in the morning, all right? I don't know," she said. "Maybe you're right. Maybe she *is* sick. But the way she's been, what in hell does *sick* mean? You know? She's as bitchy as I am, isn't she?"

"This has nothing to do with you, Fanny."

"Pardon? Nothing to do with me? Were we talking about my child, or did we have a conversation in Urdu about a baby on the other side of the world? Can you remember which, Jack?"

"I meant it wasn't your fault. I meant you shouldn't take it, you know, personally."

"I thought I heard you right," she said.

"What'd I *say*?"

"Give my baby to me, please."

"Fanny."

"Now, please."

I handed her over. I always remember that. I handed her over. Fanny took her up to bed to try it again. We were very tired and very worried, and it was probably what we should have done, Archie Halpern told me. When he said it, his round sweaty face tightened down and I thought he was going to start crying. He really wanted me to believe him. I remember I handed her over and then she went, in Fanny's arms, upstairs. It was night, but with a brightness in it—I suppose it was the moon. The mixture of light and dark was the same as now, when the dean of faculty was telling the Secret Service about the dilemma and the Secret Service was telling the head librarian that canceling the visit was not going to keep her from doing federal time and Professor Piri asked if there was anything I could suggest as our child went up the stairs.

I begged their pardon and asked them what they meant.

Piri asked if I could suggest a way out.

"There isn't one," I told them.

The dean and the head librarian looked like they knew I'd be useless and, there, I was.

Piri shrugged.

There isn't one.

And the same light as I slept under in our morris chair, falling selfishly asleep while Fanny, also burnt down and stubbed out with worry and fatigue, was upstairs with our child. I heard her snarling without words while the baby cried the same weak, tired cycle of noises over and over, Fanny crying back in what I guess you'd call frustration and the kind of anger it creates. Both of them, now, over and over, and then a new sound to the sounds, a terrible new violence. That was my specialty. I knew this. Now I heard it in our house, upstairs, and before I made a decision, I was moving out of the chair in the same light, the same sealed-in dimness, like the far-off glare of a hurricane, except inside our house.

I went up the stairs, calling to them. Their voices were blended in the rage—it was dogs snarling, except the real dog was behind me, coming up the stairs—and I went around the corner of the hallway and then I was down the hallway in three long steps and I went from the hallway into the room, our baby's room.

I went into our dead baby's room.

Then we were on our feet in the library. People discussed the irony of information sealed away in a campus building dedicated to disclosure. The Secret Service agents could not be consoled. Warnings were made and a meeting scheduled for the next day. One of the agents described it as the last. Piri said something about the right to privacy. She smiled at me shyly and I remembered how she'd told me her father was a New York cop.

And in the Jeep, driving up the campus road in second gear because, I guess, I forgot to shift into third until I heard the gearbox nagging, I thought of how in this part of the country, they keep the corpses all winter long. They don't get into the ground until April. Plants begin to bloom, and so do the graves. The frost line is high, but in April they get through the lingering snow and the iron surface of the ground by using a backhoe. Then they bury the dead. I shifted up to third, but on too steep an angle, and the engine bucked, so I downshifted and made my way very slowly to the top of the campus. I went up past the old graveyard filled with dead professors, toward the quarry where the redheaded girl had tried to kill herself. I wanted to be alone under the low, dirty clouds of the darkening day, and I was, when I turned the engine off and put both hands at the top of the wheel and leaned my forehead onto them. I must be a very bad and selfish man, I thought. I must have loved Fanny more than our child, our baby girl we had named Hannah, who was dead and under the snow.

maybe

WHEN I CAME HOME, Fanny was at work, of course. I nevertheless called to the house that I was there. The dog, who had been up with his forepaws on the inside of the door, already knew that. I let him out, and I walked with him a little. Our road had three-foot snowbanks, and he occasionally jumped up onto them and lifted his face into the winds and then clambered down. He made a series of notches in the snow that hemmed us in as we went about a half a mile up the road and then walked home. I stopped below an evergreen that had turned skeletal and brown. I hoped it was a tamarack tree. I thought they were the kind of evergreen that goes through seasonal cycles and in the spring comes back tender and green. I looked at mouse trails in the snowbanks, and rabbit tracks. I thought how much was going on when I didn't see.

"It's a kind of natural history lesson for the optimism-impaired," I told the dog. He seemed pleased to be addressed and, both of us steaming at the muzzle, we went home.

I turned lights on. After the meeting in the library, I wanted brightness, room to room. For company, I turned the TV set on and let a smooth fellow with a nasal hum tell the house about weather in

Colorado and Wyoming. Upstairs, I turned on the hallway light. I
forced myself to move with no hesitation when I went into the baby's
room.

She had cleaned it. She had used a shovel and a garbage pail
for the burnt, shredded wallpaper. They were still in the room, the
square-ended shovel with its wooden handle inside the metal pail.
They looked like a big mortar and pestle in the window of an old-
fashioned pharmacy. She had put the smaller pieces of Sheetrock
and large dried piles of joint compound into the pail along with some
of the smaller splintered chunks of stud. The rest, I thought, she
must have carried down to the garage. Near the pail was a dustpan
and a straw broom she had used to sweep the floor.

It looked like any room in process, a room in a house that someone was going to redecorate. Maybe we can do that, I thought. Maybe
it would be good for us to look at wallpaper and paint. We'll buy a
gallon of flat ceiling white, I thought. And some new rollers, and a
low-luster oil-based paint for the windows and molding and doors.
We'll take home paint chips and hold them up to the wall, and we'll
talk about colors.

I looked at the quarter-round molding I might replace with something a little more ornate. I was good at mitering cuts of forty-five
degrees. I might box in the windows with four-inch casing, I thought.
The dog had a length of splintered stud, and he chewed it, shaking it
in his teeth once or twice in case it was alive. I kept my back to the
corner of the room in which we had stood Hannah's crib.

━━━

The new one was nearly eighteen, a Filipina with a black father and
missing from a school for troubled girls in Oneida County, probably
too far from us for the maniac to be the same. Her face in the grainy,
sun-blurred photograph looked taut, thoughtful, dubious about
something. They could have printed a picture of an owl dropping a
pellet and I would have read a lot of emotions into it.

I wondered if girls had been kidnapped, murdered, preyed upon for years. Maybe it was the times, and therefore everything human and otherwise from when we began might not be at fault. Including, maybe, nature and God and the universe and Captain Marvel and Mother Teresa. Elmo gave me the details and showed me the poster, which had been mailed from the Oneida County Sheriff's Department. It was battered and stained, as if they had dug through snowdrifts to get it into the mail.

Perhaps it was the times. Or maybe it was the Tanners. They had enlisted so much help, even from passing truck drivers and people stopping for coffee on the Thruway going north-south as well as east-west. An item ran in the Binghamton papers about their posters. The reward was now $7,500, and I'd heard it was Mrs. Tanner's pension money and Reverend Tanner's life insurance, which he'd borrowed on. There was talk of a home-equity loan to bump the reward into more impressive ranges if they didn't hear something soon. They were stripping themselves to get her back. It made sense. What could you use the money for if she didn't come back? So maybe the parents of other victimized girls were following the Tanners' lead. Everyone was crying for help. That was what the Tanners were teaching them. Don't wait quietly. Do what you can. Call for help. Praying, Mrs. Tanner would call it, I was sure.

We had a run of days with temperatures closer to ten than to zero. Students walked around gloveless in what was, of course, ferocious cold, their coats open, no hats or scarves and their work boots untied. I knew they didn't believe in a dangerous world. Yet they fastened posters to their windows and they stood in corridors, waiting for class or a meeting with a teacher, staring at the faces of vanished children. Men tied up children and flayed their skin in measured strips. Women sometimes helped them. Little boys were penetrated by middle-aged men using bottle necks and broom handles. Girls were raped in the mouth by men they later called Granddad. And these children I watched out for didn't trouble to lace their boots.

I was running an equipment check on my Jeep, something I'd suggested to all of the staff. It was early in the day, and I was in the little parking lot in front of the security building, a small gray-and-

white Cape Cod cottage on the edge of the campus. I folded the
blankets, looked inside the first-aid kit for what can save someone's
life—rubber tourniquet, sharp, heavy knife for the tracheotomy none
of us thought we'd be able to perform, the inflatable plastic sleeve
that would immobilize a compound fracture and keep a jagged bone
from piercing an artery. I had a wire brush for cleaning battery termi-
nals, the extralong jumper cables that were getting a workout this
year, a miniature air compressor that ran off the cigarette lighter and
could generate pressure to swell a tire enough to get someone to a
service station. I had a folding shovel, wire grids for traction, a ten-
pound bag of ice melter, a five-gallon can of gas, a gallon of anti-
freeze. I found Sergeant Bird's summary.

I knew it had made its way into the back of the Jeep because I
didn't want to read it. I hadn't seen the Tanners in days. I'd haunted
myself with their daughter, but I'd done nothing to help them or her.
So I closed the back hatch, buckled myself behind the wheel, started
the engine, and, while it heated, I read about Janice Tanner.

It started with a detailed physical description. She was thinner
and in general smaller than I'd thought. Her underthings were white,
according to her mother. The Tanners must have hated giving that
information. Thinking why is like learning the worst in advance, I
thought. Her feet were narrow. She liked to wear a ponytail with a
velvet-covered rubber band around it.

She had no personal problems. Period. She was happy. Period.
She participated in extracurricular events. She helped her mother in
Sunday school. She was excellent in school except for math and
science, in which she was given C's and D's. I knew about those. She
volunteered two hours a week in the library, where she helped to
shelve books and do clerical work for the librarian. She played the
coronet in the middle school band. She was friendly and had
charmed all of her teachers without wooing them.

She was friendly. That was why. It was why she'd given someone
directions while standing close to his car. Why she'd gone into somebody's house or trailer or truck. Why she was never coming home.
Janice was a friendly child.

But maybe still alive, I insisted, though I didn't believe myself.

They had done a fine job, as troopers always did, of canvassing. Every house in the hamlet had been covered, of course. And two reports referred to a car the witnesses were certain did not belong to anyone in town. One talked about "one of those long, low things that makes all the noise when it starts off." Another said it had "a bump in the front." Both thought it might be black or dark blue or brown.

I went back inside and told the dispatcher I'd be off the air for a while, that I was cooperating with the state police.

She said, "That big black one? Over?"

I said, "He asked me if you dated. Over."

I had no business leaving the campus for an hour or more, but I did. Instead of filling the tank at our pump, I drove into town and filled it halfway full out of my own pocket. My conscience didn't feel twelve gallons better, but my conscience was going to have to take care of itself. I drove north, then west, and went over the hill to Masonville. I could see black clouds coming in briskly, and I knew we'd have a storm. I thought I ought to call Fanny and warn her, but warning people of storms, for the past several weeks, was the same as calling up to tell them to look outside.

In Masonville, I parked outside the post office, which was on a corner and gave me a view of the broad street that ran down from the school to the northern route to the Thruway. I was willing to bet he made his New York pickups either on the Thruway or the Onondaga Reservation, and, either way, he'd have to pass me. Of course, he might sleep until two in the afternoon. He might be out of town. He might even, from time to time, attend class. I had to respond to the report, and the car with a bump in the front, that arrogant air scoop, and its glasspacks or shot-out muffler, seemed to be the only reason to have asked for and read the report. It contained nothing. They had nothing to work with. If Janice Tanner was going to be found, a lucky accident had to happen. I was maybe their luck.

After half an hour, I figured I wasn't, and I was restless about getting back to the job. I moved the Jeep to one of the lots near the school, where I hoped to bury its blue paint job and lettering and

bubble light among a batch of bright-colored cars. You wouldn't call
me undercover. I took what I thought I might need, and I began to
walk the small campus. I stayed on its outside edges at first because
I thought to find him in his car. The buildings were pure state archi-
tecture, ugly and gray and sad, with windows that didn't look like
they'd ever been open and doors that slammed on sour-smelling hallways. Janice's poster was on every outdoor bulletin board and was
taped to the wire-lined glass inserts of the doors. Her small sad
features rippled in the winds that seemed to be getting colder.

I heard what I thought might be the car, but I couldn't see it. I
ran back from the rear entrance of what was apparently a dorm to
the walkway. Now I didn't hear it. I swiveled, turning my ears so they
wouldn't catch the wind roaring in them. Several students leaving
the dorm walked wide detours. I didn't blame them. But I did hear
the throaty, harsh rumble of his engine. I ran back to the lot and
found my car, which was about as well disguised as a hippo in a frog
pond.

I started up and aimed at what I thought was the direction. I
stopped at the driveway from the lot and turned the engine off.
Someone behind me revved his motor, then honked. But I heard the
kid's motor above the horn, and I took off. At the corner, I saw him.
He was heading to the western edge of Masonville. I went with him,
not hanging back, but not forcing the issue. The streets were plowed
and they'd been salted, and, though the nose of his Trans Am swung
out when he made his turns, the Jeep held tight. We were leaving the
business district, and then the streets of small wooden houses and
tarted-up double-wide mobile homes. The farther west you went, I
thought, the less was there. We climbed gradually and were on a
plateau that, as I remembered, had farms on it, and county roads,
and empty fields.

I was right. He was jittering now, because the roads up here were
not salted and the surface was slick. You could see for miles ahead
and around us. We were on one of the lines of a grid of small roads
that connected farms. In the late spring and in summer, these vast
fields of snow bounded by gray-black road would be creamy with soy

and wheat. The rest of the crop would be feed corn for cattle on the dairy farms. Now, though, everything was white, with the dirty clouds above, and a weak sun suggesting itself, but not with much force. We passed a few farms. I knew he was going a back way toward the Thruway as he now headed north.

Was this how children were rescued? By men baring their teeth in illegally used vehicles, chasing alleged students who, if they wore suits and sold tobacco, would be called businessmen? By men who waited in ignorance and pursued in reflex? By hook, crook, luck, and mostly mistake? Was this how children were saved? Could we find no surer way to protect them?

I was going too fast for the surface conditions, but I was worried about getting back to work and worried about Janice Tanner. I mean this: I knew she was dead, and I wanted this apprentice merchant to prove me wrong.

Prayer, Mrs. Tanner would call it.

We were on a long, empty stretch with no houses in sight. I thought to get to the end of it all instead of waiting. I put my brights on, hit the blue light on top, sounded my horn in long, even blasts, and went in behind him. I couldn't see his eyes in his rearview mirror because my car was higher than his. His legs must have been nearly parallel to the ground, I thought.

I decided to touch him a little, so I went in until we kissed fenders. It was enough to send him off the road, almost. I did it again. He pounded his horn. I hit the accelerator and did a little damage, I thought, to both cars. He skidded, he recovered, and then he lost it again. The snowbanks were high enough to keep him on the road, so what he did was slide at an acute angle, nose of the car in the ice, until he hit a soft patch and laid out on the angle. The Trans Am went over the bank and got stuck partway through it, rear wheels racing, but in the air.

I parked behind him and waited until he decided to take his foot off the gas. He tried to push the door out, but apparently he couldn't because of the snow wedged against it. He must have leaned back along the seat and kicked the door. It opened partway, and he edged out, falling into deep snow up to his elbows. His lip was bleeding. He might have bitten it through in the impact, or in anger. Because he recognized me, of course, and he was preparing to deal out some punishment.

"You ain't no police, you civilian motherfucker." He got himself up by pulling on the frame of his door. He was coming for me. "You got less rights here than fucking *cows,* you cow college rent-boy."

By the time he was out of the snowbank, stumbling on the road, I had the roll of dimes out of my pocket and in my right hand.

I held up my left, saying, "Sorry you had that skid, William. I was running an errand and I saw you lose it. I stopped to see if you needed any help. How's that bloody lip?"

He walked through my outstretched left hand and threw a long, clumsy punch at my head. I moved aside and slammed through his unzipped leather jacket and into his gut. The dimes would have broken his jaw. For the solar plexus, they were almost too much. He lost all color, he went double, tried to recover, couldn't, knew enough to make his legs take him sideways a few paces so I couldn't reach him again, and then he worked his lips like a fish as he tried to breathe.

I went after him. "Are you all *right?*" I put the dimes back in my pocket. I wouldn't need them anymore, and I didn't want to cut him a lot. I smacked his face with my gloved hand. In that cold, it must have stung the skin as well as rocked his brain. Before he could talk, I smacked him again, harder. He sat down.

"Let me help you," I said.

A big orange county work truck passed, slowed, stopped, then backed up, its warning buzzer hooting. The driver, a man with a light brown beard smeared with tobacco juice, said, "You folks all right?"

"Kid skidded off. I'll see he gets his wind back—he was scared, you know—and then I'll tow him out. No problem."

After a pause, the driver said, "Yup*per.*"

"Thanks a lot." I kept my hand on Franklin's shoulder and leaned so he couldn't clamber up, and when I'd waved with my other hand to the driver of the truck, I bent as though to give help. With the hand that had waved, I smacked him, hard, on the side of the jaw.

There's a nerve there, vulnerable to pressure, above the muscle in the back quadrant, and you don't want the edge of an angry man's hand coming down on it.

He lay in the road.

"Let me give you a hand," I said. I dug my thumb into the nerve bundle under the point of his jaw. He almost leapt to his feet. "Now," I said, "I want to ask you a question."

In spite of my anger, in spite of my urgency about finding Janice, I knew, and I think I knew from the beginning, that he was a dead end. He knew nothing. He sold drugs. He was in the hands of larger dealers, just as college kids horny for weed or maybe pills were in his. He knew nothing, he was nothing, and I knew it. But I didn't know what to tug on. There was nothing that led anywhere. There was this narrow county two-lane road going to no place and all I could do was ask him. "A little town near the college called Chenango Flats. You were seen there. Your car was seen in it on the day a little girl went missing. You know who I mean, because her posters are all over everyplace you go.

"Nod your head and tell me you know the girl."

"From the poster," he said, after drawing in a deep breath.

"You ever see her?"

"No."

"You ever drive through her town?"

"I don't know what town she lives in, man. And I don't need to steal no pussy."

I raised my hand and he flinched.

"No," he said. "I never seen her except the picture."

"You feel all right now?"

"Why?"

"Are you recovered from your accident? You were a little breathless when I came down the road and found you."

"Motherfuck," he said.

I raised my hand, then dropped it. I hadn't been this bad in a while. And he knew nothing. Then I thought, Who are you to say what he knows? So I did hit him. I slammed him in the sternum with the heel of my hand. He went gray at once. His eyes bulged. I thought for a second I'd killed him. He went over sideways and lay in the road, his legs moving very slowly. He looked like a kid making angels in the snow.

I waited. His head moved. I was afraid to hit him again, but I didn't show it. I came in closer. I said, "You can imagine what I know how to do with my feet."

He wheezed out a sound that might have been a word.

"Did you see the girl? Hear a single word about her?"

He made a sound.

"When you talk to your wholesalers, you might mention this conversation. I want you to understand: You stay off of my campus. I want *them* to understand I want to know anything they know about this girl. Who's doing what to girls, where, when, anything. You call security and have them find me and I'll come where you are and I will drop some reward on you. Otherwise, I drop the rest of me on you for ten, fifteen minutes, and you're done. You're all over. Tell me you understand."

He said, " 'Kay."

" 'Kay," I said. "Good luck with your vehicle. It seems to be stuck in the snow."

I walked back to the Jeep, and I got inside with casual movements. I drove carefully away, relieved to see, in the rearview mirror, that he was on an elbow and was moving his legs, preparing to stand. I took the first turn I came to, and I went for maybe a mile, then I parked. I let myself shake. I hadn't seen action in a long time—if you can call it action, using old skills and long training and a half-buried craziness to beat up on a wild child who made his living in sales.

Someone authentic, like Sergeant Bird or even Elmo St. John, if they had seen me, would have called me a mindless vigilante and knocked me over with a sap or just put a bullet in my leg. I was disgusted. I thought of leaning out the door and vomiting. I also thought of Janice Tanner, and the other faces on the brightly colored sheets, and I settled for standing by the front of the truck and peeing into the snow. Then I got in. I called myself a bully. Without trembling now, I drove quickly to get back to work.

———

After a little double-talk with the dispatcher, I spoke to everyone on duty and caught up, then started to patrol. It was snowing again, not heavily, and I had the wipers working in a very slow beat. Kids trudged into and out of classroom buildings and one tall woman, with dark hair trailing out behind her, ran. She was wearing a patterned dress and high heels as she went along the broad alley that connected the lots behind the academic buildings. I gestured her to get in the Jeep and I gave her a lift. She had a wide, shy smile and she left a smell of perfume in the front. I flexed my hands and took a breath and felt lonely.

I saw my English professor at the front of his long, low gray car, a new one, a Cadillac de Ville. He seemed to be puzzled, so I stopped and said hello and he gave me a little salute. His smile was embarrassed. I'd have been embarrassed, too, wearing puffy-looking sneaker things with leather trim on khaki cloth with thick soles under pea green corduroys and a kind of quilted slicker with a long-brimmed hat the color of the shoes.

"They're a new development in thermal footwear," he said. "The insulation is very lightweight, and the cloth is Gore-Tex. It repels moisture and keeps the heat in, but your feet breathe."

"Lucky feet," I said. "Is there a problem here?"

"I thought you might be coming up one of these days to talk about your grade for last semester's course."

"No," I said, "I was able to read the letter. It said C."

"Plus," he said.

"Plus."

"I was afraid you might be disappointed."

I shook my head. "I get credit for the course," I said.

"Well."

It seemed to me he was trying to figure out whether I could

understand the subtleties of all his very interesting emotions. I didn't want to name them for him, but I knew they included smugness, condescension, and superiority over the semiliterate. He looked around for a translator.

"I don't worry about my grades," I said.

He said, "*There* you go."

"Can I help you with your car?"

"I guess I popped the hood open this morning when I checked the oil and then left it open. I can't seem to close it." I found a heavy screwdriver in my toolbox and then I lifted the hood partway up. I asked him to hold it in place. The snap latch above the grillwork was closed. I used the shaft of the screwdriver to pry it open. Then I gestured him away from the hood and dropped it shut. It fell into place.

"It must have been this way awhile," I said, thinking of the witnesses in Chenango Flats, wondering if an old woman at her window at dusk might mistake the jammed-open hood for something bulbous on the front of the dark car.

"Yes, I expect," he said, ready to be rid of me now.

I tried the subtle approach. "You get to Chenango Flats a lot? I think I might have seen this car there and didn't know it was yours."

He said, "Why's that?"

"I don't know. Just wondering."

"Just wondering about me and Chenango Flats? I see." He opened his door and positioned himself to sit behind the wheel. "I appreciate your coming to the rescue," he said.

"Sure," I said. "Nothing to it."

"Why in hell would you ask me questions about Chenango Flats, Jack?"

His big strong head was ducked, as if he was trying to read his instruments. Then his head came up and he stared into my eyes. I tried to read anything there besides amusement, a little confusion, the idea that I was no longer very interesting to him. It occurred to me I wouldn't mind learning he was the one.

He took his eyes off me and started the car. I let go of the door

when he pulled it to. As he backed away and drove off slowly, with
no further word or gesture for me, I realized his car had done the
talking for him. Its insignia said I could never afford it, and the
soft-suspension trundle of its rear end had said, I turn my back on
you.

There was no reason, really, to suspect him, and stretching a
hood left ajar into a bulbous protrusion was probably silly. I wasn't
much of a cop. I knew that. Beating up William Franklin was like
beating on the world in general. My life, before I was done with him,
had shrugged and picked its teeth and waited for me to get back into
it. I was going to have to straighten up, I thought. I was going to have
to straighten everything up.

In the service, working a case was easy. It was always clear, except
for suspected theft of company funds, and one case of suspected
spying, when I went no place with either one. Usually, the guy was in
stockade for me, waiting to scrounge a cigarette and tell how scared
he was. Here was his knife. Here was the picture of the civilian
male or, sometimes, American soldier or, often enough, whore in the
hospital or medical examiner's, and here was the wound. I talked to
the prisoner, he told me what I knew, including his fear and often
enough his regret, and then I attached the transcript to the incident
report and wrote my own report, and I moved on. They always confessed to me. I was good at that part. And they were stupid. And
there wasn't anyplace a soldier could hide.

The one we thought went over to the NVA was Chinese-
American, a scared young kid who was educated and intelligent, and
we were racists and he was innocent. Everyone figured all the guys
with slanted eyes were on the same side. I wrote that in my report
when I said he was innocent. They told me I might have made a
field-grade promotion to second lieutenant, at least for the duration
of the action, except for that report. I told Fanny I thought it was the
warrior lieutenants from VMI disliking it that a guy who didn't go to
college and who seemed a little hard might get to attend their
briefings. I came out a sergeant at twenty-four and that was all right,
and I had some skills. But I didn't know what to do about Janice

Tanner, and I was afraid of making a mess. I didn't want anyone hurt because of me. Except, I told myself, William Franklin of Staten Island, New York.

The dispatcher said a professor needed assistance with a vehicle at the social sciences lot. I said I'd answer. Maybe I'd just break the arm on this one and let it go at that. But it turned out to be Professor Piri, and I seemed to have a hard time with her. She had that wide grin. It made her look young, like a high school girl. And there was something maybe mischievous in her face. It said we were both misbehaving a little.

She stood outside her runty, beat-up car, moving her feet and swinging her arms. "Thank you," she said, smiling the smile.

"I didn't help you yet," I said.

"You will. It doesn't start. It won't talk to me."

"Car won't talk to you. Does it say anything at all?"

"Nothing."

I did the usual with the jumper cables, but she was right. This was a dead car. She was sitting in my Jeep with the heater on high, and I had to open her door and reach across her for the radio. I was very careful not to touch her legs, which were in red tights. She watched my arm move in front of her. I told the dispatcher we needed a car towed. Professor Piri told me which of the two garages nearby she liked to use. I told the dispatcher to have them take it there. After I got her briefcase for her, I started driving toward her house.

I asked if we weren't supposed to be meeting soon about the threat to the Vice President.

"They're talking about putting Irene Horstmuller in jail."

"The library head?"

"She's a right-on woman. She'll go, I know she will. She'll be right to."

"What if somebody shoots the Vice President or something?"

"We're talking right to *privacy*. We're talking Constitution. This isn't just about library rules or niceties or even ethics."

"Constitution," I said.

"Why does that make you smile?"

"No," I said, "I was talking to somebody in connection with my, I

don't—well, with my duties. Earlier today. He talks about the Constitution. He also sells drugs."

"That's right. I hear you. One of them sells drugs. The other
threatens Presidents."

"Vice Presidents."

"Yes. And the outlaws are ahead, two to one, and you don't like
it." She said, "Cops."

"Whoa."

"Well, I *know* this argument. I've heard it half my life from my
father."

"Professor Piri, I am not making an argument. I'm not arguing.
All I did was, I smiled."

We were on the street, and she was pointing to houses. She had
me go up the driveway that curled around in the back of where she
lived.

"It was a fine smile," she said.

"Same to you," I said.

Here we were. I thought we were coming to it, but we were here
already. I noticed I had shut the engine off.

"Let me make you some coffee," she said.

"Please."

"Then you have to go back, don't you?"

"Yes."

"My first name is Rosalie. Did I tell you that?"

"I remember your name."

"You could call me that."

"Rosalie," I said.

She said, "Jack."

"I have to get back on patrol," I said.

"But first the coffee."

"Thank you."

"Rosalie."

"Thank you, Rosalie."

Her kitchen was small and not terribly clean. She said, "Oh! The
damned garbage."

I smelled it, too, a kind of mild decay I always associated with winter and too much snow to want to go out in. She hung her coat over a chair, and I kept mine on. She moved behind me twice while making the coffee, and I felt the hairs on my neck respond. It was a boyish feeling, and that as much as she herself was exciting.

She told me about her father, the policeman. She talked about her mother, who was a nutritionist in the public schools. She told me about Smith College and Princeton University. She talked about the politics of untenured professors.

"Tenure always struck me as a kind of baby thing. You know, do your job well and stay, do it badly and we can you." I was looking for any sort of fight, I realized. I didn't want to relax any more in this room. She sat on the counter across from me, swinging her legs in their red tights under her short black jumper.

"Say I'm a lesbian," she said.

"You're a lesbian."

"Is that a question?"

"Just saying it."

"I'm not," she said. "*Say* I am. Say my department head's a woman who wants to get me in the sack. Say she's a he who thinks a dyke is a very expendable item."

"I'll say the one where she wants you in the sack."

She almost smiled the smile, but she kept talking. She moved her hands a lot as she talked, and she swung her legs back and forth.

She said, "Say she wants me so much, and I say no, and she punishes me by seeing I don't get a new contract."

"Can that happen?"

"Not as easily as I made it sound, but yes."

"Okay. That wouldn't be fair. But wouldn't that happen in the rest of the world? Another job? Where they don't do tenure?"

"You're cute," she said. "*Here* it is. I'm teaching from lesbian theory, say."

"There's lesbian *theory*?"

"There's every theory. That's what drives a lot of work these days: theory. I'm doing a good deal of the new historicism myself."

"Oh."

"I'm sorry. Never mind that. But all it is—think of context. Anyway. Say I'm teaching a kind of theory my department head doesn't like. Say the kids complain. Say *she* complains. Say she disapproves because of how I think."

"And she gets you canned for how you think. I hear that. Okay. That's bad. But people get fired for how they think. Why should you guys get protected when the rest of us don't? Except you're better-educated and smarter and you—would you mind getting down off of the counter?"

She jumped down at once. She said, "Why?"

"You have to know why."

She did smile the wicked smile then. When she walked over to me, she leaned against the back of the chair I was sitting sideways in, and some of her touched me up and down.

She said, "I'm not a cop groupie. I know about them."

"I never met one."

"Then maybe I should be one. You could find out. They're pretty basic, I think."

"Groupy theory," I said.

I smelled her lipstick and her perfume and her skin. All of them were new to me. They overwhelmed the smell of the kitchen, which had bothered me. She put her hand on my shoulder so her fingers touched my neck. I shivered.

"I'm not careless with my personhood," she said.

I wanted to ask her what personhood was, but I didn't think she was conducting a conversation. She was delivering a message, maybe to herself and maybe to me, and I wanted to listen.

Her hand moved, but not away from me. I saw that her eyes were closed. I knew the water she was heating for instant coffee in a blackened aluminum pot was going to bubble and boil, and she would have to change her position. I found that I was moving. I was leaning up and moving my left hand. I stood, reached under her arm and pulled her against me, set my legs, leaned down, to find her looking up, and I shut my eyes and kissed her.

It seemed to me to be a lot more than teeth and lips and her small, cool tongue. It seemed to me, or maybe I was just hoping a lot, that I was going to end up with Rosalie Piri on her kitchen floor and me in big trouble. I stepped back, but slowly. Her eyes had closed again, and she kept them shut when I stepped farther back, toward the door. I heard the chug of boiling water against the side of the pot.

"Are you gone yet?" she asked.

"Here I go."

"I can't look," she said. "Can you go now?"

Her face was crimson. She looked like a child in a terrible moment who was making it go away by closing her eyes.

"Here I go," I said.

"You don't have to."

I said, "Then open your eyes."

She stood in her kitchen, slight and red. She opened her eyes, she looked at me, and she put her hands to her face and then covered her eyes with them. She laughed a grown-up's laugh. She said, "I can't, Jack. Can I—why don't I—why don't we call each other up or something?"

I did walk back across her little kitchen and kiss her lightly on the mouth and then the nose before I left. I did have to do that. I was making it a morning of doing all I could to be wrong.

———

When I saw Archie Halpern on campus late that afternoon, I asked him about people who might want to talk to one Roger Gambrelle about his rap music, his racism or his reverse racism or his racism inside out. Archie wore a Russian fur cap about two feet tall. His old-fashioned plaid mackinaw was the blue of a bathrobe I had worn as a child in 1950 something. His round face was red from the cold and his five o'clock shadow had set in. He looked like leftovers.

His little eyes were full of pleasure when he said, "I just might pay cash money to eavesdrop on you, telling this boy to lay off the famous Niva."

"She's famous?"

"Half the males in the senior class report to the infirmary with knotted testes on account of her. She's the Catch. She's smart, capable, tough, exotic as hell around here, in white-bread country, and the daughter of the president of the Denver Chamber of Commerce. Somebody said she sends for her underwear to Victoria's Secret, and guys started camping near the mailroom. No, don't go after Gambrelle. God, I can see it. The kid limps into class with a sling on his ass and two black eyes—"

"Hey, Archie, what's *that* supposed to mean?"

"It's a joke, Jack. What'd you think it's supposed to mean? You're a little sensitive."

"You're right. I apologize."

"You don't need to apologize to me. I was just pointing something out to you."

"You always point something out to me. You're usually right."

"So how come, if I'm so smart, we don't declare the campus a neurosis-free zone? You shithead. Relax. I'll whisper a word to Gambrelle in the laid-back, subtle way I'm famous for. You know: Gambrelle, stay the fuck away from Niva."

I loved it when he laughed. His laughter reminded me of feeling only good. Archie moved on, and I walked back to the truck, checked in on the radio, and continued to circle the campus slowly, top to bottom, side to side, selecting buildings randomly just to walk through. Students didn't see me because I was a support service. They were accustomed to acknowledging one another and their teachers, not the vomit-moppers or thermostat repairmen, and surely not the campus cops. Janice Tanner's face flapped in the wind outside, stirred in the hallways whenever a door was opened, and stared out of car windows over and over in the parking lots.

It was time to get to the library. I'd been summoned for three, and I showed up a few minutes early. There were two FBI agents and the Secret Service men, and Anthony Berberich had showed up as instructed by me. Our job was to keep people assembled in the big anteroom near the circulation desk while the president and the dean, who looked like men who didn't have a choice, went through the reference section toward Irene Horstmuller's office, a few feet behind the four federal agents. It looked as though they were trying to get ahead of the agents, but the agents closed up tight and edged the administrators back. Some faculty and students and library staff were behind me as I watched.

I said, turning, "We're required to stay back here, folks."

"Fuckin' fascists," a student said. He was about five feet tall and maybe Korean, with a sweet, open face. As I looked him over, he checked me out. "Cop motherfucker," he said.

I said, "What's your name?"

He didn't hesitate. "Chang," he said.

I stuck my hand out. "Hi, Chang. I'm Jack."

He let me shake his hand. He stared at me a few seconds more, and then his mouth collapsed into a smile.

One of the women at the checkout desk said, "You think they'll put her in handcuffs?"

"I think they have to," I said. "They'll serve the subpoena."

"She'll tell 'em to stick it in the great anal darkness," Chang said.

"Then they can arrest her," I said. "And take the files."

The woman at the desk, who had a round, impressively hairy face, smiled larger than Chang. "We don't have any," she said.

I said, "You shredded them?"

"No," the woman said, "they were in the mainframe. Irene accessed them yesterday."

"And had an accident," I said.

She said, "Whoops."

"Darn," Chang said.

The Secret Service men came first, the crease of their dark gray trousers cutting the air. They were followed by Irene Horstmuller, in coat and hat and gloves, looking a little tense at the mouth. Then came the FBI. When she saw us, Horstmuller's face began to collapse. She fought the tears. She raised her hands and, as the sleeves of the coat slid down, the handcuffs were exposed.

"Fascist cocksucker motherfuckers," Chang said.

As they passed and the little patter of applause died, I said to Chang, "I bet you there's a backup."

"I bet you she found it."

"That'd be good," I said. "Unless, of course, the Vice President gets damaged."

Chang said, "You can't make an omelette without breaking eggs, baby."

I asked him, "Is that one of those Harry Truman sayings?"

"Truman? You kidding me?"

"I'm only guessing," I said, gesturing to Berberich that he could leave, "but Truman's a running dog of fascism, right?"

———

When I got home, it was snowing hard again. I didn't want to be inside alone, so while the dog had his little freedom romp, I sat in the kitchen and put on the greasy old cross-country boots and used cold wax on the skis instead of heating it. I made sure the flashlight was bright, I stuck a light scarf of Fanny's in the pocket of my parka, and I fed the dog. He smelled the boots, I guess, or he read my intentions, the way he so often does. Twice when he went to the door, I had to send him back to his food. When he was done, we went outside. On the steps of the porch, I clamped myself into the skis. He checked me out, tore off in the wrong direction, came back, jumped, somehow, sideways in the air, went in a different wrong direction, then came back and waited, panting hard, for me to lean forward on my poles, imitating a man who stretches before skiing.

I headed for the field that lay to the north of the house and the west of the woods below us. It was a little sticky at first, and I was a little creaky, but I needed to work away the soreness of my arms, real or imagined, that I'd felt since beating on William Franklin. After a while, I caught something that reminded me of the old push-and-release rhythm, and though I probably panted more loudly than the dog, I went through the thick snow, and into the snow that was falling, with the mixed purpose you feel when you're skiing well cross-country. You have the effort that makes you think you're pursuing something, and you have no real destination, so you aren't worried about progress. You just row away with your arms and you step into the slide and you let it go, and everything's focused for you in your knees and, of course, breathing, which wasn't all that easy that night, what with the cold and the years and the defiantly bad conditioning.

We went over the top of a fence post I knew separated our land from the acreage of a field cut for hay by a local farmer. We were on snow at least four feet high, maybe five. The dog had started out ahead of me, predicting my moves, correcting for them, and cutting the start of a trail for me. By now, since, like me, he was no kid, he trotted behind me, usually, letting me break the wind and set the pace. My eyes were used to the dark, my ears were numb from the cold and the wind, and I couldn't feel too much of the rest of my face. My body was sweat-wet up and down. I stopped to tie the scarf over the top of my head, covering my ears. I knotted it under my chin and put my watch cap back on. Then I skied over onto the farmer's hay field and went straight ahead.

I pushed on for a very long time. I didn't want to look at my watch, but I felt it had been a long time since I'd covered my ears. My knees were aching now, but that was all right. My thigh muscles burned. Even my shoulders and arms were jumping with charley horse. I kept going. It reminded me of the runs in basic training and of the long humps with a sixty-pound pack. You got to a point where something flared up and roared for a while and then was gone, flushed out and vaporized, and you felt lighter, even if you hurt, and you knew you'd get to the end and be all right. At the finish, before your body caved in, you felt better than you had at the start.

I thought, See how good you can make yourself feel with a little work and a lot of misery? Try and do that for someone else, I thought.

I looked down as I forced the slide-ahead, slide-ahead rhythm, and I saw my skis etching lines. Ahead of me, there was nothing but snow falling very hard and dense, like a coarsely woven curtain, and snow heaped on the ground on either side, burying the snow that had fallen for weeks. I stopped and turned in my tracks because I knew you can lose yourself and die a hundred feet from your house in a storm like this. I looked behind me, expecting to see the tracks go back to a vanishing point, but I couldn't see where I'd been. I saw a big snow-covered dog with icicles of slobber at his mouth and happy eyes, a gentle fellow of huge heart who shamed me daily by believing me important. And, behind him, I saw nothing. That was what was around me. I turned in a hurry, hoping to find the forward edges of my tracks, but they were gone, too. I headed into what I thought was the nothing ahead of me that I should be pointed toward, and of course the dog came, too.

Archie would ask me something clever and psychological about what I thought I might be sliding away from. But Archie wasn't with me, and I didn't feel honor-bound to answer questions. Questions are what you have in the house where you live. Outside, where it gets a little snowy and you need a sense of direction, you don't do questions. You just slide ahead. I'd have said that to someone asking something. But there wasn't anyone with me except a dog who would run on stumps, if you chopped his legs off, to keep up with me. My face was frozen now, and I knew I ought to be heading away from the weather. You make sergeant that way, pushing off into something a little dangerous in a headstrong way and suddenly feeling more than thinking it's time to make believe you're smart.

I cut farther west, where I knew we'd come across an old right-of-way that the farmer's hands used for hay wagons. The roadway would be under snow, of course, but I thought I'd see the space in the trees that the hedgerow made—where the path was cut—against the green glare of the farmer's barnyard lights. Mostly, I saw darkness and the whirl of snow. I decided not to use the flashlight, because unless the wind is kind to you, the snow seems to blow straight into the light and all you see is snow and not the way you need to go.

Looking forward and mostly down, and seeing mostly snow, and after a while that means you see nothing, I expected to think about Hannah or Fanny or both of them at once. That was what usually happened. I thought very briefly of Rosalie Piri, and I thought it was something about her littleness mixed in with her smile, which was so grown-up and maybe had to do with sex. I was happy to be thinking of sex. I hadn't in any significant way for a long time. I wondered. If she was stretched out naked on a bed, watching a man, say me, walk toward her, would she have those little tightened breasts? Would she smile that wicked smile? Would I worry about being too heavy for her? Would I lie down beside her? Would I cover her over with me?

I didn't have the wind to talk, but I still said, "No!"

I crooked my neck, and I wondered what it was I'd said no to. You go out on cross-country skis on a very bad night in a very bad month of several bad years, and you start shouting "No!" and you realize there is a good deal you might be shouting it about.

I wondered if a man lay beside her or upon her and it was the first time together for them whether she would flush red, and whether the flush would stain the pale flesh of her chest, and whether she would cover her eyes the way she had. Maybe she would reach with those thin, small arms, I thought, and cover his.

First I saw a low glare, and then I saw the silhouette of the hedgerow. I had let us drift east, so I corrected and, not permitting myself to stop, I took us toward the right-of-way and then the narrow road it emptied into. I was hoping the town had plowed it, and we had a little luck because the snow, despite that day's fall, was plowed and packed and tamped enough for me to kick out of my bindings and stick the skis over my shoulder and walk, very slowly, up the hill and back to the house. It took over an hour of steady walking, I figured, to get there. The dog was bushed. I had almost caught my breath by the time we were home.

Fanny's car was there. I left the skis on the porch and went in, calling for her. She was at the table. I said, "What's wrong?"

"Nothing's wrong. Hello. I came home."

"It's early," I said.

"It's nine o'clock at night. Where were *you*?"

"You first, as soon as I get dry clothes on." I dumped my shirt and pants and underwear directly into the washer and, shivering, threw in more dirty clothes, tossed in the soap, and started a wash. I ran upstairs, toweled off, dressed, added a cotton sweater over my flannel shirt, and went back down in my woolen socks. Fanny had heated a pot of chicken broth, and I poured myself a cup and sat with her. The dog was lying near his half-empty water dish, panting double time, his tongue stiff and very long.

"He's too old for you to work him out so hard," Fanny said. "Where'd you go? What'd you do?"

"We did a cross-country run—well, a shuffle. Down the back field, over to the hay field, across to the old farm road and back up—without skiing, just limping—on Taft Road to the main road and home."

"I didn't know you had that much left," she said. Either I had turned only a few lights on or she had turned some off. She sat in the semidarkness, sipping at her soup, sitting in the straight-backed way that told me she had crossed her legs beneath her on the chair. It would take me two days, with pulleys and levers, to get my legs up like that. She looked square-shouldered, competent, not as frail as I knew she really was.

"I don't believe the returns are in from the outer precincts about what's left," I said. "And I may not walk tomorrow."

"Why'd you go?"

"Well, I don't know. You know. I just . . . went. But why did you come home before the shift was over?"

"Same. Just . . . came home."

"What's wrong, Fanny?"

"I missed you. I felt like I hadn't seen you for years."

"Isn't that why you took the shift?"

She drank some soup. "I wish I smoked," she said.

"It's great when you don't know what to say. You light up, you do the little business with the lighter or the match, the this and that that smokers have. I miss it."

"I miss you," she said.

I looked at my soup, saw soup, looked up, saw Fanny, didn't know where to look next. She blew her nose and he thumped his tail.

"I miss us both," I said.

Then she said, "I miss all three of us."

"But you didn't walk off the shift—"

"I told them I didn't feel well."

"You didn't walk off the shift, and leave the hospital without its most experienced ER nurse, just so you could come home and say it was a bad thing Hannah, you know—"

"Died," she said.

I said, "Died. That's right."

"But why not? Isn't that a thing we need to say?"

"Archie Halpern would think so."

"You wouldn't?"

"I mostly know what I think about things from you and from Archie. So, yeah. I guess so. Yeah. I feel shitty, too. How's that?"

"So now you feel better because you said so," she said, smiling even though her eyes were filled and her cheeks were streaked. She said, "There. It's what a nurse knows how to do."

"Is this what playing nurse means? I always thought it meant, you know—"

"Sex," she said.

"Ah."

"Remember it?"

"Sure," I said. "We used to have it. I think we had some several months ago. Well. I guess I wouldn't *quite* call it that."

"That was not your fault," she said.

"That's right. I knew that. *You* were the one with the erection and *you're* to blame for losing it," I said.

"You don't do *blame* about hard-ons."

The dog slugged the floor with his tail.

"Fanny, I wouldn't know one of those right now if it knocked me off of my chair."

"I understand," she said.

I didn't know what was in my head, but I was afraid to raise it and let her see my eyes, in case Rosalie Piri was in there looking out.

I shrugged, and she said, "I didn't come home to make love, Jack."

Trying not to look sneaky, I did raise my head, and I waited. She was waiting, too. I said, "What, Fanny?"

"Are we, do you think, are we ever going to be all right?"

I nodded hard. I said, "Damned right. Of course we are."

"Do you have any idea when?"

"We're getting there," I said. "Don't you think? Really?"

Nurses look directly at it, and they name it out loud. She shook her head.

"But maybe," I said. "Right?"

"If you want it to be maybe, we can say that."

"Is it worth coming off the shift early to come home and say maybe?"

She said, "Jack."

The dog thumped his tail.

I said, "So, then, maybe. All right?"

"All right," she said.

"Really, though. A definite maybe."

She almost laughed. She shook her head. She finished her soup. I thought, as I stayed where I was, that somebody ought to walk around the table and hug this woman hard and just hold on.

testify

W E HAD THE USUAL upstate January thaw so late in the season, it was two days away from March when temperatures went toward twenty, and people new to the region talked about early spring. Students forsook heavy coats, and some professors came to work in sport jackets with sweaters underneath and, of course, the long scarf wrapped around the neck and trailing down the back.

The dog got down to another level of dead creatures in the forest, and he came back on the second morning of the thaw with a bunch of loose but connected half-defrosted blue-brown flesh that he rolled on in the side yard. He tossed it in the air and chased it, dancing rigidly over it, back and forth, like an old brown rocking chair. Then he aimed his back at it and rolled around, his paws in the air, his back writhing. Occasionally, he took licks at it, then bites. When he came back in, I smelled him and sent him out.

So, before work, on a day when you could see, if not feel, the sun, I rubbed the old dog down with shampoo and then rinsed him off with snow. I didn't want him soaked so the lanolin ran out of his coat. I also didn't want to smell the secrets he'd uncovered. But he'd had a happy morning, and I was glad.

When I got to campus, the sun was paler, and it fell with even less weight than it had a couple of hours before. I cranked the window down and stuck my head out to look up. Clouds were massing, dirty and serrated and thick. Our thaw was about to be rescinded.

I had thought about making an appointment for Fanny and me with Archie Halpern. I had thought about it for several nights and days. I didn't drive to the Blue Bird, though, and I didn't phone his office on campus or call him at home. I read reports from the night men and I looked through the mail. The president promised us all, students, faculty, and staff (as they called us): He would move heaven and earth, he would use all powers at his disposal, he would bring to bear every resource possessed by the college, to set free Irene Horstmuller. I thought she was wrong and also a goddamned hero and I loved what she did. Archie would call this being in conflict. Apparently, no one was telling the Secret Service or the FBI or anyone in the courts that the records she was sent to jail for protecting didn't exist. This much of it, I quite enjoyed. In being guilty as charged, she was also innocent, since what she protected by going to jail wasn't on the surface of the earth or in it. Still, I worried about the Vice President.

In a sealed campus-mail envelope was a letter for me on departmental letterhead. It said:

And?

It wasn't signed with a name, only an initial: *R*. I thought it was pretty bold stuff, really. Consorting with staff couldn't be easy on any campus, and surely not this one, with its heavy burden of reputation. This was a training center for the overprivileged, underdisciplined children of large money and thick ease. They were here to learn how to manage credit cards Fanny and I couldn't qualify for. The faculty, I believe, enjoyed complaining about but also servicing the kids whose parents gave them the older Volvo to take back to school. You don't fraternize with staff. You don't lie down on a bed so when he approaches it your little arms extend above your head and stretch your small breasts tight.

I folded the letter and buttoned it into my shirt pocket. I unbuttoned it and took the letter out and tore it into many small pieces.

There was no mail about Janice Tanner or any of the other missing girls. My vice president for administration wanted my opinion on the performance of our Jeeps. I thought they were all right. They had gotten me where I needed to go, and had maybe saved a girl's life. On the other hand, pieces of them could break away in your hands. So could anything else, I thought. I chucked his letter. I read that my staff evaluations were late. I chucked that letter, too. It was a good morning for disregarding mail. Of course, I wasn't disregarding Rosalie Piri's letter. I was only trying to.

I left the rest of the mail, and I warmed up my Jeep. The sun was so pale, it barely lit the blanket of cloud cover. I thought the wind had picked up. I sniffed out the window, and I smelled moisture. We were going to end the thaw's little illusion with a giant storm. And we were locked into winter for several more months. The corpses in storage would have to wait for burial. The dog was going to have to be happy with snorting at the surface of things. It was going to get snowy and then it was going to get cold.

A sign outside the language laboratory said FREE HORSTMULLER. When I passed the library, I saw that someone had hung a bedsheet from a reference room window. FREE HORSTMULLER was painted on it in loopy red letters. Big Pete passed me and he nodded, telling me that all was well. So I didn't understand when, a few hundred yards below, where he must have passed, I found a long Crown Victoria sedan with its right-side wheels stuck in frozen mud the driver had churned his way down to, trying to get free. They were up to visit the campus with their son, a very long boy who sat in the backseat, his legs folded so his knees were almost at the level of his chin. I used the cable and I pulled them out.

I called for Pete to meet me, and we had our little rendezvous in the parking lot behind the Jewish Center. We angled so the driver's side windows were next to each other.

Pete said, "Jew-bee Jew-bee doo."

"Meaning what?"

"Nothin'. It's just Jew town here, so I'm singing a theme song."

"We can't do that, Pete. We can't talk like that."

"Who says we can't?" His little face behind thick glasses actually looked confused. He was dumber than water and too small for trouble and he got on my nerves. His job was the one I had in mind for a woman, and not only because he was too stupid to live and we needed a little courtesy on the staff. Like most colleges I'd heard about, rape here was one of the more favored indoor sports, and I thought the kids ought to be able to talk to a trained woman.

"Well, Pete, actually it's me."

"No shit, Jack."

"I mean it."

"All right."

"No. I mean I *mean* it. I'll get you canned. Actually, I'll do that myself. I'm halfway there."

"Over the Jews? Excuse *me*."

"How about the big Crown Victoria down below the library? They were halfway buried when you must have passed them."

"Jack, these fuckin' kids with their big cars . . ."

"Yeah."

"I'm not sayin' these were Jews, mind you."

"No."

"They lord it over you. You know."

"Some of them do do that."

"Like they own you."

"Well, pretty much, they do, if they pay the tuition here, Pete. Pete?"

"I shouldn't of left them there."

"No. Pete?"

"Mm?"

"I think you're fired. I want you to be. Take a sick day so you get paid, and I'm finding out if I can fire you. If so, you're gone. If not, you really have to watch your ass around me."

"You mean like *fired?*"

"Off the job."

"Fired."

"Take the car back and go home sick. Check with me tomorrow or the day after."

"You're gonna be a man short, Jack."

"Not quite a whole one, Pete. I'll see you."

I went around to the farthest dormitory, calling Anthony Berberich to tell him we'd try to tighten our rotations a little. I thought how I'd decided to suspect my English prof on account of his unlatched hood. And there was always poor William Franklin, whose chest must be black and blue from nipple to neck. I thought maybe I should add Big Pete to the list. I seemed to be trying to help the Tanners by considering the world not only a dangerous place—their daughter had proved that—but everyone in it capable of terrible acts. I was not a man you'd call at ease with the condition of things.

We pushed ourselves, and I skipped my lunch break, and we covered our patrols. Snow had begun to fall in the late morning. It came down very quickly. With my window open, I could hear it in the naked tree limbs and against the windows of the school. It accumulated with a suddenness, and all at once the streets needed plowing, and soon enough the plows on campus and off couldn't deal with the snow. By late in the day, I was using four-wheel drive on the upper campus roads. The plows left cars covered outside the classroom buildings, and we gave lifts to students and teachers leaving the campus. By four, word came that the school was closed. I walked past ice-stiffened posters that rattled on the walls. The faces of the girls were covered by heavy snow and fresh ice. The campus was deserted. I had the night shift called in early and I kept Anthony on.

The buildings were dark except for hallway lights, and the walkway lights on campus shrank in the wind-driven snow to smears of brown-orange. I checked the half-buried cars to make certain no one was trapped inside. I used the radio to remind Anthony and the night men to do the same. I called the campus radio station, which seemed to specialize in the sound of people screaming, and asked them to request that the kids stay in. The president of the college called me to ask if everything was all right. I could have said no, and I could have said yes, and neither would have been true. So I said, "Not bad." He seemed pleased.

Coming back up, very slowly and in four-wheel drive, behind the humanities building, I saw a new shape. It had snow on it, especially on top of the roof, but it wasn't buried. It looked to me like a Land Cruiser. I thought to myself, Trust a kid to drive a car worth more than a year's salary. It was broad and high and there was an arrogance to how it was set on its wheels. I thought I heard a horn, and then I saw the Toyota's lights go on and off, so I got as close as I could, pointed in at an angle you simply would have to call obtuse.

I left the Jeep running, with its lights on the Toyota, and I walked over to the driver's side. The back doors opened, and then the front passenger-side door. The driver's door came out with surprising speed and it caught me on the knee and thigh, and I went down hard in the snow.

A voice said, "Absolutely." It was *ab-so-lootlee,* and I knew it was William Franklin. He'd brought some friends for me to meet, I thought.

One of them was wearing a sweatshirt or sweater and speed gloves, what you wear when you work with the light bag. His hair was shiny in the headlights of the Jeep, and it was pulled back in a ponytail. He was either advertising he was a middle-aged vet who hadn't gotten past 1973, or he was an Indian, maybe an Onondaga, or maybe he was both. He had a big belly and sloping shoulders and those long, ropy-muscled arms. He wouldn't have stamina, I thought, but he would do a lot of damage before he tired out.

The others wore waist-length jackets, working clothes that would leave them free to pivot, spin, run, or kick. One of the jackets looked leathery; one seemed made of cloth. They were shorter than the Indian, but almost as broad, and while one of them seemed to carry a gut, the other was lean and hard-looking.

I saw this on the run or, really, on the clamber. I got to my feet as fast as I could and leaned my back against the Jeep. The light would be in their eyes, not mine, and they'd not be able to reach my back too easily. It wouldn't matter in a while, but I thought I ought to do what I knew how to do.

The roll of dimes was in the car, and so was anything else I could use, including gloves. William Franklin shouted, "Absolutely yes! It's him!"

The Indian came around his door, holding it for balance, slipping a little in what I thought were street shoes, maybe loafers. I held on to the grille of the Jeep and kicked him as hard in the knee as I could with the toe of my heavy boot. He skidded in toward me, but he was down. I let go of the car and hit him in the throat with a chopping fist. I missed the throat because he knew his business and tucked his chin into his chest. I made him uncomfortable, but I also numbed up my fist. He went facedown, then rolled back away from me. His leg wouldn't work right away.

The first squat one, the one with the bigger belly, threw a big roundhouse left to the body. Amateur, I thought. The amateur connected with the right side of my ribs and I felt him through my coat. I came over his left, like you're supposed to, with a sweet, short, crossing right. He stopped where he was. My right hand had gone from numb to sore and now it plain hurt very badly. But he wobbled. I ignored his friend, the leaner one, and followed up the right cross with a right knee. I went after that, as he dropped, with the chopping right that hadn't worked on the Indian. It worked on him, but to the side of his face. I did it again, and I thought he might be through. Something had broken with the last blow, and I was hoping it was inside him and not in my hand.

But by now, the lean one had hit me twice in the ribs, big, pounding blows. He worked the heavy bag, I thought. Or maybe he just killed people with his fists. He missed my nose but caught my temple. Then he caught my nose. I didn't want to bend over or go down, but I did both, in segments, and one of them, the Indian who was up again, I thought, caught me on the back of the neck. It wasn't the correct way to deliver that blow, which was lucky for me, but it was done quickly and with malice, which was unfortunate for a man in my position, which was down and exposed.

I was in the snow now, on my knees, and almost out of business. My head went back a few times and made contact with the car. Someone was landing feet in my belly and ribs. A shot took my elbow, and I went facedown. I tried to roll under the Jeep, and I got partway there. They pulled me out. I tried to cover up, but I couldn't see and I couldn't make my arms work. My mouth was filled with blood and I thought I was maybe breathing it in, because I started to cough.

William Franklin said, "You let him spit his blood on you like that?" It was *yoo*. He said, "You gonna let him give yez AIDS?"

One of them said, "Holy shit."

Someone else said, "AIDS motherfuckin' fag."

They continued to deliver the message with their feet. They'd let go of me by now, and I worked my body into as much of a ball as my disconnected-feeling limbs could manage. I tried to cover my head with my arms. I couldn't tell if I had. Nothing much was operational.

I thought he was whispering down one of those cardboard tubes that paper towels come wrapped around. He said something in hollow-sounding whispers, but I couldn't understand him.

Another one—maybe it was Franklin—shouted over the wind, and I did hear him. He cried, "Don't piss us off."

Another one said, "This is not about pissed off. The man understands."

My tongue was too big for my mouth. I kept swallowing liquids. I was blind. I was trying to decide about breathing, because it hurt. I knew if they did any more, it would kill me.

They did a little more. They went twice more to the body and I decided not to breathe. I wondered if they'd killed me. Someone dragged me someplace. I was cold. Someone drove a car away, maybe my Jeep, I thought. I thought if I was thinking, maybe I wasn't dead. I heard their Toyota turn over, a low, nasty rumble, and then they left.

After they were gone, I listened to the snow rattling on something, maybe the backs of my ears. I heard a low chugging noise that I thought might be my Jeep. I waited a little while longer to see if I was dead. I opened my eyes. I actually opened one. The other didn't work. I saw the Jeep about ten or fifteen feet away. You can walk *that*, I thought. I moved a little. I thought, So crawl it. I moved again, and then I thought, Roll.

I inched there. My hands were alongside my body and my face was down. I moved my knees and, each time I did, I quickly learned it was important to hold my breath. That fooled my body between the throat and the waist into believing the pain was better. A few fingers didn't work, and I couldn't lift my arms. My legs were sore, but they could push. My forehead and the front of my face got very numb from the slush and snow and ice, but that was good. Numbness was wonderful. I wanted more. I dug my head into the snow and I pushed with my knees and angled my shoulders, and within no more than a month, I seemed to be near the car.

The door was open, and I could use the running board, I thought. I did my little trick about compressing and holding a breath, but my breaths were shallow little gaggings, anyway, and there wasn't enough air on all of the campus to reinforce whatever was broken in there. I hadn't read a lot of detective stories, but I'd seen some movies on TV, especially the old ones in black and white. First thing that happens, I thought, the tough-ass, wisecracking, lone-wolf detective smacks a hood. He calls him a cheap hood so everybody understands. Then the hood gets a hundred armed men to absolutely beat the smirking detective's ass into paste. They start by hitting him on the back of the head with the butt of a gun and then they take him apart. But I hadn't seen how the guy gets up into his car when his body doesn't work and the bad guys are gone.

I apparently went off to sleep. Why not call it going to sleep? When I came back, or awake, or whatever you might say, I was on a hip on the running board. I said, "Reach up for the wheel."

Not for two years' salary and the Land Cruiser and one of the squat guys thrown in as chauffeur.

"Please reach up for the wheel," I said.

I understood the urgency. Shock was a problem. And I had lost too much body heat, so there was hypothermia, and then there seemed to be some bleeding, maybe internal, and a number of body parts and mechanical items didn't work. I thought of kidney and spleen and liver. Kidneys sounded likely, I thought. There had been a couple of hands to that region and more than a couple of feet. I really ought to reach for the wheel, I thought.

It was his whimpering that woke me up. It was my whimpering. I was on the front seat, lying down, and making a hell of a noise. It took me the rest of that week to sit up and then make myself lean far enough out to pull on the door. I was very noisy, and I vowed to stop acting out of character. Jack, I reminded myself, was the quiet one with the jumpy cheek muscles and all of that reserve that puts people off.

The parking brake was on. I released it after a while and then I was able to steer with my elbows clamped to my sides and my fingers doing most of the motion. I got it into first and I left it there. I didn't want to move my arm to shift or my foot for the clutch. I kept my foot on the gas. I was able to turn the bubble light on, and I drove. A few times, I rolled into things. I refused to shift to back up, and that seemed to work. I'd hit something and make that noise again and then I'd step a little harder on the gas and the Jeep would slide away or the object would slide away and I'd go forward. That was how I went, forward and down, forward and down.

I thought I was past the library. It was hard to tell because there was no traffic on the street below the campus, but I thought I'd passed the library. "Left," I said.

I choked a little and I spat a lot, and I tried to aim the Jeep straight. I saw the shape of the dormitories to my left, and then came the athletic buildings, then the hospital. I was a quarter of a mile away from it. All of its parking lot lights were on and the ambulance portico was bright. I almost got parked beneath it. I missed by a few feet and bent some of the fender and grille around the brick-veneer post at its right-hand side. I hit the horn and tried to open the door without moving my left arm from where it was clamped at my side. I couldn't get the door released. I moved my right hand again and pressed at the horn. I kept it there, and soon they came out.

I thought it was so lovely. The big metal door swung out and Fanny in white uniform trousers and shirt and white sweater came running. The door swung in, then out again, and she was followed by another nurse pushing a gurney. Fanny pulled the car door open, and she looked so tough, so used to finding someone like me who came spilling out of a car and almost through her arms. I waited to feel the snow again, and the ground, but I didn't because she caught me. I remember thinking how with those big shoulders and strong legs of course she would.

She said, "Jack dear god Christ Jesus Jack. What? *What?*"

Before the other nurse finished helping her move me onto the gurney, I remember saying, or gargling it like somebody in the shower with an open, filling mouth, "Fanny. Fanny. Nobody fed the dog."

——

The sleep, or whatever you want to call it, was fine. I woke and it hurt and fairly soon I went under or somebody put me there again. It went like that quite a few times. Then I came around for a longer stretch and I howled and a doctor put me under for a really wonderfully long time. Then I was awake and not enjoying it.

My nurse was named Virginia. She told me I couldn't breathe because of the cracked ribs, the torn rib cartilage, and the hematomas to my thorax. I said I thought bugs had thoraxes. Not as bad as this one, she told me. I had a catheter because I'd been pissing blood. I told her I knew my kidneys were bad and she said, yes, a kidney was bruised and bleeding. The rest of it was cuts inside the mouth from my own teeth, and the swelling of the cheekbone and nose were bruises, not breaks. I had two splinted fingers and my hands were swollen. That pleased me. When you take a beating, it's always good to have proof you gave a little back. On the whole, however, I was physically useless, and they had gotten the message across.

"They used the kid as a finger," I told the audience. It was Elmo St. John, a trooper I didn't know, and a plainclothes investigator from the sheriff's office. "I heard him say something about 'There he is,' or 'That's him,' something like that. I remember the noise, not the words. I knew he was telling them I was the guy who roughed him up."

"And the reason again?" This was the trooper. He sat rigidly, he held his hat on his lap, and he all but lifted a poster into the air that told me how much the state police appreciated rental cops like me.

The sheriff's investigator was a big, skinny man with a tan. He had long straw-colored hair that looked streaked, like a dye job or the kind of bleaching that happens in the sun on a beach eight hundred miles from us in a different season. He said, "He ran the kid for peddling drugs. He said that already."

"No," the trooper said, "he told us the kid sold drugs or delivered them. He didn't tell us why he had to knock the kid around."

I didn't say anything because my mouth and throat and face and cock and balls and kidney and back and legs and hand and arms and ribs hurt a lot.

Elmo said, "I can understand the temptation to kick someone's ass for that. If you're supposed to be protecting these kids and someone's bringing them marijuana and who knows what else."

"Pills," I whispered.

"Pills," Elmo said.

"No," the trooper said again. "I *understand* the temptation. I'm asking why *do* it."

I didn't have an answer for him. I was thinking of the coeds on campus when they came in complaining about the war against girls conducted by fellows full of beer and feeling extremely entitled. They'd be in a fraternity house or some kid's apartment and everyone would get liquored up. The girls would half pass out and feel a little horny or stimulated or happy and they'd wake up in midscrew or wake up after it and realize they'd never quite consented to getting laid. And the officer in charge, one of my people, would act like it was their fault. Why were you there with him? What were you wearing? What did you say? All the wrong questions. I remember our being told by Archie Halpern: It isn't her fault. Assume that. It isn't her fault. Some of us got confused by that. But it was our rule. I was wishing somebody was here in this hot mint green hospital room to say that about me. I wasn't going to. I wasn't about to try to figure out what blew up inside me when I beat on William Franklin. I wasn't about to drag my life out of me like a rope of intestines and tell this manly law-enforcement person, "Here."

Elmo said, "What, Jack?"

I rolled my head a little to show him Nothing.

He nodded. He told them, "He's tired. He hurts."

The sheriff's man said, "Yes." Then he said, "Except for the way he had his hair, there wasn't anything?"

"Gloves," I said.

"Terrific," the trooper said.

"Speed gloves. He's maybe a fighter."

They wrote it down, the sheriff's man nodding.

Fanny came in. Her face was pale and pinched, her nostrils wide. She said very curtly, "Please come back later."

"We're almost done," the trooper said.

"Wrong by an almost," she told him. She moved between them and me, standing with her hip against the bed, facing them down, until I heard the half sigh, half wince Elmo always makes when he stands on his sore knees. He went to the door, and they followed.

I felt her lean her weight against the bed. Then she turned, looking at the tubes that ran to me and the IV drip, and then my face. She closed her eyes. Because I am a bad person, I thought of Rosalie Piri.

Opening them, she said, "What?"

"You okay?"

"You should have seen yourself, you bastard."

"You were incredible."

"Yeah? So were you. I thought you were dead when you came falling out of the truck like that."

"I did, too."

"Nothing like this ever happened in the *war* to you," she said.

"I didn't work alone. I carried a sidearm. And I was a mean motherfucker in the war, Fanny, because I wasn't in combat. I arrested the kids who went into it and I stayed in an office in Saigon and drank real French coffee. Now I'm soft. I go around changing diapers. Well. You know."

Her face shut down when I mentioned diapers.

I said, "You know."

She went on staring at me. "Yes," she said. "Except you aren't that out of shape for a man your age."

"A hundred."

"And it was four men?"

"Mostly only three. I think the kid got in a couple of kicks to the body at the end."

"Your poor ribs."

"It only hurts when I—"

"Laugh."

"No," I said "Breathe. When I breathe or talk or yawn or fart."

"You want the bedpan?"

"I will be dead and half a teaspoon of ashes before anyone in this building delivers or takes away a bedpan. You can announce that if you like."

"You're tough."

"With doctors and nurses and amateurs, I am the toughest. I am a little less of a challenge to the semiprofessional ranks."

"They were warning you to let them sell drugs?"

"I don't think they were avenging the boy I pushed around. So, yes: I think it was a business memorandum. It didn't, of course, have anything to do with Janice Tanner, and she's the reason I rousted the kid. Someone in Chenango Flats said they saw a car that I thought might be his on the day Janice went missing. Ouch. Goddamn it."

"It *wasn't* about the drugs, then."

"No."

"The missing girls? You worry about a missing girl and they beat you up over drugs?"

"You worry a drug dealer about the missing girl, then yes. They decide it's only the drugs part, and then you get this."

"Idiot," she said.

I tried to smirk, but my mouth hurt too much. I decided simply to lie there.

"Bastard idiot. Son of a bitch bastard idiot fool," she said. She was crying, and I waited to hear the thump of a tail. "It's because of Hannah."

"You been talking to Archie?" I finally said.

"Bastard son of a bitch. If you die because of her, then it's me and a dog left in the house."

I reached to take her hand and I yipped. But I got hold of her, and I hung on. Her hand was hot and dry.

"Everything's because of Hannah," she said.

"We didn't start out because of her," I said. "We didn't have her because of her."

"What's *that* supposed to mean?"

I rolled my head on the flat pillow. I didn't know.

She said, "I have to go."

"What shift is this?"

"I didn't go home," she said. "Nobody went home. It's all right— I called the farm and they sent two of the kids over on a snowmobile. They brought him home and fed him and they'll keep him until we get there."

"I bet you he liked the ride."

"We have outages," she said. "Trees went down; power lines are broken."

"Which means the furnace went off. Which means it won't go on. You have to push the reset to make it go on again. Which means frozen pipes, maybe. It's still cold?"

"Still cold," she said. "Burst pipes for sure."

"That's upstate," I said.

She nodded.

"I'll be all right, Fanny. I'm sorry about this."

"It's the *this*," she said. "It's gotten to be so much of everything."

I swallowed a few times and she saw I was dry, and she held a glass with a bent straw to my mouth. I swallowed too fast and began to cough and it became very interesting along the right side of my body. I watched her tighten her face until I was done and lying flat again.

The door opened in and Rosalie Piri said to Fanny, "Can I see him?"

Her smile was not as broad as usual, and she looked frightened, or maybe embarrassed. She certainly was flushed. Fanny stayed pale. I closed my eyes. "He's tired," Fanny said. Then she said, "You are . . ."

Instead of naming herself, Rosalie used a pugnacious tone I thought of as New York City, and she said, "Yes, I'm a little tired, too, thank you. Can I visit him?"

Fanny looked down at me. I looked back up. My eyes were so wide, they hurt. I made a little throat-clearing noise, and I said, "Professor Piri, this is my wife, Fanny. Fanny, this is Professor Piri."

Fanny said, "How do you do."

Rosalie nodded. She said, "Hello" in a hard, cold voice I hadn't heard. Her face was as red as the head of a stick match.

Fanny said to me, "Bye, Jack." She went out the door with a very stiff back.

Rosalie came to the side of the bed. "Oh, God," she said. "I didn't handle that well." She smiled, she stopped smiling, and then she said, "Jack, is there anything to handle? Your wife's remarkable. She's so tall, she looks like a dancer."

"Can't dance," I said.

"No, she looks, I don't know, powerful. She has wonderful bones in her face."

I thought, She has shadows in her face. I helped set them there. I did my share.

"I'm too short for you," she said.

"No," I said. I thought then that I was at least one word, that last one, into someplace I shouldn't be.

"Your sad mouth," she said, touching my lip. I hissed, and she drew her hand away. "I'm sorry," she said.

"You're making my catheter uncomfortable," I said.

She blushed again. She shook her head. "This is insane," she said.

"Yes."

"I have to get out of here."

"Yes."

I waited for her to make me a promise, or to say something about her and me. She compressed her lips and took a breath. She said, "Right," and she turned toward the door and walked out.

I waited for Fanny to march in and make comments. She didn't come. About half an hour later, Virginia brought a bedpan. All right, I thought, she sent a messenger instead.

———

My doctor, who was very fat and extremely careful about hurting me, told me I was going to be all right. The kidney was bruised, but the blood in my urine was diminished. They removed the catheter, they rebound my ribs, and they told me that I should take it easy. I was to stay there another night because, although my skull X rays were negative, I was probably mildly concussed, and anyway, most of the smaller county roads were unplowed. I could sit up, the doctor told me, smiling, if I could sit up.

I was in the room's lounge chair, reading a Syracuse newspaper several days old and enjoying it. There was a lot of information about zoo animals and corruption in the county council. They didn't bother you a lot with material about inept Presidents or endangered Vice Presidents or the Senate of the United States. There were a lot of comic strips, and a crossword puzzle even I could do. I was a not unintelligent crossword puzzler.

Strodemaster came in puffing. He was dressed in ski clothes of the sort I saw the students wear, very expensive stuff in black and iridescent yellow that looked like spangles were woven into the skin-tight cloth. His goggles hung around his neck.

"Jack!" he called. "You all right, man?"

I said, "Hi, Randy, did you ski all the way in?"

"Good exercise," he said. "And I qot a lift from the snowplow for the last three miles. Jack, holy hat. This happened to you because of me, according to your wife."

"My wife said that? How is she?"

"Been busy here for her, I guess. One big emergency."

"One big emergency," I said.

He walked back and forth too fast to call it pacing. I could see his leg muscles jumping in his tight outfit. He swung his arms and didn't look at me. He moved back and forth, wall to wall, and he looked straight ahead. I couldn't figure out how he kept his hair so carefully combed under his ski hat. From the side, he looked a little bit like a movie star whose name I almost remembered. He walked, he swung his arms, and then he suddenly stopped. He faced the bed and looked at me like I was precious to him. It was something that went over his oaky-looking face.

"Listen," he said, "I know I talked you into this. I got you involved in the first place when I went to Archie. I got you involved in the second place when I came to you. You aren't a cop anymore. You don't need this kind of shit, getting mugged by hoodlums. What kind of world is this?"

"You know, I have very little idea," I said.

"I can tell you this much—it's scary. When a good man gets hurt this much on account of some blabbermouth buttinsky like me . . . Well, we were just trying to help, weren't we? Just trying to do a little good."

I had the feeling I was missing what he wanted me to hear. I folded the newspaper and blinked a lot and focused hard.

He said, "You got me feeling guilty, man."

"What are you guilty of, Randy?"

"Your whipped ass, Jack. I don't ask you for help, you don't get going into this stuff, and the hoodlums don't hurt you. It couldn't have been a fair fight."

I said, "I don't believe I know of any fair fights."

"Really?" he said. "That's a cruel, frightening weltanschauung, Jack."

"Excuse me?"

"Oh. Point of view? I don't know—view of the world, maybe. Way of looking at things?"

"Oh."

"It's German."

"It's a German way of looking?"

"It's a German word."

"Sounds it," I said.

He was walking back and forth again. There wasn't much of

anyplace to walk. It was a two-person room, and the only reason there was space for the chair was that Virginia had pushed the empty other bed against the wall. But he paced. He looked sweaty and less healthy than when he'd begun. I thought of him out there in Chenango Flats with his girlfriends and his garbage and his devotion to poor yellowing Mrs. Tanner. I tried to see him in graduate school and then his early days at the college with a wife who loved him. I could only see him alone. I couldn't imagine him with a wife or with the girlfriends he was said to bring home. I could only see him in the bathrobe with its stained front. I remembered the smell of his kitchen. I was confused by his language and his shiny-faced energy. I was disturbed by how much he wanted me to like him.

"Jack," he said, "promise me."

"What, Randy?"

"You'll get out of it, the involvement with . . . with this whole awful Janice Tanner story."

I thought, listening to him, what I'd thought when my English prof had carried on about something we'd read. It always sounded prepared, which was a silly reaction, since these guys got *paid* to come to class prepared. I guess it sounded insincere, what they thought they were supposed to say instead of what they felt. I don't know. I remember thinking I wasn't cut out to be listening to these people. And what they felt wasn't supposed to be my business, anyway.

"This is my own fault, Randy. I handled a lot of stuff wrong. Remember what I told you—I haven't been an investigator for an awfully long time."

He said, "Yes, I remember. What I thought at the time was, What's an investigator? He picks up data? I thought *I* could do it. I was trained. Investigators are like scientists. Scientists are investigators. I didn't do Janice any good, did I?"

I said, "Maybe."

"Maybe I did?"

"Maybe investigators are scientists. What I did, when I worked it seriously, I listened. I just tried to hear what they said. I did a lot of interrogations. I was good at it."

"At listening," he said, walking to the door and turning to walk back.

"At listening," I said.

He said, "Listen, then, Jack. I'm the one at fault here, not you. You have broken ribs. The cartilage that binds two of them in place is torn away. You have two simple fractures in your fingers. Fanny told me you were pissing blood. Your face is puffed and black-and-blue. You look like you can't move a lot of the rest of you. You're *out*. I hired you, for a great big nothing, and now I need to fire you. Please. All right?"

"Randy," I said, "relax. You professors. All of you. You talk and you talk. Relax."

"Get outside and go for a run on the sticks."

"What?"

"Go skiing. That's what I should do more of. That's what I'll do. But no more—what shall we call it, detective work?"

"I think you call it getting beat up."

"Good description," he said. "Good man!"

"That's me," I said, wondering if Fanny would enter the room again.

———

She'd been on for four days, and by the time the roads were cleared and most of the area's power restored, they sent her off for a couple of days' break, and they sent me with her. Security would dig my Ford out and run it a little to charge the battery. My vice president for administration had interviewed and hired a temp to fill in until I came back. When I did, I could decide whether we would keep her. I was pleased he had listened to me about hiring a woman. All I needed now was for Fanny and me to be all right, and for the missing girls to appear unharmed in their homes.

Here's what I thought. I thought about Ralph the Duck, who didn't have any feathers. I thought, Once upon a time.

I truly wished, as Virginia wheeled me to the door and helped me into Fanny's car, that I knew something about prayer. Mrs. Tanner did, I thought. Presumably, her husband did. Maybe Janice did and maybe it comforted her. I wished for that.

I knew that praying was more than wishing. It was more than talking loose and swearing careless oaths to what you wished would bail you out of the shit. When I was in the service and people fired on each other while I was working, two times I heard men scream to Jesus and God the Father, "Oh please please please don't kill me God Jesus please." I'd got in the habit, there, of using those names as messily as anyone else had, and I'd known at the time and I knew now that praying was something else.

I thought, as Fanny drove us home, that I could work as hard as I wished, bullying bad guys and giving up my rib cage and doing all the powerful listening I could, but that something else had to happen. I didn't know what it was. I wasn't thinking about God. I had no ideas about God. God worked His, Her, or Its side of the street, and I worked mine. It wasn't what Mrs. Tanner would think of as God. But we all needed more than we were bringing to the situation, I thought.

We skidded out, but Fanny caught it.

"You all right?" I asked her.

"Fine."

"Fanny, you're so amazingly pissed off at me."

"Why is it amazing?"

"Because I haven't done anything bad except get my ass kicked is why."

"And your little short professor—what's her name? Your faculty friend?"

"I find this hard to believe," I said.

"No," she said, "you should believe it. Walking into your room and talking through me like I'm hired help. Excuse me, I'm sure, pro-*fessor*. Do you knock her off in some maintenance shack or something? Or is she what you do in your truck when you aren't rescuing the daughters of the upper crust?"

"I don't knock anyone off. You, of everyone in the world, should know that. You know who I am. You know how I've been. Come on, Fanny. And how could you suspect me of something like that?"

"Oh, it's worse than suspecting you, Jack. It's *her* I'm suspecting, too. All I needed was one fast look at her curly little mouth and her tight little body and the expression in her eyes when she looked at you. That girlish little blush? Dear mercy me, Jack, you can't be that naïve. No one can. Which means you know what's going on, whatever it is."

"Which is nothing."

"Whatever it is," she said. "And you know. And *I* know. Maybe the registrar knows. Maybe she gives you a grade. And I believe that terminates this portion of the journey's conversation, thank you very much."

Fanny had apparently arranged to have us plowed out, and she was able to park close to the house. We went in together. She was near me, in case I slipped, but otherwise she was distant. The house smelled cold, and I headed for the cellar door and went down to hit the restart button on the oil-fired furnace. It started up. I walked the cellar, inspecting the water pipes. None down there had burst, and when I was back upstairs, I called up to Fanny to ask if anything on the second floor had burst and run.

From the head of the stairs, she said, "No."

I made a fire in the woodstove and it didn't take that long for the furnace to heat the water and circulate it to the radiators. The house began to warm and creak as wood and metal expanded, and it felt alive, though not as hearty as I'd have liked.

Fanny called down, "I was wrong. There's no water running up here in the bathroom."

"I'll take care of it."

All she said was, "Good."

I fetched the heat gun and wedged myself into a corner of the mudroom. That was where the pipes ran vertically, along the wrong wall, the outside wall, to the upstairs. I set the heat gun on low because I didn't want to fire up the lath inside the plaster walls, and I warmed the pipes up. If we were lucky, the problem was a kind of slush or light ice, and I could melt it.

Five minutes later, Fanny walked into the kitchen, around the corner from me, and said, "There's water now."

I turned the heat gun off and lay on my back on the mudroom floor where I'd crouched. My ribs felt worse than they had for a day. I was going to have to learn, I thought, about behaving differently. Maybe if I told Fanny I was hurt and was about to act better, she would forgive me.

I thought, Forgive you for which?

She said, "What are you doing?"

I said, "I'm resting a minute."

"What'd you hurt?"

"Ribs."

"You jerk."

I nodded.

"You unbelievable jerk."

I nodded.

Instead of coming over to help me, or to give me codeine-laced tablets, or lie down beside me and murmur comfort, she walked away.

I wished, as I worked at getting up, that she could see me. It would have moved her, I thought, seeing my difficulties. I was on my knees in the mudroom when she walked—I'd use the word *strode,* actually—around me so she could get her parka from the wall.

As she pulled on gloves and tucked her hair into her woolen cap, she said, "I'm going for the dog."

"I might lie down someplace where he won't step on me coming home."

"Good," she said.

"Or you."

"Jack," she said, "you don't have to worry about my foot or any other part of me touching you."

I was remembering a time when we were in the bar of the Christopher Hotel, which is out on a country road that takes you toward Cooperstown by way of the hills. Around nine or ten on Saturday nights, the local men bring their dates in for a hamburger and some beer and some dancing. A woman I knew from the campus bookstore,

Helena, was there with her boyfriend, who worked for the state fisheries. Fanny and I were eating a late steak, which is what they call the long, thin, greasy meat they charge extra for bringing to your table. The song that someone had punched on the jukebox was Stevie Ray Vaughan playing "Testify."

Helena is a tall and sweet-faced woman with long black hair that hangs halfway down her back and a busty, big-hipped figure. She came dancing over to the table by herself. She closed her eyes when she got to us and she said, "Jack, get up here and get some."

I looked at Fanny. She stared at me with a face I barely remembered from when we started going out in the seventies.

I didn't think you should have to be scared of your wife. You'd think I would have learned. I said, "Yes, ma'am."

What happened was, I held her away from me, and she moved in a very sexy way to get in closer while moving much of her body at the same time. I more or less held on for the ride. The music ended and I got her back to her date, who didn't look up from his conversation with some men. It was a piss-your-wife-off move on his part, and her dancing was a piss-your-husband-off on hers.

When I got back to the table, Fanny looked like she was crouching in her chair. I leaned on my arms in front of her with my hands flat on the table. She took her knife, all smeared with steak fat, and she very slowly put it into the web of skin between my finger and my thumb. People looked over at the sound I made.

Fanny handed me her napkin and said, "Here. Put some pressure on it."

I waited for her to tell me something else.

She said, "Don't expect *me* to be your nurse."

Moving up slowly to my knees on the floor of the mudroom, I told myself, You might have to expect less friendship now than you've been used to in the last little while.

daughter

WE HAD MORE SNOW on our road than I'd ever seen. I watched it from our bedroom window and our living room windows and our kitchen window. In the back room, I saw the vast amounts of snow in the field and at the edge of the woods. I saw plenty of snow. They delivered my car in it and went back to work at the campus in it, but I didn't. I stayed home and, according to Fanny, I healed. What was wounded in her did not.

While she was at work, I climbed out onto the roof from an upstairs bedroom, and I tried to shovel snow. The idea was to keep the stuff from breaking through the roof. It weighed tons. The idea was also that when the snow really began to melt, it would run under the shingles, and then if it froze again and melted, it would shove the shingles off or even break through the subroof. The dog stayed below, where the lawn would be if the snow ever melted, and he barked each time I tossed a shovelful over. That added up to five barks, because the pain was too bad. I settled for edging the stuff around with a stiff leg, then kicking sideways, in a clumsy soccer motion, to push it in powdering mounds off the roof. He didn't bark for the pushes because they were probably not very impressive.

I replaced a doorknob. That meant using a borrowed backset drill I should have returned to the hardware store half a season ago. I was terrible with it. I didn't have enough body strength to set myself and wrestle tools around. I ended up with a hole about a foot in diameter. You'd have needed a knob the size of a beach ball for the door. I did some laundry, swearing again, as I always did, when I saw the label on the softener. No matter what brand, it's always a sweet, cuddly little kid, or a bear you're supposed to want to hug. I fastened an FM antenna to the radio in the back room and hung it out a window. I listened to music for a while, but I didn't want to feel anyone else's rhythms. I cooked. I made my infamous chili con carne with about twenty-five cloves of garlic and lots of cumin and oregano and chili powder and some shavings of dried chili. I couldn't find hamburger meat or stew beef, so I hacked up some steaks I found in the freezer. Serve with ice-cold beer to someone who likes you.

It was time to take more of the little pills with codeine in them. I did that and then I put the chili away without eating it. Since I was still in my boots after working on the roof, I put on a sweater and a parka, found my gloves, used shears to cut off two fingers of the right one, told the dog to stay, and I left. Getting stuffed in behind the wheel was painful, but I reminded myself that I'd taken pills and they surely had kicked in by now. I reminded myself again, then got the car going. I backed it up by using the mirror so I wouldn't have to try to twist my body, hoped that no one was coming down the road that minute, and drove toward Chenango Flats.

It looked so small, I was thinking half an hour later, when I entered it from the south. There was the river, with heaps of ice and snow at its banks, and the crusts of ice at its edges. There were the railroad tracks no trains went over anymore. I thought of southern and midwestern towns I'd been in during the war, where the trains ran all the time. That was when I started to hear a little blues music, and to understand how much of it was the sound of trains. In the songs, they were always leaving. The fields were attached to houses, so the children grew up, if they weren't Janice Tanner, as part of the crop. I drove slowly through, passing Strodemaster's large, empty-

looking, dark Victorian farmhouse and his beautiful stone and plank-
ing barn. I passed his neighbors and came to the crossroads. I knew
one wing of it headed east toward a quiet, small lake. I'd heard that
children, if they weren't Janice Tanner, ice-skated there. Heading
south a little more, having passed maybe eleven houses, I came to
the Chenango Flats Baptist Church.

It was small; it had a stubby excuse for a spire and no cross on
top. The five-foot cross, fashioned of wood stained a piney color,
was on the clapboard out front. The congregation wasn't rich. The
glassed-in announcement board said that the Reverend B. Tanner's
Sunday sermon would be "God on *His* Knees." I wondered if Mrs.
Tanner approved. It took several minutes to emerge from the car. I
tried to keep a straight face in case someone was watching. Outside
a church, I thought, who do you expect to be watching you? I didn't
look up. I went through the narrow anteroom into the church. It was
all on one level. It was painted a harsh white. There was a set of
about a dozen pews, and behind them several rows of folding chairs,
some wood and some metal. In the front, I saw a battered black
upright piano off to the right. Few lights were on, and daylight
through the narrow unstained windows didn't turn anything awfully
bright.

I came halfway down the aisle to stand under the low ceiling
made of tin plates with designs on them, and I tried to imagine what
the Tanners said and thought when they were here. I tried to sense
their comfort but couldn't. I closed my eyes and tried to hear Mrs.
Tanner's voice. I felt a pulse beating in my ribs, I thought. Something,
surely, was banging away inside in that vicinity. I tried to hear Mrs.
Tanner praying. I tried to hear Janice. I had never heard her voice. I
didn't think I would.

Dear God, I thought, keeping my eyes closed. I thought of men
I'd known in the service who prayed. They had prayed at bad times, I
thought, and maybe to someone religious their prayer would seem
selfish, tainted by all their need. A lot of American servicemen beat
up whores. They were exhausted, frightened men, and their experience was mostly of loss. They lost girlfriends and wives at home.

They lost money over there, and they lost face. They lost some bat-
tles, though they won some. They couldn't tell because everything
was measured in killed bodies and we told them they outkilled the
enemy, but the real estate they'd thought to gain was either given
back or retreated from because goals and strategies were changed at
the level of command. So they *felt* like losers. And they lost their
friends. Men died in terrible ways, of course, and they saw them die,
and no one told them how to mourn or gave them time or occasion.
Men they loved were torn to pieces and everyone was slicked with
their blood and no one stopped a minute to say their sorrow for them.
And some of them cut up girls in the bars and brothels. They beat
them badly. And we arrested them after viewing the crime scene. And
one of us was always saying, "My God," or "Dear God," or "Jesus
Christ." I think we might have meant *something*, but I never knew
what, and I couldn't feel what this building was for.

I said her name to myself, but not out loud.

Then I said it out loud, to hear it against those ceiling plates,
maybe three feet over my head. I listened to its two syllables bounce
back down.

A low voice whispered, off to my left and behind me, "Who's
that?"

I wheeled, and of course my ribs hurt badly. I made some kind of
noise and then I said, when I saw her, "Mrs. Tanner. Damn. Excuse
me. I was thinking about you, all of you."

"Who's Hannah?" she said. "You were saying her name."

"No," I said, "Janice."

"You said Hannah."

"I did?"

I saw a motion, and I went to where she sat, in the farthest
left-hand folding chair in the church. Her orange-yellow face was
gaunt. She wore a coarse gray blanket wrapped around her, over her
coat.

"It's so cold in here," she said. "I don't know why. We pay a
fortune for fuel oil, but it doesn't warm up."

I said, "I was coming to see you. I was going to your house after
this."

"You didn't know I was here?"

"No."

"Then isn't that a wonderful sign," she said. "We're in tune with each other."

She shivered, and I went to one of the old-fashioned iron radiators at the wall and I touched it. Part was cold and part was warm. I followed the wall, feeling the radiators that were placed every ten or fifteen feet. When I got to the one at the back, where its water pipe entered the floor, I asked her, "Do you keep any tools here?"

"In the back, maybe. In an old hutch near the desk."

I saw its shape, so I didn't turn lights on. I found the wrench on a shelf, along with two hammers, a long screwdriver, a short one with a Phillips head, and a rasp. I tried to figure why they'd need a wood rasp in a church. The wrench was the right size. I thought the Reverend B. Tanner would have used it, but he forgot. He wasn't thinking of radiators. Back in the church, I fought my way as quietly as I could to my knees, and I used the wrench on the valve. The air hissed out, and a little rusty water, and then I shut it off. The radiator jumped a little. It took me half an hour to do the others. It got more difficult, each time, to get down and then up. Once, I spilled a little too much water out. I pulled myself up on the last radiator I'd bled, and then I went over to her, still holding the wrench, and I leaned against the wall to her left.

"Aren't you a miracle worker," she said.

I said, "No. If I could do miracles, I'd have brought your daughter back. Mrs. Tanner, I haven't found anything. I read the state police reports, I talked to deputies and troopers and some local police. I found two or three people to scrutinize, I guess you'd call it. I tried very hard to suspect them. I don't think they're involved. I don't know a thing."

"You warmed the church up," she said. Then, her voice dropping even lower, harsher, she said, "Who are the ones you suspected?"

I shook my head.

"I suppose you're right," she said. "I don't have too much more time to wait. Do you understand?"

I stared at her. It had been a pretty face, and I tried to find Janice in the tight, stained skin. She was waiting, and I finally said, "Yes."

"Good," she said. "Oh, didn't you make the church *warm*." And then she said, "So we all believe she was taken away. A distance away."

"It's often the case," I said.

She moved her head. "Imagine," she said, "it happens enough— little children are stolen into, I don't know, are seized and taken—so you can say the word *often* about it."

"I'm sorry."

"Will we find her?"

I shrugged, then winced, because I had moved my shoulders and therefore my ribs too hard.

"What?" she said.

I said, "Nothing."

"Will we ever find her, Jack?"

I almost said *God knows*. I almost said *By accident, maybe*. It was all about accidents, one and then another. I said, "Competent people are working on it."

"Yes," she said. I shifted my legs. She said, "And who *is* Hannah?"

The tin ceiling tiles were machine-pressed into sunburst shapes, but sunbursts made of straight lines and right angles. There was nothing round on the design that was repeated on tile after tile. Each of them was held in place with nails, I thought, and the nails were rusted. I figured they had hammered up into lath or cheap, unfinished firring strips. The radiators were chugging now, and there was plenty of heat. Mrs. Tanner kept the blanket around her, though, and I saw her mouth move slowly against the pain. And here I was, the burly fix-it guy from security, doing nothing for anyone but harm. Mr. Interrogator, I thought, who can't find anyone to interrogate. I was nagged by something at the bottom of my thoughts, and I couldn't find it. Probably some C-4 on a fuse that Fanny had planted for me.

Mrs. Tanner said, "Jack?"

I thought, You can give her that.

I thought, No, you can't.

I reached into the blanket, and I found her broad, cold, weight-less hand. I squeezed it.

"What did you do to your hand? You can at least tell me that."

"Hooligans on campus," I said. "They showed me what-for. My father always called it that when someone took a beating: They got what-for."

"Are you in pain?"

I squatted in front of her, instructing my ribs to stay out of this. I said, "*You're* asking anyone else about pain."

"Don't you talk like that to me, Jack. Don't you make me into some hero. I'm a middle-aged woman with cancer and no more child. That's no hero. God, maybe, is the hero. God makes the plan."

I said, "Maybe Janice is a hero, too, though. Since nobody con-sulted *her* about the plan."

Her face collapsed.

It seemed to me I had done more than enough damage. I squeezed her hand again, I made my body rise without too much drama, and I told her, "Mrs. Tanner, kids come back. Sometimes they run away and sometimes they come back. Sometimes they get stolen and they escape and come home. But sometimes, they, you know, don't. I couldn't be telling you anything new. You must have thought about this so much—"

Her eyes were on me. She simply nodded. I waited for her to talk about her horrible dreams of Janice, but she moved her head that one time and then she was still as she watched me.

"Your hope has to be in the authorities."

She didn't speak.

"And God," I lied.

She said, "Hannah. Is she yours?"

"Was," I said. "She was."

"Oh, Jack," she said.

"No," I said, "it was years ago."

On the car radio, one of those round, cheerful voices you hate if you aren't feeling well said the long-range forecast was warmth. Temperatures would stay in the twenties, he said merrily, and I thought that if they did, the snow would melt off in two or three weeks. It was three and four and even five feet high in places on the banks of our road, and then it would be gone. We wouldn't remember the cold or how we had to fight every day to get out and around. Though I wasn't convinced. It seemed to me we were condemned to winter. I tried to see dirt, but I could only imagine snow.

I let the dog out and I took a couple of extra codeine jobs. Maybe I would get in touch with William Franklin, I thought, and ask him for something with a heavier punch. The brain waves must have been boiling that day, because as soon as I thought the word *punch*, the telephone rang, and Sergeant Bird, telling me what a considerable courtesy it was that he took the time to call, said they had followed up on my recollection of speed gloves and they had run a fighter who looked good for it, and they were holding him for me to check out. I had to hurry, he said, because if he was the one, and if he mattered to heavy people in Syracuse or Utica, a lawyer would be there taking him out on a leash in a couple of hours. I told him I was used to either military procedure, where basically I'd arrested who I'd pleased as long as he wasn't an officer, or campus justice, where I was powerless with everyone no matter what they did.

Which, when I hung up, had me thinking of Rosalie Piri for some reason. I suppose it was the powerless part. Although that made me think of Fanny, too.

I called the dog in and gave him a rawhide stick to chew on. I noticed a great deal more white in his muzzle, and the slight thickening there that tells you how much older they are. What he did with his face, I would have described as smiling, if it didn't make me feel too sentimental. He smelled of cold and snow. I nuzzled his face and he bumped me with his head while he worked on the rawhide.

I didn't enjoy fitting my body into the seat of the Ford, nor did I like the backing-up part, where I strained to see. Letting it roll forward and steering small with my arms clamped to my sides made me feel better. So I did, shutting off the radio voice. I headed south, toward the state police barracks, squinting against a bright sun that seemed to be part of the argument—Mrs. Tanner would call it a plan —about winter ending. I screwed my face up against the sunlight, but I would not have given even money on spring.

Bird wasn't there. A square, thick uniformed trooper with very curly dark hair and a frowning mouth who called me "Sir" but didn't enjoy it took me to an office.

He said, "This guy was easy. He was the only overweight noncontender with his hair in a ponytail who limped."

"How many gyms did you look in?"

"Syracuse cops walked into one, walked out, walked into the other, and there he was."

"Was he ever any good?"

He reached for the cut-glass knob and stopped. He looked amused when he said, "You mean, were you good enough to hurt a pro?" He made sure I saw him take in the splints, the bruises, the cuts, the way I stood like a man held together with tape.

"Guy stuff," I said.

"Yeah. Well, he wasn't in anyone's stable. He trained on his own and he fought on his own. He did the circuit—Albany, Syracuse, Buffalo, Cleveland, Detroit. He lived that way for a couple of years. He still has his eyes. You're a lot older than he is."

"What was his name?"

"What it still is: Joe Corona."

"Southwestern?"

"I think he's from around here. Probably, he liked Mexican beer."

"Where's the one-way glass?" I asked him, pointing at the paneled wooden door.

"In the barracks in Wampsville and on TV," he said. "Wait here." He went into the office and shut the door behind him. Eventually, I heard furniture scrape.

As he opened the door again, he said to someone behind him, "Do not change your position. Don't move."

He left the door cracked open, and he whispered to me, "Check him out."

I looked over his shoulder, where he crouched, and I saw the man I thought of as the Indian. His face was turned three-quarters toward me, and he held himself rigidly. This was a man who listened to instructions. His skin looked sweaty; his hair was out of the rubber band and hanging down his neck. He looked strong but out of shape. Well, so was I. All he looked was uncomfortable. I was the one with busted fingers and torn-up ribs.

I said, "Yes."

"For certain," he said, closing the door.

"Yes."

"Now, you're—"

"Yes," I said. "Was he limping badly?"

"He said he sprained his knee."

"I thought maybe I busted some ligaments for him."

"You did him all right," the trooper said.

"Good."

"And he's the one. Finally, officially, for once and for all."

"Cross my heart," I said.

"You'll have to pick him out of a lineup with lawyers there."

"And be surprised when I see him?"

"If you would, please, yes."

"Isn't justice wonderful?" I said.

"I'm sorry," he said, "did anyone mention justice? We're just trying to lock the fucker *up*."

So, I thought, driving home and thinking of codeine, we had found the malefactor. He had nothing to do with Janice Tanner, something to do with the people who sold the drugs to William Franklin, who sold the drugs to the students. That traffic would continue. If the Indian knew anything, he'd be out on bail to keep him quiet. If he was a hired banger, and they were insulated from him by a cutout they trusted who'd done the hiring, he would stand for assault, and he would serve some months, maybe in the county jail. And, meanwhile, Janice Tanner was gone. The students were stoned. Rosalie Piri stretched out in the cold blue light of a room in my imagination. And Fanny was as far from me as she could get. Haven't you done well, I told myself.

If Fanny had been in the car with me, she'd have pointed to the faintest pink color in the tips of the dark trees. She would have found a willow tree on the side of the road and showed me that its branches were the slightest bit thicker at the ends. Because I was fastened immobile by the pain, I saw little of the sky. Mostly, I saw black empty boughs and white snow, and nothing convinced me of winter ending, not even the slight softening of the snow packed ten or twelve inches onto the surface of our road.

I drove past campus, and I drove to Rosalie Piri's house, and I pulled up her drive to park the car in back. I couldn't have stated a reason to anyone, much less to her, and I hoped very hard that she would be in the classroom or her office or at the market or buying new tires for her terrible car. I hoped so hard that she would be gone, I forced myself out of the front seat and over to her back door, and I made myself knock.

"You aren't here," I said.

Opening the door, she said, "Oh yes I am. Is your wife with you?"

I shook my head.

"Would you like to come in?"

I nodded.

"Can you speak?"

"I haven't figured out what to say yet."

She wore big men's boxer shorts in a yellow plaid design and a flannel shirt of green and orange that clashed horribly with the shorts. The shirt looked big enough to belong to the big brother of whoever used to own the very big shorts, and its tails hung halfway down her thighs.

"I know," she said, closing the door, "I'm a symphony of bad taste. This is what I wear when I do homework."

"You're taking courses?"

"Reading for class. If they have to do it, I have to do it. Would you like a beer? A glass of wine? Juice? Buttermilk?"

I shook my head. It was not only that I didn't know what to say but that she made me smile so hard. My face felt stretched. She was smiling, too.

She put her hand out tentatively, and she touched the side of my coat.

"It's the other side," I said.

She helped me take my coat off and she hung it on a hook in a little closet and came back to stand before me. She reached up and began to unbutton my woolen shirt. She saw the wrapping. She made a sound and put her lips together hard. She insisted on touching the ribs, very lightly, and I winced.

"No," I said as she flinched. "You didn't hurt me. I *expected* hurt, so I acted like a baby. It doesn't hurt."

"It has to." She had moved her hand, and the fingers lay gently on my chest, above the bandages. She moved them back and forth, lightly, watching my expression. I didn't know what to do except close my eyes and put my left hand on her shoulder.

I moved my hand to where her shirt was opened several buttons, and I touched her throat. She made a sound. "Has to," she said, flushing down her face and under my hand.

"Has to what?"

"I forget. No. I remember: hurt. You couldn't hug or kiss anyone or lie down with them."

"Could we stay like this awhile? Would you be willing to?"

"Willing?" she said. She moved closer and leaned in and kissed my chest. She kept her face against me and I felt her breath go over my skin as she said, "Yes, I guess I'd be willing."

I didn't know what to do with my hand. I put it loosely around her throat in a choking motion, but we knew I wasn't going to shut the fingers. They lay against her, and I could feel her swallow. Then she stepped back and took my hand in both of hers and kissed my palm.

"I felt that in my ribs," I said.

"Your poor ribs," she said. "Why did this happen to you?" She buttoned my shirt and then her own. Then she picked up my hand again, and she led me to the living room. I sat by kneeling my way onto the seat of the chair. She brought us coffee, and I almost slept, in spite of my confusion and excitement, while she made it. Then she asked me again, "What happened?"

"Payback," I said. "I beat up a kid who runs the campus pharmaceuticals supply. They sent some people, not because of him, really, so much as because of the business. Free trade, kind of."

"Couldn't you have arrested him instead of beating him?"

I liked the way she accepted the option of the beating. But of course she was a policeman's daughter. She would know.

"I hate those drug bastards. But what it was about was something else. You see the posters all over?"

"Those poor children."

"One of them, the one whose picture went up first, I'm, I don't know, I'm helping her parents."

She nodded. "Of course you are," she said.

"I felt *that* in my ribs," I said. "You do that to me."

"I want to," she said. "But you're helping her parents—"

"Janice Tanner's parents. Her mother is supposed to've died from cancer, but she keeps waiting until Janice comes home. You really end up having to do it for her. Do something, anyway. I don't think we'll get her back. But, you know. Professor Strodemaster's their neighbor. He got me into it, and I guess I got involved. I went after the kid. Jesus, I just jump around and get myself confused and end up suspecting anyone and then bagging it all and figuring no one did it, that she took off for New York or Saint Paul, Minnesota. . . . You know. I'm not doing much."

"Was she unhappy?"

"She was the perfect Christian child. She played—*plays*. I can't keep talking like she's dead. Even if she probably is. She plays an instrument. She loves Jesus. She volunteers to roll bandages and feed the hungry. You know? She's wonderful."

"So she isn't," Rosalie said. She was sitting on the footstool of my chair and she had her fingers on my calf above my boot. Her hand felt warm, and I felt warm, the coffee was filled with frothy milk, and

I would have given a great deal to be lying with my head on her chest and asleep.

"Why not?"

"Because nobody is. No young girl—fourteen, right? No adolescent girl is wonderful. Her life is shit, her parents are shit, school is a trial, minute by minute, her hormones are nuts, her skin drives her crazy, and she gets cramps all the time, or she doesn't bleed on time, or she hasn't got breasts, or all of that. She's *nice,* she wants to be nice, she's a good kid, but she's in trouble. She comes up missing, it's because she was in trouble a long time before that."

"So why didn't anybody tell me this a long time ago?"

"Your wife could have."

"Sure. I mean, a nurse would know."

"A woman would know; a nurse would know; your friend Halpern would know. I've seen you in the Blue Bird, you sitting there all pale and straight and sad and him all over the pastries. He gets so worried about you."

"How do you know? He's talking to *you* about me, too?"

"His face, Jack. He feels like me, I think."

"How's that, Rosalie?"

"Nice. I don't know how far his affections go, but *I* have in mind something like taking off your clothes and doing things, Jack." She didn't cover her face, but her eyes were closed.

"Oh."

She spat her coffee onto my jeans and the rug. "I'm sorry," she said when she got herself under control. "It was the way you said that."

"You get me wordless a lot."

"And you don't have that many words to begin with."

I shook my head. She leaned over and touched her forehead to my knee. I put my hand on her dark hair and held a handful and then let go.

When she sat up, we were quiet for a couple of minutes. I loved it, sitting like that with her. Then she said, "What's her room like?"

"Haven't been there," I said.

"But *why?*"

"I think I'm scared to. I don't know. I do know. And I am scared. I don't want to know her that well. I don't want to touch her things. She went into the worst kinds of nightmares you can have. I don't want to go there."

Her face was serious now, and it looked longer, older. Her dark eyes looked different, and I saw a little of how much there was to her. I figured her father, the cop, had scary eyes like hers. She nodded. "Makes sense," she said, "but you *have* to look at her room. Really, it's where you have to *start*. What you've been doing, whatever you've been doing, that comes later. First you get yourself in her room. It's where they *live*, girls that age. It's their *brains*. If you're lucky. If they aren't so good at hiding that even their rooms are camouflaged."

"You're tougher than I am, aren't you?"

"Maybe. I don't know. But I'm tough. Is your wife tough?"

"She has been for a long time. She's had to be. You marry me, you're in trouble automatically."

"I'll remember that. Are we finished warning each other off?"

"All right."

"Do we agree that something's going on here? Between us?"

I nodded.

"Say 'yes,' " she said.

"Yes."

"And you're coming back here? Or, we're meeting? We're going, you know, *on* from here."

I nodded.

She said, " 'Yes.' "

"Yes."

Then her face grew less beaky, her eyes less angry. Then that wide smile came out. She stood up, she took the coffee cup from me, and she set both of our cups on the stack of books on the table next to the chair. She leaned over me, supported herself on the chair arms, and she kissed me very softly on the mouth. She let herself down a little and she kissed me harder. She bit my bottom lip, then let her teeth apart, then bit me again, harder. In the same position, she very slowly licked where she had bitten me, and then she stood up.

I said, "My wife accused me of making love to you in a security vehicle and in strange places on the upper campus."

"Are there strange places up there where we could have been making love?"

"Yes."

"You know them? You have access to them?"

"Yes."

Pulling the tails of the baggy flannel shirt down straight, she said, "Well, well."

———

The dog waited at the drawer we kept his food in, and by holding on to the countertop with my fingers, I let myself down to my knees and got out the plastic bin of kibble. I gave him a lot, then put the food away. Still on my knees, I checked his water. I worked my way up and I let him out to run. It had been a mistake to get up, I thought. I wondered if ribs could bleed, because I sensed a loose, runny material inside. I thought I might feel better on my knees again, and from there it was a very short trip to my back.

I made a few unworthy noises, and I put my hand on my side. There was a scrabbling sound, and I knew it was the dog, ready to come inside and be celebrated for doing so.

"In a minute," I said.

The door bounced again, and I said, "Lie down and wait, goddamn it."

The noise stopped and I was sorry I'd shouted. I saw him, curled on the snow on the porch, lying against the door. That was interesting, because I wanted to curl on the other side of the door and surround the pain. I couldn't make that shape anymore, though, and I said to him or me or both of us, "Sorry. Sorry."

I came up from it saying that again, but it wasn't the dog. It was Fanny. Then the dog, his fur cold and his tongue wet, came over to lick my face.

"Why are you sleeping on the floor, Jack?"

"I was?"

"You still are. Look."

"Jesus, Fanny, I can't *look.* I'm in the middle of *doing* it. Why do you have to sound pissed off right away because I fell asleep somewhere?"

"And left the dog on the porch all night. You were passed out, weren't you?"

"Could I have some of those pain pills?" I asked her.

"When's the last time you took them?"

"Afternoon."

She got on her knees and worked her arms under my back and kind of pushed me forward and over, and then I climbed up from my knees by holding her hands. Her power was very impressive. She got me into the living room and onto the sofa, where I made a lot of small noises. She brought me the pills and some water. She was still wearing her opened coat when she sat down on the coffee table and said, "What'd you do?"

"I went on some errands. I guess I wasn't ready to." I told her about the Indian.

"You sound pleased," she said.

"He made a living at it for a while. He can walk. For a nobody in the fights, that's significant."

"Jack, what's this male warrior shit? The man and his friends put you in the hospital. They could have driven a rib through your lung. Did you ever watch someone's face while their lung is inflated? You could have died."

I let myself say, and I never should have, "That would be the easy way out, wouldn't it?"

She sat back. She *flinched* back.

She said, "Dying?"

"Just a thought," I said.

"Dying? As opposed to what—to life with me?"

"No," I said. "I was being, you know, philosophical. That's all. It's what happens after you accumulate two or three college courses over a lifetime. You look at the big picture. You know."

But she was not reachable by jokes, if that's what they were. Her eyes were immense and bewildered. In the near darkness of the living room, I thought, My wife has been so wonderful to look at for so many years, and now she's getting . . . scuffed. The edges have been treated hard. I wanted to cup my hand on her chin and cheek. I wanted to run my fingers over the lines between her eyes and over her nose. I wondered if she would smell Rosalie Piri's skin.

"Is this about the missing girl, Jack?"

"What this do you mean?"

"Don't stall."

"Yes. Partly. Yes. I went to see her mother."

"Why don't you go see Hannah's mother?"

"You?"

"That's who I mean. Why do you have to build yourself a fever and damage yourself, running all over the county chasing a girl who you *know* is raped and strangled and cut into pieces and, I don't know, *eaten*. Some of these creatures pickle parts of the children, don't they? They eat them and use their skin to draw illustrations on. She's so dead and gone, Jack. And I'm *not*. I'm a little crazy sometimes, and I know I'm getting harder to live with."

She was doing me the worst hurt, by then. She was weeping without covering her face or blowing her nose. The dog let his tail brush the floor, but he wasn't enthusiastic. He feared it when we fought or wept too noisily. He had a low threshold of emotional pain. Fanny sat on the coffee table and her nose ran and tears poured down her face.

"Fanny," I said.

"And I know I'm right about your little professorette," she said.

"No."

"You're not having an affair with her?"

"*No.* I told you. No, I'm not."

"Then what was the little furnace in each of her cute little eyes about at the hospital?"

"I don't know. I wasn't looking at her eyes."

"What, then? Her legs? She shows enough of *them*. Nice, if you like miniatures. I know what I saw, Jack. She was choosing between

the enema bag and the sponge bath. Miss Professorette, Girl Nurse.
If you're not involved with her—"

"Fanny, come on."

"Then she's involved with you."

I tried to shrug. It hurt a lot.

"Don't you be strong and brave and silent, you son of a bitch."

"I promise not to be brave or strong or—I forget the other one."

"Silent. That's your middle name."

"I won't be silent. What shall I say? You know, these stitches in
my mouth keep pulling. It hurts to talk."

"It hurts you to talk with or without them. We're a mess, Jack."

I said, "I'm sorry. I really am. I'm sorry."

"Here's what I was thinking. Would you like to know what I was
thinking?" She stood and she wiped her face with her woolen hat,
then took off her coat. "As soon as you're better a little bit, just so
the ribs don't hurt you so much, I'm going to stop being your nurse
for a while. You remember Virginia, the nurse on your ward. She lives
in town, it's a big house, and she has a room to rent, and I'm taking
it. I don't know how long. I'm just taking it. I can cook in her kitchen,
and I'll have my own bathroom."

"This is because of Professor Piri?"

"This is because all I am here is your nurse. Except when you're
mine. I'm very angry about that. I feel terrible that everything about
us ends up like we're two sick little people and we take turns looking
after each other. Can you understand that? Does it make any sense?"

"What we do with each other, or your moving out?"

"Oh, I'm not *moving out*. It isn't as if you're a drunk and I'm
running for my life, or I'm punishing you."

"Yes," I said. "It *is* punishment. It will be. Not living with you."

"But, really. Look what living with me is."

"Or your living with me."

She said, "Yes."

"Can the dog stay here?"

"It isn't a divorce," she said. "We're not having a custody fight
about a dog."

"Don't you want him, though?"

"You mean, don't I want you. Yes."

"Then why leave? To make the point? I know the point. Some of it. I know what you're talking about. You're trying to make something happen, Fanny. But what's going to happen?"

"You and I could get to wherever we've been going about our child."

I closed my eyes because her white face hurt me. She was so tired and sad. It had gone on so long. And the pills were softening me. I could feel me falling in on myself. "Fanny," I said, making my eyes open, "what if we're there?"

"And this is it? And we can't get any better?"

"Any better. Any closer to wherever you thought we'd go. Any smarter about knowing how to handle it. What if this is it, the whole it?"

She was shaking her head. Her hair whipped. "That would be like winter all year," she said. "I don't believe it."

"Then what's supposed to happen, do you think?" My sore lips wouldn't work right.

"What always happens," she said. "You have a hard, terrible winter; then it ends."

Someone in the dream of Fanny and me being sad talked sternly about spring.

———

Then I woke up and it was almost time for Fanny to go back to work, and then it was three days later. I spoke to the security people, and I asked the dispatcher, "Are there any other missing girls?"

"Damned if I know, Jack. You want me to ask around?"

I told her no. We talked about schedules, and I said I would be in the next day. When Fanny left for work that night, she carried a suitcase and wore a rucksack that made her look like a girl in college. I was still trying to invent a way of asking her to stay that would sound sensible when she came over to me and leaned down like she was going to kiss me good-bye. I leaned farther down toward my coffee mug. Her lips touched me on the head, above my right ear.

"Call me," she said.

"You want to talk to me?"

"I'm doing this to help, you dumb fuck. This isn't about a fight."

I said, "Oh." I said it stupidly, not with any sarcastic intentions. It was roughly what I knew during those days: Oh.

I went into the hospital next morning, but not anyplace near Emergency. The doctor unwrapped me. I had another X ray. Then he showed me the little cracks and then he wrapped me again. He examined my fingers. He asked if I needed more tablets for pain. I lied. At ten o'clock, I was in the security building, reading the dossier of the woman who'd filled in for me and who was now a candidate for Big Pete's job. I arranged to have her fill in at night and on party weekends, and I looked at the ad we would use to find other applicants. I read incident reports, and I talked to my administrative vice president.

When I went out on my rounds, I stopped first at the library to find out about Irene Horstmuller and the Vice President. When I was in the parking lot, I thought of how it would feel to climb down from the Jeep and walk up the stone steps into the library, and I decided to let the Constitution and the second in command take care of themselves for a while.

I suppose I was sitting there with my eyes closed and my mouth open when Dispatch connected me and Sergeant Bird, who reported that the kid from up north had been found dead in a motel room.

"No nightmare stuff," he said. "The guy apparently laid a pillow on top of her face and suffocated her. We've got a description and we'll catch him here or they'll find him in Toronto. My feeling about this is we've got separate perpetrators and therefore no serial crime. Which would be nice."

"The thing is," I said, "you find the serial killers at the end, when they make a mess of it because they're boiling over by then. So you get five, ten, fifteen deaths over the years, and *then* you catch them."

"I'm grateful you found the time to mention it," he said.

"Janice Tanner?"

"Zip."

"Well."

"You know how long these things can take."

"The thing is, her mother's halfway dead already. She wants to know."

"Everyone wants to know," Bird said.

"I appreciate your calling," I said.

"And I appreciate your appreciation," he said.

I was a little annoying to some students after that call. They were rolling a friend down the hill below the library. The aim, apparently, was to see how much snow would build up around him.

I hit the roof light, and I stood at the top of the hill on the edge of the road, giving them the mean-cop stance—legs apart, hands on my waist, no facial expression. When they came up, puffing and grinning and not much caring that I was there, I looked past them until I saw their friend break himself out of the snowball and start the climb up.

"You can smother someone that way," I said.

"Yeah, well, we didn't," the tall one with dark whiskers said. "We weren't trying to. We were having fun."

The shorter one said, "We were like playing. You know? I mean, what is this about, please?"

"I suppose it's about my trying to give you fellows a hard time for endangering his life." I gestured down the hill.

"We got assassins on the loose, and there's a rape every—what, four seconds? And the starving children of the Balkan nations? And you're fucking around with *us*?"

If I wasn't careful, he was going to call home and ask his father to purchase me and ship me someplace. If I wasn't careful, I was going to take my flashlight out and bounce it all over him. Then my ribs would feel worse, and I'd be unemployed, and Fanny would never come home.

"No," I said. "I'm not. Just let's all be careful."

I made myself not hear what all three of them were saying by the time I was back at the door. It took me a minute to work myself up the running board and behind the wheel, and I thought about the pain pills but decided not to take any. I finished my run up the hill, then began to circle back down. When I passed the library hill, they were gone. I saw no new posters on cars or buildings. On the other hand, I saw Janice's face wherever I went that morning and all that afternoon.

———

She said, "I'm sorry."

I was lying very still, smacking my eyelashes against myself, trying to figure out not where I was, because I knew it when I woke up, but why I had let myself go there. I was in her house and in her bedroom and in her bed. I was on my back, and she had pulled the covers away. She was leaning on an arm.

She said, "I wanted to look at you, and I woke you up."

"Not much to look at," I said. "Bandages, balls, black-and-blue marks."

"It was the balls part," she said. She cupped them in her small hand and moved her head, then hesitated, then went on and pushed her face gently into me. She said, "Mmm."

"You're being daring, huh? What I mean is, you're wonderful. But you worry about doing it."

She covered us both and lay very close to me, with her face on my arm.

She said, "It shows?"

"I don't know."

"Yes, you do. It isn't that I haven't had some men. *Ack!* 'Had some men.' But I did. I had boyfriends in college and graduate school. I've been around." I felt her lips move. I felt the warmth of her breathing on my arm. Her head shifted as she spoke. "And I can get feeling crazy and sexy. I can let myself get there. With you, for example. But something always gets me embarrassed. I don't know what. Maybe I think I have to act embarrassed. I don't know. When your father's a cop, you grow up with a major superego thing. No matter what you do."

"I get embarrassed, too."

"Maybe you're your *own* superego," she said.

I recognized the word, but I didn't know it. I was so far over my head in so many ways. I said, "I have not had a lot of women friends in my life. I've lived with the same woman since the seventies. When you were born, right?"

"No," she said. "I was born in '68. Your wife's pretty. She's sad. So are you. Aren't you?"

"That seems to be the effect she and I have on each other."

"Did I make you sad? Do I?"

"Why would I be here if you did? I came banging into your house like an accident happening."

"No," she said. "No accident. How are your ribs? Did we hurt you?"

"It was like a feather on top of me. When you say 'no accident,' you mean you were expecting me?" I thought of Mrs. Tanner and her certainty that everything was planned. "Because I didn't know I was coming here tonight. Of course, I didn't know I was coming here the other day. I thought this time I was driving home. It was like—Jesus, I haven't got your kind of words, Rosalie. It was like I was in the water and I just reached out and caught hold. I hope that isn't insulting. I don't want you to think I have some kind of tool—no, some kind of anything *practical* in mind. Jesus. The more I talk, the less I say. Rosalie," I said. My eyes were shut. "I didn't know it was possible for me to still . . . do, you know, *it*. And feel good."

"No?" she said. "Well, let me make it clear: You did do it. I felt you pump and pump." She reached for me again. Then she moved her head again and said, "I wasn't expecting you, either. I was hoping. I didn't think for sure it would happen, though. Even after the other day. I almost raped you standing up. I knew you felt embarrassed about me being on the faculty here. I knew you were the kind of man who stood back a long time and considered things."

"There has to be a lot of social pressure on you, from inside of you, about this happening to us. To be perfectly honest, I feel some of it, too."

"But, hey," she said, "tough shit, right? If it's you and me, then that's what it is."

When I shifted, I closed my eyes against what I felt.

She said, "Do you want to ask me why I was hoping for you?"

"Why were you—you know."

She put her teeth onto my upper arm and then slowly worked them up and down, like she was tasting my flesh. It felt warm and moist and in the darkness, like a baby feeding, but also there was the feel of her breast and side and groin and thigh against me. I felt myself grow and I forgot what we'd been saying.

In a whisper, she said, "Because I knew you would taste like this. I knew you'd be tough and maybe even mean but you'd try and not show it. And you would taste this good."

She moved under the covers. I almost didn't hear the muffled whisper when she said, "I'm not embarrassed when I can hide like this." Then she said, "I knew you'd taste this good."

When I woke up again, she was sleeping, too, and it was one in the morning.

I said, "Jesus!"

"Are we all right?" she said.

"The dog. I have to feed the dog. He's used to eating around five, five-thirty. He'll think he's dead of starvation."

"You're leaving me for a dog? Not your wife and not your children —you didn't talk about children." Her voice was soft and sullen. She sounded like a teenage girl.

I didn't think I could put my socks on because my side was too stiff. I stuck my legs through my trousers, my bare feet into my boots, and I balled my socks and underpants and stuffed them in pockets. I got my shirt on and then Rosalie stood in front of me, wearing my sweater pulled down over her arms and hips. I wanted to stay awhile and peel it up very slowly. I also wanted to make her promise to give it back. I thought of Fanny recognizing it someplace, and in the darkness of her bedroom, I closed my eyes. I remembered how on an earlier afternoon she had covered her eyes like a child, and now I was doing it, too. When I opened my eyes, she was closer to me, and on her toes, leaning against me, kissing the bottom of my chin.

"Bend down and kiss me for real," she said.

Her arms were on me, and my head was coming down. She

chewed on the side of my jaw, that little wet nibbling pressure of her teeth.

I drove through town at fifty, and I didn't care if I was stopped. I got up to sixty-five on the snowy two-lane highway, and back down to forty-five on the ice-packed road that went to our house. The roads and snowbanks and fields looked blue under the moon, as blue as the room in my imagination where Rosalie and I had made love. In fact, though, her bedroom was mostly creams and tans and ambers, with a little deep red in some of the stuff on the wall. I tried to see her stretched out, as I'd imagined her, but instead I saw myself stretched out, and Rosalie nibbling with little teeth on me. She looked like a child, but she acted like a veteran in bed. I got as excited as I was scared, and something was wrong with that. Something, of course, was wrong with me leaving like a kid past his curfew, and something was wrong when a man left a small, exciting woman in her bed. Something was also wrong with the way I thought of her, the tiny breasts and narrow hips, the little belly. There was something not right about her looking in my mind like a child.

I pulled in too quickly and skidded. It didn't matter. Fanny's car wasn't there to slam against. I'd been speeding home like when she lived with me in the old days, before she put herself on the late shift and before she moved to the room she let from Virginia. Fanny wasn't home, and it didn't matter, I realized, if I came home half-dressed from someone's house. She thought I did that anyway.

The dog danced designs on the floor, and I let him out, then had to come out with him and pee into the snow to persuade him to finish relieving himself before he charged past me at the door. I let him in and put down food and fresh water. I ran some water for myself and took my tablets for the pain.

I thought of Rosalie Piri telling me her father was a cop.

He probably kept a service revolver in his bedroom, I thought, but with the shells locked away someplace else because there were children in the house. I heard her say, "You didn't talk about children." I let the dog out for a run, and I went upstairs. I was moving slowly because I had done a little damage to the ribs. I couldn't begin to think what else I had done some damage to.

I kept the pistol wrapped in a greasy fatigue T-shirt in our closet. The shirt stank of gun oil. It was in a cardboard box, in which a pair of women's white soft walking shoes, size nine, had come to our house in a United Parcel Service truck. I carried it downstairs. I let the dog in, gave him a biscuit, and then I poured myself a drink. I'd been careful about using whiskey for a while because I thought I might be able to dive into a bottle one night and not come up. I put some sour mash over ice cubes in a tall glass, and I put the bottle away. I spread newspaper on the kitchen table, and then I put the revolver on top of it.

Taking the brushes and the oil from the shoe box, I saw the dog watching very carefully. He seemed to be. His head was aimed at me. I saw his nostrils work in and out.

"I'm just cleaning it," I told him.

He moved his tail in almost a wag, and then he lay down. His groan told me he had suffered a terrible day and please don't make it worse.

I took the empty cylinder off and worked the extractor spring with the tip of an oiled brush. Sometimes they rusted in there, especially when you haven't looked at the piece in years, much less used it or cleaned it. I took off the butt plate and worked the coil spring to the hammer mechanism. I cleaned each chamber of the cylinder and inserted six Fed 85 JHP cartridges, which the man in Utica had sold me. I remember he wanted me to buy 85-grain wad cutters and I'd said no without understanding the difference. He'd enjoyed it too much and I was interested in fear, not fun. It was a .32, useless for anything but close-in work unless you were a good marksman. I wasn't. I took it away from a kid who broke apart about a week before the end of my tour. Somehow, he had been able to take it with him, from the day he reported to the bus station in Houston until the night in a room above a place called Gaspard he impaled the foot of a fifteen-year-old girl to the wood at the end of her bed with a Finnish folding knife and her screaming brought the pimp, and the pimp laid out the soldier with a wooden hammer used for tenderizing meat and then sent word for me. I got the whore cared for, I arrested the boy, I impounded the knife, and when I found the gun on him, I said nothing and kept it. He said nothing, too, because the gun would have worsened the charges. I brought it home with me because I was enough of a cop to like the idea of an anonymous weapon that no one could trace to me. I didn't have intentions. I was simply being thoughtful. I'd have bet our mortgage that Sergeant Bird had one and that Elmo St. John didn't.

It was a Taurus, a .32 Magnum Taurus 741 with a big front sight that made it clumsy. For a little gun, it was large. They called it a "banker's gun." They used to call it a "belly gun." It was cleaned and loaded now. The dog was looking at me under his eyebrows, winking. You'll hear the cops in movies call it a "throw-down piece." I never heard it called that on the job. I thought, Men go nuts with a gun, and all of a sudden they shoot the family dog. I thought, They shoot everything and then they shoot themselves.

I had forgotten to drink the sour mash. I tasted some. It was almost three in the morning. I drank the rest and shuddered it down. I decided not to put on underwear or socks. I emptied the clothing from my pockets and left it on the table next to the cleaning apparatus and the box of shells. I told the dog, "This time, you get to ride in the car."

He danced in a circle, took off for the door, then came back and ran around me. When I took out the car keys for confirmation, he circled again and ran to the door. We went out together onto the blue snow, and he worked his way back and forth between the front and back seats a few times while I waited for the defroster to warm up. Then we went, and he settled for the front seat, as I had known he would, and he sat with his nose against the window I had opened a little so he could get some cold air.

"They sometimes shoot the shit out of the house," I told him. "Blow up the cat and the dog and the fish tank and then they do the wife. When they see how dead she is, they get filled with sadness. The poor little kids, how am I gonna tell them what I did to Mommy? So they do the kids. Then, they either do themselves or they go on TV."

The highway branches a few miles outside of town, to the north, and you can either take the lefthand fork and go to school or the hospital or, say, Virginia's house or you can take the right and go a dozen miles to the little farm road that dips west and takes you into the river end of Chenango Flats. I didn't know until we came to the fork which way I would go. I went to the right, away from Fanny, away from school. I went toward where the Tanners slept.

But they didn't, or they didn't appear to. Lights were on downstairs, and I thought I saw a shadow move on a wall of their living room, which looked onto the shallow front lawn that ran to the road. I drove past and looked at Strodemaster's: no lights, no motion, a sleeping house. I was envious, and I thought I might stop the car and lie in the backseat a while. But I realized I was tired, not sleepy, and I didn't think a nap had anything to do with my kind of fatigue. I drove on to the church and made a U-turn and parked in front of it.

"Sometimes," I said, "they go into churches and shoot up God and recite poetry and then they surrender themselves. It takes them maybe thirty seconds to figure out the God they had in mind didn't notice."

I started up again and turned on my lights. I drove very slowly toward the Tanners' and I saw their lights were off. I pictured Mrs. Tanner coming downstairs, or the Reverend Tanner rushing downstairs, to get her medicine. I thought of her face in its pain. I backed up very slowly and looked over toward Strodemaster's. His house was dark, too, and now the Tanners' was dark, and the only lighted house I could think of where someone might want to talk about girls gone missing was my own. I drove home to talk myself to sleep.

briefs

N THE HOSPITAL parking lot, the dog sat with his nose out the window while I drowsed behind the wheel. I hadn't slept much, what with my driving around to shut-down towns and my sipping more sour mash, and I'd made myself waken early because I wanted to be here when Fanny came off shift.

"Sometimes," I told him, "they go after their estranged wife and they shoot up the hospital, the parking lot, the family dog, and then themselves. You sure you should be here?"

He ignored me. He knew we were waiting for something, and he didn't want to miss it. He kept his nose out the window, flaring at whatever was on the wind. I saw her first because he was so near-sighted. She was walking directly to her car, behind which I happened to be parked. The sky was gray-yellow, and I found myself hoping for snow, since I'd been predicting that it never would end. Then he saw her, and his tail began to go, and then he bounded into the backseat, over it, and back to the tailgate, and then he came back to half-stand on the seat beside me, winding his hind end into his tail.

She saw us. She slowed, then picked up her pace and went to her car. She held on to its door handle and then she came over. I rolled my window down. He came across me, leaned in fast to be sure and

dent a rib, and then he was outside and up and down beside her.
They do look like they're smiling, and she was smiling back. I got out
of the Ford and stood beside it, not sure whether I ought to approach
her. But nurses look it in the face and they act. She walked to the
passenger's side and got in. I took a breath and got behind the wheel.

"Good morning," she said. She was looking me over. I waited.
She leaned in and sniffed. "You're a little disheveled, Jack."

"I had sour mash for dessert last night."

"You'd been staying away from it for some time, too. That's a
shame."

"A couple of months, I think. But it tasted good."

"Well, good, I guess. I hope you didn't do anything dumb."

"Oh, I probably did, Fanny. How's work?"

"Jack, it's been two days."

"It seems longer."

"I'm a tough habit to break, huh?"

I nodded. "You like the room?"

"I think of it as an apartment. That way, it doesn't feel as small."

"It's small?"

"If I had a pet, say a gerbil or a parakeet, we'd have to take turns
sleeping there."

"Good thing you don't have a pet, then."

"Yeah," she said, "it worked out. I see you're driving with a partner
these days."

"Jesus, Fanny, I got so screwed up on campus what with one
thing and another, I didn't get home until so late last night, he must
have thought he was abandoned."

"One thing and another," she said. "You're still keeping the peace
and finding the child."

"Janice Tanner."

"I know her name, Jack." She yawned and folded her arms across
her chest and let her eyes close. "She's what screwed you up on
campus? The kid who never set foot there? God. You're so fucking
transparent. You do something you feel bad about, and you tell me
inside of *hours*. I mean, it's twenty years, Jack. I know you. What'd
you do that you had to come and confess about?"

The dog, I think, took this line of questioning as an example of interrogator's art, and he banged his tail against the backseat, where he sat watching Fanny.

I said, "I wanted to see you, that's all."

She stared ahead, as though we were moving.

"There's plenty of space at the house, Fanny. I don't have any boarders or anything."

I was thinking of Fanny alone in a room and me coming up the stairs in my socks. I was thinking of the echo of her cry in my head as I ran. I was so late getting there. I knew it on the way. I was running underwater, like somebody was dreaming it and I was in their dream. And then I got down the hall and to the door and pulled myself around and through the doorway to find them.

I said, "What?"

Fanny, beside me in the car, sat looking at me. She seemed very tired, and her face was defenseless.

"I didn't say anything," she said.

"I thought I heard you say something."

"You were over the left-field wall," she said. "You were far away. Where was that?"

I shook my head. Then I said, "Couldn't you come home? I don't think we'll get it done this way."

"You don't believe there's any it to *get* done."

I wanted to shake my head again. I didn't. I said, "I have this really terrible thought. I have this idea I can't even say about the missing kid."

"Why can't you say it? No, that's a ridiculous question! What *can* you say?"

I love your long, narrow face. It makes me sad. I've watched the skin loosen from its bones for twenty years. You were the girl I made love to in the Hotel Albert in Greenwich Village and in Hawaii twice, on the big island in the borrowed beach house with the roof of galvanized tin, and in cars too small for all our thrashing around. You told me you were going to teach me how to shout and cry and you did. I read a terrible poem to you over a telephone wire running under the Pacific Ocean. You and I said Ralph the Duck to our baby and then we couldn't anymore, and then we couldn't talk about rubber ducks or children or say our daughter's name for so long. Your hair used to shine with the life in us and now the light rolls away from it. I could make you smile then, and now I can't.

I said, "Fanny. Listen to me."

She grew so still.

I said, "When you think about Hannah. When you think about the worst of it."

"What?"

"Can I keep talking? Is it okay?"

"How can it be okay? Yes, though. Go ahead."

"What do you remember?"

"Oh," she said. She sounded disappointed. "We've done this before. I thought we could maybe get someplace new."

"But can you tell me? What you see?"

"I don't want to, Jack."

"No, it's all right to. Really."

She had her tissues out, and the dog was slapping his tail against the seat. "You," she said, "and the baby. You holding the baby against your chest."

"You don't see anything behind me."

"What?"

"You know, any special furniture or part of the room or direction or anything. You just see me."

"And—the baby."

"Hannah."

"Hannah."

"And I'm holding her against my chest."

"Too hard, Jack," she said. She covered her face with tissues and fingers. "Too hard. Poor Jack," she said. "Poor Jack."

"No," I said, reaching and refusing to wince. I got my arm around her partway and I pulled her over. She let herself lie against me with my right arm over her shoulder. I got my left around a little, and I covered her cheek with my hand. I tried to hide her from it. I was afraid to go after more. I wanted to be sure she didn't know. I was the cunning interrogator of bashed-up whores and bad-boy soldiers, knife fighters and sexual deviants. I wasn't very good with wounded people brighter and braver than I was. "I'm sorry, Fanny," I said.

"I know, Jack."

"Come home."

She sat back away from me. It felt, as my arm came down again, like I'd torn the cartilage a little more.

"So you can nurse me and I can nurse you?"

"Christ, Fanny, what in hell do married people *do*? Isn't comfort any of it?"

"Sure."

"So?"

"So is getting better."

I shouted, "How in the fucking fuck do we *do* that? By saying it over and over? By staying away from the people we need? You do need me, I guess. Don't you? Or is that where I'm wrong?"

"I need you," she said, low and with no expression, looking straight ahead. I saw in the rearview mirror how the dog lay flat beneath the storm.

I said, "I'm sorry I shouted."

"I'm sorry I'm giving you such a hard time."

"We're so sorry for each other, maybe we should be having breakfast together in bed or something."

She nodded. "Probably we should," she said. "Why did you make me remember that?"

"You remembered it without me."

"Why did you need me to say it? Do you think we can get past it? You know, learn something beyond the standing there, all three of us, dead and everything?"

I said, "You want me to drive you home? We can come back and get your car later on. I'll call in sick."

"You just got back. You can't be sick so soon. Anyway, I'm going to Virginia's house. I'll drive my car there. I'm going to sleep, Jack. I'm really tired now."

I let my breath out so long, the window of the car fogged up. I started the engine to work the heater.

She leaned over and kissed the side of my face. She said good-bye to the dog. She got out and closed the door so softly, the lock didn't catch. I didn't want to reach anymore, so I left it that way.

I told the dog, "Either stay in the back or close the front door better." *Stay* kept him back there. I got into reverse as Fanny sat in her car. She drove away and then I went in the same direction until I came to the campus, where I turned.

What I had seen on a rear window of her car and what I saw now on doors and campus utility vehicles were the new posters. They were larger, bright white, with the same picture of the girl with sad eyes who wanted to please people. They offered a bigger reward. I knew she was going to be everywhere today.

Irene Horstmuller was back on campus. They couldn't keep her in jail to make her give up the information she withheld because the information didn't exist anymore. That was the difference between us, I thought. The Secret Service wanted to cancel the speech unless Horstmuller remembered the name of the last person to use the book the threat was written in. My terrible poem to Fanny that I'd read from Tokyo, where I was very drunk and very lonely, had been better than the poem that Rosalie found. At what the Secret Service cutie with the long hair threatened would be our last meeting, Rosalie looked dangerous. She sat across the seminar table and put her finger in her mouth and sucked the end. I didn't know if she looked twelve or a thousand years old, but I knew how dangerous she looked. What I felt when I saw her smart face go clever, then naughty, then brilliant about making me dance in place where I sat was telling me a truth I didn't want to know.

"Jack?" the dean said.

"What I said last time. You tell us to do it, I'll organize local people, deputies, security, student aides, the whole ball of wax. J. Edgar Hoover over here can put the sharpshooters in the balcony of the chapel and he can talk tough into his little radio."

"Now, Jack," the dean said.

"Take it back," the Secret Service man said.

"Take it *back?*" I said. "Like in the schoolyard take it back? That kind of take it back? Is that what we're doing? Okay, no. Now it's your turn."

The one with the short hair said to the dean, "He is not cooperating."

"Sure I am," I said. "I just think the two of you are sissy boys and poops. Pushing around a librarian so you can get your rocks off. *You* go find the shooters around here. *You* protect the President. Vice President. Whoever. You don't come onto the campus and act like we're the problem. *You're* the problem. You're a bunch of incompetents. You're clowns." Turning to the dean, I said, "Is that better?"

Piri's mouth was in its huge wicked grin. I looked away. She was outlaw as much as policeman's daughter, I thought, and she was too deep for me.

You stud, I thought, crawling to her house, whining your way into her bed—

—where she wanted you—

—and *then* you decide she's scary.

I shook my head.

Ms. Horstmuller said, "Yes, Jack?"

"Nothing," I said.

"You can say that again," said the one with longer hair.

"You need help with the spelling?" I asked him.

The dean smiled, looked down, lost the smile, and looked up. Ms. Horstmuller suggested that we'd run out of talking points. The dean told us how much he wanted the Vice President on campus and he spoke as well for the president, who was away.

Rosalie said, "A college is supposed to be a place where we want to *give* information. So's its library." Horstmuller nodded vigorously. "It's ironic, then, that we end up feeling we need to suppress information for the sake of a functioning society of unfettered individuals. Which is what the Constitution's about. Keep the information in so we can continue to give the information out."

Short Hair said, "So?"

"Ironic, as I said."

"Gee. Right. Thank you," Short Hair said. Long Hair was silent, probably deciding how I would die. "Now the Vice President is safe."

Rosalie said, "You know, our director of security spoke for me when he made some ad hominem characterizations."

Long Hair looked at her, working it out, and the dean dismissed us.

Near the circulation desk, Rosalie caught up with me. She said, quietly and looking away as if embarrassed again, "I thought about you."

"Yes, ma'am," I said.

"Jack."

"I have to get out there and protect the campus from people like me," I said.

She whispered, "Where are those secret places on campus that your wife was worried about?"

"Damn," I said.

"When will you be near one?"

"Maybe we could run into each other later by accident," I said.

"I get out of my next class around twenty after one. I hope my car, which I parked behind social sciences, will start." She batted her eyes like an old-fashioned movie heroine.

I was thinking of her beneath the covers, and how I had loved her thin, light limbs on me, the head with its heavy brain and the small, child's fingers and toes that I felt, the little girl's tongue and teeth and mouth. I felt greasy with sweat when I started the truck.

The dog pushed into my face, but I moved my head toward the window that I'd rolled almost all the way down. I took some breaths. Then I looked in the glove compartment to see that the pistol was there. And then I drove from the library onto the road that went to the top of the campus, bracing myself to see, on the posters they and Strodemaster and their other volunteers had taped up everywhere, the little girl's sad mouth.

———

I had a half-gallon plastic jug of cold water and his dish, and he drank when we took our breaks. Then I'd let him out of the truck and he'd tear around on campus, always circling back to see where I was. Students threw snowballs and sticks for him, and professors waved, and he made a little bit of an ass of himself. He acted like a puppy. But you can't live in a kitchen or even on the sofas all day, every day. You have to come out and pee in new places and run some circles to a little applause. He seemed to enjoy our patrolling, and he was perfectly willing to sleep in the corner of my tiny office, his ears jumping a bit as the radio buzzed and issued voices full of concern that alternated with boredom. He didn't mind my random trips into buildings, either, although some of the older marble floors seemed to feel treacherous to him, and he waddled and panted as we walked. He liked it better when we were in the Jeep, and since we spent most of our time there, he had a happy day.

Archie Halpern had a big bright office in the back of the counseling suite. Sometimes I found him in a soft, brown reclining chair, his feet up, watching television, especially during basketball season, when he watched taped games on a VCR. He claimed it helped him counsel the jocks on campus. I think it was because he was devoted to the New York Knicks. This time, though, he was watching a pretty roughly made film. I thought I recognized the campus and then I saw one of our trucks roll past on icy ruts. The film zoomed in clumsily to the face of a man in a high bearskin hat. It was Archie. It showed his nose, which was running. It came in closer but lost focus. He stopped the machine with his remote.

He was wearing the turtleneck over jeans that were rolled at the bottom. I could see the blue flannel of their lining. He wore soft bedroom slippers and blue woolen socks. Squirming in the chair, shoving on a wooden lever at its side, he rocked forward and sat up.

"Are you here to arrest me?"

"For bad acting," I said.

"That wasn't an act. My nose was really running. The auteur behind this particular piece of shit is someone I'm supposed to be helping. Now he's completely outraged by me and he won't talk to me. So he gives me this. He says, 'Check it out.' *Chuck* it, more likely. How's life?"

"Fine," I said.

"So how come you look like dog shit?"

"I'm undercover. It's my disguise."

"You've never been much good at disguise," he said. "For example, how's Fanny? You see?"

"She's fine. What do I see?"

"What I see. You set your face. It's like a fighter taking a stance. I ask about Fanny, you get set to defend yourself."

I nodded. I sat down in a chair in front of his desk. He was in a corner decorated with pictures of his children. They were all squat and thick-necked and roundheaded.

I said, "Fanny moved out for a while."

"How long a while?"

"Maybe the rest of our lives, I think. I think she doesn't know. But it's not terrific."

His telephone buzzed. I looked at it, at him, and he said, "Fuck it. For a couple of minutes." He waved his hands. "I'm booked solid. These are healthy American children, which means they're all pulsating with neurosis. But just sit there a minute."

"Did she move out to get away from you?"

"I guess."

"Or to force your hand?"

"For sure, that."

"To do what?"

"To make me talk to her. To make me be happy. So we don't keep nursing each other, she said. To make us get to springtime. Well, it was a figure of speech. To get *better*."

"You think it'll work?"

I shook my head.

His phone buzzed and then rang.

He held his hand up and I sat again. His eyes were focused, and his big face was tight around them.

"You know it won't work?"

I nodded.

"You have a purpose in all of this. I've always thought so. You never told me. Can you tell me?"

I said, "The last thing I can ever do is let her remember what happened."

"When your baby died."

"When our baby died."

"Because you love her," he said.

"Yes."

"Fuck, Jack. I mean, did—"

"Absolutely last thing, Archie. I keep testing her every once in a while, and she doesn't remember it all. She sees me holding her. Hannah. Our daughter. She sees that, and then on from there. She doesn't remember it, and I don't want her to."

Archie picked up an extension of the phone, which was on the floor beside his recliner. He lifted the receiver and hung it up to stop the buzzing. The radio in my back pocket made its static hush and said my name.

I turned my radio down, and he said, "Can you tell me what you're protecting her from? Or yourself?"

I looked at him. I was trying to think of the best words, and I couldn't. At times like that, I never could. Finally, I said, "Can you think of any way of convincing her we're better off together than alone?"

"Saying that," he said. He wiped his chin with the back of his hand. "If it's true."

"You think it's better for couples to split?"

"Sometimes it is. Will she be happier without you?"

"She never lived without me, except when I was overseas. We lived half our lives together. It must be more than half."

"A lot of people split in their forties, some in their fifties, their sixties. Later, even. But what you're saying is she moved out to get you better—in her terms, Jack. I'm not choosing sides. My point is, if she wants you to do something for the two of you, maybe she wants the two of you to go on. It would be good if you told me what you don't want her to know."

"To remember."

"To remember," he said. He picked up the receiver and said, "In thirty seconds."

"I can't, not now."

"You should try. Maybe it would help with Fanny."

"Guaranteed: no."

He said, "I have to throw you out, Jack. Come back. Find me."

"One question," I said.

He nodded.

"Do you pray?"

"You think it'll help?"

"No. I don't know how. I don't even want to."

"Bullshit," he said.

"But do you?"

He leaned back hard and worked his shoulders and seat into the cushions. He said, "I'm a Jew. I was born a Jew. Definition of Jew: They can come to your door and take you away to a camp and kill you. Do I pray? I argue. I spend a lot of time arguing with whatever you want to call it. Yahweh. Shithead. Father. I don't know. I argue about bad deaths and terrible diseases. I say, 'How can you *permit* it?' and I don't get an answer because maybe no one's there. And if He is, He disgusts me. Or I disgust Him and He doesn't want to argue. And I keep arguing. Would you call that prayer?"

I knew he didn't expect an answer. I didn't have one. I went over to his chair and stuck my hand out. He shook it. His hand was gentle and wet.

———

I did drive over to the social sciences lot, and I did find her standing next to her car. When she saw me, she shrugged. I left the dog in the car and stood beside her, asking dumb questions and getting laughter back.

"Well," I said, "we sure can't leave you here."

"I've got my briefcase with my negligee and vibrator and leather handcuffs inside, so we can go wherever you say, Officer." I drove us out of the lot while the dog introduced himself to her hair and the nape of her neck. I told him to lie down and Rosalie said, "Why don't we all?"

We drove up toward the quarry, above the cemetery. The truck skidded a little, and I put it in four-wheel low, and we got through. Halfway toward the quarry, you can cut through some low brush and you're at the top of the old ski lift the school no longer uses where there is a low wooden equipment hut. I saw how the snowy brush had sprung back behind us.

I said, "We're invisible."

"I'm surprised the students don't come here."

"They don't mind using motels. Or classrooms. Storage closets in the administration building."

I found the right master key on my ring and let us in. There was a small mound of sand, a rack of chain, hose from the old snow machines, a few plastic tarpaulins, and a very excited colony of mice.

Rosalie said, "I thought maybe Chanel No. Five, or Poison, not the smell of cold mouse." She held her nose with a mittened hand, and she looked about ten.

"It's the only pretty much hidden place where we can get kind of risky and wild the way you wanted."

"That's what I wanted, huh?"

"I think so. Yes."

"You're right. I guess it was a bluff."

"No," I said, "you were turned on and risky-feeling. It's possible we might get nuts up here, but I think what we'd get is cold asses and sore skin and smelly."

"This is the first scripture lesson, then."

"In what?"

"In taking it easy? I'm not sure. Maybe in just being us and not some idea about us that one of us might have?"

"I didn't intend that. I'm not sure I could even come up with it."

"You really wanted to do what I wanted to do."

I nodded.

She reached under my coat and cupped my ass and squeezed, then patted it. She said, "Let's do second best."

"Anything you want," I said.

"Let's go back down and I'll drive my car home and we meet up later and be whoever we are."

"Could I kiss you first?" I asked.

She said, "I think you have to."

——

I said to the dog, when I drove the Ford off campus after work, "You won't starve. I promise." I had taken the gun from the Jeep, and it was angled uncomfortably in the pocket of my coat. I put it in the glove compartment of the Gran Torino. "But we need to make a stop." When I pulled into the Tanners' driveway, I left windows open halfway down and told him to stay.

She was in bed, the reverend told me.

"Thank God they took her off the chemotherapy," he said. "It was killing her. This way, she's in her own house, and when she feels strong, she can putter. And, of course, she's supervising the search."

He was probably right. In terms of full-time concentration on Janice Tanner, she was doing more than anyone in the state. Maybe, I thought, the man who took Janice had done more. The reverend went upstairs and I stood in the living room. There were no pictures on the walls except one of Jesus that looked famous and one of Janice that was famous for sure. It was the one with her glad eyes and sad mouth. I saw hooks where other pictures had hung. On the coffee table in front of the thin wooden settle, there were posters and news-papers. The top paper had an article about her parents' efforts to find her. I had a metal taste in my mouth, and the saliva kept running.

Tanner was back. He gestured to me, and I followed him up the steep, narrow staircase. I could feel the thermal current of the house as cold air rose behind us. I waited for the heating system to kick in. I was worried about how cold Mrs. Tanner felt.

He gestured me to a rush-bottomed ladder-back chair beside the bed. The only light in the room came from a weak bulb in the lamp on the bedside table, which was a cracked cherry stand. The shades in the two windows were drawn and the overhead light was off. She lay on her side, curled up, her fists on the sheets, outside the layers of blanket she was under. In that dim light, even, I saw how sparse her hair was. She licked her chapped lips with her tongue. The skin of her face was the color of old oranges, and it looked like it would split and start bleeding if someone pushed against it. Her eyes, though they weren't bright, were still smart, and they grew large as she fixed them on me.

"No," I said. "I'm sorry. Nothing new. I just wanted to say hello, I guess. It's only a visit."

She raised her brows and moved her head on the pillow a little, like she was saying she understood.

I said, "And maybe look at Janice's room. I never did that. Maybe I should do that."

Her smile was tired but real.

"I hear the real cops do that."

She nodded.

"So I thought I'd come and get real."

She said, in more than a whisper, "Did you want to pray?"

I should have said yes, of course. But the thought of her God made me angry. I felt mad enough to wail like a child. I said, "No, thank you, ma'am. I can't."

She said, "I would pray on your behalf."

"Thank you."

"I have a confession."

"You already did."

"You're easy to want to take care of," she said.

"That's what my wife once said."

"Lucky woman," she said.

"Isn't she. I'll ask your husband to take me to the room." I leaned over and kissed her temple. She smelled like wood that's been in pond water too long. She was coming apart inside.

The reverend said, in the hall, outside her closed door, "I didn't know Mrs. Tanner was praying for you."

"It's an arrangement we have."

"I'd be pleased to pray for you, too."

"You're very kind, Reverend Tanner."

"But you ought to make the effort also."

I nodded, but I didn't have anything more to say because we were in the room now. I put my hand up and he looked at it, and then at my face.

"I'd like it if I could be in here by myself a minute."

"Clues," he said.

"Clues."

"Randy told us about the uncertainty principle."

"I have a lot of that."

"The observer of a phenomenon changes it through the act of observation," he said.

I said, "That sounds reasonable."

"So I'll leave you to your *own* uncertainty." He smiled to be sure I understood the joke.

I nodded. I didn't.

"I'll be outside," he said.

"Thank you."

"In the hall. If you need me."

"I'm not going to touch anything, Reverend. I understand it's precious to you. I'll keep my hands in my pockets."

"Less alteration of the phenomenon observed," he agreed.

He flipped a light switch, and he closed the door. I took my hands out of my pockets, but I did keep them to myself. I couldn't find her here. I saw paperback books and school notebooks on a cheap maple desk. On the wall I saw pictures of her parents outside her father's church, and I saw clipped photos in dime-store frames of people I guessed from their hair and clothes were rock singers. There was, of course, a Jesus in a wooden frame. I looked in some plastic-covered albums at pictures of junior high school kids. In the books on the shelves were some postcards. They were scrawled on in round inky writing by kids writing to Janice over a summer. There was a book called *Generation X* that looked a little difficult for her. There was a book called *I Know Why the Caged Bird Sings* and one titled *The Light in the Forest*. I learned from them that maybe she felt trapped. But most of anything I'd ever read was about someone who was trapped, so I wasn't making much progress.

I didn't think I was going to find stuff taped under drawers or glued inside the covers of hardcover books, and I relied on the state police for that kind of search. I did do the obvious—look between the mattress and the box spring, feel behind the wooden headboard, lie down on the floor and move slowly in a circle, looking for something that might have slid down. Zero. What I'd expected, plus some extra sensations in the ribs. I smelled one of the little bottles of cologne on a painted metal tray on her bureau and it was sweet and sad.

But it could be anyone's room, I thought. What made it Janice's?

I looked at her coronet. It seemed to me to be tarnished. I held it in front of my mouth. I smelled her saliva. I put my lips where she put hers. Then I put it back and I sat on the bed. I lay on it. I turned my face to the pillow and sniffed for the smell of her hair and soap and skin. I pressed my face in and down. Then I sat back up because I didn't want to be found like that. I smoothed away my impression on the pillowcase. I looked across at the little wooden bookcase she used. English books and history books, a book on earth science and one on physics, a clutter of photocopied sheets that I reached for and looked through: math quizzes with bad grades and handouts for English, and no invitation from a psychopath to meet after school. I opened and closed some bureau drawers.

Here's what the great detective, the interrogator of mysteries, the famous payer of attention, came up with: Janice had been hiding while she lived here. Her parents knew the good little girl and maybe that's what she was, but she was also someone else. The room was like a set for a high school play called *Typical Girl*. Of course, Rosalie had already known this. When I came into the hall, the reverend reached around in front of me and turned off her light.

He said, "Clues?"

"Sir, did you change anything in there? Add anything, take anything out? You know, after you became worried? When the police started investigating?"

"That would be Heisenberg on a huge scale!" he said.

"Yes, wouldn't it. Did you?"

"That's how she left it. Socks to saxophone."

We were on the stairs. I said, "I didn't see a saxophone."

"My little joke. I liked the alliteration."

But I did think of socks. They'd most of them been white, though she had some bolder colors. "Could I go back up a minute, Reverend?"

I went to her room, telling him to wait downstairs for me. I got the light on and the door closed, and then I looked through her socks. I found one pair of stockings. The drawer contained the things of a child, not a fourteen-year-old pushing to be grown. I went to the drawer beneath it, which I had already looked through, but very hastily. I wondered why. I thought, You would have been a shy father.

The drawer held little brassieres, sad small things that looked like models of the genuine item. I looked through them and found, on the bottom of the stack, a brown paper bag. In it was a bag from a chain I'd seen in the Syracuse mall. Inside that bag was a little black bra made mostly of lace. Under it was a matching pair of underpants. I looked at her stacked underpants: all white. This pair, in the bag, looked narrow-cut, like they'd come up thin at the crotch, and again very lacy. She had kept the receipt. She must have worked hard baby-sitting to save up for them.

The great payer of attention read the receipt three times before he figured out what worried him. The bill was for "2 pr wmns pnts and 2 brs."

So now I knew what she was wearing when she left: the other set. She was wearing sexy underwear. Her mother would have been the one to pry in a daughter's underclothes, and she'd been too sick. Her father would be as frightened of poking as I was. Though, finally, I hadn't been. Had I? Good of me to find the courage to try to smell her body on her bed, to finger her little sexy disguise.

But maybe she hadn't *been* disguised. Maybe the real kid was the one in dramatic lingerie. Why would a child wear clothes like that? Who'd get to see them? I listed on my fingers. One, the girlfriend she has the secret with, and they giggle and they make believe. Two, herself, but maybe not worth it for the money. Three, the boy who takes her clothes off. I found myself moving slowly in a circle in the room, the underpants rolled in my fist.

The door moved, and I barked, "Wait!"

The door closed. I kept circling. She was wearing the other set of matching panties and brassiere because she was going to meet the boy, or go someplace with the boy, and he was going to take her clothing off and see what she wore for him.

Or man, I thought.

I thought of Rosalie Piri.

A man like me, I thought. I was going to wipe at the sweat on my face with her panties, when I stopped myself. I put the clothes back in the package inside the brown paper bag, and I replaced it in the drawer.

"Sorry," I whispered.

I stopped and looked at the books again, running my finger from poetry to the thing about the caged bird and on through her school-books. I was on my knees, holding on to the edge of the bookshelf.

I said, "Sorry."

Then I stood. It took me a long time. I tried to make the room look like I hadn't been there. The cops might as well not have been. They'd assumed, as I had, that she had run away or been taken and that no clues were going to help. Probably, I thought, they were right. Unless what they wanted was to find the guy and kill him or break his body up. I thought I might be close to wanting that. I thought I might be close to doing it.

When I came into the living room, the reverend said, "She's asleep."

"Would you say good-bye for me, please?"

He looked as pleasant as he had when he was making his terrible jokes. But he said, "I really can't. I can't bring myself to use that word with her."

"Would you tell her, then, I sent my best?"

"You're very decent to us," he said.

I could only think to thank him, and I did.

———

I had bought a small bag of kibble for the dog, and Rosalie put out water for him in a thick white bowl. He wagged as he ate to show he knew he was with company. I went outside with him and he checked out her little yard, then climbed through sparse hedges into the neighboring yard to pee and snoop. When we went back inside, Rosalie had changed into her terrible outfit of boxer shorts and flannel shirt. She was wearing ankle-high fleece-lined soft leather cabin boots, and I admired the hard muscle in her calves.

"I feel you looking at my legs," she said from the stove, parting them.

I went over to her and was compelled to reach down and stroke her inside the back of the shorts. I felt her harden the muscle and then relax it. The way she trusted me with who she was when she relaxed it was as exciting to me as the skin I stroked.

"Do you want pubic hair or anything with your scrambled eggs?"

"Everything," I said.

"Good. That was the right answer." She shut the burner off and turned from the stove to stick her hand out. Her eyes were closed. I took her hand and shut my eyes to join her, and we led each other to the bedroom. "Stay," she called to the dog, "if you don't mind."

I loved the darkness, and I loved the feel of her skin. I kept denying that we made my ribs hurt, or my fingers burn, and we made love with her riding me, her hands, at the end, in my hair and her body on top of me, bandages and ribs and all. It hadn't taken long, because I was filled with urgency and hungry for as much sensation of her, inside and out, as I could have. It occurred to me to ask if we should do it differently to be better for her, but I was led to be quiet by the way she pulled the covers up and rolled to the side of the healthy ribs, wrapping her legs around my left thigh, rubbing her toes on my right calf. I heard the dog sigh and lie against her bedroom door.

I came out of the sleep because I'd heard a question, but not its words.

"Hmm?"

"The little girl."

I thought of Professor Rosalie Piri, her small body under and around my own, which was big and ugly and busted.

I made more noises and touched her tight skin where I could.

"Tell me what you saw in Janice's room," she said.

"Stuff."

"Cops know how to brief one another," she said. "Come on."

I sighed. I wanted to sleep beneath her and above her and smell her breath and kiss her stomach and make love again.

"Brief me," she said.

I recited the room. I told her about the sexy underwear and the coronet and the books and Heisenberg and Mrs. Tanner.

"So all we really know," I said, "is she went voluntarily."

"So we have to backtrack. Boyfriends, teammates, the girls she might have confided in."

"No, the state police are good at that. They'll be doing that anyway. They always look for boyfriends. So we don't have anything much, except it wasn't, probably, a stranger who killed her."

"You should always try and get killed by a friend."

"I'm your friend."

"And you wouldn't hurt me. You adore me, Jack."

"I do?"

"Tell me how much you adore me or I'll crush your balls."

"Your hand's too small."

"I warned you." But her hand on me was gentle and then very exciting.

"Oh dear," I said.

"I warned you," she said, moving on me. And then she said, "You don't have to love me. It's all right if you can barely tolerate me."

"I *can* barely tolerate you," I said.

"I can stand you, too. About this much. About this far. Well, no. Maybe, oh my, maybe we can—*this* far. Yes, I can stand you this far."

oracle

SCUTTLING IN Janice Tanner's room hadn't done my ribs any good, nor my fingers. Neither had scuttling under Rosalie Piri. Because it felt too good with her. Because it all led to seeing Fanny's face. Fanny when our baby died. Fanny feeling old because Rosalie wasn't. Fanny needing to lift me and shake me, Jesus Christ, and get me well. Fanny moving out to make me move.

I said to the dog, "Sometimes they take these things and climb up into the upper floors on college campuses and they take out targets of opportunity." I made sure the safety was on and then I put it in the pocket of my coat. The problem was its front sight, which was too high for easy working in and out of coat pockets. A belly gun is supposed to clear for action without getting caught on clothing or equipment. That, and a size that makes for hiding it, are its excuses for existing. Otherwise, nobody needs a .32-caliber piece. And this one was too broad and too heavy. It was guaranteed to do nothing much for anyone unless you were ten or twelve yards, at most, from your target, and you put a cluster into him—all, or most, of the cylinder. In the service, I had refused to carry the standard issue to the military police for close-in combat. I'd taken the idea from pilots

who wouldn't carry their standard-issue .38 in its shoulder holster.
Like them, I lugged the World War I .45-caliber Colt with its horren-
dous kick that made for buck fever and that tended to intimidate
more people than it wounded. You looked into its bore, and you
obeyed. I didn't know what the .32 would do if I fired it in anger,
because I'd never wanted to. Now I did.

I fed the dog and let him out to run a while. I filled his plastic
jug and stuck a bottle of aspirin in my other coat pocket. I swallowed
a couple of the remaining codeine jobs to convince my ribs I'd enjoy
bending myself behind the wheel. In the refrigerator I saw margarine
and peanut butter I could spread on toast, but I couldn't imagine
who would eat it beside the dog. I swallowed a little orange juice
from the carton. The carton flap was pulpy and most of the juice was
gone. "Bachelor kitchen," I said, making a face, but I didn't think me
funny and I didn't reply.

I drove to work slowly, and I squinted into a white sky. The sun
was strong behind it. My eyes felt sore from not enough sleep, and I
thought of lying someplace with my hands on them to keep the sun
out. Which reminded me, of course, of Rosalie, and how she'd
shielded or shut her eyes like a child and how, later on, I had shielded
my eyes like a grown-up under the covers with a child.

And Fanny's sad face that had been so easy once, and not so
breakable-looking.

"It's because I'm looking into the goddamned sun," I told the dog.

I listened to sheriff's deputies talking about road wrecks and
house fires. It was a way of not listening to me. I knew a local man
with a scanner who would sit in his chair at night and drink beer and
listen to catastrophes. He never went to bed unhappy, he said, because he was alive to do it and somebody else, between seven and
ten, would have died in a stupid way while he sat in his chair.

The branches were thickening a little, just as Fanny would have
pointed out. I saw the tops of grasses in the fields off our road. They
were scoured by driving winds after the storms, and then the winds
polished them. At dusk or dawn, they gleamed. As spring came on,
as no new snow was deposited and as the winds diminished, the tops

of the fields grew coarse and started melting down. It seemed a likelihood, I was ready to admit, that winter *might* be ending. But we had suffered snowfalls in April with some frequency, and I could remember May snow that took saplings over into twisted shapes that looked all spring and summer like suffering. So, yes, it was possible we'd have some spring. But I was ready for winter to go on.

At the Blue Bird, where I had my thermos filled and bought some doughnuts for the dog, I saw Archie Halpern and I waved. I didn't go over because I felt like one of those patches of grass-topped swamp ground you intend to step on and instead you step into. I was brimming with it and trying not to let it show. I figured if I sat with him for half a sip of Verna's sour coffee, I'd be shouting into his shoulder and crying out loud. Just thinking of it made me turn away from him. He knew. He knew something was up. He just let his eyebrows go up and come down the next time I looked over.

I read every piece of campus mail, and I signed off on everything I could—rosters for night watch, extra-duty rosters, an agreement with the student rape-prevention service that escorted girls to and from the library at night. The head of the political science department must have hand-delivered the announcement that the Vice President of the United States of America would not be appearing on campus because of unalterable schedule conflicts. "For more information," his memo said, "consult Head Librarian Horstmuller." I hadn't ever much liked him because of his schedule. He was one of those professors who came to work at nine and left at five, like a man who had a job. That kind of trying to act like a businessman annoyed me, since I figured this guy, like most of the others, couldn't balance his own checkbook. Of course, neither could I. Anyway, I thought Ms. Horstmuller had some balls, even if I didn't agree with her holding back the information, so I didn't appreciate the chairman's tone. What a pity for him, I thought.

Then, letting the dog have one more run before we settled in to cruise, I warmed up the Jeep. The temperature was rising, but the moisture in the air was, too, and my elbows and knees reacted to it. I didn't even want to think about my ribs, and I wondered if they were

going to have to put a screw into the little finger of my right hand. I
kept thinking I could feel the pieces of bone shift and grate against
one another. I moaned and hissed a bit when I got into the car. This
made the dog very pleased and he sat up prettily to pose for the
students and teachers we passed.

"She had to have a diary," Rosalie had said. "They sometimes stop
after a while, but most of them at least begin. Girls that age keep
diaries." Rosalie had also said, "I wouldn't be surprised to hear her
parents had found it and suppressed it. They'd hate her sad little
cries of ecstasy about the tenderness of whoever was committing
statutory rape with her."

"You're not bad in the ecstasy department," I had told her.

"Those aren't little cries, Jack. You made me *come*. And this is
not rape. Is it?"

I thought again of Janice and I pictured the cheap, sexy underwear. I thought of Fanny's sturdy, reliable underpants and bras. It had
been a very long time since I had seen them except in the washer or
dryer. It felt like a very long time since I'd seen *her*. And Rosalie: I
thought of her in the oversized boxer shorts. I thought of her naked
with me.

I deserved to live alone with my dog, I thought. I lived with a dog.
I rode patrol with a dog. That was who I talked to. Except when I was
two-timing Fanny.

Down at the bottom of the campus, on its back end, where the
street ran parallel to the main street of town but was separated from
it by the width of the college, I saw the black Trans Am with its
spoiler and scoop. I stopped and backed up so I had a little cover
from some old maples. It seemed to me I saw Everett Stark, the black
kid who was tired of white folks and cows. It seemed to me he leaned
into the car, then straightened, looked around, and then leaned in
again.

I was not about to let him do that to himself. I hit the accelerator
hard, and of course I skidded out as I took off. I got control, pretty
much, and the slight swerve I stopped with added to the look of law
enforcement on the move. I told the dog to stay and I was out and
walking, and hurting pretty much, before either of them might have

expected me. My Jeep was in front of the Trans Am, so he would have to back up to get away. I walked around behind his car, and I stood there.

I had not realized that I planned to do that. I hadn't understood that what I was going to do was plant my legs, aim the pistol at the back window, and tell Everett to walk around and stand beside me.

"William Franklin," I said as Everett came over, "stand outside the car. Shut the door. Place your hands on the roof."

Franklin came out slowly. I said to Everett, "You stand to my right, behind me, and you stay there. And shame on you, Everett."

"On the roof," I told Franklin. I walked a wide circle so I could come in directly behind him. That way, he couldn't tell whether I had the gun in my pocket, which I did, or aimed at him. I reached for his left hand—I remembered him as a lefty—and I took hold of his little finger. You can make a man the size of a left tackle walk on his tiptoes and sing falsetto with a grip on that finger. I kept hold of him and patted him down. He had a lot of cash, which I threw on the snow behind us, and I found the plastic envelopes I'd expected to. I also found brown pharmaceutical vials.

"Everett, what in hell are you doing with your life?"

Franklin said, "Since when do you guys go armed?"

Everett said, "It was a little speed. Very mild stuff. Ask him. I got to study more. I got to stay up late. I keep falling *asleep*."

"You work a job, right? You go to classes all day, you work in the cafeteria, of *course* you fall asleep. That's what you need."

"I can't afford to sleep," he said. "I need to study harder."

"I know where *that* is," I said. "But you can't buy medicine from Dr. Doom out of Staten Island, New York, over here. How do you know what goes in those little items he sells you? You lie down with dogs like this, Everett, you get up with only fleas, you're lucky. This guy gives you rabies and worms and all kinds of shit. I want you away from him. You hear me?"

Franklin said, "This is a fuckin' restraint of *trade,* Ev."

I tightened a little on the finger, and he was on his knees, his head sinking.

"It'll break, William. You know it."

"Okay," he said.

"Okay what?"

"Okay whatever you *want*."

I let up enough for him to raise his head.

"Go away, Everett. All right?"

"Jack, you're a little, like, *enthusiastic*, you know?"

"Sign of a craftsman, Everett. I take a tremendous amount of pride in my work." I tightened on the finger a little and Franklin made noises. "See you," I told Everett.

When I saw him make progress up the campus walk, I let go of Franklin's finger and I told him, "Sit in the back of your car." I worked the gun out of my left-hand pocket while he got in, shaking the hand I'd been working on. I got in, too, and I was pleased to note I made no sounds that could be mistaken for the lamentations of a man with broken ribs. He was looking at the gun.

"You're fucking crazy," he said.

"I figure one of these, two of these, and you bleed to death fast. Yes? Two, I think. I don't want to go for the head shot on account of that means broken glass, blood and brains all over it, and they find you sooner. This way, you just go over and shake your legs a lot because of the pains in your intestines and your spongy little inner organs, and then you're dead. I really would love to get rid of you."

"Three guys beat the shit out of you—"

"Give yourself credit, William. Four. Don't I remember a couple of field goals you kicked before you guys called it a night?"

"And you figure—what? You're Superman?"

"You couldn't begin to imagine what I'm figuring, son. It begins with you, though. Let's see. You kicked me in the ribs as hard as you could. Why don't I put two of these in the same place on you? You ready?"

His handsome white bullyboy's face was sweaty. That was a good sign. He swallowed a lot, and that was a good sign. His feet were pointed toward me, not at the door to his right, and that was another good sign—he wasn't about to push off and come at me. And I was pretty certain he believed me. I believed me, too. I was going to do it.

That's part of it, when you take someone on. You have to make yourself believe you're ready to do it. So we were believers in there, in the smell of his cigarettes and lotion, the air freshener that hung from his rearview mirror stanchion next to his cross. Soon, I was going to smell his sweat, and then maybe the gas he'd begin to leak or even the filling of his pants.

I said, "Ready?"

"Tell me what to do, I'll do it."

"Go away."

"I know how to do that."

"What about your heavy friends?"

"I have to tell them you ran me."

"And?"

"I gotta say it. Don't—I'm just telling you what I think."

"Speak your little heart, William."

"I think they'll try and take you down."

"Except now you're not so sure they can. You said *try.*"

"I'm not so sure."

"So tell them that."

"Okay. Right. I will."

"Don't come here anymore."

I cocked it. I let the barrel wander up in the direction of his ribs. I brought it down and tapped his knee. He jumped.

"I promise. I swear it."

"Cross your heart, William."

"Cross my heart."

I was beginning to make myself sick. I backed out, and this time he heard me answer to my ribs. That seemed to impress him more. He shook his head as he crawled out and then got in front behind the wheel.

"You really must love this place," he said. "All the shit you put up with for a bunch of fuckin' preppies."

"I'm supposed to take care of them," I said.

"Okay," he said. "Well, you did that, all right. I'm gone. You got it straight up and down. I'm gone."

He backed up, made a K-turn in the little street, and rumbled toward the corner. I let the hammer down, put the safety on, and stuck the pistol in my pocket. When I looked up, across the street, a man with white hair and glasses was looking through his front window at me. When he saw me focus on him, he started, then stepped behind the curtain. I saw him peeking out when I turned the Jeep around and went back up the hill. He would talk to someone. I would probably lose my job.

But I can always find work in a nightmare, I thought of telling the dog. I didn't. I was sick of gestures.

I was also scared. I had forgotten what the weight of the .32 made me remember—the kind of power a weapon concentrates at the end of your arm. You move it, and you're Mrs. Tanner's heroic Lord. You make decisions. Let this person's chest be opened. Let there be bone fragments in the air. Let his chest breathe, sucking for air through the maroon spittle on his sternum. The fear on his face begins at the end of your arm with the gun's dead heaviness, and you're scared, too. I'd even liked the fear. I had enjoyed it more than I should have. His fear, my fear, the stink of our dry mouths in the back of his car, even the pain in my side and my heartbeat in my fingers, which brushed against the blue-black butt of the pistol. Where I'd gotten to was the cellar of the haunted house, and what was haunting it was me.

———

Rosalie Piri drove her little tan clunker onto campus too fast. We had a twenty-mile-an-hour limit, and the security people were supposed to enforce it. I didn't think that writing her a citation would be useful to our further friendship, so I followed her up the steep, slithery, narrow college road, staring from the greater height of the truck down into her car. I thought she knew it was me, but I couldn't find her eyes in the mirror. She began to slide in the melting, slushy ice and packed snow where the road bent around the administration building. She must have gunned it then, because her rear tires spun and the rear end of her car slid left. I dropped back to avoid her as she went into a backward-turning skid, but you can't predict a skid, and I figured wrong. She had turned directly around, and she came down into the front of the Jeep. I let us go, not working the brakes, but getting into the clutch and downshifting, then working it into four-wheel drive. I hit the lights and pounded the horn to try to warn anyone behind me. When we slowed a little, I began my tap dance on the brakes, and I worked us into an angle against the softening snowbank, and we stopped. There was Rosalie, poised above me on the incline of the road, half of her left wing in snow, her car apparently pinned beneath the truck at the grillwork, and her eyes very large, her mouth in the wonderful dirty grin.

I walked over to her car a little slowly. The impact hadn't been bad, but enough for the rib cage.

I said, when she leaned over to roll down the passenger-side window, "You're in trouble with the law, little lady."

"Are you going to take matters in hand, Officer?"

I said, "Professor, sweetheart, you go too fast for the surface conditions and the shittiness of your vehicle."

"I called, but I couldn't reach you anyplace," she said. "I had a terrible idea. I mean, it's terrible, but it's also maybe right. It's about a book."

"A book?"

"And Janice Tanner. I think I could maybe guess who did it. Even though it sounds stupid."

"That's what I thought. About my idea."

She said, "It's time to debrief again. We'd better get into bed and talk."

I stepped back, looked at traffic, and said, "If you put it in reverse and just barely touch the accelerator, I might be able to push you back up. Then you can park it at the ad building, and I'll drive you up to class. If you would like me to."

She said, "Jack, did anyone ever accuse you of standing around and watching them and looking a lot like you could drive them anyplace you wanted to?"

Two teachers drove past, honking and waving. One was my English professor. They came to a sloppy stop and waited.

Rosalie said, "Shit. I guess I have to go with them."

"I'll catch you later on."

"Please do," she said. She got out of her car and hauled her briefcase up to her rescuers.

A minute later, behind the wheel, I made a few noises about how my chest felt when I breathed or moved. I rubbed my face and nudged the fingers and made the sounds again. I'd been talking to the dispatcher about a wrecker for Rosalie's car, and she said, "Say again, Jack? Over."

"Pissing and moaning is all. Over."

I thought of my professor, who would probably call her Rosie, and maybe tell her what kind of killer I'd been for the Phoenix Project, or how I was this wonderfully naïve character, this rough country fellow, who came to class with essays about corpse rape and a little duck who didn't have any feathers to protect him when the cold winds blew—not an uninteresting campus cop.

I drove north after work, to a little country road about half a dozen miles outside town, where I swung west, then south and west, on a road they kept plowed. I suspected someone on the town's road crews lived there, among the eight houses I counted, and that was why they cleared it. I stuck the Ford as close to the verge as I could get without stranding myself, and I let the dog go out onto the frozen marshy edge of the big lake. Dead reeds shook in the warming winds and I heard game birds under scraggly cover begin to squawk as the dog approached, then go silent when he was on them. His tail went up and he stuck his chest out, demonstrating his savage alertness. He couldn't see too far past his muzzle, and whatever he smelled he didn't recognize, but we waved his brushy tale in those short, choppy strokes reserved by dogs for showing humans that they're tracking.

I went out after him, not caring about the birds, just wanting the emptiness and the silence. The road was a good distance from the far side of the lake and no one came past where I was parked. I worked at letting my shoulders collapse under their own weight from where

they'd bunched around my stiff neck. I was contemplating the last of
the pain pills. I was contemplating Fanny and Janice Tanner, Rosalie,
and the gun that was in my coat pocket. The dog had his face into
slush and was snorting it away. I knew not to go as far out as he was,
and I walked parallel to the shore, hearing the ice crack under my
feet. There was a smell of something soft—I didn't know what, but it
had to do with spring. Either something was rising up from under
the ice and snow and black water or something was spilling off the
trees and plants. It was possible that spring would come. It might. I
didn't know. Mrs. Tanner was going to die, though. She wouldn't see
Janice. I knew that. I was certain she was dead. I wondered if one of
them really had a diary she'd written.

Why not? I might have done the same if Hannah had become a
girl and an almost-adolescent and sneaked away to crawl around on
top of some naked man with her hands and mouth working.

You're thinking of Rosalie, I thought.

But of course I knew that. I had known it. That was what had
tipped me off. The little girlness of it. That was what he had loved.
That was what had frightened me about some of my pleasure with
Rosalie. I wondered what had finally scared him.

Sergeant Bird had questioned and dismissed a man in Vestal,
New York, who had been accused of molesting a child. He had sworn
at me for pestering him, and then he had read me a summary of the
state detective bureau's file survey: zero suspects placed on the scene.
We had congratulated each other on our fine police work. And I
thought that if Mrs. Tanner was going to die and not see a live child,
she could possibly see the person who had killed her, if I was right. I
had not told Sergeant Bird about the guess I was arriving at. I had
barely told myself.

The worst I could be was wrong, I thought.

Who cares that terribly much if I take out the ugly dark handgun
and put a few rounds in him and then they say I'm wrong?

The dog came back with a bright yellow wrapper from a fast-food
sandwich. His tail swung slowly back and forth to signal not hunting
but the hunter's return with his prey.

"You're brilliant," I told him.

He agreed.

"Drop it for me."

He deposited the wrapper on the softening ice, but he kept an eye on it. When I picked it up, he watched as I put it into my coat. I shoved it in with the pistol. I didn't care. I wouldn't need to draw the piece with any speed or fire it with accuracy. I was simply going to brandish it, as they say. I was going to wave it in somebody's face until I was satisfied. Or maybe I'd just kill someone.

———

I expected to find her in a coma, but she was sitting up in a rocking chair in her kitchen. I'm not what you'd call a man of taste. I like light. I like to feel warm from colors. I don't like living the way someone in a cubicle decided I ought to. But I don't know much more. Whatever I learned about the way the larger, man-made pieces of the world fit with one another, I learned from Fanny.

Still, when I was in the Tanners' house again, I wondered why you wouldn't just shoot yourself or hang yourself or drive yourself into a deep lake if you worked from your adolescence on to surround yourself with what I saw. There were crocheted armrests on the rockers in the kitchen, near the stove. They were made of the kind of tan, white, gold, and black wool you can buy for not very much in the little intentionally homespun general stores you find in small upstate towns. There were braided rugs you could buy from the smaller catalogs printed on coarser paper. Imitation-brass fire tools stood near their heavy iron woodstove in a fake wrought-iron stand. Their pottery mugs did not discuss Christ, salvation, or sin, but they did sport cheerful red-white-and-blue Pennsylvania Dutch designs.

Reverend Tanner was feeding her oatmeal. She was frowning at him and flapping her hands. When she saw me, a smile changed her face, and then—like Rosalie and then like me—she covered her face with her hands the way kids do.

"You see?" she said to her husband. "You see what you've done? Jack might as well have caught me in a high chair."

The reverend said to me, "I thought she might eat if I did it this way."

"It isn't the dying," she said. "It's the terrible cooking."

"I can fry French toast," I said. "I can make stew. Corn chowder. Some kind of a roast. I'd be pleased to try. Vegetable soup? My wife taught me how to make soup."

Her husband nodded encouragement to her. She closed her eyes and shook her head.

"And don't talk that dying nonsense," he said.

She didn't bother to answer, and he didn't bother to say any more. He put down the crockery bowl.

"How about a drink?" I said. "How about a shot of whiskey?"

"We don't drink," he said. "We never drank."

She whispered, "Maybe we should have."

I didn't know if she heard him talking about his own death in hers. I noticed when he stood that his belly was soft and bulging a little. His thin-looking blue shirt and feed-store dark blue gabardine pants were hard-folded, as if he'd worn them for many weeks. There were stains on his shirt and the lap of his trousers. Before he carried the bowl and long-handled iced-tea spoon to the sink, he looked around, his eyes big behind his glasses, and I thought he was trying to find where he was, or where the sink was, or the table she sat at. The shape and drift of the stains on his clothes reminded me of Randy Strodemaster's bathrobe. The reverend was getting ready to be alone. No. He wasn't setting himself or preparing his mind. It just was coming. It was like a storm. He knew it was almost there.

Mrs. Tanner was wearing boot socks and pajama bottoms and a sweater under the blanket that was wrapped around her shoulders. It was a bright gold blanket, and I knew it would feel soft and almost damp, the way those machine-made fabrics felt. She seemed a lot stronger than yesterday, weaker than days before. Her almost-orange skin, with something darker underneath its soft top layer, looked tight.

And like someone trying to make sure she would haunt me later on, months later and years later on, she looked at me with her tired eyes with their brown-gray semicircles underneath and she said, "You look terrible, Jack. What hurts so much? What *did* you do to your fingers?"

"The fingers are fine," I said, sitting across the table from her. The room was very hot, but I kept my coat on. I guess I was trying to join her in some of it. "There was what you would call a fracas. Law enforcement waded in and busted up their fingers."

She shaped a little bit of what might have gone on to be a smile but didn't.

"I hope you didn't hurt any of the students."

I shook my head. "I take care of them," I said.

"Yes, of course you do. You must, apparently."

"Must?"

"I'm being a soothsayer. It used to be my role. He would comfort them, and I would be an oracle of certainties. You need that kind of teamwork in the country-pastor profession. I hope you feel all right."

"I hope *you* do."

She put her wide hand, which was so light, out on the table. If there had been a newspaper, I thought, I could have read it through the back of her hand. The fingers were relaxed, almost curled. I took hold of it. I let my hand lie under hers. It weighed so little, my broken fingers felt almost nothing. I would have held her up if I could. I would have breathed for her.

Find her daughter, I told myself. That's what she wants.

When I let my breath out, it sounded shaky even to me.

Her husband sat down. He put tea in shallow cups on saucers in front of each of us. He held the edge of the table.

He said with a hardness, "What." It wasn't really a question.

Mrs. Tanner said, "He knows something. Jack? You know something."

I got the next breath in, and then I got it out.

"Maybe," I said. "Possibly. I don't know. Possibly. Can I ask you something?"

Nobody talked.

"Did she wear fancy underwear? Grown-up perfume? Did she read about love affairs in the supermarket newspapers? Did she watch about them on TV? Did her girlfriends talk about it? Sex? Love affairs? Sexy men—you know, movie stars, anchormen, sports people."

"Oh," the reverend said. He sat back. He lifted his teacup by the tiny handle and then he put it down. "Well, Jack! In my experience, all girls of that age—"

"Nobody ever talked about her acting like all girls before." I added "Sir," figuring it would make me seem more respectful and the questions less disrespectful. "You see what I mean? I never heard she was an average girl before."

"Was," Mrs. Tanner repeated.

"Damn," I said. "Excuse me."

"Damn," she said. I don't think she meant to be funny or comforting.

"She's the perfect all-around kid," I said. "She plays the coronet, she serves the underprivileged, she teaches Sunday school, and she's a friend to all her neighbors. That's unusual. Well, nobody added anything about her being a normal fourteen-year-old girl."

"No," her mother said.

"I don't think of her as normal," her father said. "She's better than normal."

"Normal isn't bad," her mother said.

"No," he answered. "Not at all."

"No," she said.

"It's just she's a little . . . well, better, I guess you'd have to say. I'd have to say, anyway."

That routine performed, they sat and waited for me to talk. I thought of the dog in the car, the ride home, the dark house. I suppose I sighed. I leaned away from the feeling in my right side. I thought of what might be opening up in there.

"I'll be by tomorrow," I said. "Maybe I'm getting at something. I haven't got there yet. But I'm working. I'll come by tomorrow." I tried to be smiling when I said to her, "You plan on being home?"

"Above ground," she said.

Her husband said, "My God."

She said, "And there isn't anything to tell us tonight? There is, Jack. I feel it. I'm sure of it. Why? I mean—you know very well what I mean. Please tell us now?"

"Let me get there," I said. "I have to get *there*."

Her hand had stayed with mine. I'd felt it start beating, moving inside, when she thought I was going to tell her. I'd felt it slow after she knew I wouldn't. Now she moved it so I'd let her go.

"You be here," she said.

"You be here, too," I told her. I was trying to think of a way to apologize for being so bad at all of this. It seemed to me I could start here, with Janice's mother, and go on all night with anyone who cared to show up.

I backed us slowly out of their drive, and I went to Strodemaster's. His house was lighted up. He was in his kitchen, moving slowly but regularly. When I opened his storm door and stuck my head in, I heard a loud hissing and I smelled onions and peppers. The cooking odors covered the stink of rottenness I'd expected. Over the sizzling of what was cooking in a smoky wide black skillet, I heard music. In his loosely tied flapping blue bathrobe with its pattern of toothpaste stains and food smears, he was moving in place at the stove. He seemed to be slicing a long sausage to the rhythm of the music. When I closed the door, I slammed it.

He jumped. He dropped a bright broad knife. When he saw me, he did a big motion with his shoulders to show me his relief. He held up a finger, then went to the radio on top of his refrigerator.

"Gene Harris," he said, over noises of frying, which he didn't turn down. "You know his stuff?"

"I don't know much music," I said.

"Piano," he said. "Beautiful jazz piano. And he's from *Idaho*. Who'd expect it? You know? From someone in Idaho?"

I didn't care. I said, "Randy, can I talk to you?"

"Town-to-gown? Town-to-town? Or beer-to-beer?" His big eyeglasses were smeared. I saw he was wearing corduroy pants under the bathrobe, and a white T-shirt. Nothing looked like his food had missed it. The chalkboard had all kinds of fine wobbly lines on it. I thought it was a very complicated map. There were darker spots on it that looked slammed into place with the chalk. He finally turned the light off under the onions and peppers. He got us very expensive San Francisco beer from the refrigerator. He expected us townies to drink it from the bottle, so I sipped. I hadn't tasted it before. It was wonderful, almost sour but not quite, and it got into my thirst. It was the first time any appetite of mine for anything except a short, thin woman felt satisfied.

He was watching me. "*Pas mal*, huh?"

"Excuse me?"

"French. Gown stuff. Forgive me. I meant, not too bad."

"I don't speak French," I said.

"No problem," he said. He leaned back in his chair and he pulled another bottle out of the fridge. He had an opener at the table. "These things don't have the little cutesy screw-off tops. You want a beer, you can open the mothers the old-fashioned way."

"It tastes wonderful," I said. I unzipped my coat, and when it swung behind me, it clanked.

"You sound loaded for bear," he said.

"That's me," I said.

"So how're you feeling, Jack? You got kicked to shit, halfway. You feel a little better?"

"I feel a little better," I said. "Except I just came here from the Tanners'. Man."

"Terrible," he said. "I'm over there a couple of times a day. Terrible."

"I didn't give them the news they wanted," I said.

He sat forward, pushed his glasses up, probably smearing them a little more. The way he looked at me, I thought I understood why his students liked him. They probably didn't buy half of his absent-minded professor act, or the local guy of good heart number. But when he listened to you, he really listened. Someone could do a lot worse than listen like that, I thought with what I would have called professional admiration. His big, strong face was set, and his bright eyes were wide and locked. His hands, I saw, were clasped at the edge of the table. He looked like a giant joke about a good boy in school.

"Then what kind of news, Jack?"

I shook my head. "Gas. Wind. Noises."

He nodded. "I know what you mean," he said.

"I think you came up with the wrong man, Randy. You should have looked for a real detective. Or advertised, I don't know, in *Soldier of Fortune* or someplace. You know? A real damned cop. All I do, I wander around, I get into trouble, I make people sad, and I bring that woman nothing."

He leaned in, shaking his head. His loud, hard voice got softer. "You're the man," he said. "I knew you. You were the guy I wanted from the beginning." He leaned back. "Jack, think of it this way. They have all those professional cops. They're already working on it. I wanted a man with brains who knows the community, who has a *heart*."

"You're a gent to say it."

"Really," he said.

"No lie?"

He said, "Come on, Jack. For chrissakes."

I sipped some more beer. I knew it cost about seven dollars a six-pack in the market, when you could find it. I thought I might buy some one day if there was something to celebrate.

Name it, I thought.

"Well," I said, "you got me, I'm afraid. I didn't help Janice, and I didn't help her parents, and I surely didn't help you."

He watched me again, all eyes and brain.

He said, "I'm a man whose family left early in the morning while I was at school. My wife and my son and my daughter. In the car I'm still paying off in installments. One of those big Buick station wagons nobody needs unless they have to run errands before the country club dance. You know the kind of shit I mean? I know about screwing up so they never forgive you. I'm saying never. They never will."

I wanted him to tell me what he'd done. We can sit here, I thought, and drink designer beer and tell each other how much of other people we broke.

He said, "So I know about fucking up, I'm saying. You didn't."

I said, "Randy, I couldn't have done less if you went from town to town and took a collection up and *paid* me to fuck it up."

"You want another beer, guy?"

"I have to feed the dog."

"Bring him in," he said. "We'll all three of us have some sausage and peppers and beer. Your dog drink beer?"

"Not this kind, that's for sure." I had to be in the car, driving home with windows open for me and the dog. I had to feel cool. My armpits and crotch felt clammy, and the ribs underneath the bandages were just broken in two and the parts bumping into each other, it felt like. I'd had enough. I'd done enough. And none of it was any use.

Strodemaster said, "You feel all right, Jack? You're pale as hell."

"Gotta sleep, Randy."

"Want to sleep here? I meant it about staying for dinner."

"You take good care of your detectives," I said. "Thank you. No. Gotta get home."

"You want a ride? You look peaked. You look like about a yard of shit in a pickup, Jack."

"Considering how I feel, that's a compliment."

He got up when I did, but he did it more smoothly. My right side felt like it moved in several sections. I leaned on the chair, then pushed myself off.

He told me, "You stay in touch, pal."

I swore to him I would, so he let my shoulders go and I worked my way down off the porch. It was a long trip to the car. It was a long time getting my legs under the wheel and the rest of me straight up, more or less. I couldn't tell you now whether I drove home or the dog did.

———

I don't remember a lot of the dream. It had to do with pieces of girl. I knew in the dream they were all over the floor and I had to keep from stepping on them. I ran down the stairs; I almost jumped them, getting away from the crudely cut wet bits that made the noise of soaked washcloths hitting a floor when I couldn't help stepping on them. They were the consistency of old, soft fruit. I was on my way down when the pain in my knees and then ribs woke me up. I was on the floor beside the bed in our bedroom, and I knew I was awake, because the dog thought we were playing a game. He had his face in mine and he was nipping gently to show me he understood the rules.

It took me a while to stand. I settled for sponging at myself from a basin of soapy lukewarm water. I did brush my teeth, and not in the same water. I don't remember what clothes I put on. It was dark and it was five in the morning, almost. When I was dressed, I let the dog out and then in and fed him. I figured on breakfast at the Blue Bird, coffee at least, so I filled his water jug and told him he could come in the car. Outside, he did his circling around himself, then got to the car ahead of me in case I needed reminding.

We were in town before quarter to six. I drove to the hospital, told him to stay, and went in. They were beginning to make noises in the hall outside the ER, just in case the patients in the adult ward were sleeping. In the emergency room, a woman who was not Virginia sat at the desk to the left of the door, typing at a word processor. In the little rooms down the small corridor from her, just off where they stopped the bleeding or set the bone, I heard the scrape of a chair against the linoleum floor. The bright lights bouncing their glare off aluminum equipment hurt my eyes the way the oncoming lights of a couple of trucks and some cars on Route 8 had hurt them. I wondered if I'd hit my head against the floor or bureau while running the stairway out of my dream.

The woman at the desk said, "Yes," which sounded like No. I pointed past her and nodded, the way I would if I agreed with her. She made some wait-a-minute sounds, but I was past her and into the office I thought I'd heard her in.

I was right. She was sitting on a high table with paper stretched out from a roller at the top that covered it. Her face was down; her arms were holding the edge of the table at either side of her legs. She didn't swing them. They hung straight down from the knee. I thought she was asleep sitting up.

I said, "Fanny."

She jumped or winced, and she knew it was me by the time her face was level. Her eyes looked awful.

She said, "Since when don't you shave?"

I asked if she could get away a little early. "Maybe we could have some breakfast at the Blue Bird," I said.

She said, "Why?" She looked at my face and I guess she saw me looking at hers. I didn't know how to walk closer to her. I wanted to. I hoped she would see that along with whatever else she was seeing. "Is something wrong? I mean—something else?"

I said, "Did any more posters go up that you noticed? Did you hear anything from any cops coming in about more girls missing?"

She shook her head.

"It isn't a serial thing, I think. Mass killings or just a girl for every phase of the moon. I think it's a guy—I'm talking about Janice Tanner —I think it's a guy who snapped one time. The others—Christ, I don't know. I don't know. It isn't fair. You're a small person, a little girl person, and you go outside of your house but where it's supposed to be safe. It's *supposed* to be safe! And people come and they hunt you. They pull up next to you in a car and the back door opens and your nose is peeling off and they're fucking you to death or making soup from your brains. It isn't *fair*. Christ. Listen to it, huh? I don't —I got involved here a little, I think. I shouldn't have done it, but they knew I would. I was a natural to get into this up over my head and drown inside of it."

She looked the way you do when someone talks to you in a foreign language but for a minute you thought it was English and you couldn't figure out why you didn't understand.

She said, "You're crazy, Jack. I think you're going crazy with this. Or us. Or the combination. Jack, what was that about you shouldn't have done it? What were you telling me?"

"Shouldn't have—is that something I told you?"

"Just now."

"Shouldn't . . . Oh. *Oh*. Shouldn't have taken the job. Shouldn't have let them talk me into, I don't know, investigating, I guess you'd say. The Tanner girl. Janice Tanner? I didn't need that, did I? Of course, Archie would say I did."

Her head dropped. Then she got her chin level again. She shook her head very slowly. "I would say you didn't."

"I would, too, right now. It's just, it didn't seem fair. I couldn't figure out why somebody couldn't look after these kids a little. I know. It isn't fair. It isn't. Their parents didn't want anything bad to happen. I sure know Mrs. Tanner's hanging on to her pain just to find out something good so she can die. Damn thing is, there isn't anything good for her to learn."

"You know about it? I mean you know who?"

I nodded. I said, "Yeah. I do. I think I do." Then I said, "Fanny." I said it like a kid who was waiting to get his nerve up and ask for a date. "Could you come home again?"

All she said was "Jack." I'd known her so long. But I couldn't make out what she was telling me. "Jack," she said again.

"Could you drive home from here instead of going to Virginia's? I promise not to go there and bother you. Just go there and take a bath and go to sleep. Take the dog. I'm really boring for him, and he hasn't seen you in a long time. Just go to the house. When I come in tonight, stay there. Don't go to work. And we can talk. Or we don't have to. We can hang around together. Or just be in the same place. Or you can go to work and you don't need to see me."

She said, "I gather you're giving me a series of options here, Jack."

I shrugged. I made sure not to wince, because the last thing I wanted was for Fanny to see me move strangely, and then for her to unbutton my shirt and run her hands along my skin and then undo the bandages around my chest. It was also what I wanted nearly the most. I confused myself by remembering how Rosalie had opened my shirt and put her hands and then her mouth on my skin. I put my left hand in my pocket and let the right hang by my thumb to my belt buckle, and I waited.

She said, "Did you leave any out?"

I waited.

She said, "I'm not really cracking jokes. I'm trying not to cry." I would have bet a week's gas money that the dog was slapping his tail against the seat of the station wagon. She asked me, "Do you think I did us any good by moving out?"

I said, "Not for me. Maybe you saw things clearer or something. Except I don't think you were having any seeing problems. You said it when you left. You wanted to force me into understanding our situation differently. Something along those lines. Do *you* think it helped?"

She said, "No."

"Do you want to stay away from me forever?"

"No."

"Do you think it's my fault she's dead?"

She closed her eyes. The tears ran under her lids. Her voice sounded like she was trying not to cough. "I don't want to know. I don't want to remember."

"You remembered, though."

"I can't. I don't want to anymore."

I said her name. I said, "Hannah."

It didn't make her cry harder. I don't think anything could.

I heard voices outside, near the entrance. She whispered, "Change of shift."

"Come outside with me?"

She didn't answer. She got down slowly, and she went down the hall to the right. After a few minutes, she came back with her coat on. She was wiping her face with a paper towel. She walked past me and past the people at the desk and out the big doors. I went after her. I felt them looking at me, and I knew they doubted I was human.

Outside, she was at the Torino wagon, opening the tailgate so the dog could get to her. He went up in the air, wriggling like a puppy. He went around her, then he took off. He went to the far edge of the parking lot, kicking up slush and snow, skidding on the ice, dragging his tail and rounding his hips when he turned. He was making the signal of playing a game. He looked like a ball carrier giving the dead-leg juke to a defensive back. I waited next to Fanny, not touching her.

When he stood next to her, panting, waving his tail, banging his head into her coat, I said, "Where to?"

She said, "I'm going to get into my car. I'm going to turn the engine on. When it's warm enough, I'm going to let it roll. At the entrance to the road, I'll either turn left to Virginia's or I won't."

"Turn right," I said. "Take the dog with you. Make a right."

I went to my car and I kept my mouth shut when I got in. I watched the dog jump into her car. I started the engine and shut the window so I wouldn't hear her motor. I held on to the wheel and looked at my hands. I closed my eyes. I counted one Mississippi two Mississippi three Mississippi four Mississippi five Mississippi six Mississippi, but I couldn't get myself to ten.

I opened my eyes. I looked for her car, but she had left. I thought I saw her gray-violet exhaust smoke in the air. It blew raggedly on the wind, like the smoke from the hospital's heating plant. You can tell it's the dead of winter when the smoke stands straight up, stiff. When it blows apart, you can think of warmer temperatures. I thought it made a lot of sense for me not to wonder why she'd hurried.

field

H E WAS IN THE BLUE BIRD and eating something I think is called a horn. It was large and crescent-shaped and it seemed to have a great deal of shiny material on top of it. He wore a dark blue chamois shirt with frayed broad collars. It was opened several buttons, showing the mesh of the long-sleeved thermal undershirt that also showed beneath his sleeves rolled to the forearm. He had a lot of hair on his arms and wrists and it sprouted around the undershirt. The heat was high and wet in the Blue Bird, and the smokers were laying down a screen. Verna screeched her jokes; senior citizens laughed in what was probably among the pleasantest times of their day, since now they weren't alone.

I wanted to be happy I was there, looking at Archie's brilliant eyes in his ugly round face, but the heat was choking me and the smoke and lights made my eyes and forehead ache.

He said, "You look like a set of defective bowels."

"It's one of my favorite disguises."

"At least you haven't cut yourself shaving the last few days."

"They took our razors away. Belts, shoelaces, you know the routine. Can you get out of here with me awhile?"

"I'm on my first pastry," he said.

"I'm about on my last, Arch."

He pointed a finger in the air. He performed a horror. He stabbed the horn into his coffee cup, brought up the dripping, shiny, melting cake, and, tipping his head back, stuffed it into his mouth. He didn't swallow it, though. He did something like straining it, because although I saw him swallow, the cake clearly remained bunchy in his mouth. He got his coffee cup up and tipped the remaining coffee through his gritted teeth. It made the noise of a garbage-disposal unit in a sink.

Then he said, "Ah." He put money on the table, slid sideways, and we went. I drove him out of town, past the frozen lake I'd gone to, and he didn't talk. I didn't look at him. We got to Johnnycake Hill and went up about a half a mile before I pulled off near a field where loggers deposited trimmed evergreen trunks for the local mill trucks to take with their huge oily grippers.

We walked. It used to be an empty road, and then, for years, an almost-empty road. Now there were new houses, all of them with those semicircular windows that look like winking eyes and don't admit enough air to make a difference when it's warm. The winds were gentle. I didn't want to seem optimistic about anything, but it seemed possible that we might be approaching the end of winter.

He said, puffing a little, "Tell me."

"You've been saying Fanny and I have to talk about our baby."

"I've been saying so much, I decided not to tell you anything anymore. I can't figure out whether you want to and can't or you really just don't give a flying fuck about it and you want something else out of this incredible analytic mind I keep serving you from for no additional charge."

"You never charged me a penny."

"You're my friend. And you work for the school. I'm giving you the service you're entitled to."

"Sure."

"And you're my friend."

I stopped. We were at a level part, where someone building a house had been caught by winter. The framing was done but not the roof, and they'd have damage to contend with. It didn't seem to me that anybody capable of building a house ought not to be capable of understanding a little about weather.

"I know I am," I said. "You've been great."

"You leaving town?"

"No."

"Good. You sounded a little valedictory there for a minute."

I shook my head.

"Like you were saying good-bye?"

"That," I said.

"Tell me, Jack."

I felt the same hesitation as when I'd asked Fanny to come back home. But I pushed through it. I said, "I didn't kill our little girl."

His hand came up on its own, it looked like. He seemed to me surprised to find it on my face, just touching my cheek and part of the side of my neck. If he had pulled, I'd have stepped closer and set my head on his shoulder. He just touched me like that and then he dropped his hand.

"I didn't think you did."

"She died."

"Dying doesn't mean killed."

I walked ahead, and I heard him follow. We went on to where the hill climbs again, and I stopped because I heard him breathing harshly. I didn't mind not moving because of how my ribs felt. He stopped and caught his breath a little. I heard him open his mouth, then close it. I turned to look at him.

"You can kill a kid, sometimes, by shaking her. You don't mean to. Your life's crazy, or you're sick, or you haven't slept in—forever. However many nights."

"I know," he said. "It happens a lot."

"You can be half dying because you're *worried* about the kid, but she's going on with that sick little tired little nagging kind of crying, over and over, and nothing you do does her any good. Nothing. Hold her, put her down, try to feed her, sing to her, turn on the radio, dance in the bedroom with her, sit and touch her so she knows you're there."

He said, "That's right."

I looked anyplace else. I couldn't see. I felt the wind, I felt him very near, but I couldn't see anymore.

He said, "Jack."

I said, "That's all right."

"Fanny doesn't remember?"

"She thinks she remembers me doing it. I went up. I heard something when they were up there. Then I went up. By the time I got there and got hold of Hannah because Fanny was crying and crying . . . by the time . . . by the time I got there, all I could do was breathe into her mouth. I held her and I breathed. I breathed and breathed. We drove to the hospital. They called it, I—"

"Sudden infant death syndrome," he said.

"Yes."

"Instead of shaken child syndrome."

"Archie. She turned and found me. When she came out of it, or came to. Whatever happened. I think she went into this blackout so she wouldn't see what had happened."

"She saw you."

"Holding her dead baby."

"She thought you did it."

"When she lets herself remember that much."

"But nothing about herself."

"Nothing."

"That's why you can't talk to her about it," he said. His hand came up again, and he put it again on my face. It wasn't warm up there—the temperature was below freezing—but his face was running with sweat.

"I don't *want* her remembering what happened."

"So she remembers what didn't happen." He was very cold, I saw. I realized he'd been wearing sneakers, not boots, and they were soaked dark. Shifting his feet, he said, "God. She needs help, Jack."

"Help? You think Fanny needs help? You think I do, Arch? You think I didn't stumble onto that insight by myself? Yeah. I think we need some help. The thing of it is, I can't come up with any ideas about help that don't have to do with locking us both up for murder or craziness, or shooting us full of drugs and killing whatever's left of us, which isn't a fucking whole hell of a lot right now to begin with."

He brought his other hand up, and he stood there with me, shorter and fatter and smarter by a dozen lifetimes. He couldn't seem to think of anything to say.

So I told him, "I didn't expect you to come up with a, you know, a miracle cure for her. Or something that maybe would freeze my memory up so I could be the same as her. That's what I want. To remember the same as she does. I know she doesn't want to hurt me. She knows I don't want to hurt her. The way it is now, I know what she knows, and she has no idea of what I know. If we can even stay that way, that fucked and fouled, I'll take it."

He said, "A marriage often dies when a child does."

"You were good enough to share that insight with me before."

"It's why you pay me," he said, squeezing my face and letting his hands drop.

"I wanted you to know," I said. "You've been good, helping me. Talking to me the way you have."

"I haven't helped," he said. "I'm not sure there's help for this."

I nodded.

"Something else," I said.

"Jack, there can't *be* anything else."

I said, "Tell me one more time you were the one wanted me worrying at the Tanner girl thing."

"You're still pissed about that?"

"No. But you were the one, and because it might help me."

He said, "Yeah. But of course that was when I thought all you were coping with was this unbearable, shattering loss. I didn't know it was some kind of a Greek goddamned play."

I made myself look at him again. "Whatever happens," I said, "I want to thank you."

"What's that mean, Jack? The 'whatever' part?"

"Thank you," I said.

"What's that 'whatever' mean?"

"I think I'll be in touch with you later, Archie. Maybe you can think of something you could do for Fanny?"

"When you get the boulder to the top of the hill, don't let it roll back."

"What boulder?"

"That's about all I can think of," he said. "Make sure I hear from you soon."

———

I knew that I wasn't going to work when I dropped him off at the Blue Bird. He got out without talking because I think we'd run out of words. Instead of driving onto the campus, I stopped across from the Blue Bird at the public phone and called the dispatcher. I didn't tell her I was sick. I told her I wasn't coming in and then I hung up. I drove out of town to the south and east and I went to the Tanners'.

She was in the same chair and wearing the same clothing and blanket. He was at the little woodstove, putting in a thick log that might smolder most of the morning. I liked the smell of the smoke but not the heat. My ribs and fingers were hurting and my headache was worse. The brightness of the sun behind the cloud cover moving in seemed to make my eyes throb.

I didn't sit with her because I was afraid I'd end up with my head in her lap.

They said good morning, and I said it. They waited. The reverend, on his knees at the stove, sat on the three-inch brick fire floor like a little kid on the sidewalk, knees up near his face, his arms around his legs.

He finally said, "Oh dear."

I said, "Did you know your daughter was having an affair? I don't know if that's the right word. I'm sorry for this. I think she was let's say *seeing* someone. I figure she wouldn't have bought expensive lacy underwear for a boy her age, right? They don't do that. I figure the boys are so grateful, they don't require anything like what I saw upstairs. Maybe I'm wrong. I'm going on one fact, one nonfact, one guess, and one lie. I'm figuring, to start, that a perfect girl who isn't like any of the other girls in America wouldn't get involved with seductive underwear unless it was something to do with sex and an older man. I'm sorry."

"Whose lie?" Mrs. Tanner said. She had the blanket around her now, so I could hardly see her face. Her voice came out of the shadows it made, hooding her.

"Don't you want to know the fact?" I was angry at them for not knowing, and I must have sounded it. "Wouldn't a mom and dad want the *fact* first?"

She said, "All right, Jack. Please."

"The sexy underwear in her bureau. Why didn't you know about it?"

"I don't pry," she said. "*We* don't."

I said, "Why not? I thought you took care of her. Couldn't you have looked? And let's one of these days ask someone in law enforcement why *they* could look, and see the underwear and not read the receipt and know she had two pairs of it. That meant she was seeing this person a lot, maybe. Or maybe thinking about it. Figuring, knowing her, she'd need to wash and dry the one while she wore the other. Right?"

Mrs. Tanner took the upper part of the blanket down. Her hair looked like it was made of something artificial. Her complexion was changing, from the orange with a darkness underneath it to something like the skin of a lemon going bad. Her husband had his face down on his knees.

"The nonfact," I said, and I almost whispered it. My voice didn't want to come. My throat didn't want to let the air out. I said, "The nonfact is what you don't know. Or the diary you saw and burned or hid or made yourselves forget about. Or the diary she didn't write because she was too smart. Or the underwear you didn't know about. It's something like that. It's what this family didn't ever talk about. That could be a guess, too.

"Except I'm guessing about who the man is. So it can't count as a guess and it has to be a nonfact."

She said, "I know you're as upset as we are, Jack."

"Could be," I said. "And just because I sound like I hate you, or me, or everybody, I don't want you thinking that's all of it that I feel. Understand? Can we have a deal on that?"

The reverend looked at her.

I said, "I want a *deal* on that."

The reverend nodded. His wife said, very low, "Yes. Thank you, Jack."

"You wanted to know the lie?"

They waited.

"I'm going to come back in here in a minute or two. Will you wait for me?"

I turned. I left the car where it was. I walked in the road because they didn't have a sidewalk in that town, and I had the gun in my left hand. I couldn't have held it in my right. I went up Strodemaster's drive and I opened his back door. He was in the bathrobe, frying bacon. I smelled the sausage and onions from the night before. Under it, I smelled what had rotted in the room.

I put the pistol into my right hand, though it didn't want to hold it. I didn't feel very much about the power of it this time. I wasn't howling inside about my primitive strength. I couldn't have been happy for a price. Maybe if someone gave me back my life with Fanny and Hannah. But that wasn't in the small, smelly kitchen that was crowded with two big men breathing like cross-country runners, one of them in unlaced boots and a bathrobe. I simply wanted to be sure I fired it with some accuracy. But I couldn't. It seems I closed my eyes.

I stuck my hand out and cupped the bottom of my fist where it met with the bottom of the pistol grip. My eyes were shut. I squeezed the rounds off slowly. It felt like every shot was a word or as close as I could come to words.

After four of them, I opened my eyes. I had put a gray-blue puckering hole in the enamel of the stove. I had placed a round in the wall behind the stove. I'd heard a ricochet off the frying pan. And the last one had disappeared. I wondered if it had gone into the cork rim of the chalkboard or into Strodemaster. He was crouched in front of his burning breakfast, with his hands on his ears. We could line him up with me and Rosalie, our hands in front of our eyes, I thought, and make that joke about monkeys not doing something. I smelled the cordite as well as the garbage now, and of course the burnt bacon in the greasy pan. I smelled the stink of my sweat. He wasn't moving, and I was still in the firing stance.

We'd been taught in the MPs to startle people in rooms we broke into by shouting in those up-from-the-navel sergeant voices to stand still, put your hands on your head, et cetera. I didn't have any strength today. I needed the audiovisual effects, I told myself. I hadn't known, walking through his door, what I would do. I think maybe I was trying to kill him. I pretended to myself it was all a part of my plan—the door kicked in, the shots fired, the attention he would give me now.

He was still crouched, standing up at the stove, and his face was really a series of funny faces. He looked like a man pretending to be a clown in a spattered blue bathrobe.

I said, "Turn it off. And close your slovenly bathrobe."

He said, "Jack."

My ears were still full of the shots. I could smell the used loads and I could smell his last night's sausages. And I was certain I could smell the rot I had smelled here before. It was Janice. We were standing in her. I let the pistol come up and I squeezed off again. The solid sound of the round striking into the floor at his feet, the spray of wood and linoleum splinters, made a strong argument.

I said, "Tighten your fucking bathrobe, goddamn it. No. Wait. A man shouldn't dress like a boy. Don't tighten it. Take the fucker off."

He slowly stood. He pushed his glasses back up on his nose. He took his bathrobe off and held it out. I pointed to a chair and he dumped it. In a voice that sounded tinny after the shots, he said, "What's wrong, big guy? Why the gunplay? Why the anger? I understand I got you into a search you didn't want to be part of—"

"You lied to me two or three—I think it was three times," I said. "Archie got me into it, not you. You wanted me *out* of it. That must be a compliment. I don't care. I heard it and I heard it, and then I used what's left of my brain to think about it. You. Archie thought it would help me out if I did something about getting back a missing girl. You were talking to him, and he made the suggestion. You were supposed to be so eager to find her, you had to say yes. Jesus, what's not to say yes to? A broken-down campus cop who takes a week to find his dick in the men's room. Right? So you came to me and asked me and then as soon as you had an excuse, like when I stuck as much of my body as I could in front of a bunch of arms and legs, you came crying over to turn me free. *That's* the part that's the compliment, you fucker. That anything about me worried you. That you actually thought I could *do* anything. See anything. Hear anything.

"But you're finally so goddamned convinced you're smarter than everybody. Than the little girl you fucked and killed. Than her parents. Than half the law-enforcement officers in a couple of counties. Surely smarter than me. So you had to repeat the lie about who engaged my useless services. But you know, Professor Strodemaster, sir, Ph.D., even a poor dumb fuck like me sooner or later hears it when a wormy, phony, arrogant cocksucker lies and lies and lies."

I saw spit pop out of my mouth. I heard my voice climb higher and higher. I did not forget I had a round left in the cylinder.

"And you sliced her apart here. And what'd you do after? Did you can her in her juices? Freeze her crotch so you could take it down to remember her by?"

He shook his head and gripped his glasses over the ears like they were coming off. He looked down an inch or so with a sorrowful face. "Jack, boy," he said. "You're talking to a fucking associate professor of physical sciences with tenure for life and an NSF grant in his package. We don't do dismembering. The guys in biology do that. And *they* don't do it to people. This is fucking college life we're talking, Jack. You and I are employees of a *school*. The worst cutting up gets done is at parties, unless they're scoring on one another's wives. I'm a wronged, innocent associate professor, guy. I'm also your friend. Remember? And here. Consider this. I heard this, and I believe it to be true, seeing how punchy you've got. We are both of us men whose wives walked out. We're both wronged. Are you hearing me, Jack?"

I always admired how some people could open their mouths and talk. They could talk and talk. But I didn't think I wanted, now, to hear about my dreams, and especially not from Strodemaster. I tapped him on the soft part of the temple with the gun.

I said, "What'd you do, butcher her in the kitchen? Clog your septic up with her body parts? That's why it stinks like that. You used some kind of scientific knife thing and you cut off her arms and legs first, and then I guess her head. Her head next? Did you slice off those tiny nipples? Didn't you at least let her wear that sad little sexpot brassiere when you cut her up?

"You know," I said, and I tapped him again, at the bridge of the nose, kind of hard, "sometimes they notch people up with their gun sights and then they go absolutely crazy a little and shoot up a tenured-for-life associate professor's house. They let them bleed to death on the kitchen floor, where the girls got sliced and diced."

I lifted my foot in its hard boot and I ran the lug sole down his leg, from the knee to the instep inside the loose tongue of his boot.

He vomited onto his boots and it spattered onto mine. I didn't move back. I've had worse on my feet from drunks and speed freaks and I was taught to see it as a tactic. "Barf and run," we used to call it.

He wiped his mouth on his sleeve, knocking his dirty glasses off. They fell into the vomit. He left them there, though he reached for his face a couple of times as if to adjust them. His face looked incomplete, a little younger. I felt like I could see it better. But I couldn't read it, and I was glad. I didn't want to understand his thoughts.

I'd raised a welt on his nose and a little dark streak on his temple. His leg was probably red down the shin, and that would hurt for a good part of a week. I thought at first the tears were from his vomiting, but he was crying for real.

"I could never hurt that child like that," he said, snuffling. "Cut her *up*?"

"Well, I haven't met that many killers," I said, "and I never was smart enough to figure people out. That's why it took me so long with you. What is it, you get off better with little girls? It's some kind of psychological thing with you? Or was she one of those secret-rebellion kids who's a miracle in the sack? And you of course were the super father physicist local community guy with the prick that was tenured for life and you were instructing her in whatever she couldn't get in the preacher's house. Holy shit, Randy. Did I leave any of it out?"

"Oh yes," he said. He moved to the wall and stooped the way nearsighted people do. He picked up the chalk at the end of its red string and he faced me. He erased the map lines on the board with the side of his arm. Vomit and mucus ringed his mouth. His eyes looked soft and unfocused. He pointed with the chalk to the chalk-board and, peering in, made an X in a circle in the upper left-hand corner of the board. "Let this represent the emotions between us," he said in a pleasant and even eager voice.

"Jack," he said, "she was both a child and an adult. She was a woman. She was. Truly. The emotion is a difficult one to name, but not to feel, and we felt it. I'm trying through this crude iconography to suggest the flow of emotional power—" He made an arrow point from the X to the right of the board. "Here. This might represent the field of power that flowed from her house to mine and, naturally—" He made an arrow that moved back to the X.

"Let me add this for clarity," he said. He circled a Y. "I'll be Y," he said. "Understand?

"Now." He made a crude drawing of a house under X and another, sloppier, under Y. Below them, he crosshatched an area. "The corn-field behind our houses. We'll assume the snow." He looked up, smiling a boy's shy smile. "I don't know how to indicate the snow."

He looked back at the chalkboard. "No," he said. He wiped with his hand and forearm until most of his marks were gone.

"Try it this way," he said, drawing a box with a rectangle in it. "Let X represent the bed." He chalked an X into the rectangle. "Y, of course, is the house around it. And these"—he stabbed sharp small marks around the rectangle—"are tears. Not mine. I was the father, and the father never weeps. Well," he said, looking at me with a friendly smile, "not that they know of, eh? She wept, Jack, like a baby. I comforted her, of course. That was what I did. But remonstrations, condemnations, *confessions!* She wanted us to confess. I think it was a momentary lapse to childhood from the small adult she'd become. I've seen it happen before. Children are *like* that, and we *understand* them.

"Jack, I urged her to be silent. To consider our pleasures, our friendship. We really shared a lot. We were silent, though. It was one of our conditions."

I saw her sad mouth and the eyes that wanted so much to be happy. I saw her in the underwear her mother would call vulgar, and I closed my eyes against it. When I opened them, I saw Strodemaster bending to his board. But I couldn't help seeing him roll her face into the bedclothes and lean on the back of her head until she suffocated. Or take her jaw in one large hand and cover her forehead with another, and jerk, so that her neck snapped and her eyes emptied out. Or, maybe, shake her and shake her and shake her and shake her until she simply broke.

He said, "Are you understanding all of this?"

He continued to lean down toward the chalkboard and study it. He slowly shook his head. With his forearm, he wiped and wiped.

"I don't think I've made this clear," he said. He looked at me and smiled sweetly with embarrassment. "And I'm the one they call a master teacher!"

I stepped toward him and my hand was up.

His face changed. When he spoke, his voice sounded thicker: "You can kill me, Jack, if you need to. But I have to tell you. It looks to me like something about this turned you on. Like you were with me for a while. Their little titties and their hands in your mouth."

"I wouldn't be you."

"No, you can hit me all you want. I'm just tell—"

I used my left hand like a stiff board and I didn't hit him all I wanted, maybe, but I hit him. I slapped his face. I was imagining how Mrs. Tanner would do it if she could. Left side, right side, left side, right side, left side, right. His face jolted. I was angry enough to do some damage.

"I don't want to hear from you anymore how I'm your twin maniac brother. Because I am not a bad person. I am not, goddamn it. I am not a bad man."

He had stumbled against the chalkboard, then moved forward to lean against the kitchen table. His feet were back in his vomit now. His smell had begun to rise. His face was bright red, with white spots on it from my palm and fingers and knuckles.

I said, "I want you to say now where she is. You can tell the state police about your love and then the terrible accident that happened when you were naked with but not meaning to fuck a fourteen-year-old girl who you killed without meaning to kill her. Your lawyer will tell you what to say so nobody believes you but you get off with time served and a free psychiatrist for life."

"I wrapped her," he said. "It was a sign of respect." He turned toward the chalkboard but then faced me again. "I wound her in a sheet."

"You buried her?"

"Of course."

"Where?"

He pointed. The sleeve slid on his arm, and I saw strong muscles move. He was pointing toward the barn.

"In it?"

"Behind it."

"In the ground?"

"In the snow above the ground. I'd have buried her properly, come spring."

I saw her sad face come rising as the snow melted around her.

"You'll have to show them."

"I will."

"First you have to walk to her mother's house. Her mother and father's house."

"Not and talk to them."

"Jesus, Professor, I hope I'm not making you uncomfortable or anything. I will not hesitate to fucking kill you. Putting your ass down would solve all kinds of problems, I want you to know. So just let's do this."

When we went down his back steps, we had his neighbors watching us. I guess they'd heard the shots. In little towns, they tell each other the news, and we had people in coats over bathrobes and nightgowns, pajamas or work clothes, on their porches or standing in their front walks when we covered the short distance to the Tanners'. Strodemaster was ahead of me, not wearing his glasses, wearing his dirty white T-shirt and holding his hands in his trouser pockets. He stumbled once because he stepped on his bootlace.

We went up their drive and I told him to stand in front of their back door. I reached around behind him and knocked. I wasn't careful about keeping distance between us. I knew if he moved on me, I would hurt him. It would hurt me, too, but I didn't care and I wanted to break him up and he knew it.

I only wanted the Reverend Tanner to open the storm door and hear me say, "Bring your wife."

He moved. She came slowly to the door and her husband held her from the side and from behind.

She looked down the steps, and she looked. The feeling was of a focus being tightened and held. She finally said, "Oh God." It took her a long time to say. What I hated most about that minute or two was that I couldn't be in the kitchen and hold on to her.

I marched him back to his house and through his vomit. I was determined to step on his glasses and I did, dragging the frames along with his stink through the kitchen. I sat him at his table while I phoned.

I left a message at a number I had never called, the dean of faculty's office. I said, "Please tell him that Associate Professor Randolph Strodemaster, with tenure for life, is about to be arrested for killing the girl he used to rape every night."

When I hung up, I turned to him. I was going to say something smart about his not minding if I made some toll calls. He was sitting with his legs crossed, one smelly boot hanging beside his torn-up shin. His hands were folded in his lap, and he leaned back in his chair like a man waiting for breakfast. I smelled the vomit, the old food, the stink of his garbage, the new, dark smell of his urine.

"How could she crawl around with you?" I asked him.

"Are you jealous, Jack?"

I didn't bother to threaten him. I'd become too tired. We were both so weak, I think we could have gone to sleep where we were.

He said, "I can be charming, I think is the answer. I know a lot." His voice was leaking up now, like gas escaping. I thought I could even smell the process of his bowels inside him. "And I loved her. I'm a daughter's father, don't forget. I know how to love a girl."

I was too dizzy to turn around to him again. I leaned on the wall beside his phone and called Elmo St. John's office to leave a courtesy call. Then I phoned the state police barracks and asked for Bird. They told me he was supervising the execution of a warrant. I told them to get another warrant, this time for Professor Randolph Strodemaster, and to get here soon. He'd confess.

He said, "My attorney's in Norwich. I'll want him here before I say a word to the fuzz."

I said into the phone, "Tell Bird I might shoot the professor before he gets here."

Then I hooked a chair with my foot and pulled it over to the phone. That cost my ribs a bit. I probably made a noise, because Strodemaster looked sharply at me. "Never," I said. "You'd have to murder me to get one yard away. I'd leave maybe a pint of all of you for them to arrest. You don't understand. I *want* to kill you. Sit there and be quiet."

I got Archie Halpern's assistant. She was ordinarily a very patient woman, but she didn't understand why I didn't understand how when Archie was with a patient, we none of us were supposed to disturb him.

I told her it was a matter of life and death. She said it always was. I said I meant death for real. No more breathing, I said. She told me I had to be nuts. I reminded her what office she worked in.

After a few minutes' wait, Archie came on and I said, "I found the guy who killed her."

He said, "Did you hurt him?"

"Hardly at all."

"Did you kill him?"

"Not yet."

"Do you feel any better, Jack?"

"You know, I really don't," I said.

"After what you told me, I didn't think you would. On the other hand, I didn't think you'd catch him."

"Why should you have?"

"It's wonderful you did."

"I suppose," I said.

"Don't do anything rash."

I started to laugh, and I didn't know how to stop. I giggled pretty stupidly, and then I was crying.

"Jack," he said.

"Don't worry," I said. "You should see *him*." That made me laugh again, so I hung up.

———

Someone brought a chair out for Mrs. Tanner. She lay back in it with her bright golden blanket around her, sitting on her throne like the queen of nothing.

Strodemaster and his lawyer talked to Bird. Strodemaster made marks on a topographical map the state police insisted on using. I didn't try more than once to point out how on a map like that you need to see the shape of the land like you're looking from above, and with all the snow, of course we couldn't. The cops were in charge and all of us did what they said. And Mrs. Tanner watched us.

We waited two hours for a state roadworks bulldozer to be brought up on its tractor trailer. By then, local men had brought in wood by pickup truck, and they'd started a fire just behind Strodemaster's barn to keep Mrs. Tanner and most of the rest of the hamlet warm. The dirty smoke blew back at them and up, but they sat in front of it, accepting the heat and watching us through the raggedy darkness of the early afternoon.

Archie had come out. He'd been held away from the house by
the police and he'd argued awhile and then left. I didn't like seeing
him go. I thought he could talk to Mr. and Mrs. Tanner. I thought he
could talk to me.

We were out now where the bulldozer had pushed a poor road
through the snow. Bird was the least of the law now, he and the cop
he'd arrived with. There was a captain, and we'd been told a colonel
was on his way. There were a number of plainclothes investigators
wearing bulky jackets under the bright, thin windbreakers labeled
STATE POLICE. Some of them also wore baseball hats that told them
who they were. They carried notebooks and wrote in them. I couldn't
imagine what they could think of to say.

I looked back over to the local people at their fire. If you could
look down from above, the way the topographical map did, you would
see Mrs. Tanner in her chair and the rest of them standing in a loose
semicircle. Then you would see the road cut through the snow like a
wound, showing corn stubble and even in places the frozen mud
below it. Then you'd see us, and we'd look as small as the rest of
them if you saw them from above, working a hundred yards or so
away from the fire and the parked vehicles and what in that hamlet
would pass for a crowd. It was growing. Word had spread on the
scanners and people were driving in.

The investigators agreed that they thought he was lying about
how far he'd carried her when he laid her into the snow, planning to
come back in late March or early April and use the laws of physics to
bury her at night for good. But we all thought it was right to start
looking where he'd indicated and then move back toward the house.

The snow was to be moved toward the south end of the field. We
would move it back while moving ourselves north and west toward
the barn. The police had brought shovels and so had the state road
crew, and people in the hamlet had loaned us some. There were
twenty men and women, middle-aged or younger, most of us cops,
who dug shallowly, almost scooping more than digging. Behind us
were the people with shovels and buckets who moved what we
dumped while we widened our circle at the end of the road in the

snow. If you were looking from above, you would have seen us making awkward motions and not getting very far down.

I began to have a kind of daydream. I'm in Hannah's bedroom, in the plaster dust and pools of Sheetrock screws and splintered wood and the clawed-looking walls. I'm in there alone and Fanny is gone, at Virginia's, and then the dog comes clicking down the hallway, his tail wagging as he rounds the corner into the room, because he's happy about showing Rosalie in.

She either says she was lost for forty minutes finding the house and then her car went into a snowbank and she walked the rest of the way or she doesn't bother. I can never decide. She's holding a shopping bag in each hand. Her face is bright from walking in the cold and because she wants to see me.

I'm sitting against a far wall, near the window, but not looking out. I don't know what to say to her, so I raise my hand a little and then let it drop back to my lap.

Rosalie says, "Your wife isn't here."

I shake my head.

"I don't care if she is."

"You'd care," I say. "She'd be at least a battalion's worth of mean if she found you."

Rosalie says, "Found *us,* you mean. And let her be. I brought you soup. The makings of soup. I make wonderful vegetable soup, and I have a bottle of Barolo that we deserve to drink, and also my toothbrush."

"This is really dangerous," I say.

"No. It's really wonderful."

"Well, yes. It is. And dangerous."

She has set the bags down and is letting her coat drop down her arms.

"Fine," she says, "dangerous."

She goes to her knees, then lies between my legs and along my chest. I put my arm around her. We lie in the corner where the crib had been, and I wonder whether to tell her.

"Faculty don't do this," I say instead.

"Faculty do anything they want, Jack. And I can tell you something."

"Do you have to?"

"This is the real scene of the crime," she says.

I don't answer. I know that what I want to do is not think about the crib, or Fanny coming home, or Fanny never coming home, or the truth of what she has just said. I want to unfasten Rosalie's jeans. I want to do it so much that I start and she helps, standing to slide them down her legs more easily. While she stands above me, I unfasten my own, and she holds the top of my head and slowly, not closing her eyes or looking anywhere but into me, she slides slowly down until we are locked to each other, wet and then not moving.

"How long can we sit like this do you think?" she says.

I start to buck up, but I want to feel everything slowly. Her small hands are strong on me, her muscles move powerfully. I want to hear us be together. So I stop. I lean forward, forgetting my ribs, and I listen to her heart through her shirt. She adjusts a little, and I hear the sound of our wetness.

She says, "Jack?"

I nod against her shirt, maybe make a noise.

"Is the dog watching us?"

I stopped myself, but I was happy a minute, though my ribs were naturally not cooperative. This wasn't a comfortable motion for them. No motion was. I worked at not making noises and at scooping the snow. I looked down into it, seeing grit and pieces of vegetation and coarse crystals of ice. I was looking for a small young face with a glad mouth and unhappy eyes. She would come up, I thought, like someone floating in a pond. She would rise while we dug, and if you were looking from above, you'd see her surfacing. I stopped and took some very short, choppy breaths. That was the best way to regulate it, I had found. I was looking down the road toward the fire and I saw Archie's car return. It was followed by Fanny's. Archie parked his sloppily. He usually drove it like that. He got out and he went around to Fanny's car and opened the door for her. At that distance, she looked like anyone else at the end of winter in a heavy coat. But I knew it was Fanny and then I saw the dog. Archie looked at a patrol-man and shook his finger and talked awhile. They got passed through.

Now, dogs can't see as well as nearsighted old people. And he surely couldn't have smelled me over that long distance. But he came down the sloppy, raw roadway straight toward me. Two investigators began to wave their hands and call commands. Stop. Sit. Get that goddamned dog away.

I whistled. He stopped, he searched the wind with his muzzle. I whistled again. He found me and barreled in. We said hello a little. Then I pointed to an area we'd scooped through down to nubs of corn, and I told him to sit there and stay. The first few shovels of snow he saw powdering toward the south of us, he was up and ready to chase. I pointed at him and he saw me and he sat. After a while, he understood what we were doing, I thought. His big chest stuck out and his muzzle was raised as he watched us sift the snow. He knew this kind of work.

If you watched us from above, you would have seen the small men and women making themselves move slowly and carefully. There was the huge field out behind the barn. There were the little crea-tures hauling some of the millions of tons of snow. There was the dog, watching, like an expert consultant. There we were, scooping up ounces from the tons.

Fanny and Archie stood in the bulldozed road now, partway be-tween the people in the hamlet and the people performing the actions that were required because it wasn't safe to be a girl. The sky behind them and around us looked like somebody had poured milk straight down along it to the ground. The sun was in it, and I suppose it was strong and spring was going to come. But I didn't warm up, even when I was shoveling. I stopped more than I should have, but my ribs were moving in sections again and my fingers had no grip.

I thought, We could dig here forever. Then I thought, No, only until full spring. All we had to do was wait. But we couldn't. We wanted our girl back.

Everyone wanted someone back. It would be a hundred degrees of dry heat and I would be in an air-conditioned motel in New Mexico called the Arroyo, a little less than a year from now, and all those miles from the field we worked in that looked as big to me as North America, and I would still want our Hannah back, and so of course would Fanny. Mr. Tanner would be alone with only his church and his jokes and his heaven, wanting back his wife, who watched us now, wanting back the daughter we were reaching for under the snow. And Rosalie, who is a better cop than I am, would find me in my hiding place and get me talking on the phone.

Are you eating well? Are you sleeping well? She would stay on my trail. She would find me. She would call. And I would begin to suspect myself of counting on her. The phone would ring, and when I answered, I would hear the distance behind her voice and begin to regret it, and then Rosalie would say my name.

In this winter, though, in the field behind Randy Strodemaster's house, I leaned on the shovel. I was looking at Fanny, who talked while Archie listened. I wouldn't ask them where he had gotten her from, Virginia's place or ours. Wait and see, I told myself. I knew I couldn't. Look at me and these other people, what we were doing when all we had to do was wait and see.

I went back to work and then I had to stop again. When I looked toward the road, I saw Archie with his hands in his pockets. Fanny was gone, and so was her car. I wasn't completely sure I could move anymore. I made my fingers close around the shovel. I made myself breathe the short, choppy breaths, and I scooped some snow.

I thought I should remember to tell the Tanners about the physics book in her shelves. I didn't think of it, I would tell them. I would mention Rosalie and it would please them, I thought, knowing that a stranger had pondered so hard about their child. They would want to know it was maybe another clue. Rosalie had been certain Janice wouldn't have taken physics, since she'd been less than capable with numbers. Strodemaster gave her the book, since numbers were what he knew—Rosalie was sure of it. Teachers do that kind of passing their books along to kids. The young are so lucky, I thought. We so love teaching them. I would want to ask Archie why a little girl would buy her underwear in a fuck-me clothing store for a man like

Strodemaster. Maybe I would also ask Rosalie. I felt like I needed an expert to tell me about anything human, though on all other information, I was absolutely informed. I wondered where Fanny had gone. I wondered if Strodemaster's wife had moved out because of something with him and his daughter. It could happen, I thought. I leaned over to spit onto the snow and moved it off behind me where somebody breathing hard was moving it farther away.

People were talking, but not very much, and I could hear the rushing sound of the big fire back near the barn. The dog sat very still, watching the hole slowly grow. He was getting ready.

Here's what I thought. I thought about Ralph. I thought, Once upon a time.

I made myself work. I was like the others. Whether we believed in spring or not, we did not want to wait. If you watched us from above us, you would have seen it. Spring or not, ribs or not, fingers or not, we were going to move the entire field.

Girls

FREDERICK BUSCH

A Reader's Guide

A Conversation with Frederick Busch

Q: Upon finishing the book, I recalled the first chapter, which I then re-read. I realized that it now felt like the "last" chapter. What was your plan with this design?

A: I first wrote the book going from the beginning of chapter two to the end. And I was dissatisfied—as I worked on the beginning—with plunging the reader too quickly into so much grimness. And although the first chapter doesn't make you sing, it has a little bit of humor to it, and it seems to me to help set the scene for who this man was, and whom he became, and to give the reader...the slight sense there was hope for him after the events of the book.

Q: Why not bring Jack and Fanny back together? They clearly loved each other.

A: Because people who so clearly love each other nevertheless do not always know how to live together. That's reason one. Reason two is the plot I created made it impossible to bring Jack and Fanny back together. The only way they can live together is for her to not think he killed their baby. The only way they can live together is for him to not know she killed their baby. Now how can you undo those two things? I wanted it to be a kind of paradox: He loves her so much he takes the blame for what she did, to the point where she can't take him because of it. And she can't take what it does to him: It makes him a very bitter and difficult man.

I loved Fanny, and I wanted him to stay with her more than my readers imagined...the short story] "Ralph the Duck" appeared in 1989...and became chapter two. And you see Fanny is a little softer in that story, a little less self-protective, more accessible to Jack. I wanted Jack and Fanny to have a possibility of happiness. But they kept returning to me, and the more I thought about them, the more I wondered, why had Jack made her cry? A lot of people noticed her sorrow, so I must have made her sad without intending to make her quite that sad. I learned from my readers who Fanny was, and I began to want to know about her sadness. Whenever a storyteller wants to know something, he or she tells a story to find out the answer.

Q: **Let's talk about the dog. A great dog.**

A: Good, I liked him, too.

Q: **Why no name? Why a chocolate Lab? And how on earth did you manage to get into its chocolate head so well?**

A: It had no name…I hadn't given him a name for a couple of chapters—I realized that suddenly I was used to hearing Jack refer to him as "the dog." And I thought, "Wow, I'd better give him a name," and then I thought, there is no name Jack could give him. Jack is a man who is unable to name his dog. And that tells us a lot about him. He's a guy who can't say "I love you," who can't say "Fanny, let's go to counseling together." Because he doesn't quite believe in speech. He's not a man of words. He's absolutely a man of actions and thoughts. It's the other people around him who are people of words.

How do I get inside his head, and why a chocolate Lab? I've always wanted to have a chocolate Lab and never did, so I decided it was time to have one. Also, Judy and I have always had two and sometimes three Labradors, and they've always been black. And I didn't want to make the dog in the book a black Lab because if my Labradors ever got wind of it, they might be embarrassed. So that's why it's a chocolate Lab. And how did I get inside his head? Because we've lived with Labradors for about thirty years.

Q: ***Girls* examines the darker side of life. Why?**

A: I live in a dark part of the country. My ancestors come from a dark part of the world, which is Russia, and I am a serious artist, which means that what I am looking to understand is the bad news, not the good news. I think by and large if you distinguish between serious writing and not-so-serious writing, you would find that the serious writing—even though it might be a love story—[has] room in the book for darkness, for bitter moments, because I think it is that side of life that the artist tries to explore. There are moments of joy, and he or she may bring explosions of joy to the page; but by and large I think our responsibility is to explore the more frightening moments on behalf of our readers. I think that's why they may value us, if they do.

Q: **They value us because we do it *for* them? Sort of like a surrogate?**

A: Yes. We do it with them—if you're a good writer, you get your readers to care as you do about certain huge facts or factors that are at stake in your book. Big values: You're worrying about love and death and need and all those huge abstractions. And the courtesy that good writers perform is to make them concrete, instead of abstract, through characters and events. And the courtesy readers perform is to permit writers to take them on that dark and sometimes frightening ride. Now, not only do I live in a dark part of the country and am, I guess, a man with a proclivity for those dark thoughts, but I was living here at a time when actual small human girls were being stolen from their safety and raped and murdered and eaten and butchered and god knows what happened to them. And I became inconsolably involved in the terrible loss that their families were going through, and I wanted to do something. This is all I could do. And that's why I created a man like Jack, who at best would be clumsy and only get halfway near the bitter truth, because that was all I could do.

Q: **You say that "serious" writing is writing that portrays the darker, more frightening side of life. Then you would agree with the person [Margaret Atwood] who said "A novel about unalloyed happiness would have to be either very short or very boring."**

A: I would argue that you can find fascinating happiness in the midst of sorrow. So she's right. Her word, "unalloyed" is the key…what makes us interesting to each other is the trouble we get each other in, just a little bit, and then the way we console each other.

Q: **You said before you used the Colgate campus for the setting**

of this novel. How was that received by the Colgate community? Did you get any complaints?

A: I got a lot of questions; a lot of students and faculty tried to identify people in the book as belonging to the faculty. And I had to tell them—and this is the truth—that nobody in the book reflects anybody living or dead…except one person, who is a model of great human decency, and he has just retired as the head of the campus counseling service. He was the model for Archie. The other was Rosalie Piri—she came in part from a faculty person with that particular nose and mouth. I asked permission and she gave me permission to use those in the novel.

Q: **You're a very prolific author. What is your inspiration and how do you get started each time?**

A: I'm one of those Jewish puritans—I feel like I have not earned my oxygen and food and water unless I've written, and so I try every day to make language—whether or not it's a successful piece every day. I write essays, book reviews, and letters, I have a novel and short stories under contract. My life is writing. The professional life is writing and it flows into my teaching.

My home life is absolutely different. It involves Judy and me traveling or cooking or just talking—our boys are grown…. My poor kids were aware from their infancy that periodically every day the old man disappears from sight, and if he comes out surly it means he didn't do so well, and if he comes out beaming it means it'll be a better afternoon and evening. They called me "the bear" all through their childhood, because I'd come lurching and lumbering out of my writing room. I have a very nice writing room on the second floor of our barn across a field from our house. The house is a low, white farmhouse, with a white picket fence. We're five miles from the nearest town on a small country road. The main part of the house was built about 1810. The rest has been added over the years. It sits all alone in the middle of about one hundred acres.

My first writing room was a bathroom in Greenwich Village…while Judy slept, I would put my portable typewriter on the toilet-seat cover and sit on the bathtub, and that's where I wrote my first novel.

Q: What advice do you have for young and aspiring writers? Any secret tricks of the trade to share?

A: I think aspiring writers, young or old, ought to read all they can. If you don't love to read, I cannot imagine that your imagination would be fed enough to write. That's the first piece. Second piece: Assuming you have some talent—you can never grow it, or make it bigger—have enough courage to dare to look straight in the eye what your talent causes you to see. The most important component you can develop is energy, to get up at 5:30 in the morning. It's hard work, brutally hard work. And it's frustrating and you fail most of the time. Most of what a serious fiction writer does is fail. But in spite of rejection by yourself, your editors, agents, and readers—the first novel I published was the fourth I wrote—you have to keep going. That's the hardest part. Finally, try to treat writing like skating on very thin ice: Keep moving or else you'll fall in. And finally, finally: Don't be precious, believe you're writing to be read, believe in the needs and thoughtfulness of your reader, and honor your reader.

That's it from Busch Central. That's all I know.

Reading Group Questions and Topics for Discussion

1. The weather in *Girls* is severe and relentless. What role does this weather play in the novel, and why? What other books have you studied in which the weather was such a large part of the story? How do climate and landscape tend to affect the lives of individuals as well as larger societies?

2. Jack is a Vietnam veteran, a self-educated, blue-collar kind of guy. His wife, Fanny, is an emergency room nurse, a job requiring considerable education and training. In what ways do you think their differing backgrounds affect their relationship? Are these effects beneficial or damaging? What commonalities can you find in their backgrounds and/or jobs? Do you think these are sufficient to keep them together?

3. Did you want Jack and Fanny to get back together? Why or why not, and why do you think Busch arrived at the ending?

4. Do you think this book fits into the typical detective-novel genre? Why or why not? Why do you think readers like to categorize types of novels? Do you think *Girls* belongs to any distinct category or genre?

5. The first chapter directly follows the final chapter in chronology. Why do you think the author placed it at the beginning of the book? Did you go back and re-read the first chapter after completing the novel? Did doing so alter your perception of the book? If so, how?

6. Why do you think Jack and Fanny couldn't discuss the death of their baby after so much time? Has there ever been something you or someone you know couldn't or wouldn't discuss? Why do you think people close themselves away like that? How might people avoid doing so, or help each other overcome it?

7. In recent years there unfortunately have been many highly publicized cases of missing girls like Janice Tanner. Do you think these cases have always occurred and that are just being

played up by the media today? Or do you think something has shifted in our society that is causing an increase in such tragedies? Do you discuss these disappearances with your friends or your families? If so, how do you respond? Do you feel safe in modern society?

8. Jack lives in a world of extreme coldness, bleakness, and silence. It seems that the only lightness in his world is his nameless dog. Why do you think this is so? What function does the dog serve in the novel as a whole? In Jack's life? What do you think the author had in mind when he chose to include the dog in this story?

9. When did you as a reader think you knew who was responsible for Janice Tanner's disappearance? Who did you think did it, and why? Were you right?

10. What role does Professor Piri play in this drama?

11. Fanny is repeatedly described as capable and competent, and of course, her job is one of helping to save lives. Juxtapose this with the circumstances and aftermath of their daughter's death, and discuss what effect this combination has had on Fanny.

12. As this is a work of fiction, the writer could do with his characters whatever he wished. Why do you think the author let Jack get beat up so badly?

13. Jack and Fanny's marriage is a paradox: two people who love and are bound to each other, and yet cannot seem to live together. Discuss this paradox and why it exists. Do you know anyone with such a paradox in their lives? What is it like, and how do they resolve or live with it?

14. Why do you think Jack found Rosalie Piri so irresistible? He obviously loved Fanny and really wanted to make it work with her; yet he barely hesitated before he got involved with Rosalie. What do you think motivated him, or prevented him from resisting the affair with her?

15. Why didn't Jack drag Fanny in to talk to Archie? Why didn't

Archie push for them to get counseling together? Many people in our society often resist counseling when they most need it. Why do you think this is so?

16. Jack goes into the Tanners' church, and still finds himself unable to pray. Yet he really wants to. Why can't Jack pray?

17. Identify all the different girls in the book who could contribute to the book's title. What do they all have in common? How do they differ? Do you think *Girls* was a good choice of title? If not, what might you have named the book?

18. Why does Jack harass William, the drug dealer from Staten Island? Jack knows he's not really guilty, at least not of being involved in the Janice Tanner case. Yet he knowingly beats him, and quite brutally at that. Why would Jack, who is basically a good man, do such a thing?

19. What do you think was the author's purpose in including the subplot about the vice president's impending visit?

© John Hubbard

ABOUT THE AUTHOR

Girls author Frederick Busch has written over twenty books, including numerous novels and several collections of stories. His works include, *Closing Arguments*, *Rounds*, *Absent Friends*, *Long Way from Home*, and *Sometimes I Live in the Country*, as well as his recent collection, *The Children in the Woods: New and Selected Stories*, which was nominated for a 1995 PEN/Faulkner Award. He has also written a book called *The Mutual Friend*, which is a novel about nineteenth-century English writer Charles Dickens.

Mr. Busch has received the PEN/Malamud Award for achievement in short fiction, as well as an award for fiction from the American Academy of Arts and Letters. He has won the National Jewish Book Award and has held Guggenheim, Woodrow Wilson, National Endowment for the Arts, and James Merrill Fellowships.

Frederick Busch has served as the acting director of the Writers' Workshop at the University of Iowa and has read and taught extensively at college and university campuses. He is currently the Edgar Fairchild Professor of Literature at Colgate University (which served as the campus setting for *Girls*), where he teaches creative writing and fiction of the nineteenth and twentieth centuries. He is the founder of Colgate's Living Writers program and the annual Chenango Valley Writers' Conference.

Mr. Busch was born in Brooklyn, New York, and was educated at Muhlenberg and Columbia. He lives with his wife, Judy, a high school librarian, in rural upstate New York, and he writes in a studio on the second floor of a barn on his property. Mr. Busch is a dedicated fan of the New York Giants, and he and Judy have two grown sons, plus several black Labs.

Excerpts from reviews of Frederick Busch's
GIRLS

"*Girls* is about as close to perfect as a novel gets. Its prose is clean and strong but never advertises its own quiet brilliance, its characters are sharply defined and irresistible, and its plot is suspenseful enough to keep you up until dawn."

—*Men's Journal*

"Combining the quick pace of a detective story with the bold poetics of literary work, Frederick Busch's taut new novel, *Girls*, is a dark, compulsively readable drama…. From the makings of an all-too-common evening-news item, Busch has fashioned a novel of considerable weight and dimension. By imbuing the lurid with the introspective, he has given a stock story intelligence, humanity, and terrific range."

—*Elle*

"When a book is this successful it's impossible to detect any sign of artistic struggle…. Jack is such an absorbing and sympathetic narrator…. nothing [Busch] has published in the past has quite prepared me for the seductive beauty of this very disturbing book…. Its pitch-perfect dialogue, skillfully contrived plot, and authentically wintry atmosphere are all exceptional, but a great deal of its strength comes from the moral complexity of its characters…. The highest compliment a reader can pay a literary thriller—or any novel, for that matter—is to claim that the book is nearly as intricate and mysterious as life itself, that the reader has lived in the book as if it were a particularly lifelike dream, and cared about its characters as if they were real. All these claims are true about *Girls*".

—*The Washington Post Book World*

"It is a dark tale, but it's told with an economical mastery and intensity that only a few current novelists can command. Busch even manages to create a dog who is real, touching but never cute, and the perfect life-enhancing foil for the human sorrows around him."

—*Publishers Weekly*

"The novel's social realism gives it the page-turning pace of a mystery. But Busch's masterly pairing of dark wit and tender mercy is what makes *Girls* a great work."

—*US*

"This well-written and engrossing novel is part mystery and part exploration of how grief can manhandle a marriage."

—*Booklist*

"*Girls* is about pain and what happens when pain can't find its way out of the human vessel.... *Girls* is unusually entertaining.... In the end, this is a chilling story about the guilt of adulthood."

—*Time Out*

"Though the crime story is intriguing, it is Jack's growing insight about his marriage, his town, and himself that transforms this page-turner about lost children into a tender and eloquent examination of the even greater mystery that is the human heart."

—*Glamour*

"Fierce, wise, gripping and true, *Girls* marks the continuing evolution of a first-rate American storyteller.... the triumph of *Girls* is in its clear-eyed compassion for all those who try to flee from the bedrock realities of their lives."

—*The New York Times Book Review*

"A complex and disturbing vision of the world as a place filled with danger powers this fascinating novel.... It all works superbly as a conventional thriller, though the story's most effective as a harrowing expression of the fragility of our defenses against loss and death, and a moving characterization of its memorable protagonist, a decent man who struggles against powerful odds to remain one."

—*Kirkus Reviews*